MURDER

·IN·

Murrells Inlet

Anthony,

I hope you enjoy
the story I've written.

Peter F. W

PETER F. WARREN

outskirts
press

MURDER in Murrells Inlet
All Rights Reserved.
Copyright © 2016 Peter F. Warren
v2.0

Cover Photo and Author Photo © 2016 Jayne Smith. All rights reserved - used with permission.

Outskirts Press, Inc.
http://www.outskirtspress.com

ISBN: 978-1-4787-7911-7

Library of Congress Control Number: 2016911254

Outskirts Press and the "OP" logo are trademarks belonging to Outskirts Press, Inc.

PRINTED IN THE UNITED STATES OF AMERICA

To Nora June

'We've been waiting for you to join us!'

Peter Warren Books

www.readpete.com

Other novels by Peter Warren include:

The Horry County Murders

The Parliament Men

Confederate Gold and Silver

The Journey North
(Written with Roy McKinney and Edward Odom)

Peter Warren often speaks at libraries, schools, book and civic group meetings, and at other events. He has spoken numerous times to Confederate Civil War groups and camps, and at Gettysburg. As well, he often attends, and participates in, Civil War reenactments and other events across South Carolina.

If you would like Peter to speak to your group, please contact him at **www.readpete.com**, by email at **peterwarrenbooks@yahoo.com** or through his Facebook pages.

LIKE the author on Facebook.

About the Author

Peter Warren, a former resident of Connecticut, retired from the Connecticut State Police Department after serving for many years in several command assignments. He is a graduate of the University of New Haven, of the FBI National Academy, and is an Honor Graduate of the Connecticut State Police Academy. He is a past national president of the National Alliance of State Drug Enforcement Agencies; a past member of the CT Chapter of the FBI National Academy; a past member of the American Association of State Troopers, and served several terms as President of the CT State Police Academy Alumni Association. Like many Civil War enthusiasts, the author is a member of the Civil War Trust.

Currently he resides in South Carolina with his wife Debbie.

A Civil War enthusiast, and an avid golfer, the author has combined those interests, along with his law enforcement experience, to write several novels. *Murder in Murrells Inlet* is the author's latest exciting and suspenseful novel. His previous novel - *The Parliament Men* - closely followed on the heels of the author's well-received murder mystery, *The Horry County Murders*. First appearing in the author's Civil War novel, *Confederate Gold and Silver,* several characters from that story also appear in each of the author's murder mysteries. With the exception of *The Journey North*, all of the author's novels occur along the South Carolina coast. Like *Confederate Gold and Silver*, a novel that has been very well-received by many historical groups and history buffs, ***The Journey North***, is a Civil War novel written with Roy McKinney and Edward Odom. Suspenseful and intriguing like all of the author's novels, they are stories that readers of most books will enjoy.

The author routinely speaks at libraries, schools, social events, book events, Civil War reenactments, and at many other similar types of events. Individuals and organizations interested in having **Peter Warren** speak at your event may contact him directly at <u>**www.readpete.com**</u> or by sending him an email at <u>**peterwarrenbooks@yahoo.com**</u>   See the author's Facebook page - ***PETER WARREN BOOKS*** . Twitter : @peterfwarren1

Single or bulk copies of this book may be obtained through the author, through Outskirts Press, or through the worldwide web.

Some of the Characters within the Novel

MURDER in Murrells Inlet is a story set within Georgetown County, South Carolina. Some of the characters in this story have lived there their entire life. Some speak with the rich flavor that so many Southerners have in their voices. A few of them, for several reasons in their personal lives, have received little in the form of a formal education; hence, their speech has been intentionally designed to be rough. Those characters, who add so much to the story being told, are designated below with a * next to their names. I hope you enjoy those characters as much as I do. Like most of the others in this novel, they are honest and hard-working folks; just the kind of people I enjoy having as family and friends.

Paul Waring
> First appearing in the author's novel *Confederate Gold and Silver,* and again in *The Horry County Murders* and *The Parliament Men,* Paul is the principle character in this story. He is a retired Connecticut state trooper who now resides in Murrells Inlet, SC. One of his closest friends is Bobby Ray Jenkins.

Donna Waring
> Paul's wife. She is a bank manager.

Captain Bobby Ray Jenkins*
> A close friend of Paul's. He is the commanding officer of the Georgetown County Sheriff's Departments Major Case Squad. Like Paul, he is one of the principle characters.

Sheriff Leroy William Renda*
    The sheriff of Georgetown County.

Solicitor Joseph Pascento
    A South Carolina prosecutor.

Carl 'KD' Adkins
    The owner of an ACE Hardware store.

Betty Repko*
    A waitress who is a close friend of Paul & Donna's, as well as with
    Bobby Ray.

Carter 'Sonny' Pratt
    A carpenter.

Mickey O'Keefe
    Sonny Pratt's boss.

Ziggy Bagrov
    An employee of the South Carolina DMV.

Walter Barber
    Georgetown County's deputy coroner.

The Victims
Roger Platek, Kevin Holland, Father Jonathan Guyette, Uncle Johnny

The Investigators
Sgt. Kent Wilson, Det. Frank Griffin, Det. Blake Stine, FBI Agent
Thomas Scozzafava, Det. Darren Edwards, Det. Bruce Davis, Sgt. Don
Elmendorf, Det. Ron Nanfito, Douglas Vane, Det. Doug Lancelot,
Det. Roy McKinney, Trooper Edward Odom, Det. David Wagner and
Det. James Dzamko.

Glossary of Terms and Abbreviations

GCSD	Georgetown County Sheriff's Department
HCSD	Horry County Sheriff's Department
MBPD	Myrtle Beach Police Department
NMBPD	North Myrtle Beach Police Department
SCHP	South Carolina Highway Patrol
SLED	South Carolina Law Enforcement Division
PIO	Public Information Officer
DD	Detective Division
ME	Medical Examiner
MP	Military Police
SAC	Special Agent in Charge
NCIC	National Crime Information Center
XO	Executive Officer
FTO	Field Training Officer
RPG	Rocket Propelled Grenade
RTC	Round the Clock
PEG Tube	Percutaneous Endoscopic Gastrostomy (a feeding tube)
ISIS	Islamic State of Iraq and Syria

Prologue

Like so many others around him, Corporal Gideon Squires, of the 1st Minnesota Volunteer Infantry Regiment, struggled to maintain his position alongside his fellow soldiers. Ordered at first to fill a widening gap within the Union line along Cemetery Ridge, Squires, like his fellow Minnesotans around him at Gettysburg, now moved bravely forward. Advancing under withering fire, they attempted to beat back the ferocious charge thrown at them by Brigadier General Cadmus Wilcox's Alabamians.

In the chaos of the hot and dusty afternoon, like in so many other places along the Union line, from the Round Tops to the copse of trees sitting slightly more than a stone's throw away from Squires' position, Union and Confederate soldiers alike struggled to keep their regiments together as cohesive fighting units. Around them, just as it was across the entire battlefield, the whiz of minie balls flying close by, as well as thunderous cannon fire and the screams of soldiers falling injured, contributed to the confusion of the afternoon. Further adding to the day's confusion was the thick acrid smoke which lingered in the air like soft grey clouds. The smoke, the result of thousands and thousands of rounds being fired from a variety of different infantry regiments, both blue and grey, blanketed the area where nervous soldiers hastily fired their weapons; each soldier trying to survive the bitter fight so they could live to fight another day. Around them, smoke from hundreds of cannons angrily firing their shells at an enemy they often never saw enveloped the fields where thousands of young men worked hard to maintain contact with others from their respective regiments.

As evening approached, Gettysburg's second-day of bitter fighting drew to a close. Across the battlefield, from along the Emmitsburg Road to the Wheatfield, from the Peach Orchard to Spangler's Farm, and from all along the Union line, soldiers like Gideon Squires, as well Private George Adams, from the 10th Alabama, struggled to keep in contact with their regiments, and with others supporting them. While some were fortunate enough to walk away from the deadly fight that had ensued for hours, others were not. Limping or crawling from the field of fire, many shot or injured by a minie ball which seemed destined to find them, soldiers dressed in a wide variety of blue and butternut colored uniforms anxiously strained their weary eyes across the blood-soaked ground to find a source of comfort amongst the epic ordeal they had managed to live through.

That comfort, found on poles and wooden branches, or on fancy wooden shafts carved before the war, came in many different shapes and sizes. No matter what the colors displayed were, or what the shape and size of these banners and flags were that were borne by the standard bearers of both armies, those flags gave comfort to all who saw them at the end of that horrific day. For others that day, the flags of their nations, one legitimate and one imagined, like the flags of their home states, allowed their respective sons to rally around them. Whether while marching in retreat from the field, or advancing forward to fight again, soldiers had reason to once again have hope. While our flags still continue to offer us comfort and pride, for those fighting in the American Civil War flags were often their sole means of communicating with each other.

From the start of the Civil War, in Charleston, South Carolina, to the South's surrender at Appomattox Court House four long years later, the day most often recognized as the end of organized hostilities between the North and South, the American flag has brought pride to the hearts of a countless number of its citizens. It is only right that it does. Most importantly, in the years following the war, the American flag played an important role in helping to reunite the two bitter factions who had once tried their best to destroy such a beautiful symbol. Like the flags flown by other nations, our flag represents the very principles our nation is based on.

For many others, like those who fondly remember the devotion rendered to the South's fight for independence by their ancestors, or those who proudly honor their Southern heritage by continuing to display a symbol of times past, the Confederate Stars and Bars battle flag still brings pride to those who proudly wave and display it. Flown still in many parts of the South, as well as in many other areas of the country, the Stars and Bars remain, more than one hundred and fifty years after the defeat of the Confederacy, a symbol of pride for many. It is only right that it does.

For others, especially for those whose relatives and friends grew up under a symbol of repression, one which required them to be treated vastly different than those who served under it, the Confederate flag is viewed as a sign of oppression. For the grandsons and granddaughters of former slaves, and for others, whether liberal or progressive in their views, the Stars and Bars of the Confederacy, the flag of a defeated army, is one that has no honor to it. That is especially true in South Carolina.

The horrific events which occurred at Emanuel African Methodist Episcopal Church, on June 17, 2015, caused many people to finally see the hatred that others have for one of the many Confederate battle flags. For others, it would only cause the existing rift between the two sides to grow wider. For those determined to preserve an important symbol of their Southern heritage and of times past, their opinions would be vastly different than those of the politically correct.

Already existing for well over two hundred years, this rift is, perhaps, even more disturbing than those injuries sustained by our nation's soldiers as they fought against each other during America's most painful war. Like the thousands of injuries the war caused, this rift would cause the nation's pain to continue for many more years after the flags had been formally furled on April 9, 1865.

During the Civil War, battle flags were carried into battle for purposes of identification and pride, as well as honor. Today, for many similar reasons, we fly our nation's flag over our schools and town halls, over our churches and government buildings, outside our homes and within our cemeteries. For all of the right reasons, we proudly fly our flag at Arlington National Cemetery and at so many other places where brave men died fighting a tragic war on our nation's soil. Like we often do here at home when we honor our dead, we are routinely brought to tears when we see our nation's flag proudly flying over the graves of brave American soldiers at the Normandy American Cemetery and Memorial in Colleville-sur-Mer, France. The same is true at many similar locations across Europe where the remains of our soldiers have been laid to rest. No matter how big or small they are in their size, we fly these flags as a tribute to all of our veterans who have perished while protecting our freedoms. Until recently, several southern states continued to fly a flag of historical significance at similar venues as a means of remembering their past. Despite its resentment by certain groups and individuals, the Confederate battle flag still flies today as a means of honoring the thousands of sacrifices made by many Confederate soldiers.

Just as the sight of the Stars and Bars caused resentment from so many Northerners during the war, today that same flag breeds similar hatred from many others. In 2016, in Georgetown County, South Carolina, that same flag would continue to cause pain and suffering to occur. This time the pain and suffering would be caused by another son of ours; a person intent on causing problems by destroying the fabric of our peaceful way of life.

1

The loud blare of a tractor trailer's air horn brought Paul Waring's focus back from where it had momentarily drifted off to. The horn's loud noise had been sounded angrily by its driver after being abruptly cut off in heavy traffic. Like others in traffic with her, the young college-aged female who committed that particular infraction had been far more focused on her texting than her driving.

Looking up from where he was standing, Paul watched as the white smoke out on the road began to slowly dissipate. It had been generated as a result of the tractor trailer's brakes being quickly applied during the operator's attempt of avoiding a collision with the offending vehicle. Despite the momentary lapse of judgement on the young female's part, traffic quickly returned to its normal steady flow across the busy four lanes of Highway 544.

Despite his vantage point, Paul could barely hear the steady flow of traffic as it moved along the busy stretch of highway. On the far side of the highway across from where he stood, perhaps less than a half-mile away, two tall light stanchions and the outline of Coastal Carolina University's Brooks Stadium, the home of the Chanticleer football team, could easily be seen. Inside the multi-purpose stadium, one being renovated to accommodate the school's recent move to the Sun Belt Conference, coaches and other staff members were finalizing plans for the third-day of spring football practice.

Returning his gaze to the small granite slab in front of him, Paul suddenly realized the irony of what he had witnessed over the past several moments. As he did, he could not help noticing the early morning's rainstorm had now caused his brown leather loafers to become stained with mud and bits of recently cut grass. As he stood reflecting on why he was there, a warm breeze from out of the west gently caused a large number of colorful flowers to sway in a garden off to his left.

Looking up from the granite grave marker, Paul could not help thinking how the busy stretch of highway running immediately outside the cemetery was so full of life. A quick glance at the nearby college campus soon gave him the same thought. Like the other roads around it, Highway 544 was filled with an assortment of passing vehicles of many different shapes and sizes. Despite the brief momentary chaos he had witnessed outside of Hillcrest Cemetery a few moments earlier, an abundance of life existed along the busy stretch of highway. But chaos had always been a part of Paul's professional life, and the near accident he witnessed had been the second interruption to the early start of his day.

Settling back into somewhat of a regular routine after taking life in retirement easy for the past few months, Paul nervously toyed with his cell phone as it vibrated in the right front pocket of his blue jeans. Earlier, it had also been the source of his first interruption. Fingering the phone as the call went to his voice mailbox, his thoughts bounced back to the call he had received earlier. Then, for no particular reason, he thought of his wife and of the busy day she had in front of her. Kneeling down to brush away a few leaves which had gathered around the granite marker, he soon listened to the brief new message which had been left for him.

Moments later as he stood up, Paul spoke to his friend. "Well, Audrey, I guess our visit has been interrupted enough for today. We'll blame it on Bobby Ray again, just like we always do."

For several moments, Paul fussed over the placement of the freshly cut blue and white flowers he had placed next to the upper left corner of the gray-colored stone. Neatly etched into the granite, directly under the name that had been centered on the highly polished stone, were the dates April 18, 1988 to October 21, 2015. Under the dates, also etched into the stone were the words "GONE, BUT NOT FORGOTTEN BY YOUR BROTHERS AND SISTERS IN BLUE". After her untimely death six months earlier, Lieutenant Audrey Small's co-workers and friends from the Georgetown County Sheriff's Department had chipped in to pay for her memorial stone. Outside of that painful morning when she had been laid to rest, this was Paul's first trip back to the cemetery to visit his friend.

Months earlier, Paul Waring, a retired state trooper from Connecticut, headed an investigation that Audrey Small had been a major part of. So had her boss, Captain Bobby Ray Jenkins, the commander of the Georgetown County Sheriff's Department Major Case Squad. It was during the time of this investigation, when others were struggling to identify who the killer of five young men had been; she had left to enjoy her honeymoon in Hawaii. Three days into her honeymoon, Small was tragically killed when the sightseeing plane she and her husband had rented crashed into the ocean. As it had for others, including his best friend, Bobby Ray, Small's death had shocked Paul.

Satisfied his flowers were now properly displayed, Paul spoke to his friend again. "I'll be back sometime soon for another visit, Audrey, after I bail your boss out of trouble again. I'm not sure why, but it seems like trouble always has a way of finding Bobby Ray. Now that trouble has turned into some kind of an emergency he needs my help with, so while I'd rather stay and chat with you a bit longer, I've got to go." Turning to leave, he paused for a brief moment to look down at Small's grave. Like many others who had known her, Paul still struggled to make sense of the painful loss of his friend. After a quick nod of respect, just like the flowers he had set down next to her cold stone marker, Paul began the short walk back to his pick-up truck. As he did, his cell phone announced another call from Bobby Ray.

******

Living in Murrells Inlet, South Carolina for the past six years after retiring from the Connecticut State Police Department, Paul's life in retirement had been everything but what he expected it to be. Spending most of his thirty-plus years with the state police in a variety of command assignments with several investigative units, Paul had seen firsthand the senseless violence that was often inflicted upon so many innocent victims. While much of it had been perpetuated by family members and friends, on other occasions it had been inflicted by complete strangers.

Along with his wife, Donna, Paul had moved to South Carolina to enjoy a different and slower kind of life. He had dreamed of a quiet life, filled with only the stress of trying to figure out how to spend his time. The hardest decisions he had hoped to be making in retirement were ones related to whether he was going to be spending his days playing golf, fishing, or taking his pontoon boat out on the Waccamaw River. Spending time with Donna, his wife of thirty-eight years, at the beach was another option he also looked forward to. But life in retirement had proved to be everything but that, for both he and Donna.

Shortly after getting settled in South Carolina, while out on the river with his new boat on a Friday afternoon, Paul had accidentally discovered the remains of a Confederate soldier. Mixed in with the remains were documents which had carefully been protected from the weather. They were papers Paul soon managed to decipher by successfully navigating his way through a series of complex clues hidden within the documents. Doing so allowed him, with help from Donna and Bobby Ray, to discover where the long lost treasury of the Confederate States of America had been hidden.

Moved out of Richmond near the end of the Civil War, the treasury, comprised of millions of dollars of gold and silver coins, had been found in North Carolina and South Carolina after an extensive search. The discovery of the lost treasury, while exciting to Paul, a passionate Civil War enthusiast, also brought fame and media attention that he cared little about.

While it was due to Paul's tenacity, along with his well-honed investigative abilities which had caused the treasury to be found, the discovery soon led to the Georgetown County Sheriff's Department seeking his assistance on two separate murder investigations. In their own way, both had been equally brutal and confounding. These requests for Paul's assistance had come directly from Captain Bobby Ray Jenkins and Sheriff Leroy William Renda. While Paul had agreed to offer his assistance in both of those investigations due to his friendship with Bobby Ray, it was his canny ability at understanding the unique complexities of each murder suspect that soon helped to solve the difficult and lengthy investigations. In addition, Paul's extensive experience in working homicides back in Connecticut had allowed him to see things Bobby Ray's detectives had not. Most notably, he had seen how several fragments of evidence in each of the two cases were connected to each other. In both cases, some of the evidence which had been seized had been intentionally left behind by the killers as a means of taunting the cops. Connecting some of this evidence to other evidence had led to the successful capture of those responsible for the murders that had taken place along the Grand Strand. Quite strangely, Donna Waring, a banker with no law enforcement experience whatsoever, had helped her husband significantly in both investigations.

Unlike her husband, Donna had barely known Audrey Small. The two women, distinctively different in every way possible including their career choices, had only met on two occasions. Despite that, Donna was aware of the pain Small's death had caused her husband, and for others within the GCSD.

It was due to the void Small's death caused for her department, especially in Bobby Ray's Major Case Squad, that Paul agreed to continue on with his temporary assignment after the two significant homicide investigations had been closed. Realizing his investigative skills might be needed once again, he had agreed to stay on until Bobby Ray was able to fill Small's position, and two others, within his unit.

While he had only worked a handful of routine criminal investigations since his friend's death and the arrest of Zeke Payne, the person responsible for senselessly murdering five young men in North Litchfield, Paul had managed to keep his in-service training up-to-date in order to maintain his law enforcement standing in South Carolina. This he had also done as a professional favor to both Renda and Bobby Ray. Despite doing so, and after years of managing a wide variety of criminal cases that included brutally senseless murders, drug assassinations, bank robberies and a host of other crimes involving far too much violence, as well as too much bloodshed and other atrocities, Paul cared little about working many more cases like them. What he had seen during his career in Connecticut had numbed him. For his own sanity, he knew the time was coming for him to call it quits.

Now as he started his truck, Paul took one last look back in the direction of Small's grave. Like it had when it first happened, it now pained him even more to be the person replacing her on Bobby Ray's staff, even if it was only going to be for a short period of time. Briefly staring at her grave, he wished things had gone differently for his friend. "If only things hadn't played out like they did, Audrey. If only you hadn't gotten on that stupid plane."

As traffic momentarily eased, Paul pulled out of the quiet peaceful cemetery, with its manicured lawn and gravel driveways, and back into the cold chaotic world he knew was waiting for him. As he headed east on Highway 544 towards his destination, he listened to the newest message Bobby Ray had left on his phone. It would prove to be only one of many that he would receive from his friend over the next several weeks.

Five minutes later as he neared Socastee, a small community within the geographic boundary of Myrtle Beach, Paul realized he was once again back in the game. But unlike others, he knew the murder game never had any clear rules or happy winners. It was simply a game filled with blood, violence, long and painfully frustrating days of tracking down leads and witnesses, and, as

Paul hoped for, an occasional ending of satisfaction. Satisfaction was always what those caught up in the murder game needed. Cops included.

What Paul could not realize at this time was how much satisfaction he would soon get from working this new case. What he was about to experience was something that had never before confronted him in life.

2

Asked to participate in a promotional oral board the North Charleston Police Department was conducting for the rank of detective, Bobby Ray was clearly, through no fault of his own, in the worst location possible when he first received news of the latest murder confronting his department. A week earlier, the GCSD had been called to investigate a similar murder that had taken place less than a mile from this new scene. It was an investigation that was still in high gear.

Despite the beautiful weather that had followed the morning's rainstorm, and despite his own heavy foot, Bobby Ray's ride from North Charleston to the new crime scene on Richmond Hill Drive, in Murrells Inlet, took nearly an hour to complete. After passing through McClellanville on Highway 17, and after being updated twice on what was confronting Sergeant Edward Kindle at the scene, Bobby Ray called Sheriff Renda to advise him on what had actually transpired that morning. Like his Major Case commander, Renda had been out of the office that morning attending a meeting at Conway High School on school violence with other area law enforcement officials.

"Is Kindle sure there's only one victim?" Renda asked Bobby Ray from where he stood in the hallway outside of the school's auditorium. "And is he sure the guy died for the same reason our other guy did?"

Frustrated from having to negotiate his way through traffic that was backed up on Highway 17 from an on-going highway construction project in Pawleys Island, Bobby Ray bit his tongue before responding to Renda's questions. They were ones the veteran investigator found rather premature for his boss to be asking.

"Not sure what Big Ed knows and doesn't know right now, boss. He's only been at the scene for about forty-five minutes so far. I'm sure he's had his hands full up to now just getting the scene stabilized. He's likely just getting a handle on the big picture." As he finished speaking, and despite having activated both the audible siren and flashing blue lights on his unmarked vehicle, Bobby Ray was forced to brake hard to avoid striking a motorist who had pulled out in front of him from the local Fresh Market parking lot. As he did, he silently cursed at the inattentive driver for nearly causing an accident, one he did not have time to be a part of.

After listening to a few of Renda's other comments and questions, Bobby Ray, having regained his composure, again spoke to the sheriff. "Boss, you know Kindle's as good as we've got. He'll get the scene stabilized for us as soon as he can, and then he'll let us know what it is we're facing. Besides, it's kind of foolish at this stage of the game to expect him to know why our newest victim croaked, isn't it? I'm sorry, but I'm not calling him to ask him any foolish questions right now. He's too busy for that. Besides, I'll be there in just a few minutes. I'll find out the answers to your questions myself." Bobby Ray could not help shaking his head at the foolish questions his boss had expected him to know the answers to this early in the investigation.

"OK, OK," Renda said as he stood off to the side watching as a large number of students passed by in one of the school's busy hallways. Reluctantly responding to the warning a series of hallway bells were making, each of the students began moving more deliberately towards their next class. "Call me later when you know more. I'm going to be making a few calls before I head back to this meeting I'm attending. And, just so you know, I'll probably stop at the scene on my way back to the office. Have some answers for me when I get there."

"Will do. I'm less than a minute out from the scene. Talk to you later." Clearly annoyed at being bothered, Bobby Ray disconnected the call before Renda had time to reply. After doing so out of pure frustration, he cried out in anger. He did so as a means of trying to force himself to calm down before arriving at the scene. Frustrated by the heavy traffic, and from nearly being struck by another vehicle, the normally patient Major Case commander had become testy after having his time wasted by having to answer Renda's ridiculous questions.

"As long as I've known him, and for as long as he's been a cop, that man has asked some of the lamest questions at times," Bobby Ray muttered to himself as he pulled up to the scene. As he did, he saw Kindle, the department's day shift uniformed patrol supervisor, standing with several others in their newest victim's front yard. While it was too obvious for him to miss, Bobby Ray also saw the immediate area around the residence had already been cordoned off twice with yellow crime scene tape. This had been done not only to define the scene's inner and outer perimeters, but had also been done to keep on-lookers and the media as far away as possible.

Walking to where Kindle stood near the victim's body, Bobby Ray heard the veteran sergeant ordering his deputies to make sure the immediate area around the neighborhood had been completely closed off to traffic. This included a nearby intersection where three streets merged together. Having been broken in by Kindle years earlier, he knew the sergeant's orders were primarily being issued for two reasons. The first was to make it difficult for the probing eyes of the media to be able to photograph the victim's remains before his family could be given the courtesy of learning about his death the right way. Despite doing so, Bobby Ray knew the long range and low-light capabilities of the media's camera lenses made it difficult to protect the scene from being viewed by the outside world. Like most cops, Bobby Ray believed that a victim's friends and family members should not have to learn of their loved one's demise from seeing a gory and upsetting news clip. By doing it the right way, by making personal contact with their victim's next of kin, two detectives would prevent them from learning about it on television. The other reason, the more important one for Bobby Ray's detectives, was to prevent the destruction, or loss, of any evidence that had yet to be recovered along Richmond Hill Drive.

Seeing the small group of reporters and satellite trucks who had already begun to congregate at the scene disgusted Bobby Ray. "Freaking vultures," he muttered out loud, "the poor bastard's been dead less than two hours and these people are already swarming around the scene. They always have to be in the way, don't they?"

Having already discarded his tie, Bobby Ray rolled up the sleeves of his blue dress shirt as he moved closer to Kindle and the others. As he did, he unwrapped two sticks of Juicy Fruit gum. Placing the sugary sticks inside his mouth, he gave a quick but friendly nod to those hovering over their victim's body.

"What's it look like, fellas? Anything like the one we had last week?" Bobby Ray asked, donning a pair of blue latex gloves as he shooed a couple of his evidence technicians out of the way.

As they moved further away to give him some room, the Major Case commander knelt down to examine what was now lying at his feet. As he did, out of the corner of his eye, he saw Kindle pointing to a broken flagstaff less than six feet away. Looking at it, Bobby Ray could tell the blood soaked upper section of the wooden pole had likely been the instrument used to inflict the massive head injuries he now saw the victim had sustained.

"Looks like this poor bastard took quite a beating, Bobby Ray," Kindle said as he watched his good friend lift a once clean white sheet further off the victim. While it had only been in place for a short amount of time, blood now stained the sheet bright red in several places. Lifting it revealed several other significant injuries to the victim's chest and arms. "Besides the obvious wounds you see on his face, take a look at his hands. It looks like at least seven of his fingers have been broken. Our vic apparently tried to protect himself by putting his hands up in front of him as he was being beaten. You're the expert here, but my guess is those are all defensive wounds you're looking at. When you're done looking at his fingers, take a look at the guy's mouth. Poor bastard also lost several teeth. When you finish looking at him, take a look at the lawn over here," Kindle said, pointing to a spot less than ten feet away. "There's a bunch of blood over there, likely it's blood that was cast off the flagstaff during the beating."

Bobby Ray's gaze moved up and down the victim's body as he took mental note of the brutal beating that had taken place in the front yard of the nearby home. Quick looks at both the victim's hands and mouth confirmed Kindle's assessment of what had occurred.

"Do we have any witnesses? What do we know about our vic?" Bobby Ray asked to no one in particular as he continued to kneel on the ground.

As before, it was Kindle who spoke first. But before he could finish answering the questions that had been asked, Bobby Ray asked his next two questions. As he asked them, the Major Case commander stared at a fixture mounted on the exterior of the house. Mounted at eye level on the home's exterior siding, a polished metal bracket sat just to the left of the still opened front door. A door sitting less than twenty-five feet away.

"Probably a couple of stupid questions to ask, Big Ed, but that bracket I'm looking at by the front door, that's where this broken pole came from, correct? We do know this is our vic's home, correct?"

"Yep, this is . . . sorry, Bobby Ray, I meant to say this was his house," Kindle offered, correcting himself due to the victim's recent demise. "Our guy's name is Kevin Holland. He's a sixty-eight year old white male with a DOB of August 23rd. He was born in 1948. From the little we've been able to learn about him, he's lived here alone for the past six years. One of the neighbors told us our vic moved here from Jersey after his wife supposedly died in some kind of work-related accident. Just so you know, I already have one of my senior guys checking that out. We're also being told our vic was a career military guy; supposedly spent thirty-plus years in the army. Maybe that's why this yard, the home as well, looks so neat. Looks like this guy was a spit and polish kind of guy, kind of wish I was more like that at times myself." Kindle said with some regret as he closed the pad he had been reading from. Taking a moment before slipping his small black pad back into his pants pocket, he took another look around the manicured premises their victim had obviously taken great pride in caring for.

Standing up after covering Holland's body back up with the sheet, Bobby Ray again took notice of the broken flagstaff.

Splintered badly, and nearly broken in half, it had been discarded in a small circular flower garden a short distance from where its owner's body now rested. Around it, in what looked to be freshly laid mulch, several well-tended flowering plants bathed the garden with their bright yellow and red colors. Stirred by a gentle breeze, an American flag, and just under it a black POW flag, waved at the top of a twenty-foot high flagpole. Standing erect in the middle of the garden, the white flagpole was surrounded by the many colorful plants and flowers Holland had carefully tended.

The sound of a car door being closed out on the street caused Bobby Ray's attention to shift in that direction. Almost immediately he saw his friend, Paul Waring, making his way towards where he and Kindle stood.

"Morning, fellas! At least, I think it's still morning," Paul said cheerfully, glancing at his wristwatch as he moved closer to where the others were waiting for him. Reaching them, he shook hands with Kindle as he gave a friendly nod to Bobby Ray. In moments, Paul's attention shifted to what was once again covered up by the bloodstained sheet. As he did, his eyes picked up on the broken wooden pole lying nearby. "I'm thinking if you boys called me down here to help you with something, more than likely it's what I see lying under this sheet that you need my help with. The fact that these bloodstains are seemingly expanding in size as we stand here also tells me whatever is under this sheet is likely pretty dead. Am I correct on those assumptions, Captain Jenkins?" As he waited for his friend's response, Paul put on a pair of blue latex gloves that Kindle handed him.

"You're pretty smart . . . very observant too . . . for a damn Yankee, ain't you?" Bobby Ray deadpanned.

Smiling at his friend's good-natured shot, Paul, without asking for permission, removed the sheet covering Holland's face and upper torso. Doing so revealed the significant damage that had been inflicted upon the retired soldier's face. Having already seen far too many similar injuries in his career, what he now stared at did little to make Paul flinch. His lengthy career with the Connecticut State Police Department, as well as the two recent murder investigations he had helped Bobby Ray with, had dulled his sensitivity to the brutality inflicted on man by his fellow man. The stoicism he now displayed as he examined Holland's body was not meant to be a reflection of any indifference or lack of concern, but was rather a means of dealing with the inhumanity he was once again witnessing.

Despite realizing what was now confronting Bobby Ray and his staff, Paul, at first, could not figure out why his friend had summoned him to the scene. From all accounts, this was a routine murder investigation he was now present at, one the sheriff's department had competently handled many times in the past. But then, as he surveyed the scene around him as others continued to stabilize it, Paul's eyes focused on the broken flagstaff. More than just the murder weapon, it was the one clue present that only a veteran criminal investigator like him could pick up on without being told much about it. As he continued to stare at it, Douglas Vane, the GCSD's senior forensic examiner, quietly walked up and stood by Bobby Ray's side.

"This why you called me here, Bobby Ray?" Paul asked as he pointed to the flagstaff before shaking hands with Vane. "Did you call me here because of that, or because Audrey's not here to help you guys sort this mess out?"

The mention of Audrey Small's name caused a slight grimace to appear on Bobby Ray's face for a brief moment. Next to him,

Vane, who had been especially hit hard by their friend's death, shifted uncomfortably on his feet as he turned slightly away from Paul. Seeing his friends react as they did at the mention of Small's name caused him to make a mental note about mentioning their late friend's name too often.

"Both really," Bobby Ray replied in answer to one of Paul's previous questions. "Audrey's death has certainly left me short in both the experience and supervisory departments. It's all on me, but I just haven't had the time or the inclination to fill her position within the squad as yet. I know it has to be done, and I know Renda wants her spot filled for all the obvious reasons, but out of respect to her I've left it open. Perhaps I've left it open too long."

"I understand how you feel, Bobby Ray, but Audrey, if she was here today, she'd tell you to get your butt in gear and take care of business. It was somewhat classy of you to leave her spot unfilled for a time due to the circumstances surrounding her death, and I know you know this, but we're all replaceable. Don't get upset over what I'm about to tell you, but I think you need to get moving on what needs to be done."

Forcing a smile, Bobby Ray complimented Paul on his astute observation. "Looks like you've still got it, Yankee Boy." While his comment was meant to be a friendly jab at his Northern friend, it was also said to get them back to the matter now confronting them and away from thinking about the painful absence of their mutual friend.

Taking a moment, Paul cast a furtive glance at the damaged flagstaff before speaking again. "My gut is telling me there's more to this mess than what you're telling me, fellas. I'm thinking you need to tell me what was on this pole before we go any further."

Looking at Bobby Ray, then at Vane, and then at Kindle, Paul added, "And, if it wasn't what was on this pole that got this old-timer killed, then tell me what it was that caused us all to gather here on his front lawn today."

Their friend's perceptive comments caused Kindle and Bobby Ray to exchange brief looks with each other before offering a response. It was Bobby Ray who finally let Paul in on what had caused Holland's death earlier that morning.

"It's what was on the flagstaff that apparently caused our vic to be murdered, Paul. I'm afraid it's just like the one we had last week when you and Donna were back home . . . at least I suspect it's for the same reason." Pointing at Kindle, Bobby Ray then continued by giving his friend more information to digest. "Ed's deputies have already spoken to the two neighbors on either side of Holland's home. Doing so confirmed it for us; at least I think it did. While we haven't found anyone who saw or heard Holland fighting with anyone out here, they did confirm one important thing for us. Seems like a poor excuse to murder someone, but I . . ."

Frustrated by Bobby Ray's long-winded explanation, Paul impatiently cut him off before he could finish with what he had to say. "Hey! We're burning daylight here. While I'm still young, OK? Are you going to tell me what was on the freakin' pole or do I have to find out for myself?" Well aware of Bobby Ray's tendency to be verbose at times, Paul's sarcastic comments caused Vane to briefly laugh out loud.

"The Stars and Bars, old buddy. The Stars and Bars are what likely got this poor old SOB murdered right here in his own front yard." While he already knew why Holland had been killed, Bobby Ray's answer caused Kindle to shake his head in disgust.

His doing so finally told Paul the reason why he had been called to the scene.

"You're talking about the Confederate flag, right? You're telling me the Confederate battle flag, the one we all recognize as being the flag of the Confederacy, that's what got this poor bastard killed? Is that what you're saying?" Paul asked incredulously, not sure if he should believe what he was being told or not.

"Afraid so." Bobby Ray replied as he stared down at the sheet covering Holland's body. "At least, that's why we think he was killed. Until I hear otherwise, I'm focusing our investigation around that motive for now. I hate to admit it, but that flag has stirred up everyone's emotions recently. We're obviously going to be taking a look at everything, just like we always do, but that dang flag is likely what caused Holland to be bludgeoned to death right here on this very lawn."

Like many others, Paul had closely followed the events surrounding the tragic shootings that recently occurred in Charleston at the Emanuel African Methodist Episcopal Church. While he understood the fervent historical support the flag still received, as well as the hatred others directed at the principal symbol of the Confederacy in the wake of the tragic deaths of nine innocent victims, it confounded the veteran investigator as to why the flag had been the cause of Holland's death.

"Was Holland a guy, and perhaps it's too early for you to know the answer to this right now, but was he vocal about his support of the Confederate flag? I mean, you said he was from Jersey, right?" Paul asked, still perplexed over why the flag had caused Holland's death.

"Not that we know of right now," Kindle answered, looking directly at Paul as he spoke. "I had one of our intel analysts back at HQ run his name through our database to see what she could find. I was told the guy doesn't even have a record of getting a traffic ticket or for even being involved in an accident over the past ten years. He certainly isn't on our radar, or anyone else's that I know of, for being a white supremacist or anything remotely close to that. I suspect Bobby Ray's folks will do a more thorough check on Holland's background with the feds, but for now our guy looks like he lived a quiet but boring life."

"Why'd he fly the Stars and Bars then, any idea?"

"Not yet, Paul. No idea." Kindle answered as he scratched the back of his head with his left hand.

Having not seen what he was looking for, Paul scanned the yard once more before asking his next question. It was an obvious one to ask. "If he flew the Confederate flag, where is it?"

"We haven't found it yet," Bobby Ray answered as he stared at a group of neighbors collecting on someone's lawn across the street from Holland's home. "Haven't found a trace of that flag, or of any other flag that might have been with it. Hate to guess at things because it clouds your objectivity during investigations like this, but I wouldn't be surprised to learn our killer, or even killers, took it with them."

As Paul went silent, processing what he had seen and was told at the scene, Bobby Ray gave Vane his marching orders. "Doug, we'll be done here in a minute. When we are, I'm going to get our folks together over there in the driveway so we can get this investigation going. I'll hand out everyone's assignments then. No need for you and your folks to be there though, you've got a pretty good size scene to start processing. Do me a favor, start from the area around the front door and then work your way to where we're standing now." Collecting his thoughts for a moment, Bobby Ray then spoke again to his forensic examiner. "Dougie, I know I don't have to tell you this, but make sure you bag both of Holland's hands after you're done with your photographs and sketch map. Who knows, maybe we'll get lucky and find some asshole's DNA under our guy's fingernails."

As someone who hated attending meetings of any kind, Vane was pleased to hear his presence would not be required at Bobby Ray's strategy session. Because of that, the fact that Bobby Ray had needlessly told him he wanted their victim's hands bagged to preserve any potential evidence from being lost did little to dampen his spirits. Being told he did not have to attend a meeting he would have likely considered a painful waste of time brighten Vane's day enormously. While bagging the hands of a murder victim was an obvious part of processing any scene, a task he had completed many times already during his career, Vane, by way of his usual dry and sarcastic wit, assured his boss it would soon be taken care of. "Not to worry, I'll make sure that happens as soon as possible. Thanks for reminding me to do that."

Vane had barely finished speaking when Paul spoke again. He did so after giving some thought to a statement his friend had made regarding a similar case already under investigation. "Bobby Ray, a few moments ago you made reference to this being the *second* murder of this sort. Did I hear you correctly? Is this really the second such murder you've had like this?"

"Yep, you heard right. That one and this one are the real reasons you're here. I'm thinking this issue with the flag, no matter what position you're taking, is one that's only going to get worse. Those folks in Charleston . . . doesn't matter if their black folks, whites, liberals, Civil War buffs or whomever . . . they're the ones with the cool heads. They're dealing with a very flammable issue down there. For whatever it's worth, I'm proud of them for dealing with it like they have. They're using their faith in God, and in the judicial system, to comfort them. In our case, we're the ones dealing with a whack job right now. A whack job who, in my opinion, is apparently intent on killing again." Taking a moment to look at the sheet covering Holland's body, Bobby Ray then turned to look at Paul as he started speaking again. "As we have in the past, and even more so now because of Audrey no longer being with us, we need your help again. We need to put an end to this madness ASAP."

While comprehending what his friend was telling him, Paul sought to learn more information before committing himself to the GCSD again. Despite being eager to help, he needed to learn more about what had already happened. "Tell me more about the first murder, Bobby Ray, especially any similarities between that one and this one." As Paul finished speaking, Vane moved off to give his crime scene techs and the two detectives assigned to the Major Case crime van their instructions.

For the next couple of minutes, Bobby Ray, with an occasional comment tossed in by Kindle, explained what had happened eight days earlier on Fire Thorne Drive, in Murrells Inlet. Like their current location, the first scene had also occurred on a normally quiet residential street. "Our first vic, a guy by the name of Roger Platek, was a forty-seven-year-old white male who had been born and raised here in the inlet. Unlike Mr. Holland, Platek was something of a redneck. He'd been arrested seven times, maybe it was eight times, over the past six years for stupid shit, mostly victimless crimes. But he was also a loudmouth who liked to drink too much beer. Much to the dismay of several of his neighbors, he was also someone who often drove his piece of shit pick-up truck too fast."

Shifting on the balls of his feet as he listened to what he was being told, Paul struggled to find a connection between the two murders. "Bobby Ray, once again you're telling me everything but what I need to know. I'll worry about the first guy's pedigree later. What I'm waiting for you to tell me is how or what connects these two cases together. Is it the manner of death? I mean, did you also find a broken flag pole at that first scene? Did this Platek guy, or whatever his name is, did he also fly the rebel flag?"

Like his friend had done before him, now it was Bobby Ray's turn to shift uneasily on his feet before speaking. "Yeah, that's about it. Platek took a serious beating before he died. From the amount of blood we found at the scene, he apparently gave someone a good beating as well. Presumptive tests Doug ran showed we had two different types of blood at that scene, both human. Just like here, we also found a broken flagstaff in Platek's driveway. It was smeared with blood just like the one we found here. Like I already told you, Platek was what you Yankees would call a redneck." Pausing to look up and down the street in front of Holland's home, Bobby Ray then added, "Down here rednecks . . . and many others, still fly a certain flag because of their Southern heritage. I guess that answers the last part of your question, doesn't it?"

Glancing at the broken flagstaff still lying in the garden near Holland's now cold body, Paul asked his next question. "You said you found the first flagstaff in the victim's driveway. Was it near his body like this one is?"

"We found the bottom half lying about ten feet away from where we found Platek and . . ." Somewhat upset now, Bobby

Ray looked at Paul for a couple of moments before finishing the answer to his friend's question. "The other half, the half with the sharp splintered edges, had been used to stab him several times in the chest. His killer left it there after stabbing him for the final time. If you ask me, and Lord knows I've seen a lot of people who've been killed, but that was a pretty brutal way to kill someone." Despite his years of investigating horrific crimes of violence, Bobby Ray's voice trailed off as he finished speaking.

＊＊＊＊＊＊

Seeing that his detectives had finished photographing Holland's yard, and were now doing the same to document the injuries their victim had sustained, Bobby Ray, accompanied by Paul and Kindle, walked several feet away. This allowed the next set of detectives, assisted by Vane's crime scene techs, to carefully plot on the crime scene map the locations of Holland's body, the broken flagstaff, and the various places where blood now stained the front yard.

Along with the map, they would be photographs that would be referred to many times over the course of the next several weeks.

3

While some were real, many perceived reasons contributed to Sonny Pratt's dislike for several groups of people. Among those he disliked, and there were many, he hated pedophiles and the Catholic Church the most. He also despised those whose vehicles and yards were adorned with bumper stickers and flags of the Confederacy, symbols of a time he detested.

Most people he viewed as simpletons; people he believed as being foolish in their beliefs regarding God, country, and family, as well as others who they idolized. In his opinion, these were people who were often uneducated and barely scraping by in life, the unsophisticated morons who had yet to learn his adopted ways of living. It did not matter that he was one of them, for now he abhorred them, the people who worked menial minimum wage jobs and who often lived in single and doublewide trailers. To him, they were the real threat he and others like him were now facing. Dismissing the fact that he still continued to live and work amongst the people he now hated, he viewed himself as being vastly superior. "For now," he thought, "I'm just disguised amongst them, waiting . . . waiting for the right time to act."

For similar and vague reasons, some even too vague for him to justify, he hated cops as well. Despite the handful of innocuous tickets he had received in life for speeding and other motor vehicle violations, his dislike of cops had been formed from years of listening to the liberal ultra-left views of his father. His father, David Pratt, who had died five years earlier, had been a hippie, someone who had never managed to escape the late sixties lifestyle he adopted years earlier. Even as he was dying from an incurable form of cancer, an illness he elected to treat with only herbs and marijuana, as well as with daily and healthy shots of tequila, his father had been someone who continued to rail against the system and its oppressive form of government. Like many of his rants and raves, David's claims about police misconduct, especially when they spoke of the systematic mistreatment of Blacks and American Indians, were often flawed. Along the way, David Pratt and his wife, despite advocating a lifestyle of peace and love, routinely abused their children.

While he knew his father's family ties had been traced back to the Black Creek Indians, and to one other now extinct east coast tribe whose name he had long ago forgotten, he also knew his father's uneducated views were often filled with hate and bias. They were also views that had become exaggerated over the years in their size and scope. They had grown from perceived slights occurring years earlier.

Now at age thirty-nine, and often to his own dismay, David Pratt's son found himself hating people as much as his father had, and often for the same benign reasons. But unlike his father, he knew his own contempt of others was due to his growing distrust of any form of governmental sanctions and policies imposed at any levels. Stubborn, short-tempered, and increasingly cold towards his few remaining friends and family members, he gradually retreated further away from those who were still left in his life. As he did, his views became more radical than ever.

Despite his distrust of cops, Carter Pratt was addicted to shows on television which featured cops and attorneys in both traditional and non-traditional settings. CSI, Chicago P.D., Law & Order, and other shows like them were among his favorites. For the past twelve years, Pratt, nicknamed Sonny by his late mother, and for reasons far different than her son's outlook on life, devoured as much as he could each day regarding police procedures, the handling of forensic evidence, and courtroom tactics. He was, by all accounts, a television junkie. He was also becoming a religious zealot and a brutal murderer.

******

Purposely parking his black Chevy Tahoe in a parking space half-way between Old Time Pottery and a nearby McDonald's restaurant on Highway 17 in Surfside Beach, Pratt hid behind his vehicle's deeply tinted windows for several minutes. As he did, he placed the bloodstained clothes he had been wearing, an orange-colored long sleeve Clemson pullover and a worn pair of blue jeans that he had recently purchased at a nearby Goodwill, into a large black garbage bag. Mindful of the possibility about transferring grass clippings and blood from the scene he had just left, Pratt had already placed the red sneakers he had been wearing inside the bag. Like his other clothes, including his white socks that were now splattered with blood from the violent struggle, he had also purchased the sneakers at the same store two weeks earlier during the planning phase of his twisted operation. Aware of the blood that had been cast off the flagstaff as he repeatedly beat Holland with it after gaining the upper hand in the fight, Pratt checked his face and hands for any blood he had previously missed. Soon satisfied he was free of any blood, Pratt awkwardly changed into the clothes he had placed in his vehicle early that morning. As he did, he repeatedly scanned the large parking lot around him, making sure he was not being watched. Paranoid of still having miniscule drops of blood on him, he carefully wiped his face and hands with several hypoallergenic baby wipes. Like his clothes, the wipes were quickly placed inside the garbage bag when he was finished.

Exiting his vehicle after again checking the area around him to assure himself that he was not being watched, Pratt walked the short distance to the rear of the fast food restaurant. Nearing the restaurant's large metal dumpster, which sat strangely close to one of the two vacant drive-thru lanes, he nonchalantly flipped the black plastic bag inside it without breaking stride. Pleased with himself over what he had accomplished that day, and for not being caught doing it, Pratt allowed a smile to cross his unshaven face as he approached the side door of the restaurant.

Pausing to hold the door open for a young couple who were experiencing difficulty with a combative stroller holding their young daughter, Pratt's eyes quickly focused on a bumper sticker displayed on the rear window of a newer model Ford F350. The sticker, intentionally printed in vibrant red and white colors, proudly told others how the truck's owner felt about his Southern heritage. Featured prominently on the left side of the sticker was an accurate representation of a Confederate battle flag.

Minutes later, as he took the first bite of his Quarter Pounder, Pratt watched as a middle-aged white male opened one of the truck's passenger doors for his teenaged daughter. Watching her as she climbed inside, Pratt quickly estimated her age to be between eighteen to twenty years old.

"Probably going to grow up to be an asshole like her father," Pratt thought as he stuffed several French fries in his mouth. Sitting in a booth next to a window, he watched as the truck began to back out of its parking space. As it did, he quickly jotted down the truck's registration number on a grease-stained napkin.

Watching the truck pull away as he chewed his fries, Pratt paused from eating to take a long sip of his Coca-Cola before finishing his thought. "Guess I'll have to ask Ziggy to run another plate for me. It'll cost me a few bucks, but he'll do it. It's always a help to know as much as you can about your next victim before you start the hunt." Finished thinking about his next target, Pratt's attention returned to the meal in front of him. Despite his food growing cold, he quickly focused back on his unfinished burger and fries. Nearby, the Monopoly sticker on his drink cup still waited to be peeled off.

******

While Pratt would easily learn the identity of one of his future victims, the surprise he would soon face would be an unexpected one. It would prove to be one that would soon be delivered by his intended victim's young daughter.

4

After learning of the similarities that existed between the two recent murders, Paul walked to where the GCSD's Major Case van had been parked. Besides the electronic roof rack mounted on the van's roof, large colorful markings on all four sides told others what the vehicle's purpose was. Inside the large vehicle, which had been carefully designed to carry the specialized equipment needed to process a wide variety of crime scenes, two techs were hard at work.

Standing in the rear of the vehicle, Paul saw the next two people he expected to see arrive at the scene. Like others he knew in life, respecting some more than others, he respected one of the newest arrivals far more than he did the other.

First noticing the arrival of Solicitor Joseph Pascento, the chief prosecutor for most of Horry and Georgetown counties, Paul then saw the sheriff of Georgetown County, Sheriff Leroy William Renda, as he walked to where Bobby Ray was talking with several of his detectives. Noticing Paul watching him, Pascento shot a smile, and then a friendly wave in his direction. They were greetings which Paul acknowledged in similar fashion.

From his work on the Melkin investigation, but perhaps more so due to Paul's ability to make a positive connection between a handful of the most obscure clues in the recent multiple murder investigation that had taken place in North Litchfield, Pascento had come to respect Paul's experience and skills in investigating the most violent of crimes. The tenacity Paul had shown in following up on all types of clues, as well as his ability to predict what each of the murderers was going to do after killing several of their victims, were traits the veteran prosecutor had not seen demonstrated by any of the cops he normally worked with within his judicial district. It was those skills, coupled with Paul's exhaustive work ethic, which caused Pascento to finally warm up to him like several others already had.

Likewise, Paul had come to respect Pascento as well. The aggressive youthful-looking prosecutor, who took pride in his trim and fit appearance by dressing the part of a successful attorney, had proven to Paul during the previous two investigations he had worked that this was a prosecutor who was very supportive of the law enforcement community he worked with. Unlike some of the prosecutors he had worked with back home, Pascento had demonstrated that he was someone who was willing to listen to the opinions and thoughts of others.

After briefly speaking with Vane's crime scene techs, mostly to exchange friendly but sarcastic greetings with each other, Paul returned his attention to Renda. Unlike Pascento, who Paul often thought shied away from too much attention being lavished upon him, Renda's loud arrival at the scene let all who were present know that the sheriff of Georgetown County had touched down. Now in his tenth term in office, Renda had exited his vehicle barking orders at both his uniformed deputies manning the roadblock outside the Holland residence and to those detectives starting to work on the drawing of the exterior crime scene map. Perhaps due to the task at hand, or due to their years of experience in dealing with him, Paul could not help but laugh as he noticed the detectives continuing on with their work, paying little, if any, attention to Renda's loud and superfluous comments.

Realizing he was likely prolonging the inevitable, Paul made the short walk from the crime scene van to where Bobby Ray and Pascento had just started talking. As he did, Renda took notice of the former trooper from Connecticut.

"Good to see you, Paul." Renda said as he moved closer to the briefing Bobby Ray was giving Pascento. "Bobby Ray told me he called you. I just cut short a meeting I was at in Conway to get down here. Thought it was important for me to be here. What happened here today is just terrible, just terrible. What makes it even more upsetting is that our victim is someone who dedicated a large portion of his life to serving our country."

"Afternoon, sheriff," Paul said, offering a brief but polite smile as he glanced at his watch, still not sure of what the exact time was.

For the next twenty-five minutes, the four veteran law enforcement officers discussed what had occurred at the Holland residence. As they did, Kindle and one of Pascento's inspectors quietly stood off to the side of the conversation that was taking place. As Bobby Ray and the others spoke about what little evidence had been found at the scene, they also discussed the possibility of the Holland murder being committed by the same individual who had killed Platek. Despite the minor differences in the victims' manner of death, it was not hard, especially for these seasoned investigators, to see the similarities between both investigations.

As they finished their conversation on what direction the Holland investigation was going to take, the noise of several car doors being closed nearby was heard. Looking in that direction, Paul was surprised to see Sergeant Kent Wilson, along with Detectives

Blake Stine and Frank Griffin, standing by their vehicles as they geared up to start working Holland's murder. Their unexpected presence pleased him significantly. First meeting Wilson and Stine, cops from Myrtle Beach PD, and Griffin, a North Myrtle Beach PD narc, when they had been assigned to the task force working the Melkin murders, Paul had been impressed by how each of them approached their roles during the difficult investigation. Later, when he was asked to head the North Litchfield murder investigation while Bobby Ray was recovering from a back operation, Paul had made one unequivocal demand to Renda. Asked to come into an investigation after Audrey Small had made a few early questionable calls due to her inexperience, he had made it clear he needed some experienced cops working that investigation with him. Paul had demanded, and got, Wilson, Stine, and Griffin, as well as FBI Agent Thomas Scozzafava, assigned to the case.

"Surprised to see those ugly faces out there, Paul?" Renda asked in his deep Southern voice. As he stood there, a smile creased the sheriff's worn and tired face.

"Kind of," Paul freely admitted, "but I guess you kind of know me by now, don't you?"

"For what it's worth, I like those fellas as much as you do. They're all good cops. Kind of wish they'd come work for me someday. I could use some more experience on my staff right about now," Renda said wishfully.

"Ever tell them that, sheriff? You know, how much you appreciate them and all." Paul asked as he shot a look towards the three cops who had just finished fiddling around with their gear. "Doesn't cost anything to have a conversation with them, does it?"

"No . . . I guess not," Renda admitted. "Say, that reminds me. I know you're here because Bobby Ray called you, but I could sure use your help again, Paul. My budget is kind of tight right now, especially in my Personnel Services account, but I'll be glad to pay you what I paid you for helping us out in North Litchfield. I'll also pay you for any expenses you incur, but I'm afraid I can't do any better than that. At least, not now I can't."

Paul smiled at Renda's concern about not being able to pay him properly for his time and experience. But to Paul's credit, money was never an issue, or even a concern because of his healthy pension and Donna's salary. Being able to stay in the game, and being able to use his acquired investigative skills to help solve brutal violent crimes like the one now facing the GCSD, was what drove Paul. Police work, especially investigative work, and having the ability to outfox the bad guys was his reward for the time he spent away from home. His only real concern involved another issue.

"Don't worry about what you can and can't pay me as I'm good with what you paid me during the last investigation. I have no complaints with how you've treated me." Somewhat embarrassed, Paul then added, "I'm more worried about having to tell Donna that I'm working another investigation. She wants me to lighten the stress in my life so I can enjoy the retirement I worked so hard to get. But I expect she'll be fine about all of this; she knows I enjoy what I do and knows its stuff like this that keeps me going. It'll all work out, there's nothing to worry about." As he finished speaking, Paul wondered who he had been trying to assure more, Renda or himself. Silently he prayed that Donna would be fine with him committing to help Bobby Ray with another investigation of this magnitude.

In the previous two investigations he had been involved in with the GCSD, Wilson, Stine and Griffin, along with FBI Agent Thomas Scozzafava, had each been assigned significant roles. In the Melkin investigation they were part of a regional response to the five random murders their suspect had committed. In the North Litchfield investigation, one which involved the senseless murders of five young men, Paul had brought them on board for several reasons. Among them were Wilson and Griffin's interview and interrogation skills, and Stine's relentless pursuit of every kind of evidence imaginable, including hearsay and testimonial. While Scozzafava had been brought into the first investigation due to early concerns regarding the killer crossing state lines, he had quickly proved to be an extremely competent investigator. His ability to access federal databases had also been a welcome source of help.

Realizing early on that Paul would have again demanded their presence in this investigation; Renda beat him to the punch. This time he contacted their respective departments immediately after learning of Holland's murder. To his credit, even Renda had seen the possible connection which existed between the two recent murders.

"Where's Scozzafava?" Paul asked, wondering if the FBI agent he thought so highly of had been contacted. Like his friend standing next to him, Bobby Ray was also pleased to see the extra help being assigned to his growing and complex investigation. But unaware until now that any of the cops he saw walking towards him had been contacted by Renda, the blank look on his face told Paul he did not have the answer to his question.

"Relax, Paul," Renda offered as he watched Walter Barber, Georgetown County's deputy coroner, get out of his truck.

"Scozzafava will be here tomorrow. He's just out of town today with his family, that's why he's not here now. I spoke with his SAC earlier this morning; he's promised me Scozz will be here for the duration." As often was the case, Renda's rich Southern accent caused most of his words to flow together, making it difficult for Paul to sometimes understand what he was saying right away.

"Thanks for the help, boss." Bobby Ray said as Paul gave Renda a polite nod of appreciation. The sheriff's actions in reaching out for the extra help also pleased Pascento.

"Good idea you had, sheriff. I like each of those guys. Just as Paul has been, they've certainly been a big help to us on the two previous cases. I'm sure they'll do the same again with this mess we're facing. Hate to say this, but their presence will help to offset Audrey not being here to help us." The solicitor's words caused Renda and Bobby Ray to briefly exchange silent looks with each other.

As he let his two bags of gear fall to the ground, Walter Barber surveyed the scene around Holland's body. A horse enthusiast, and a part-time cowboy at heart, Barber, nearing seventy-eight years of age, was dressed as he normally was. Sporting a light brownish-colored cowboy Stetson on top of his thick head of hair, he had on a dark blue long sleeve denim shirt and blue jeans. From the looks of them, Barber's cowboy boots had obviously spent a great deal of time being worn around his small farm in southern Georgetown County.

"What the heck have we got under this blood-soaked thing that used to be called a sheet," Barber asked, already knowing it was not anything good.

As Bobby Ray began briefing Barber on the events surrounding Holland's death, Pascento politely excused himself. Due back at his office in Conway, he needed time that afternoon to prep for a Probable Cause hearing on an unrelated murder case scheduled to begin the following morning.

"Call me if you need anything, sheriff." Pascento said as he politely shook hands with someone he had clashed with professionally in years past. Then, not wanting to disturb Bobby Ray as he spoke with Barber, Pascento spoke to Paul. "You've got my numbers. Call me when you've got something that I need to know."

Spending most of the next thirty minutes with Barber, Bobby Ray, with Kindle's help, detailed what they had found at the scene as the deputy coroner closely examined the significant injuries Holland had sustained. What he saw and heard made the seasoned coroner shake his head in disgust. Despite his years of service to the county, and despite the number of dead and mutilated bodies he had examined, Barber was sickened by what he was being told.

"Just amazing, just freaking amazing. Twenty-eight years I've been doing this, and man's inhumanity to his fellow man still shocks and offends me," Barber said as he took off his hat. Moments later, out of pure frustration over what had happened to Holland, the deputy coroner ran his fingers through his thick gray hair. "Did this poor guy really have to die just because he flew a flag, albeit an offensive one to some, in front of his own home?" Barber's rhetorical question only drew stares from those around him.

"OK, OK," the veteran coroner soon said in disgust after finishing with his examination of the sustained wounds. Pointing at Holland's body, Barber asked, "You boys about done here with this fella? You know, with your photos and measurements, or do I need to give you some more time? I'm not rushing y'all, but I've got a hundred or so bales of hay to put up before I call it a day."

Looking for a response from Vane, who was now searching the victim's front yard with a metal detector for any small bits of evidence that may have been overlooked, Bobby Ray saw Sergeant Don Elmendorf for the first time. Arriving at the scene only minutes earlier, the senior member of Bobby Ray's Major Case Squad had been testifying in federal court down in Charleston when word had gone out about Holland's murder. Immediately jumping in to help process the scene, the seventeen-year veteran, who had processed hundreds of crime scenes already during his career, was assisting a crime scene tech with carefully packaging up the splintered flagstaff. They were doing so in hopes of not losing any of the bloody fingerprints or other evidence that had been left on the staff.

"Dougie, Don," Bobby Ray hollered out, "you boys all set here with the vic? Walt wants to start packaging him up so he can get him down to the ME's office. We good?" Seeing the thumbs-up he received from Vane, Bobby Ray gave Barber permission to move the now cold remains from the front yard.

As Barber got to work, he spread out a large clean white sheet on the ground next to Holland's body. Unlike the two young deputies watching what was taking place from where they stood several feet away as they took in the sights and sounds of their first visit to a murder scene, Paul knew exactly why the sheet was being used. Patiently he took a few moments to explain the sheet's purpose to the deputies. He did so by asking them each a couple of questions.

"Know why he's doing what he's doing?" Paul asked, catching the attention of both deputies, ones whose youthful appearances had already caused many to question whether they were really old enough to be cops.

"No, sir," the young female deputy answered. Tall and thin in build, Deputy Lydia Swanson had only been working the road alone for the past four months after successfully completing her FTO training. Barely looking at Paul as she answered his question, Swanson kept her eyes fixed on what Barber was doing, and on Holland's badly beaten body.

"What's our victim's body hopefully have on it?" Paul asked, hoping one of the deputies knew the correct answer to his fairly simple question.

"Bruising?" The twenty-something-year-old male deputy replied, not really sure if his answer was remotely correct or not.

"Well, we know that's true from the beating he took," Paul answered, realizing from the answer he just heard that both deputies were likely even greener than they looked. "The correct answer is evidence. Trace evidence, in fact. The purpose of the sheet is to collect any and all amounts of trace evidence that our killer may have unintentionally left on Mr. Holland's body; evidence that's sometimes hard for the naked eye to discern. He's using a white sheet simply because any evidence that's been left on the body, even if it falls off our victim's clothing like it often does, will stand out more on a white background than it would if he used a darker color sheet. The sheet also helps to keep any evidence, such as hair follicles, dead skin, and clothing fibers, from being lost. In this investigation, just like in any homicide investigation, even the smallest amount of trace evidence can sometimes help us identify who's responsible for what happened."

"Sir," Deputy Ray Clarke asked, his face growing redder by the moment due to the embarrassment he was feeling, "I'm not really sure what you mean by the term trace evidence."

Not trying to be rude, but at the same time chuckling over what he considered to be one of the most basic of terms in both law enforcement and legal jargon, Paul, as politely as he could, answered Clarke's question. As he did, he caught Barber motioning to him. "Deputy, I'm afraid that's a term I'll have to explain to you at greater length during our next basic crime scene processing session. Right now, I've got work to do."

As soon as Paul moved back to where Barber and Bobby Ray were standing, the coroner spoke to them regarding the autopsy that would soon take place. As he did, he began packing up his equipment.

"I spoke with Doc Symthe on my ride up here, Bobby Ray, he's gonna do the Post tomorrow morning. Have whoever's gonna watch him do his magic there by nine. For me, it's an obvious call . . . he'll rule this as a murder, and likely list the cause of death as blunt force trauma to the skull. The tox report will obviously take a couple of weeks to come in as you know, but I'd be surprised if that tells us anything more than this poor guy probably liked to have a cocktail or two in the afternoon despite possibly doing so in conflict with medicine he was taking for his diabetes or for some other medical condition he had. It really doesn't matter though as none of those issues had any bearing on what took place here today." After exchanging looks with Paul and Bobby Ray, the wannabe cowboy turned coroner looked down at Holland's remains one last time. "Guess I've got another chapter for the book I've been telling myself I'm going to write, don't I? I'll probably have a drink or two myself later tonight, maybe that will finally get me motivated to start writing. Doubt it, but we'll soon find out, won't we?"

Shaking his head at Barber's comments, Bobby Ray laughed before jokingly adding, "You're a sick old man! You know that, don't you?"

Assisted by his student intern in zipping up the black plastic body bag, Barber chuckled softly after hearing his friend's comment. Then nodding at what still rested on the ground next to him, he said, "Kind of have to be when you do what I do for a living."

After finishing with everything that needed to be done with Holland's body, Barber discarded the latex gloves he had been wearing as he stood next to his vehicle. Grabbing an old plastic milk jug from the bed of his truck, one long devoid of its original contents, he poured the lukewarm water inside it over his bare hands. Then pushing the plunger of a small glass bottle several times, Barber quickly lathered his hands with a thick layer of puke-green antimicrobial soap. While the gloves had protected his hands during the examination of Holland's body, the veteran coroner carefully scrubbed his hands clean, protecting himself from any bodily fluids he may have come in contact with.

After rinsing his hands with some of the remaining water, he dried them by using an arm's length of paper towels. Soon satisfied they were clean, Barber spit out the wad of smokeless tobacco he had inside his mouth; carefully replacing it with a generous amount of fresh tobacco. He did so by using several of the fingers on his right hand, ones he had used minutes earlier to poke and prod inside the recesses of Holland's still bloody mouth.

* * * * * *

After the removal of Holland's body, Bobby Ray, assisted by Paul and Vane, supervised what still had to be done to finish processing the crime scene correctly. This was done both inside and outside the Holland residence. Playing by the rules, Mincey warrants had been obtained from Pascento's office, and later signed by a local magistrate, so Holland's residence, his surrounding property, and his two vehicles could lawfully be searched. By obtaining the warrants, Bobby Ray knew the seizure of any evidence would be far less likely to be attacked or contested than it could be if it had been seized without the court's permission. While he was confident that none of Holland's relatives, if there were any, would have contested the victim's residence or property being searched, or any evidence being seized, Bobby Ray never really gave much thought to how relatives would react when it came to processing crime scenes. Instead, he thought of his victims, those people who could no longer speak for themselves. He also thought of those responsible for committing the violence, and the games and baseless objections their defense attorneys would attempt to raise during their client's Probable Cause hearings, and during the actual trial itself. Like Paul, he would never allow a technicality, or a question about the legality of how a crime scene had been processed or how evidence had been seized, to be the focus of any trial. Doing so would have been unfair to the victims he now served.

While four of Kindle's deputies had already completed a very basic neighborhood canvass in the early stages of the investigation, as the others were busy processing the crime scene Wilson and Griffin spent time retracing the efforts made by the less experienced deputies. After interviewing the residents of several nearby homes, including one family who lived directly across the street from their victim's home, the two veteran investigators reported their findings to Bobby Ray. What they soon told him was not much to base an investigation on.

"Talk to me, fellas. Tell me you've found the bad guy's wallet or something special like that." With far too many years as a cop under his belt, Bobby Ray knew there was little hope of his wish coming true. Seeing the expressions his two investigators wore quickly confirmed they had little, if anything, of substance to tell him.

"That'd be nice, wouldn't it? Imagine finding a smoking gun like that, that'd make life far too easy for us," Griffin remarked, referring to Bobby Ray's comment regarding the wallet.

"Learn anything?"

"Sorry, boss, not much, certainly nothing to point us in any specific direction," Wilson said, shaking his head in disappointment. Pointing to a small single-story home directly across street from their victim's residence, Wilson told Bobby Ray about the one lead they had learned.

"A couple by the name of Whitmore live there; Frank and Cecilia Whitmore to be precise. Like a few of their neighbors we spoke to, they weren't home when Holland was murdered. The good news, and this is all of it, is that when they were driving home from having lunch down in the inlet, they saw a white male running through two of their neighbors yards. The individual they saw looked like he was running pretty fast, but they have no idea if he's our suspect or not. They described this guy as being around six feet tall, rather thin, and wearing some kind of a white shirt. It's not much, but that's all they could tell us. None of the other neighbors saw or heard anything, not even this guy Mr. and Mrs. Whitmore saw. No one heard anything until they heard the sirens coming up the street."

"That's about par for the course," Bobby Ray offered somewhat dejectedly, realizing from his years of conducting such canvasses that more often than not the effort put into them was generally not rewarded with much to go on. "At least in real life that's how they play out," he thought. "Cop shows on television, well, that's a different story. Most often, a different result as well."

******

To support the newly initiated investigation, the meticulous search of Holland's home and property was time and money well-spent. But while Bobby Ray's detectives had no way of knowing this at the time, just like the neighborhood canvass they had conducted, it would soon prove to be a wasted effort.

5

Unlike its religious neighbor which sat less than a mile away, St. Thomas Aquinas, the sole Catholic Church in Pawleys Island, was a relative newcomer to those Christians practicing their faith.

Built in 1988, the church sat on a small parcel of land that had once been part of a twenty-five hundred acre plantation, stretching during its heyday from the nearby Atlantic Ocean to the Waccamaw River. Built in the early 1600s, and first carved out of an old-growth forest that was comprised mostly of *Quercus virginiana*, Southern live oak trees, the plantation prospered for years, growing, among other things, rice and indigo until shortly after the end of the Civil War. It was one of several plantations which had lined the old King's Highway, a historic road once stretching from Boston to Charleston.

While the beautifully built church on Waverly Road was the centerpiece of the current parcel of land, several other smaller buildings, including the church's large community and recreational hall, also stood on the well-maintained piece of property. Like its nearby neighbor, All Saints Church, an Anglican church built in 1767, St. Thomas Aquinas was revered by those who fondly referred to it as their spiritual home.

******

After parking his Chevy Tahoe behind a home that had sat vacant for some time on Martin Luther King Drive, Sonny Pratt stared down at the front page of the local newspaper as he turned his ignition off. Having picked up the paper off the table next to him as he finished his lunch two hours earlier, Pratt's anger rose as he read the paper's sensational headline for the second time. The large bold headline, *'Boston's Catholic priests accused of sexual abuse'*, was supported by a lengthy detailed story displayed just below the sensational eye-catching banner. Spread out over three-pages, the story told how the church had allegedly protected five priests who had been accused by several of their victims of multiple counts of wrongdoing over the past eight years.

"Miserable no-good perverts, that's what those disgraced bastards are," Pratt screamed out loud as he angrily threw the newspaper across his front seat. "Sexually abusing kids whose parents trusted them to care for their children . . . trusting them to teach their kids about the church only to later find out these bastards abused their positions of power. I hope they all go to hell! Send the other bastards who kept the truth from being made public to hell as well! They're just as dirty and corrupt as most of our so-called politicians. Send those bastards with them . . . let them all visit the devil together!" Sufficiently worked up over what he had read, Pratt's bright red face was now drenched in sweat. In his twisted mind, it was now time to make someone from the Catholic Church pay for what had happened.

Placing what he needed inside his coat, Pratt quietly closed his car door. After doing so, and by way of a wireless remote, he activated the small unobtrusive spy camera he had mounted inside his vehicle. Purchased online from an electronics store who shamelessly promoted themselves as being the leading supplier of a host of electronic spy equipment for use by private detectives, and by wives who suspected their husbands of participating in acts of infidelity, the small camera was designed to run for several hours on its batteries. Growing more and more paranoid that he was always being watched, Pratt had purchased the small camera in the event his car was broken into or tampered with by either the cops or his neighbors.

Soon finished with the needs of activating the recording device, he began making his way through several adjacent run-down pieces of property. Several moments later he stood safely inside a small stand of trees lining the western end of Waverly Road. Soon confident that he had not been seen, and wearing a maroon windbreaker he had stolen from a coat rack at a local diner in Murrells Inlet, as well as a pair of black dress pants and a blue shirt, Pratt crossed the quiet two-lane road in front of him. Walking slowly through another wooded tree line which hugged the ball field adjacent to the church's main parking lot, he paused in the shadows for a brief moment to make sure he was not being watched. Then, despite the day's bright late afternoon sunlight, Pratt moved steadily across the large open rec field and three parking lots as he made his way to the church's main entrance. To his relief, he did so without being seen.

Entering the main vestibule at precisely 5:30 pm as he had planned, Pratt was pleased to see only one elderly couple remaining inside the church. Soon finished with their weekly penance, they exited the pew they had been sitting in and turned to walk outside. As they did, they barely took notice of the person quietly sitting less than fifteen feet away from where they had said their prayers.

Now alone, Pratt remained seated in the second to last row of pews for several moments as he stared down the church's wide center aisle at the alter in front of him. High above it, and off to either side of the main alter, hung colorful and stunning hand-painted images of God's son, Jesus Christ. As he stared at them, Pratt angrily began shaking his fist as he stood up. "You . . . you betrayed them," he murmured softly under his breath. Then, as he turned to leave the pew he was in, Pratt heard the one noise he had hoped to hear. Walking slowly towards it as he cautiously tried minimizing the noise his own feet were making, he could tell behind one of the confessional doors feet were softly being shuffled.

Pushing aside the red privacy drape, Pratt quietly moved inside the left confessional booth. Kneeling down inside the darkened space directly in front of the metal screen which separated his booth from the one next to him, he began his act of Penance as a small wooden door behind the screen slowly slid open. Making the sign of the cross first, Pratt then spoke by saying, "Bless me Father, for I have sinned. It has been five weeks since my last confession."

Behind a thin wooden wall, and barely visible to the penitent in the booth next to him was Father Jonathan Guyette. In his late sixties, the popular priest had over thirty-eight years of faithful service to the church. Due to his growing responsibilities with the church evolving with each passing year, Guyette had only recently been assigned to St. Thomas Aquinas by Bishop Francis O'Halloran, of the Catholic Diocese of Charleston. As he heard Pratt begin his Penance, Guyette also made the sign of the cross. As he did, he unintentionally touched the small gold crucifix suspended around his neck by a chain of the same color.

Then, as carefully as he had rehearsed, and without a hint of remorse, Pratt spoke again. "Father, since my last confession I have committed two murders. My venial sins are that I have repeatedly taken the Lord's name in vain. I have also missed church on every occasion possible. For these and all of my sins, I am deeply sorry." As he finished speaking, Pratt knew he had just lied. "Another sin to confess at another time," he thought as he waited for the priest next to him to react to what he had just confessed to.

The confession of sins he just heard stunned the parish priest. For a brief few moments, he lacked a proper response. Finally mustering the courage, he asked, "My . . . my son, did I hear you correctly? Have . . . have you really committed the act of murder as you have confessed?" As he waited for a response, Guyette shifted nervously in his chair. Immediately, sweat began to bead on his forehead.

"Yes, Father. But while I know what I've done is wrong, I'm not truly sorry for any of the harm I've caused. I've simply done the Lord's work for him," was Pratt's calm response to Guyette's questions.

"You're telling me the Lord spoke to you . . . he . . . he told you to commit murder for him?"

Smiling to himself, Pratt moved closer to the confessional screen before whispering, "Yes, Father, he did. He always speaks to me, but I don't always listen to what he has to say." After a brief moment of awkward silence between them, Pratt's voice rose as he added, "Excuse me for feeling this way, but I don't believe you think he speaks to me like he does. He has also told me it is you who has the dirty hands . . . the dirty mind, the perverted mind, not I!"

Stunned by what he was listening to, Guyette did his best at keeping calm so as not to upset the person in the confessional next to him. "My son, I can only pray for your soul at this time as your words tell me that you are not ready to make a proper act of Contrition yet. I'm sorry to have to tell you this, but while our Lord does forgive those who have offended him, I cannot offer you his forgiveness at this time."

While not unexpected, Guyette's words caused anger to immediately appear in Pratt's words. "You are the one with the dirty hands, Father, not me!" Standing up, Pratt pointed his right index finger at the priest as he continued to speak. As he did, he unbuttoned his windbreaker at the same time. "I came here to seek the Lord's forgiveness, forgiveness I deserve . . . forgiveness I know he has for me. Why do you . . . a true sinner in the Lord's eyes, refuse to grant me absolution?"

Finished with his tirade, Pratt moved outside the confessional, angrily ripping open the door to the confessional booth where Guyette now cowered. Raising the .22 Smith & Wesson pistol he had removed from under his windbreaker, he pointed it directly at the priest's face. Then, speaking loud enough for his words to echo across the vast interior of the empty church, Pratt angrily yelled, "It is you, you and your fellow priests who need absolution, Father, not I. For it is you who have violated the faith so many people had in you . . . it is your kind alone who have committed the most heinous of sins against the church!"

As Guyette turned slightly away from the person now mocking him, the cotton Pratt had wadded up inside a homemade silencer quickly filled the air inside the small confessional. Firing twice, Pratt's bullets first struck the priest in the upper left shoulder before exiting through his back and embedding in the oak paneling behind him.

Making the sign of the cross with his pistol still in his hand, Pratt then spoke again. "For your Penance, Father, I want you to say four Hail Marys and five Our Fathers." Then, pointing his gun at Guyette's chest, he added, "Give thanks to the Lord for He is good."

Instinctively raising his hands in front of him in hopes of protecting himself as Pratt took a step closer to where he sat, Guyette slunk as low as possible in his chair, trying to make himself as small a target as possible. As he did, despite the pain in his shoulder sending shock waves throughout his entire body, the priest tried focusing on the person standing in front of him, but all he saw was an angry face staring back at him. It was a face hidden under the brim of an old fedora hat and behind a pair of heavily tinted sunglasses.

"Why? Why have you shot me?" The stunned priest now angrily asked. "I have done nothing to hurt you!" Close to going into circulatory shock, Guyette gasped for air as his white surplice grew stained with his own warm blood.

"Because your hands have become stained just like the others!" With that, Pratt fired his third shot, one which quickly tore through the palm of the defenseless priest's right hand before coming to rest in the right side of his chest. As before, bits of cotton again floated in the air around the confessional. Gasping twice for air, Guyette slumped sideways in his chair before crashing to the floor in an awkward heap.

Quickly looking around as the unexpected sound of the church's air conditioner kicking in startled him, Pratt saw no one at first. Then looking outside, he saw someone walking towards the front of the church. Looking back at Guyette for a brief moment, Pratt started panicking over being seen inside the church. Quickly reaching for the improvised silencer that he had duct taped over the front sights of his pistol, Pratt struggled as he tried tearing the thickly wound tape away from around the neck of the silencer, a small Pepsi bottle he had previously packed full of cotton. Getting his idea for the silencer from a movie he had watched, he had used the heavy tape to keep the bottle from flying off the end of his pistol when he fired it.

Afraid he was about to be caught inside the church, and with the other exits too far away, Pratt briskly walked outside as the church's elderly cleaning lady carried her supplies down the front sidewalk. Not having time to hide his bulky pistol inside his windbreaker, he held it tightly against his left leg as he pushed himself further away from both the church and Guyette's body. As he did, the cleaning lady, lost in her own thoughts as she struggled with a plastic bin holding her cleaning supplies, managed only a brief glance at the stranger she saw walking several yards away from her.

Retracing his earlier steps, Pratt moved back towards his vehicle as quickly as possible. As he did, he took notice as the cleaning lady opened one of the church's large front doors. Doing so caused a low hanging branch to knock the brown fedora hat he had been wearing off his head. Startled by the sounds of children playing on the other side of the tree line, Pratt elected to ignore his fallen hat that was now being pushed further away from him by a blustery wind. Briefly hiding in the tree line as he waited for two cars to pass by, Pratt was soon across the road. Within moments he was turning off the small camera he had placed inside his vehicle. Confident his face had not been seen by anyone, and wasting little time, in less than thirty seconds he was slowly driving away from where he had parked.

As he did, he gave the church one last look in his rearview mirror. While doing so, three sets of young eyes watched him from where they stood hidden from view. At the same exact moment, inside the church a scream of terror filled the large cavernous building. Father Guyette's badly shot up body had been found by Millicent Causing; almost immediately the elderly cleaning lady fell to the floor unconscious, overcome by what she had seen.

******

Despite his fondness for cop shows, and the amount of time he spent reading mystery novels, Father Guyette's shooter would make one huge mistake. He would do so when he dumped most of the clothes he had been wearing into a dumpster located in the rear of a nearby strip mall. But then again, souvenirs taken or worn at crime scenes have often led to people being caught for their misdeeds.

6

Just a few miles away, Bobby Ray's team of detectives now put the finishing touches on the processing of the second murder scene. Satisfied all of the available witnesses and neighbors had been interviewed, and that the scene itself had been thoroughly combed for evidence, Bobby Ray called them together for a brief meeting in Holland's driveway.

After briefly speaking with Paul on what needed to be done the following morning, Bobby Ray began advising Stine, Wilson, and the others with them what he wanted them to focus on. As he handed out the next day's assignments, his cell phone chirped to announce an incoming text. Checking his phone as he continued to speak, the message he saw displayed caused him to pause before he could finish handing out the assignments.

"Hang on a minute, fellas, I've got to make a call. There might be something happening that we need to know about." Walking inside Holland's garage, Bobby Ray speed-dialed the Georgetown County Dispatch Center.

"Georgetown County Dispatch, Dispatcher Herman speaking. How may I help you?"

"Hey, girl! It's Bobby Ray, y'all just sent me a text. Talk to me."

For the next three minutes, Bobby Ray listened as Herman told him about the shooting that had just taken place at St. Thomas Aquinas. Soon frustrated at listening to her lengthy description of what had occurred, Bobby Ray, short on patience and already tired from a long day, began to pepper the veteran dispatcher with a series of questions. Among them were questions about the victim's condition and the integrity of the crime scene.

"Vicky, has anyone told you for sure if the priest is actually dead?"

"No, sir, they've told me he's been shot up pretty badly, but I haven't been told he's dead."

"Who is at the scene and . . . tell you what, disregard that question for now. Just tell whoever's there that my folks and I will be there in a few minutes. Just make sure they don't muck up my crime scene."

Disconnecting the call, both out of frustration and disbelief over what he had been told, the wheels in Bobby Ray's brain began spinning. Far too experienced not to do so, he had already begun to question whether the scene at the church was possibly connected to the one at Holland's home. It was a thought that was soon replaced by others far more important for the exact moment. For now, his principal focus was on moving his personnel from one scene to the other, and to extending their already long and demanding day.

******

After contacting the uniformed patrol supervisor who had responded to the shooting at the church in an attempt to get a more accurate description of what he would be facing, Bobby Ray broke the news of what had just happened to his staff. Like Paul, the others, including Vane and Elmendorf, were less than pleased to learn their plans for another Saturday evening had just been cancelled. Despite having experienced such similar situations in the past, the prospect of facing another ten hours of work was less than pleasing.

It would soon prove not to be their last long day of chasing shooters and others, or of processing scenes left behind for them to clean up.

7

With Bobby Ray electing to respond to Waccamaw Hospital in hopes of being able to interview the critically wounded parish priest, Paul responded to St. Thomas Aquinas. With Elmendorf, Griffin, and Wilson, along with two evidence techs, responding to the hospital with Bobby Ray, Paul, acting as his friend's second-in-command, took charge of processing the scene at the church. After being briefed by Sgt. Orlando Mo that the scene, like its only witness, had been secured, Paul got to work. Quickly he issued his first order, instructing Mo, the uniformed patrol supervisor who had been one of the first emergency responders to arrive at the scene, to deploy his personnel so a grid search of the entire church property could be conducted. Specifically, Mo was told to look for any footprints, blood droppings, clothes, shell casings, and any other discarded items.

As Mo walked off to round up his deputies, Paul moved towards the front of the church. Moments later, after entering through a side door so he and the others with him did not compromise the integrity of any evidence inside the front vestibule, he assigned Vane, along with Detective David Wagner and three crime scene techs, the responsibility of searching the interior of the large church. "When you're done with that, then we'll start our processing of the confessional booths," Paul said as his eyes took in what had previously happened in the rear of the church.

Like Paul and a handful of other cops along the Grand Strand, Wagner had started his law enforcement career in Connecticut. Originally from Woodbury, a small town in Litchfield County, he had served a total of twenty-eight years with two different departments before moving to Surfside Beach. Much to the displeasure of four other younger deputies who were hired before him, Wagner, who had been hired less than eight months earlier by Sheriff Renda, was immediately assigned to work with the Major Case Squad due to his significant experience as an investigator. Despite their past careers, the two former Nutmeggers from the Constitution State had never crossed paths with each other until now.

After imaging the horror Guyette must have gone through, Paul instructed Stine and Detective Bruce Davis to interview Causing, the elderly cleaning lady. For Davis, a young detective with less than a year in grade, this was the third homicide he had been a part of in such a short period of time.

"She's supposedly still pretty upset over finding Father Guyette shot up like he was," Paul said as he walked into a nearby foyer with his two detectives. "Tread lightly with her due to her age. You'll find her next door in the rectory; she's in one of the offices. Blake, you're the lead on this. When you can, let me know what she has to say." As Stine and Davis started to walk away, Paul gave them one more task to complete. "While you're there, better hustle up the other priests and see what they have to say about our vic. They may not have heard or seen anything based on what we're already being told, but you'd best find out what they might know about what went on here."

As he acknowledged Paul's instructions, Stine took note of two low profile surveillance cameras mounted near the foyer's ceiling, ones the church had installed two years earlier after a rash of minor thefts.

"We'll talk to the old lady first," Stine offered as he stared up at the cameras. "Then we'll talk to the other penguins and get the skinny on the priest and everything else. We'll find out what his background is, how long he's been here, any arguments he might have had with anyone, you know, the usual bullshit we're always looking for answers to when shit like this hits the fan." Pointing up at the cameras, Stine added, "When we're done asking our questions, we'll take a look at what these two suckers captured as well."

Rubbing his chin, Davis could not help smiling over how his partner had described what they were about to do. In a more politically correct, but friendly and sarcastic manner he rephrased Stine's comments. "Boss, I think what my veteran partner meant to say is that we will afford our elderly witness, who's also our most important witness, a safe and comforting environment in which to speak with us in. Hopefully she'll be able to regale us with a host of information regarding our victim's near demise. Then, as my partner inappropriately described them, we will speak with the other penguins . . . I mean those other members of the priesthood who are dressed in black and white. It is our hope they will be able to inform us even more about the good Father's background, and about whatever else it is that transpired here earlier today. Then we will finish our pleasant late afternoon by sitting and watching a video, hoping we'll be lucky enough to ID the miscreant who harmed the good Father Guyette."

As hard as he tried not to laugh at what Stine and Davis had said, Paul could not. After bursting out laughing at the somewhat unique sense of humor two of his favorite cops had used as a means of helping them keep their sanity after another day of seeing two more people either murdered or seriously injured in acts of senseless violence, he sent them on their way.

"Come on, you freaking moron," Stine playfully directed at Davis, ignoring as he did the sanctity of the place where he was now standing. "Quit your brown-nosing and let's get to work!" While his comment drew another quick laugh from Paul, it caused Davis to shake his head in mock disgust over what he had heard.

With all of the scene's processing needs now being addressed, Paul paused outside on the front steps to call Bobby Ray with an update on what he had learned, and to get his first update on Guyette's condition. They had barely started talking when a young deputy, in a loud and excited voice, yelled from across the far side of the rec field.

"I found something! I found something!"

Realizing something positive had been found, Paul sought to terminate his call with Bobby Ray. "One of your deputies over near the ball field is yelling that he found something. I'll call you back with an update when I have time."

＊＊＊＊＊＊

Shortly after the brown fedora hat had been seized from near the line of trees bordering the church's rec field, Paul received his first update from Stine.

"We've finally finished interviewing the cleaning lady. It took longer than it should have, but like you said, she's still pretty upset from seeing all that blood. Bruce is just now putting the finishing touches on her written statement."

"Learn much else?" Paul asked, hopeful of hearing some additional good news.

"Not much, not much at all," Stine sighed, his voice reflecting his own disappointment over not learning more than he had hoped to. "The one thing we did learn of a positive note is that Reverend Hale told us he walked through the church after Mo and the others got here. He told us there's nothing missing, and nothing's been vandalized or desecrated. Small victory there, I guess. On the other hand, our witness really didn't see too much; heard even less. She told us she only saw one male leaving the church as she was nearing the front doors. Our problem is she claims she was so focused on not dropping her cleaning supplies that she paid little attention to the person she saw."

Paul's facial reaction showed Stine the disappointment his friend was experiencing. Hoping for more, Paul asked, "She tell you two anything else useful?"

"Two things really. She claims the guy was wearing a hat . . . she called it a dress hat of some kind." Stine's mind briefly went blank as he tried recalling the proper style of hat their witness had seen.

"A fedora?" Paul asked.

"Yeah, that's it. A fedora, a brown one. She also claims she saw him holding a plastic drink bottle of some kind close to his left leg. Funny thing though, because when I asked her more about it she claimed it was upside down. She also told us she saw it down around his knee, but then she questioned how this bottle could have been down by his knee as she thought it was too far down his leg for him to be holding in his hand. She was adamant it was empty as well. If she's correct about seeing our shooter, and about seeing him carrying an empty drink bottle, why's he carrying it? Was he concerned about leaving it behind with his prints on it? Not sure about all of this right now, I haven't quite figured it out yet." Stine stood scratching his head, perplexed about the presence of the plastic bottle their witness had claimed to have seen.

Paul remained quiet for several moments, allowing Stine time to complete his thought before finishing with what he had to say.

"I've got a few more things to tell you. This is all from Dougie and Wags, not her. They both stopped me on my way over to see you. Dougie wanted me to tell you after they had finished their sweep of the church for any evidence which hadn't previously been found, they found three .22 rim fired Remington shell casings. He found all three of them in the area outside the confessional booths. He's pretty sure they've been fired from a pistol, but he's holding off on his official call of that for now." Stine told Paul this as he watched the uniformed deputies patiently searching the grounds for any additional evidence. After taking a quick sip from a bottle of water he was carrying, the MBPD detective added, "Those two guys also have two other things they want you to know."

"What's that?" Paul curiously asked, hoping their shooter had left behind a critical piece of evidence for them to find.

"Two of the rounds our shooter fired came to rest in the wooden panel in the rear of the priest's confessional booth. The other round they haven't found as yet. They're still looking though. Might still be inside our vic, I guess."

"What's the other thing they want me to know?" Paul asked, anxious to learn as much as possible about what Vane and Wagner were finding in and around the confessional booths.

"Cotton. They told me they've found a bunch of cotton, small wads of it. By the sounds of it, they apparently found most of it inside the confessional booth where our vic was found. What's that all about?" Stine asked as he again scratched his head.

First telling Stine to relay a message to Vane for him, and to then view what the security cameras had captured, Paul placed a call to Bobby Ray. As he did, he told Stine his theory about the cotton.

"Yeah, Paul, what's up?" Bobby Ray asked from where he was sitting within the nurses' station inside the hospital's ER.

As he explained what Vane and Wagner had found inside the church, Paul asked what, if anything, the x-rays of Guyette had shown.

"A bunch of broken bones for sure. For being shot three times, he's lucky to still be with us. They're still not sure if he's going to survive the surgery they're prepping him for due to his age and because of the amount of blood he's lost, but we'll know soon enough, I guess."

"How about any bullets?" Paul asked hopefully. "Did the x-rays show any bullets still inside our vic?"

Turning to the ER head nurse sitting next to him, Bobby Ray sought to find the answer to Paul's question. Her check of Guyette's x-rays soon gave him the answer he was looking for.

"The answer to your question is yes. I'm looking at one of his x-rays as we speak and I can clearly see a bullet lodged in our guy's chest. I'm not sure if this means anything to you," Bobby Ray offered, "but he also sustained bullet wounds to his left shoulder and to his right palm. Why are you asking if he has a bullet stuck inside of him? Did you guys find something?"

"Yeah, I think we did," Paul answered as he began explaining what had been found inside the church. While most of what he told his friend was concentrated on the shell casings, as well as the bullets that had been found lodged in the wall, he also told Bobby Ray about the wadded pieces of cotton Vane and Wagner had found.

"Cotton?" Like Stine had been, Bobby Ray was at a loss over Paul's mention of the wads of cotton found in and around the confessional booths. "What's that all about?"

"Think about what I told you, Bobby Ray. The cleaning lady told the guys she saw our shooter leaving the church carrying a plastic bottle. It's one I'm guessing he hadn't been drinking from."

"Sorry, buddy, I'm still not getting it. Help me out here." A tired Bobby Ray said as he slumped back in the chair he was sitting in.

Despite knowing his friend was bushed from a long day, Paul shook his head in frustration. Slightly irritated over the fact that Bobby Ray could not make the obvious connection between the wads of cotton that had been found and the plastic bottle, he bit his tongue. Instead, Paul jabbed his friend with a sarcastic barb in lieu of saying something he might have later regretted. "Guess you've been sitting behind a desk too long, Johnny Reb. Looks like you need to get out in the field and do some honest police work for a change."

"Screw you! I'm just bone-tired right now," Bobby Ray said, rubbing his eyes as he waited for Paul's explanation. "How about you just telling me what the dang cotton means so I don't have to tax my already overworked brain too much more tonight." Sitting next to him as she reviewed some paperwork, the ER nurse chuckled as she listened to the words Bobby Ray had used while speaking to his friend.

"Our shooter probably packed the plastic bottle full of cotton after he taped it to the end of his gun barrel. He probably tried making a crude silencer in hopes it would muffle the sounds of the shots inside the church. When he fired each of his shots some of the cotton was obviously carried out the end of the bottle, one he had already cut the end off so the cotton could be easily stuffed inside it. Maybe he didn't cut the end of it off correctly and that's why some of the cotton has been found or maybe it's because of the force from each of the three discharges, but that's the reason for the cotton being found. If I had to guess, and it's not a hard one to make, I'd have to say the wads of cotton were discharged out of the bottle as each shot was fired. In fact, I'll bet when the boys dig the two rounds out of the wooden paneling they'll find at least a few cotton fibers there as well." Then Paul asked one more question, one related to the plastic bottle itself, "I haven't been told about any pieces of plastic shrapnel being found, have you?"

Despite being tired, Bobby Ray felt embarrassed that he had not made the connection between the two items. Clearing his throat as he sat up in his chair, he was pleased Paul was not there to see the sheepish look on his face. "No, no one's told me about any pieces of plastic being embedded in our vic's clothing or his skin. But I'll check on that after we get done talking." As he finished his comment, Bobby Ray saved himself any additional embarrassment by realizing why Paul had called in the first place. "Now I get it. The bullet that's still inside the priest . . . perhaps inside his other two wounds as well, you want me to ask his surgeons to check for any cotton fibers that may have been transferred from around the bullets to any of his wounds when he was shot. If they find any, we might be able to tie those fibers to the ones you guys found inside the church."

Paul smiled over Bobby Ray finally being able to figure out what it was that he had been hinting at. "It took you a bit, Johnny Reb, but now you're cooking with gas. Get those fibers for us, and that bullet as well. That way we can send them up to SLED so they can hopefully connect the shell casings to the bullet, and then to our shooter's weapon. That's if we can find him, of course." Then pausing a moment, Paul added, "Who knows, maybe we'll get lucky and SLED will already have the info we need from both the casings and the bullets in their firearm's library, that's if they've tested that particular firearm in the past. It's not likely, but let's hope so."

A thought quickly passing through Paul's head caused him to ask one more question. "Bobby Ray, I know this wasn't the case earlier today at our first scene, but what about your previous victim. Did you find any cotton wadding or any cotton fibers at that scene?"

Without a moment of hesitation, Bobby Ray answered his friend's question. "Nope, not a lick of anything like that. But remember, our first guy wasn't shot like the priest was, he was beaten to death just like Holland was."

"Yeah, I know," Paul replied, disappointed over what he had been told. "I just wanted to make sure, that's all. I was just holding out hope that some of the cotton might have been transferred to the first guy's clothing or to something else like that."

* * * * * *

As Paul walked back towards the front of the church from where he had been standing in the parking lot, Vane was slowly walking backwards out the large double front doors. Moments earlier, using two boxes of church bulletins, he had managed to prop them open. As he stepped outside, a large wooden panel which had been part of the back wall of Father Guyette's confessional booth was carefully being carried out of the church. Even with Wagner and a uniformed deputy carrying one end of the large polished piece of thick oak paneling and two of Vane's evidence techs carrying the other end, the four men still struggled under the weight of it.

After carefully escorting them down the six granite steps outside the church's main entrance so they did not fall, or drop the important piece of evidence they were carrying, Vane opened the rear doors of the GCSD's Major Case van so their largest piece of evidence could be slid inside it.

Finished wiping the sweat from his brow after safely securing the section of oak paneling, Vane explained to Paul why that part of the confessional had been dismantled. "I spoke with Reverend Hale . . . he's the head man here, and explained that it was going to take some time cutting with a saw, or maybe with a chisel, to get the two rounds out that are lodged in the paneling. He understands why we need the rounds, and he's certainly been very supportive with everything we need here. He also realizes the section we're taking with us is pretty much destroyed from the wood splintering when the rounds struck it. To his credit, the good Father wasn't too keen about us doing what needs to done inside the church. He also didn't want any of his parishioners getting upset if they saw it damaged like it is, so he was good with us removing it. We'll get it back to my evidence processing area tonight and then start working on getting the slugs out of it tomorrow. To be honest, I'm glad we're doing it there. Just doesn't seem right to be destroying the Lord's furniture right in front of him, even if it is for all the right reasons." Using his handkerchief to wipe the remaining sweat off his brow, Vane paused from speaking for a moment to complete his task. Soon finished, he told his friend how he felt. "What I've said may sound silly to you, Paul, but I'm a church-going guy, a believer and all of that. Ever since I was a young man, I've accepted Jesus Christ as my Savior. I know I would've felt funny doing what I know I have to do right in front of him and all. To be honest with you, I feel better knowing I can take care of business in my own controlled environment. It's definitely a place where I feel at home."

Patting Vane on the shoulder, Paul told him he respected his friend's feelings. As he did, Stine and Davis walked to where he and Vane stood next to the Major Case van.

"We've got the footage the two cameras shot," Davis offered, holding up a CD to show Paul. "Looked at it with Reverend Hale the first time we watched it. Our shooter's a white male. Mrs. Causing, the cleaning lady, she's confirmed for us who our guy is when she viewed it with us. Even though Blake and I are of the opinion that our shooter may not have known about the cameras, the video doesn't show his face very well. We could tell he was wearing sunglasses, and we could see he was definitely holding something by his left side, but due to the position of the cameras they weren't able to capture what it was."

As Davis handed the CD to one of the evidence techs so it could be logged in as a piece of evidence, Stine added another couple of important points to the conversation taking place.

"When we asked our cleaning lady to describe the clothing our shooter was wearing, she told us she could only remember him wearing the brownish-colored hat I've already told you about and a windbreaker. Like Reverend Hale, she has no idea who this guy is, nor could she tell us how tall the guy was or if he had any facial hair or anything like that. She's still pretty upset from what she saw inside the church."

"What'd the video show you when you watched it? Was the guy wearing the hat and windbreaker like she told you about?" Paul curiously asked, trying to paint a mental picture of the person responsible for shooting Father Guyette.

Stine and Davis exchanged brief looks with each other before Stine answered Paul's question. "Yep, sure was, has to be the same guy who shot Father Guyette. The only other people we saw on the video were a handful of folks either Hale or this woman knew as members of the church. The video showed them coming and going during the time period Father Guyette was hearing confessions. Our guy was the last guy in and out of the church before we saw the cleaning lady enter. The times all match."

"You're both sure the guy you like for this was wearing the items Mrs. Causing described?"

"Yes, there's no doubt he was wearing the same hat and jacket she had told us about." Anticipating Paul's next question, Davis added, "We showed her the part of the video twice where our guy is seen walking out of the church, but like we've said, she doesn't know him. Outside of telling us he's the guy she saw leave the church, she can't tell us anything else. She can't even tell us if he left in a car, on a bike, or by Pony Express. Hale doesn't know our guy either. I think we're going to have to ID our mystery man by different means as for now we have no idea who this guy is or why he came here to do the damage he did. Maybe Father Guyette knows him, but I'm not betting any money that he does. You may want to talk with Bobby Ray about showing the video to a few of the other parishioners to see if they can ID our shooter, but that's a call someone above my pay grade is going to have to make."

＊＊＊＊＊＊

As Paul gave Davis' idea some thought, and while the others finished their tasks at the church, Bobby Ray and his team did as much as they could to learn the identity of their shooter.

After easily obtaining Guyette's blood-soaked clothing so it could be air-dried and then processed for cotton fibers, blood, hair samples and other forms of DNA, Bobby Ray began working his contacts at the hospital. He did so in an attempt to briefly speak with Guyette before the seriously injured priest underwent surgery, politely arguing with two doctors over the fact that their patient might not survive the procedure they were about to undertake.

Granted three minutes with Guyette, Bobby Ray, accompanied by Detective Griffin, quickly donned sterile surgical gowns and face masks to reduce the possibility of introducing any germs into the sterile pre-op room where their victim waited. As they did, their semi-conscious priest rested uncomfortably on a gurney close to the operating room entrance. Hanging from a stand next to where Guyette rested, two IV bags were already delivering glucose and pain medication into a clear plastic port that had been placed inside a vein on top of the priest's right hand. Two large pieces of white tape held the port firmly in place.

"Father, the person who shot you, do you know him?" Bobby Ray softly asked as Guyette moaned in pain despite the dose of pain medication he was receiving. "Have you ever seen him before?"

"No . . . no, I have no idea who he is," Guyette weakly responded, wincing from the shooting pain in his left shoulder. "I've . . . I've never seen him before. His sunglasses hid his face, but I don't ever recall seeing him before."

"Father, we know this is difficult for you, but can you describe him for us? Is he a white male, a black male? Did he have any facial hair or any other distinguishing marks you remember?"

Grimacing from the increasing pain he was feeling, Guyette was slow in answering Bobby Ray's questions. "He was white, maybe in his early to mid-forties, but I'm not really sure." The steady pain he was now feeling made it even harder for the priest to concentrate. "I'm not sure I'm right on this, but he sounded like he was angry at me for something. He . . . he told me my hands were dirty, but I've . . . I've done nothing wrong to hurt anyone. My . . . conscious is clear with how the good Lord looks upon me."

Realizing their victim was weak and exhausted from his ordeal, Bobby Ray quickly asked his next question. "Father, the person who shot you, do you recall how many times he fired his weapon? Can you describe what kind of gun it was?"

Before he could answer, Guyette suddenly gasped twice for air. As he did, the alarm on one of the instruments monitoring his vital signs began sounding loudly. Quickly moving out of the way of the doctors and nurses rushing to the priest's side, Bobby Ray watched as the digital readings of Guyette's heart and respiratory rates began dropping dramatically. In moments, the monitor's audible alarm began sounding a steady warning as the priest's heart rate dropped to a critical level. From where he now stood, it was easy for Bobby Ray to tell the condition of their shot up priest was failing fast.

* * * * * *

Even though Father Guyette was not a racist, nor a history buff like his shooter's first two victims, he was a symbol of the Catholic Church, a religion despised by his attacker.

While the first two victims at least had something in common with each other, albeit an obscure one, the fact that a member of the priesthood had been violently attacked in Pawleys Island was a problem which would confound Paul and Bobby Ray for many days.

8

Rising before daybreak after only sleeping for less than four hours, Bobby Ray met early the following morning with Lt. Ty Ryan, the GCSD's Public Information Officer, to brief him on the events of the previous day.

The large squad room where they met, known affectionately to everyone who worked there as the bullpen, housed the desks assigned to Bobby Ray's detectives. At the far end of the spacious room sat a large wooden conference table. Like the table which had seen better days, the hodgepodge of chairs haphazardly arranged around it reflected their age as well.

The purpose of this god-awful early morning meeting, one orchestrated by Sheriff Renda, was for Bobby Ray to update Ryan with the latest news concerning each of the investigations. A veteran cop with far too many years under his belt, Bobby Ray knew the real reason for the meeting was so Ryan could put together an accurate press release for Renda to read from when he met with the media later that morning. For some reason, one that even Bobby Ray did not have the answer to, Renda, a typical Southern sheriff who seldom turned down the opportunity to have his face on television, always liked to have a news release ready to hold up as a prop while conducting his interviews.

Shortly after meeting with Ryan, someone who Bobby Ray often thought would have had far more success in life as a school teacher or as a minister, he drove north to Murrells Inlet to meet with Paul over a working breakfast. Despite the shortcomings Bobby Ray believed the GCSD's PIO had as a street cop, by the time the Major Case commander reached the diner where he would soon be eating his breakfast, Ryan, by way of his skills and abilities as an effective PIO, already had an updated press release in the hands of every media outlet in Horry and Georgetown counties. Among the details it contained was a vague description of the shooter and of the clothes he had been wearing.

******

Drifting into the Waccamaw Diner shortly before seven that morning, Paul gave a friendly wave to Bobby Moniz, one of the diner's new owners. A longtime cook at the diner, one well-known for its oversized portions and friendly service, Moniz, along with two of his brothers, had recently purchased it from a family who had grown tired of the long hours required to keep the popular eatery open seven days a week. Now running the kitchen with one of his brothers while the other ran the front of the house, Moniz was sitting at the lunch counter taking a short break and enjoying a cup of coffee before the morning wave of customers barged through his front door.

"Yo, Bobby! What's up this morning?" Paul's friendly, but loud voice startled Moniz whose head had been buried in the sports pages of the local paper. An avid Boston Red Sox fan, Moniz had just finished reading an article regarding his favorite sports team being swept at home in a three-game series by the New York Yankees. Teasing his friend as he walked to his favorite booth in the back of the diner, Paul added, "Taking another break while everyone else does all the work, I see. Must be nice to be the boss, huh?"

"What's this going to be, another free meal on the house or what?" Moniz sarcastically asked as he watched Paul slide into his booth.

Placing his New York Yankee hat on the seat next to him, one he often wore to and from work, Paul's next shot brought a hearty laugh from an elderly couple seated not far from where Moniz sat. "You don't expect people like me to have to pay to eat this stuff you cook, do you?"

"Morning, Paul!" Betty Geier said, snapping the gum she was chewing as she intentionally interrupted the banter between her boss and Paul. As she did, she gently shooed Moniz back inside the kitchen while at the same time pouring a hot cup of coffee for one of her favorite customers.

Years earlier, Betty was one of the first people Paul had become friendly with when he first started having an occasional breakfast at the diner. A constant gum chewer, the former heavy smoker had just celebrated her fifty-ninth birthday three days earlier. Like one other gal she worked with, she was a career waitress, part of the dying breed of waitresses who still knew how to make her customers feel welcome each time they came in for a cup of coffee or a meal. Appreciating her many skills, especially the friendly interaction she had with her customers on a daily basis, Betty was one of only five people Moniz retained after buying the diner.

"Morning, Betty. How are things going so far this morning? Good, I hope."

Setting down Paul's cup of coffee, Betty could see the fatigue in her friend's face. "I hope you don't mind me saying this, but you look kind of beat up. I'm guessing you probably worked those two horrible cases yesterday, the ones I heard about on the news this morning, that right?"

"Yep, and quite a long day it was, a strange one as well. I'm afraid that I didn't get much sleep last night. Too wound up, I guess." As Paul finished speaking, Bobby Ray slid his equally tired body into the booth opposite him.

"Morning, Bobby Ray!" Betty said somewhat too cheerfully to the person she liked almost as much as Paul. Looking at him, she asked, "You want some coffee to get you started or would you rather just give me your order now? If you're ready to order, I promise I'll bring some coffee back this way in a minute. Just tell me what you want to eat as I already know your buddy is having his usual blueberry pancakes and bacon."

"I need some coffee bad, but I think I'll have some cheese grits . . . the real ones, not the ones out of the box . . . make sure you tell Bobby that. Tell him to burn a ham steak for me, and I guess I'll take an order of rye toast, dry, no butter. I need some sugar, so you'd better bring me an OJ as well. But, Betty," Bobby Ray pleaded as he tried stifling a yawn, "please hurry up with that coffee, will you." Despite his fatigue, Bobby Ray still had enough left in him to flirt with his favorite waitress as she started walking towards the kitchen. "You keep losing weight like you are and I might be tempted to leave my wife for an older woman. Besides, she can't cook nearly as good as you can."

Bobby Ray's comment caused Paul to shake his head in mock disgust for a brief moment. It was also a comment that made their slightly overweight friend's day.

"What's the latest on your priest?" Paul asked before cautiously sipping his hot coffee for the first time. "Heard anything yet this morning on his condition?"

Wiping his bloodshot eyes, Bobby Ray told Paul what he had learned less than an hour earlier. "He's hanging in there for now. I know he surprised the surgeons and the nurses in the recovery room by how well he handled the surgery and the anesthesia, especially after it got off to such a rocky start. I was kind of responsible for what happened as his vital signs crashed while I was asking him a few questions. They had to delay his surgery for nearly an hour while they waited for his vitals to improve. Anyhow, I've got Griff and Wilson at the hospital in the event the good Father feels up to talking after he wakes up."

After taking another sip of his coffee, Paul asked about the bullet that had been removed from Guyette's chest during his surgery. He followed up by asking if any cotton fibers had been found in any of their victim's wounds.

"They managed to get the bullet out with no problem. The good thing is there's little damage to it. That should make it easy for SLED to match it to one of the casings Vane and Wags found, and hopefully to our shooter's gun when we find it. The lead surgeon was very cooperative, very helpful, regarding our interest in trying to find any cotton fibers within any of Father Guyette's wounds. I was told he thoroughly examined each of the wounds, and that he ended up finding four fibers. It's too early to tell if they are or aren't the same kind we're looking for, so we'll have to wait to see about that. At least we've got a couple for SLED to use when they start looking at the cotton we found in the church. I've already got Vane working on getting all of the evidence inventoried as exhibits this morning. When he's finished, he's going to personally drive them up to the lab later today. He's going to ask them to put a rush on the testing as we need as much information from SLED as we can get."

As Bobby Ray finished speaking, Betty appeared with their meals. After putting their plates down in front of them, she topped off their cups with fresh coffee. Then making sure they had everything they needed, she started walking back towards the lunch counter before suddenly stopping. Almost immediately, Paul noticed what she was doing. Seconds later, as Betty began walking back towards their booth, she stared at her two friends sitting there.

"Everything OK, Betty?" Paul asked, chewing his first mouthful of warm blueberry pancakes. As she stood next to where they were seated, Paul saw in Betty's eyes that something was bothering her.

"Guys, excuse me for bothering y'all while you're eating, but I've had something on my mind for a couple of weeks. It's probably nothing, but after hearing about what happened yesterday I've got to get this off my chest. Can I bother y'all for a couple of minutes?"

"No bother, Betty. Want to sit down?" Bobby Ray asked, sliding to his left to make room for her in the booth

"In your line of work I know this probably happens to y'all all of the time . . . you know, that creepy feeling some folks give you when they're talking to you. Y'all know what I mean, right?" Betty asked, not totally convinced she had properly explained what she was referring to.

"Sure do, Betty. Happens to us all the time." Paul responded as he set his fork down on his plate, more interested in where the conversation was going than in his pancakes.

Over the next couple of minutes, Betty described a series of encounters she had recently experienced with a fairly new customer. "He's only been here a handful of times, sits at the counter each time he comes in. Once or twice I've seen him here during the week, but I seem to recall him being here more often on Saturdays. He never orders any food, just one coffee . . . always black, no milk or sugar, and stays here for far too long after he's done drinking his one measly cup of coffee. Creeps me out the way he stares at folks some times. I started thinking about this guy when I heard the news about the priest being shot because this weirdo has spouted off a couple of times about his dislike for organized Christian religions. The other thing that's strange about this guy is he's a white guy, but I overheard him telling one of our customers a week or so ago that he wants to become a Muslim. Don't know why, but that's what I heard him say. Clear as day, that's what I heard him say."

As Betty finished speaking, Bobby Ray, like Paul had already done, placed his fork down on his plate. Staring at her, he immediately hoped she had more to tell them about the person who had worried her enough to tell them about him. Like his friend, who had already dove back into his pancakes; he also wanted to hear more about one of Betty's newest customers.

"Anything else about this guy you think we should know, Betty?" Bobby Ray asked impatiently, hoping there was more to the story than what she had already told them.

"Yeah, maybe, I guess. Actually two more things really. See that coat rack by the front door?" Betty asked as she pointed at the simple chrome-colored coat rack standing to the right of the diner's front door. "Well, that rack seems to collect coats, sweaters, umbrellas, and all sorts of stuff from time to time. Folks are always leaving stuff in their booths or hanging their jackets and hats on their chairs and then leaving it all behind when they walk on out of here. Sometimes we find it before their gone, but most times they're gone before we find what we find. So that's where all of that junk gets put after we find it. Sometimes folks just hang their stuff on it when they come in and forget it's there when they leave. The rack can only hold so much, so if I or one of the other girls notice something's been there a while we'll either toss it in the garbage or, if it's something nice, we'll walk across the street and toss it in the Goodwill clothes bin that's sitting there."

Finished with his breakfast, Paul pushed his nearly empty plate off to his left, pulling his coffee cup in front of him as he did. "Betty, I think we understand what you're telling us about the coat rack. But what we need to know is what it has to do with this guy who concerns you."

First shooting Paul a look which implied she was not finished with what she had to say, Betty said, "I'm fixin' to get to that if you'll let me."

"OK, sorry, Betty," Paul said with a grin on his face as he shot Bobby Ray a puzzled look. "Please continue then, we're all ears."

"Well, this creep walks up to me one day after he's spent almost an hour drinking his one cup of coffee and wants to know if he can have a windbreaker that he's seen hanging on the rack for about three weeks. The weird thing is he asked me that on a Thursday . . . might have been a Friday, but earlier that same week I saw the jerk trying it on before putting it back. Because it wasn't his jacket, but mostly it's because this guy is a total creep, I told him he couldn't have it. Well, whatever day it was, I got busy with a rush of customers and later when I looked at the rack for some reason I noticed both the creep and the windbreaker were gone.

I can't say for sure that he took it, but I expect he did. The reason I'm telling y'all about this is because I was wondering if the guy who shot the priest was wearing a windbreaker. Or what about the person who killed that man in his own front yard, was he wearing a windbreaker?" The realization that it might have been the same person hit Betty hard for the first time. "OMG! Was it the same guy who hurt both of those men yesterday? Was . . . was he wearing a windbreaker? Do . . . do you know if he was?"

Exchanging glances with each other at first, both cops simultaneously took sips of their coffee as they thought about whether they should answer Betty's questions. It was Bobby Ray who finally did.

"We know the person who shot the priest was wearing a windbreaker, but . . . and this needs to stay between the three of us for now, but we're not positive yet on what the person was wearing who killed the man in his yard. At this time we're thinking it's the same person who's responsible for both incidents, but that's just a hunch based on some similarities which exist. At this point, we can't say it was or wasn't the same person, but listen, Paul and I are telling you this only because we know we can trust you to keep this quiet, and because of what you've told us about this customer of yours. You simply cannot mention any of this to anyone, understand?"

"I understand." Their somewhat frightened waitress replied as she finished making the sign of the cross.

His curiosity already piqued, Bobby Ray asked Betty his next question. "This windbreaker you think this creepy guy took, do you remember what color it was?"

"Maroon."

"Notice anything unique about the windbreaker?"

"Nope. But I never touched it, or even looked at it too closely. I just remember what color it was."

"OK, you've told us far more than what we knew when we walked in here," Bobby Ray replied as he placed a hand on Betty's left hand in an effort to calm her down. "You said there were two things you wanted to tell us about this guy you don't like. What's the other thing?"

Composing herself after looking over her shoulder to make sure she was not ignoring any of her other customers, Betty told Paul and Bobby Ray about the most important observation she had made. "He's missing his left thumb."

"He's what?" Bobby Ray loudly asked as he pushed his coffee cup away from where it had been sitting in front of him.

"He's missing his left thumb. He's just got a really ugly scar on his hand where his thumb used to be. No stump, no nothing, just a big ugly scar that even a blind man could see." Betty lightly chuckled at the metaphor she had used.

"He ever tell you how he lost it?" Paul asked, pleased by the additional and somewhat unique descriptive feature Betty had told them about.

"Boating accident. Claimed it happened a couple of years ago; said it happened after he got out of the service. But I didn't want to know or hear any more about how he lost it. I simply don't like talking to him about anything. This freakin' guy even freaks me out when I look at him. I figure what I don't know, won't hurt me."

As Betty stood up to get back to work, Bobby Ray asked her one last question. It was immediately followed by one more. "If I send a couple of detectives over here to have a talk with you, would you be willing to give them a written statement about this guy? I'd like you to put down on paper his physical description and everything else you can remember about him. And, if you wouldn't mind, can we get you to spend an hour or so with one of our sketch artists so she can put together a sketch of what this clown looks like? It would be a huge help to us if you would do this."

"Not a problem," Betty replied, suddenly excited by the thought of being a small part of the investigation her two friends were heading. As she processed Bobby Ray's requests, she waved to three customers who had just sat down in a booth not far from where Paul and Bobby Ray were seated. "I'd be happy to do both, but after I get off work. I don't want Bobby getting upset with me, you know, doing all of this when I should be working and all. That OK?"

"Sounds perfect, sweetheart," Bobby Ray replied, again smiling at her in an attempt to calm her down even more.

"Thanks for your help, Miss Betty," Paul chimed in with. "We appreciate you telling us what you know about this guy."

As Paul polished off another cup of coffee that Betty had refreshed before moving on to her other customers, Bobby Ray used his cell to call Griffin. He did so to update him on what they had learned from Betty.

"Griff, we need to know if the guy who shot the priest was missing his left thumb." Despite realizing that Griffin knew the importance of validating what Betty had told them, Bobby Ray still felt the need to explain what needed to be done. "Forgive me for saying this, but get this out of the good Father before you ask him anything else. I certainly don't want you putting any thoughts in his head, especially if he's still woozy from being doped up, so let him tell you this when you ask him about his assailant. Call me as soon as you know something. If he tells you he saw his assailant's thumb missing, then I'm going to start working a few new angles to help us try and find our guy."

"Got it, boss. I'll get back to you as soon as we're done talking to our favorite priest."

******

After contacting Stine, a MBPD undercover cop when he was not working cases in Georgetown County with Paul, so he could arrange for his department to send their sketch artist down to meet with Betty, Bobby Ray and Paul briefly discussed their plans for the rest of the day. They were plans which now focused on trying to identify their murderer.

After leaving the diner, Paul followed his friend over to St. Thomas Aquinas so Bobby Ray could have a visual picture of the church's interior. A Southern Baptist who attended church in Georgetown when his job allowed, the Major Case commander had never set foot in the church where Guyette was now assigned. With Reverend Hale's blessing, Sunday's masses had been moved to the church's large recreational building due to the previous day's shooting. Because of that, the church had been sealed off from the public. This had also been done in the event Vane or Elmendorf needed to obtain any additional evidentiary photographs or measurements in the hours after the shooting. With Wagner's assistance, and that of two evidence techs, they had already completed calculating the angles and trajectories of the three shots fired inside the church. Now, with the chaos of the shooting, as well as the processing of the scene no longer issues, Bobby Ray was free to do a leisurely walk-through of the church's interior. Despite the plan to do so, the noise of his cell phone ringing soon interrupted what he had just started.

Near the front of Guyette's confessional booth he answered the call, doing so without looking to see who had disturbed him. "Jenkins, here." As he began listening to what he was being told by Detective Bruce Davis, Bobby Ray hoped to hear news of an important break in the investigation. While it soon proved to be good news he was being told, it quickly proved to be news that was not that important.

"OK, Bruce, I understand what you're telling me. I know the place you're describing; it's just around the corner from the church. It's been boarded up for years now; if I remember right I think some kids tried torching the place years back after it had sat empty for a year or two," Bobby Ray said as he scribbled some notes in a pad he always carried with him.

"The gal who told me this earlier this morning is the same gal who pointed us in the right direction in the last case she helped us with. Remember? She told us about seeing that prick, Payne, in one of the bars down in Murrells Inlet. He was shooting his mouth off about how all of those kids deserved to die." Davis said from the other end of the call.

"Yeah, that's right, I remember. Sandy something, wasn't it?"

"Yep, that's the same gal, Sandy McDavid is her name," Davis said with a smile on his face, pleased his snitch had again supplied him with some useful information. "She and her husband own a few pieces of property in the area, so she hears a lot of news from folks. Like many others this morning, she's pretty upset after hearing about what happened to Father Guyette."

Placing his phone in speaker mode so Paul could hear what was being said, Bobby Ray asked his young detective his next question. "What else did she have to tell you?"

"The only other news she told me about was what I've already told you regarding the vehicle those three kids saw leaving from around the back of that abandoned house. She said the kids described it as being a beat-up Chevy SUV of some kind. She also said the kids didn't know what model it was, but they did tell her it had a South Carolina license plate on the back of it. I'm going to get a couple of uniforms to help me canvass MLK and a few of the other nearby streets in the event anyone else saw this vehicle cruising the area. If I have to, I'll ask Sandy for help rounding up the kids she talked to earlier so we can get their statements. I'll call you if I find anything I think you should know about."

******

With their hands already full of tasks related to the two murders that had taken place, and the shooting of Father Guyette, Paul and Bobby Ray's efforts at identifying who was responsible for those despicable crimes would soon take a back seat to a new problem which soon would confront them.

It would prove to be a problem that would test Paul's endurance more than any other problem ever had.

9

Six years earlier, Donna Waring had been a reluctant participant in her husband's plans of starting a new life together in South Carolina. While retirement started earlier than she had planned, it also forced her to move several hundred miles away from their children. It was a move she had been very reluctant to agree to.

While her husband had spent a long and successful career as a state trooper in Connecticut, Donna had just celebrated her twelfth-year anniversary with the bank she worked for. After spending close to seventeen years as a full-time mom to their boys, Brian and Sean, Donna had returned to work as a banker, quickly rising to become one of ten branch managers for the local bank she worked for that was based in scenic Newtown, Connecticut.

Partially due to her previous career in the banking world, Donna soon became one of the bank's most trusted employees, often being consulted by both her customers and others within the bank for her opinion on a variety of financial issues and programs offered by her employer. Less than six months after returning to work, and due to the number of astute and savvy financial decisions she had helped the bank and her customers with, she was promoted to the position of Assistant Vice-President.

As she found it difficult to leave her position with the bank, Donna had found it even harder to leave her children and the daily interaction she had with them. Despite her reluctance to leave so much of her life behind, including the host of personal and professional friends she and Paul had made, Donna acquiesced, wanting Paul to have the opportunity to fulfill his retirement dream.

Shortly after moving to Murrells Inlet, and despite not having the need to do so, Donna began working for the Murrells Inlet National Savings and Loan, serving as the manager of the Garden City branch.

******

Making her way to work on Monday, two days after Holland had been killed and Father Guyette seriously injured, Donna found herself smiling at the wonderful things that were soon going to be happening in her sons' lives. Her oldest son, Brian, a captain in the Southbury Fire Department, had recently announced his engagement to his longtime girlfriend. Then, during a quick visit back to Connecticut to see the house Sean and his wife had purchased, she was told she was soon going to become a grandmother for the first time. Both announcements had pleased her greatly. While she was excited about having one of her sons getting married, she was tickled to death about becoming a grandmother. Now, as she parked her car in the bank's parking lot with the smile on her face even wider than it had been just a few moments earlier, Donna secretly hoped these events would trigger a move back home. Locking her car, she quickly decided it was an idea she would start talking with Paul about over dinner that night.

After making her rounds to say hello to each of her employees, Donna got settled at her desk. Soon hard at work preparing for a Managers' Meeting the following day, she was interrupted by a friendly face staring at her from just outside her office.

"Steve! How nice to see you! This is a surprise," Donna said, walking to the doorway to greet a friend she cared dearly about.

Dressed nicely as he always was, Steve Alcott was an elderly businessman in his late eighties. Many years earlier, his family members were among the first handful of white settlers who established Murrells Inlet and Pawleys Island. Becoming friends with Paul first, Steve had met his new friend shortly after Donna and her husband had moved to Murrells Inlet. Paul and Steve's chance encounter on a rainy summer afternoon soon led to all of them becoming fast friends.

Helping his new friend become established in South Carolina, including selling him his first pontoon boat, and then giving him a part-time job at a local golf course he owned, had caused Paul and Steve to become friends. Days later, after being introduced to each other over dinner one night, Donna soon became fast friends with him as well. Alone in the world, Steve took an immediate liking to her, coming to think of her over the next couple of months as the daughter he had never been blessed with.

It was because of their friendship, and because of Donna's strong business sense, that Steve had moved a great deal of his rather extensive financial portfolio to Donna's bank. Doing so gave him the opportunity to occasionally surprise her with an unexpected visit. This morning was such an occasion.

After helping Steve complete several large cash deposits he was making, deposits from the marina he owned in Murrells Inlet, and from a small waterpark his family had started years ago, as well as a large rent deposit he was making from a handful of other properties he owned, Donna sat talking with her friend for several minutes. As they did, she excitedly told him about her soon becoming a grandmother.

Having to get to his next appointment, Steve soon began collecting his deposit slips from off of Donna's desk. As he did, Donna's eyes caught the first flicker. The small, but intense flicker of red light came from a non-descript alarm panel that had been intentionally hidden from view for anyone else to see except Donna. Staring at the panel that was mounted underneath a wooden shelf directly opposite from where she sat, Donna saw the red light flash a second and then a third time. In all of her years in banking, this was the first time she had ever seen such a warning light activated. Fear immediately gripped her as she turned and stared at Steve.

"Oh, no!" Donna softly whispered. Both frightened and upset by what she was seeing, she spoke just loud enough for Steve to hear what she was saying. As she did, he saw the look of concern on her face.

"What's wrong, Donna? What's happening?" Steve asked, unsure of what had caused the pale look of concern to appear on his friend's face.

With her eyes now staring back at the red light, in hopes she had seen something she never cared to ever see or experience, Donna softly answered her friend's question.

"I . . . I think the branch is being robbed."

The look on Steve's face immediately mirrored the one he continued to see displayed on the other side of the desk.

Realizing the small red light was the result of one of her tellers activating one of several strategically placed panic alarms along the floor of the teller line; Donna sat quiet for a brief couple of moments. Anxiously she waited, hoping to hear the sounds of police sirens responding to the bank's call for help.

While many other banks had elected to remove most types of panic alarms and other devices for their tellers to use when activating silent alarms during robberies such as this one, Donna's bank had not. While others had chosen to do so in order to minimize the risk of any of their tellers or customers being hurt, or being taken hostage if a robbery attempt went bad, some had not. While progressive in many ways, the small family-run bank that Donna worked for had continued to maintain the age-old policy of requiring their tellers to activate one of the branch's many panic alarms when confronted with a robbery situation. They chose to do so as a way of protecting their financial interests, and, in the thinking of the bank's management team, as a means of deterring future such robbery attempts.

Trained in all aspects of the branch's operations, Donna knew the bank's panic alarm had been hard-wired into the phone system, one designed to by-pass the bank's alarm company in times like this. Doing so, in a time of crisis, eliminated precious moments from being wasted. By doing this, the alarm company, who would have wasted time verifying through a pre-arranged code that an actual robbery existed, was no longer a step in the actual process of notifying the police of the real emergency which existed. It also eliminated the opportunity for a bank robber to pose as a bank employee if challenged over the phone by either the alarm company or the police. Now she prayed the call for help would be handled seriously by the Garden City Police Department and not be taken as another routine false alarm.

Peering cautiously out of her office doorway after dialing 911 and then handing the phone to Steve with instructions for him to talk softly so he would not be heard by anyone outside her office, Donna got her first look at the middle-aged male standing in front of the teller line. Dressed in black pants, and wearing a pair of old white Converse All-Stars, as well as a maroon windbreaker which hid from view the color and style of shirt he was wearing, and a pair of tinted sunglasses, the person she peered out at was nervously waving a black pistol in his right hand. Just out of view, Donna stood frozen as she watched the pistol being waved in the faces of three of her tellers. Watching what was unfolding less than twenty feet away, Donna knew behind closed doors in the office next to hers, Kati Keller, her assistant manager, was hard at work. Unlike Donna's, Keller's office had not been equipped with an alarm panel or other types of warning lights to warn her of a robbery taking place. As Donna continued to watch, the gunman loudly yelled orders at the young female teller he had indiscriminately thrown a small red pillowcase to moments earlier. As he did, his eyes scanned the lobby and front doors for signs of any threats. Almost immediately, he noticed his first real threat, an elderly couple who had come inside the bank at the worst possible moment. After addressing his first problem by locking the couple inside a small closet just off the lobby, Sonny Pratt angrily dealt with his next one after noticing Keller had come out of her office. She now stood frozen less than ten steps away from him. As she realized what was occurring, several pieces of paper slowly fell from her hands.

Motioning at first with his pistol before pointing it at her, Pratt pointed at a spot on the floor where he directed her to sit. As he did, Donna slowly backed out of sight as her assistant manager sat down.

"Nice of you to join us, young lady! Now that you have, stay quiet and stay where you are so I can see you! Try something stupid and like my poor misunderstood urban black brothers often like to say, I'll pop a cap into one of these pretty faces standing right in front of me. *Got it?*" Pratt loudly yelled before turning both his attention and his pistol back on the young teller filling the pillowcase with money. Not even bothering to wait for her response, as he realized Keller was too nervous to be a threat to him, he again yelled loudly, threatening everyone in his presence with harm if they tried something they should not.

Now frightened more than she ever had been, and with her head bowed in fear as she was unaware that Pratt had turned his attention elsewhere, Keller barely managed a slight nod as she cowered on the floor. As she sat there, her curly dark hair hid the tears beginning to stream down her face. Like her fellow employees, she had never seen Pratt before.

After making several irrational but loud demands to no one in particular, Pratt zeroed in on the young teller nervously trying to fill the pillowcase. "Make it quick, bitch! Forget the singles, and don't give me any rolled coins either. Just big bills, all the big ones you all have in your cash drawers!"

As the pillowcase was being filled, Pratt climbed partway up onto the counter that separated the teller line from the bank's customers. Speaking brusquely again to the young teller as she nervously tried complying with the unwanted demands thrust upon her, he said, "And don't do anything stupid like putting any of those exploding dye packs in with the dough! Do that and I'll come back in here and blow all of your freakin' brains out! You hear me, missy?"

As the pillowcase was nervously being handed back over the counter, Donna made her move, bursting out of her office and walking straight towards the threat still existing in the bank's lobby. Knowing it was a bold move to make, she did so as a means of trying to protect Keller and the rest of her employees from any harm.

Despite being scared, Donna spoke loudly, and with a boldness that even caught Pratt off guard as he turned to face her. *"Get out!* You've got what you want; now get the heck out of here!" Pointing to the bank's double front doors, she screamed, *"Get out!"* As she did, four security cameras caught her bold move and angry words.

Now less than fifteen feet away from a pistol being pointed at her, Donna's loud demands were met with a burst of two wildly fired rounds. Flying high over her left shoulder, the bullets harmlessly penetrated the painted gypsum wall outside of Keller's office before smashing against the inside of the bank's exterior brick wall. While the noise of Pratt's weapon being fired was deafening, the smell of burnt gunpowder quickly permeated the air inside the bank's lobby.

"Next time I won't miss!" Pratt calmly said before making his way towards the front doors. "Next time, neither your Lord, nor your asshole husband, who I've read so much about in the papers, will be able to save you from what I'm going to do to you!"

With the threat soon out the front doors, Donna quickly helped Keller up off the floor as she checked to make sure her other employees had not been hurt. As she ran to her office to grab a set of bank keys lying on her desk, Donna began barking a series of orders to her assistant manager before running outside in an attempt to identify the kind of vehicle Pratt was driving. "Call 911, tell them what's happened. Tell them we need help here now. Then call the main office and let them know about this. I'm going to try and get this jerk's license plate number. I'll be right back."

Cautiously exiting the front door and then locking it from the outside so Pratt could not get back inside if something went wrong, Donna saw off to her left the reverse lights of Pratt's Chevy Tahoe come on as he began to back out of the parking spot his vehicle had occupied. Apprehensively, Donna slowly moved down the bank's front sidewalk in an effort to get a clear view of the plate she saw mounted above the bumper. Forcing herself to calm down and to focus on just the plate, she realized it had been placed upside down on the back of the Tahoe in an attempt to discourage anyone from being able to read it.

"You son of a bitch, you did that on purpose, didn't you?" Donna angrily mumbled to herself as she inched closer down the sidewalk.

As she strained to read the first three numbers of the inverted license plate, the Tahoe's operator raced his vehicle backwards across the parking lot. Frozen by what she was now seeing, at first, Donna was slow to react to the danger now facing her. Finally realizing the operator was intentionally attempting to strike her, she turned to step out of the way just as the Tahoe violently jumped the curb. Barely three steps into her flight out of harm's way, Donna was forcefully struck by the Tahoe's rear bumper. Thrown through the air for several feet, she landed hard, her head and left shoulder taking the brunt of the impact as her body struck the ground. Still out of control after landing, Donna's body roughly tumbled though a small garden, striking several shrubs and bushes before finally coming to rest in an awkward heap after bouncing off a large decorative planter just to the right of the bank's front doors. Scattered across the sidewalk behind her were her keys, one of her high heel shoes and a broken silver bracelet, one she always wore on her left wrist. Like her shoe, her bracelet had been ripped from her body. Briefly conscious, she gasped hard for air as her heavily bruised and battered face rested in a soft bed of wet cedar mulch. As blood began to seep out of her nose and mouth, Donna briefly groaned in pain. In moments, the excruciating pain she felt drove her body into unconsciousness.

******

For nearly two minutes, Donna's body laid there unattended before several of her employees, as well as a young mother and her son who had witnessed what had happened, finally came to her aid. Scared and unprepared for what had happened, they did little more than comfort her. Wisely they let her shoe and bracelet lie where they had come to rest. In a small strip mall less than one hundred yards away, another set of eyes carefully watched what was occurring.

As Donna's co-workers rushed to her aid, three police cars and two ambulances, all responding to the silent alarm that had been triggered, also arrived to render assistance. Moments later, in response to the frantic 911 calls for help, other units arrived to begin addressing what had just occurred.

Help had finally arrived, but Donna's attacker was already gone. In some respects, help had come too late.

10

Barely pausing to watch Donna's battered body come to rest, Pratt quickly threw the Tahoe's transmission into drive, punching the accelerator hard to the floor at the same time. Immediately the vehicle's rear wheels started spinning, working hard as they attempted to gather traction on the relatively smooth surface of the bank's asphalt parking lot. Moving quickly forward, with the sounds of responding sirens drawing closer, the Tahoe was driven across the bank's front lawn and out onto the business section of Highway 17.

Lucky to enter the normally busy road just as four nearby traffic lights changed their sequence from green to red, the Tahoe quickly sped north. Weaving in and out of morning traffic present on the four-lane road, Pratt recklessly plowed through the busy intersection where Highways 17 and 544 meet. As he did, the angry blare of horns from a handful of motorists whose vehicles had nearly been struck in the busy intersection briefly sounded.

Quickly approaching the highway's intersection with Farrow Parkway, Pratt braked hard as his vehicle slid sideways and momentarily out of control. Fighting hard to complete the left turn that was being made much faster than it should have been, the Tahoe's rear wheels were again asked to gather traction as it turned in the direction of Valor Park. Soon regaining control of the vehicle, and aware that he was not being pursued or followed by either law enforcement or by witnesses to his reckless operation, or to what had just occurred at the bank, Pratt reduced his speed in an attempt to minimize any unwanted attention. In moments, the Tahoe began moving through The Market Common area of Myrtle Beach at the posted speed limit.

Approaching a residential section of the large complex still under construction, a complex which had once been part of a large tract of land comprising the former Myrtle Beach Air Force Base, Pratt signaled his intention to turn left onto Shine Avenue. It was the first time that morning he displayed his intention of making any sort of turn. A marginally proficient finishing carpenter employed by the general contractor responsible for building several upscale townhouses, Pratt was one of over fifty carpenters working at the site.

Reaching into his driver's door pocket with his left hand, Pratt grabbed the garage door opener he had stolen two days earlier. Assigned to complete most of the crown molding in a three-story home that was nearing its rough completion, the Stanley garage door opener had discreetly been placed inside one of his tool boxes when his fellow workers had left for lunch. Pressing hard on the opener's button as he slowly made his way down the street, Pratt nervously glanced side to side as he neared his destination, hoping none of the myriad of tradesmen working in the area were paying even the slightest amount of attention to what he was doing. Satisfied he was not being watched, and seeing the nearly finished garage was still void of any building materials being stored inside it, the Tahoe was quickly driven inside. Just as quickly, the garage door responded to its second command, slowly closing to prevent any prying eyes from seeing inside the stick-built townhouse. As it closed, another vehicle, one being driven by the person whose eyes had watched what had happened earlier from the strip mall next to Donna's bank, slowly drove down the street. Seeing the garage door closing as he expected caused the operator to allow a smile of approval to cross his face as he drove away.

Already late for work, Sonny Pratt quickly changed into his work clothes. Soon finished, he placed the clothes he had been wearing into a black plastic garbage bag, tightly tying the bag closed when he was done. Within moments, it was tossed inside the Tahoe's rear cargo compartment. Grabbing the pillowcase containing the stolen money, he tucked it under a small pile of dirty work clothes on the backseat floor before placing a couple of crumpled up fast food bags on top of them. For now, his count of the money would have to wait until later in the day. Finished with the rest of his tasks, Pratt grabbed one of his screwdrivers. Concerned over someone coming into the garage during the day, and wanting to minimize any unwanted attention, he used his screwdriver to return his rear license plate to its normal position.

Walking outside with one of his tool belts suspended over his left shoulder, and carrying a black plastic case in his right hand that had been designed by its manufacturer to hold his finishing saw tightly in place, Pratt slowly made his way down the sidewalk of the still yet to be finished street of homes. Told the previous afternoon to assist another carpenter first thing in the morning with a small task before finishing what he needed to finish in the townhouse he had been working in, he moved towards the unfinished house sitting less than eighty yards away. As he did, others already busy at work filled the air with a variety of sounds as nail guns, power saws, hammers, and other tools made their respective noises. America, at least this small segment of it, was hard at work.

******

"Hey, asshole!" The loud Irish sounding voice yelled from an unfinished second-story balcony. "You're freakin' late, *again!*" Despite his years of living in the United States, the foreman's thick brogue was undeniably present.

Unlike the others hard at work installing the balcony's custom wrought iron railings the new homeowners had painstakingly searched high and low for, Mickey O'Keefe was just there to watch the progress being made. In his early sixties, the veteran carpenter had gone from owning his own small construction business to becoming the eyes and ears for a reputable engineering firm who operated a subsidiary by the name of East Coast Construction Company. O'Keefe's firm had been hired to build the seventy-three town houses that would soon complete Phase 3 of The Market Common development plan.

"Sorry, Mick," was the extent of Pratt's insincere reply to being caught reporting to work late for the fourth time in two weeks. Grudgingly, the response had been offered with a half-hearted wave. "I ran into a wee bit of a problem earlier, and then ran into some heavy traffic out on 17. It won't happen again, I promise." A brief but unnoticeable smile crossed his mouth after realizing the words he used to describe what had happened less than thirty minutes earlier. Whenever possible, like he had just done, Pratt took the opportunity to mock O'Keefe's accent.

"Sure it will, you prick bastard! It'll probably happen by Thursday, won't it?" O'Keefe's upper arms bulged as he helped to move a large section of metal railing into place. As he did so, a large colorful tattoo, red, white and green in its colors and large enough to show the pride he had in his Southern and Irish heritages became exposed around the bicep of his right arm. "Pray that it doesn't happen again, asshole, for if it does you're history. There's plenty of others like you . . . and I don't care if they're Mexicans, Russians, Irish assholes like me, or who or where their sorry-asses came from, at least I'll know they'll be here on friggin' time." Finished saying what had to be said, O'Keefe glared down at the one person in life he cared little for.

"Nice tat, you've got there, Mick! Real nice, in fact. We'll talk more later," Pratt said sarcastically as he continued walking towards his destination. As he did, he turned to stare one more time at the tattoo he had previously seen on his boss' right bicep. It was one he detested almost as much as his boss detested him. Mumbling under his breath as he moved closer to where he had to be, Pratt saw O'Keefe's brand new white Dodge Ram was parked further down the street. "Forget the guy I saw at McDonald's two days ago, he can wait. You're next, or maybe your truck is, you Irish asshole!"

******

As things in The Market Common reached a near boiling point, emergency responders, including on and off-duty cops from a handful of departments, along with EMS and fire personnel, and officials from Donna's bank, continued to race to the scene of the robbery and to where Donna had been seriously injured.

Several miles away, Paul and Bobby Ray would soon start their own journey north.

11

As he tried finding time to do his walk through of the church on Monday morning, two days after Father Guyette's shooting, Bobby Ray's attempts at doing so had been interrupted by two phone calls already. The first had come from Griffin, the next from Davis, and, now, a third one came from Scozzafava. Like the first two, the call from Scozzafava kept him from being able to finish what he barely had time to start. Frustrated by the number of interruptions, the tone in Bobby Ray's voice clearly showed his patience was being tested as he answered his phone.

"OK, Scozz, it's your turn, I suppose. I've heard from everyone else this morning it seems! What can I possibly do for you this lovely morning?"

As he began listening to what the FBI agent was telling him, Bobby Ray stared at Paul twice, deflecting his gaze elsewhere each time his friend looked at him. While he knew he would likely be doing the same if the roles were reversed, he also knew Paul was likely trying to figure out why Scozzafava was calling.

After listening to what Scozzafava was telling him, a now visibly upset Bobby Ray responded to the news he had been told. In a hushed tone, he said, "Yeah, he's here with me. I'll take care of it, Scozz. Keep me posted. We'll be there in about twenty minutes, maybe less."

Putting his phone back into his coat pocket, Bobby Ray watched for a brief couple of moments as Paul continued to examine the area around the confessional boxes to see if anything had been missed by Vane or Wagner the day before. Doing so gave him time to figure out how to break the news to Paul. Finally summoning his courage, Bobby Ray hollered to his friend.

"Paul, that call was about Donna. We need to go. *Now!*"

At first, not comprehending his friend's unexpected loud comment, one which caught him totally by surprise, Paul was slow to follow Bobby Ray's move towards the vestibule. But then, realizing something bad had likely happened to his wife, he moved quickly towards the vestibule and the church's front doors. Catching up with the fast pace Bobby Ray was setting as he made his way towards the parking lot, Paul, somewhat apprehensively, asked about his wife's condition.

"Is she . . . ?"

Grabbing Paul by his left arm, Bobby Ray interrupted his friend before he could finish his question. As he did, he used his key fob to unlock the doors to his assigned undercover car. As they moved closer to it, it was Bobby Ray's turn to speak anxiously.

"Get in. I'm driving. I'll fill you in on the way with what I know."

In moments, Bobby Ray's black Dodge Charger quickly sped down the driveway of the church, barely pausing as it turned towards Martin Luther King Drive. Turning onto MLK, Bobby Ray punched the accelerator hard as he flicked on the Charger's low profile blue strobe lights. Moments later, the vehicle's audible siren began to whelp as its driver pushed the vehicle down the nearly deserted residential street close to 75 mph, and closer to Highway 17.

Navigating the Charger through heavy traffic at the intersection of MLK and Highway 17, Bobby Ray again punched the accelerator hard as they sped north on 17. As they did, Paul nervously asked his next question.

"What happened, Bobby Ray? Is Donna OK?"

******

The marked Myrtle Beach PD cruiser had been in place along the right shoulder of Highway 17, just south of the Myrtle Beach International Airport, for less than five minutes when its operator first saw the Charger's flashing lights as it was being driven north.

While Donna's branch was located in Garden City, just south of Myrtle Beach, and closer to Waccamaw Hospital, the EMTs who had evaluated her injuries at the scene decided to have her transported the extra few miles to the Grand Strand Regional Medical Center. They had made this decision due to the hospital's well-known reputation of being able to successfully treat a large number of patients who had sustained a variety of serious head injuries similar to the kind Donna sustained.

Pulling out well in front of Bobby Ray's Charger, Officer Susan Twine, the MBPD cop assigned to run interference to the hospital, activated her overhead roof rack as she made her way into the far left lane of four northbound lanes. Despite the hour of the day, Twine's bright flashing blue lights bounced off the vehicles and reflective signs around her, warning others in her path to move out of her way as she slowly moved north, patiently waiting for the Charger behind her to close the small gap between them. As it did, with the flip of a switch she activated the siren mounted under the hood of her marked Ford Taurus. As the two vehicles raced loudly across the bridge above it, traffic on Highway 501 barely knew whatwas taking place. Soon heavy traffic in front of her began to give Twine's cruiser a wide berth; the nine-mile sprint to the hospital would soon be over with just as fast as it had gotten started.

* * * * * *

Sprinting into the hospital's emergency room, Paul was immediately met by Scozzafava, and, most importantly, by an ER nurse and two surgeons. Close behind him followed Bobby Ray and Twine.

Taking charge, the younger of the two surgeons, Dr. Samuel Ellis, a forty-six-year-old doctor who had been a member of the hospital staff for close to twelve years, quickly escorted Paul into a nearby examination room that was no longer being used. As he did, and as Ellis introduced himself and the others with him to Paul, Bobby Ray and the two cops with him followed a short distance behind, respecting the privacy the moment required.

Formalities finished, Paul started by asking three of the many questions running through his mind. "How's my wife, doctor? How bad has she been hurt?" Scanning the large and empty ER room, one large enough for three patients to be treated at the same time, but not seeing his wife, he asked, "Where's . . . where's my wife?"

"Mr. Waring, for the immediate moment, your wife is doing as well as can be expected based on the injuries she's sustained. She's just been taken up to our surgical unit. She's being prepped for surgery." Ellis replied matter-of-factly.

Already fraught with fear, the words Ellis used to briefly describe Donna's condition cut deep into Paul. "Is . . . is she going to be OK?" While Bobby Ray had told Paul all that he knew about Donna's condition, and about what had happened earlier at the bank, Paul pressed Ellis for more on his wife's condition.

"Mr. Waring, I'm going . . ."

"Doctor, let's you and I get started off on the right foot," Paul said nervously, cutting Ellis off in mid-sentence. As he did, Paul shifted uncomfortably on his feet, scared by the bad news he was expecting to be told. "I'm a pretty low-key kind of guy. Mr. Waring was my father's name; unfortunately, he's deceased. My name is Paul. I understand that you're just being respectful, but, please, I'd rather you just call me by my first name. Now, I'd like you to tell me what my wife's condition is without trying to sugarcoat it in any way . . . just tell me the truth, tell me what we're facing. I need to hear it plain and simple, and I'd prefer to hear it that way from you."

Despite his years of experience in having to explain difficult news to a countless number of relatives whose loved ones had been seriously injured in a variety of accidents and mishaps, Ellis uncomfortably nodded his head after hearing what Paul had said. Placing his clipboard down on top of an EKG machine which minutes earlier had been affixed to his newest patient, Ellis paused a brief moment before speaking.

"OK, Paul, I'll give it to you as straight as I can. Your wife has been seriously injured after being struck, intentionally I'm being told, by the person driving the vehicle which hit her. It appears the initial impact was to her back, her lower torso to be precise, and that she was sent flying through the air a short distance as a result of this first impact. Understand that I'm somewhat guessing at the sequence of events after that, I'm just trying to paint a picture for you based on the tests we've run so far, and from what the EMTs have told me."

"I understand. Keep going, doc. Please." Paul said, anxiously looking at Ellis, and then at Bobby Ray who was now standing just inside the doorway of the examination room.

"We've just completed a CT scan of your wife's head to help us evaluate the amount of swelling in her brain, as well as the extent of it. We've also had an MRI done. Because of what those tests have revealed, and as I've just told you, your wife is being prepped for surgery." Pausing to gather his thoughts, Ellis then continued. "Paul, I know you must have a great number of questions for me, but please just listen to me for a moment. You need to realize there's a sense of urgency which exists right now, so you need to trust that I know what I'm talking about." Pointing at the nurse with him, Ellis said, "Mrs. Jensen is the admitting nurse here in the ER. She has a few forms you need to sign. The most important being the one which gives us permission to operate on your wife. I'll be joined by two orthopedic surgeons in the operating room, they'll be working on Donna's other injuries after we address the injury to her brain. I've already called Dr. Randolph Tillengast, one of the best neurosurgeons along the Grand Strand, if not in South Carolina. He's on his way here now. But, for now, I need you to sign these forms as time is growing critical. We can talk more on the elevator."

Hearing what Ellis had to say caused Paul to momentarily grow quiet, but then his resolve, along with his law enforcement training kicked in. "OK, doc, I get it," Paul said as he started signing the three forms Jensen placed in front of him. "I expect folks to trust me when I'm conducting my investigations, so I guess I have to trust you."

As Ellis started walking towards the elevator that would take him up to the hospital's surgical floor, Paul walked with him. As they stepped onto the elevator, a worried husband asked his next question.

"Before I let you get off, I need to know what my wife's biggest problem is right now. I'm certainly upset about her leg and shoulder injuries, but those aren't reasons to be bringing in a neurosurgeon. Tell me what we're facing here?"

"Mr. Waring . . . I'm sorry, Paul," Ellis said, catching himself on how his new patient's husband preferred to be addressed. "Paul, your wife, like you've just said, she has a broken leg and a broken arm; both are on her left side, the side she apparently landed on after being struck by the vehicle which hit her. But she also appears to have sustained a traumatic brain injury, a TBI as it's commonly referred to as. It was likely caused by the blunt force of her head striking the ground hard when she landed. As a result, she's sustained at least one fracture to her skull, but that's not what concerns us the most. What concerns us is the internal bleeding we're seeing inside her brain, that and the other fluid we're seeing collecting there is not good. The fluid that's collecting amongst her brain tissue is called cerebral edema; it's not a problem we doctors like our patients experiencing. That's the biggest problem she's facing as it can quickly lead to other problems. We're trying to prevent those problems from occurring by doing this surgery. During her operation we'll be making sure her brain is getting the proper flow of blood and oxygen it needs. To do that, if her swelling is as bad as I'm afraid it's going to be, we may have to temporarily remove a portion of her skull to relieve any swelling or pressure her brain may be experiencing."

Stopping outside the entrance to the surgical unit, Paul asked his last question before letting Ellis leave to attend to Donna. "Doc, what if this brain injury is as bad as you think it might be? Is it going to have an effect on her ability to walk or talk, or . . . God forbid, her ability to think normally?" The thought of Dr. Ellis or one of his colleagues having to remove a portion of his wife's skull scared Paul. Even if it was for all the right reasons and even if it was for only a short period of time.

After tapping the door sensor mounted on the wall to his right so he could gain access to the surgical unit, Ellis put a hand on Paul's right shoulder. It was an act of compassion not only from a doctor to a patient's relative, but it was also a gesture from one husband to another. "Paul, let's just hope for the best right now. Let me and the other doctors do what we do best, and then we'll talk. I'll tell you what; we're going to be working on her for a few hours so go take care of yourself for now. Grab some coffee and some rest. I promise I'll come find you when we're done."

"OK, but please take good care of my girl for me." Angry and upset over what had happened to his wife, Paul's voice cracked from the wide range of emotions he was starting to feel. "Please take good care of her as I'd . . . be lost without her."

Too numb to say anything else, Paul watched as Ellis disappeared behind the surgical unit's doors as they closed. After they did, he stood in the hallway for several minutes as others came and went through the doors he was now afraid of. Standing there, he tried fighting through the emotions he was feeling. As any spouse would have gladly done, he would have been happy to change places with Donna. Finally rounding up the courage, he moved back towards the bank of elevators and to the two phone calls he knew he would have trouble completing. As the elevator doors closed, tears began streaming down his face as he thought of his wife, and of their two sons back home.

For Paul, this was a day he had hoped would never have happened to his family.

* * * * * *

Having only met Ellis under a brief but trying circumstance, and barely comprehending what little he had been told about

Tillengast, Paul had no way of knowing these two dedicated physicians were complete opposites in both their personalities and appearances.

While Ellis was the more outgoing of the two, friendly and confident in all types of social settings, Tillengast was not. Occasionally viewed by those who barely knew him as being someone who was not as affable as his colleagues, often due to his tendency of allowing others to be the focus when a patient's medical history was being discussed, the brilliant physician was generally witty and warm with his close circle of professional friends.

Unlike Ellis, who dressed conservatively, and who kept his hair neat and reasonably short, Tillengast was sometimes perceived as being a throwback to the 1970s due to his scraggly beard and bushy moustache. Often wearing a variety of different framed eyeglasses, and never the same pair two days in a row, Tillengast also dressed as casually as possible on most days. While always wearing a freshly pressed white lab coat when dealing with his patients, his manner of dress generally made him look more like a high school gym teacher than the well-respected neurosurgeon he was. Unlike Ellis and the rest of the hospital's medical staff, Tillengast, nearing seventy-two years of age, always wore his greyish hair tied in a short ponytail.

How they dressed and interacted with others, just as how they wore and combed their hair, mattered little to Paul. All he cared about was his wife's health, and how these two doctors who had been unexpectedly thrust into his life could return her back to him just as healthy as she had been a few hours earlier.

12

As Bobby Ray waited for Paul to return to the ER, he used the time to make sure certain tasks were being completed by his detectives. After contacting Sgt. Kent Wilson on his phone, he assigned the seasoned MBPD investigator to assist the Garden City Police Department, SLED, and the FBI, with the investigation of the bank robbery at Donna's branch of the Murrells Inlet National Savings and Loan.

"Give them whatever help they need," Bobby Ray instructed Wilson, "but make sure you keep me informed. If you need more help, call me. I'm staying here with Paul for a while, but I want this son of a bitch caught, and caught soon!"

Soon finished speaking with Wilson, Bobby Ray dialed up Detective Blake Stine on his cell phone. As they spoke, he told Stine of the conversation he and Paul had with Betty at the diner earlier that morning.

"Get in touch with her to find out a good time to meet with her later today. Then get a hold of that forensic sketch artist we used a while back. Get hot on this as I want all of this done today while Betty still has a good mental picture of what this guy looks like. I'll send Wagner down to help you, but make sure you guys obtain a written statement from her as well." Remembering how fond Betty was of both Paul and Donna, Bobby Ray gave Stine one last matching order. "Blake, after you and the sketch artist finish with what needs to be done, it's best if you tell our favorite waitress what's happened to Donna. I'd rather she hear it from us and not from seeing it on the news later on. Tell her I'll swing by to see her when I get the chance."

As Bobby Ray finished handing out what he wanted done, Paul had made his way to the hospital's cafeteria. Choosing to sit alone in one of the back corners of the large utilitarian eating area, one almost void of any creature comforts, but immaculate in its appearance, he barely paid attention to the hot steam rising out of his coffee. Sitting quietly for close to five minutes, he forced himself to make the calls he dreaded having to make. Finding his sons, Brian and Sean, both at work, he did his best at telling them everything he knew about what had happened to their mother. As he had told Ellis to give it to him straight about Donna's condition, he now gave the news to his sons the same way. After answering the multitude of questions they threw at him, Paul did his best at suggesting they hold off on jumping on the next plane to come see her. After explaining why he wanted them to wait a day or two, he promised he would call them as soon as he knew more.

"I promise, guys," Paul said in a rather impromptu and awkward conference call he had arranged with his sons by way of their Smartphones, "I'll call you as soon as I can after mom comes out of surgery. Just give me time to talk with her doctors about her prognosis, and then I'll call you. We'll figure out a game plan for when it's best for you to come and see her."

Despite his sons' protests, Paul got them to promise to wait until they heard back from him before making any travel plans. While significantly concerned about their mother's condition, both reluctantly agreed to wait until later that afternoon at the earliest before deciding when they should come to see her.

As Paul wiped away the tears that had formed in his eyes after speaking to his children, Bobby Ray appeared carrying two cups of coffee. Soon tasting it, both men quickly agreed the hospital's coffee could not hold a candle to the kind Betty served them during their visits to the diner. While neither of them thought of themselves as connoisseurs of fine coffee, it was apparent to each of these two cops that the hot bitter black liquid in their cups had not been made by a barista, nor had it been brewed in a fancy expresso machine. Like his first cup that sat untouched, Paul did little more than toy with the one his friend had brought him.

"You call the boys?" Bobby Ray asked, noticing the redness in Paul's eyes. As he waited for Paul to compose himself, like any experienced cop does in an unfamiliar setting, Bobby Ray's eyes scanned the cafeteria for any threats. He did so by taking notice of who was seated around them. As his eyes briefly scanned the large cafeteria, just as he always did at other places he visited, he also took notice of where the emergency exits were located.

"Yep. Just got done talking with them when I saw you walk in. Naturally they're upset, both of them want to be here right now as a matter-of-fact, but I told them we'll talk about that later. I promised them I'd get them down here to see her soon enough. It'll do them and, hopefully, her some good." Paul said, forcing himself not to become any more emotional than he already had been in front of his friend.

"It will do you some good as well, partner." Bobby Ray offered as he wiped jelly from a stale jelly donut off one side of his mouth. Tossing the napkin aside, he took his next bite of the sugary donut as Paul changed subjects on him.

"Bobby Ray, I'll do my best to keep helping you with what we've been working on, but you know I have to be here with Donna as much as I can, at least until I know she's out of the woods from the head injury she's sustained." As distraught as he was over what had happened to his wife, having to distance himself from his commitment to his friend was almost as painful. Unlike others, Paul was not the type of person who liked leaving a task unfinished or a friend hanging.

"I wouldn't let you help us even if you wanted to. You need to be here . . . here with my girlfriend." Bobby Ray smiled as he finished speaking, knowing Paul was well aware of the fondness that both he and his wife had for Donna.

After quietly drinking their coffee for a few moments, Bobby Ray told Paul what he had done to address the issues of the morning. He started by telling him about assigning Wilson to assist those who were working the bank robbery at Donna's branch, of assigning Stine and Wagner to work with the sketch artist when they met with Betty later that afternoon, and, finally, of the tip Davis had gotten from one of his snitches.

"Listen here, partner, I've got to go and ride herd on these cops of ours, but I'll be back later. You call me if you need anything," Bobby Ray said as he pushed his chair back under the table they had been sitting at. "I'll call you with any significant news I learn. Maybe it'll help serve as a distraction of some kind for you."

******

Six hours after signing the surgical permission form, as well as several other related bureaucratic forms which assured the hospital they would be paid whether Donna survived her surgery or not, Paul met with Ellis again. This time it was to be updated on how well the various surgeries had gone. Twenty minutes after finishing with him, Paul briefly visited his wife for the first time in the hospital's ICU ward. Like two other areas inside the hospital, each of the private rooms in the ICU ward had recently received a fresh coat of paint and new privacy drapes.

Despite being nervous, as well as frightened by the various tubes and monitors attached to his unconscious wife, Paul knew Donna was going to survive what had happened to her. While he knew she would remain in a medically induced coma for an unknown period of time until the swelling in her brain went down, and while he also knew her broken bones had been properly taken care of, Paul knew his wife was a fighter. Earlier, he had been pleased when Dr. Ellis had also described her that same way. Staring at her heavily bandaged head, and then at her broken arm and leg, he spoke gently to his wife.

"It may be a long and difficult row for you to hoe, but you'll make it . . . we'll make it, I promise."

13

Despite realizing he had likely pissed off a couple of the Garden City detectives responsible for conducting the investigation at Donna's bank, Wilson cared little about their personal feelings toward him. Arriving at the scene upset and angry over what had happened to Donna, he had made it clear to everyone around him that Paul Waring was one of his best friends. He quickly followed that up by telling them that if Paul's wife had been intentionally run over outside her branch, then no arbitrary jurisdictional line was going to keep him from helping to identify who had hurt her.

"Besides, she's my wife's second cousin. That makes her family, so I'm not leaving. Call Solicitor Pascento, or my boss, Bobby Ray Jenkins, if you've got a problem with me being here. Even if they tell me to leave, I'm not leaving," Wilson said, blatantly lying to the Garden City police chief about the family connection that supposedly existed between Donna and his wife.

Several minutes later, after making a weak and less than sincere effort at apologizing for barging in on their investigation, Wilson stood off to the side as two Garden City detectives interviewed the young teller the bank robber had tossed the pillowcase to earlier. Listening to what was being said as the teller did her best at describing both the robber and the weapon he had used,

Wilson's ears suddenly perked up as he listened to one unique characteristic being described.

"I . . . I was focused on the gun he was pointing at me," sobbed the still scared young teller, "so I'm sorry, but I can't remember what his face looked like because of the sunglasses he was wearing."

Frustrated by what he was hearing, but realizing he needed to keep his cool so he did not upset his witness any more than she already was, Detective John Bears, an often irritable and slightly overweight Garden City detective with nearly twenty-two years in law enforcement, continued with his line of questions. Calmly and politely he phrased each of them. Like any cop investigating his first bank robbery, he was anxious to solve the biggest crime to hit the small town in years.

"It's OK, you're doing fine, Carrie. Just tell us what you remember," Bears said, trying to boost the young teller's confidence. "What about the gun he was using, do you remember what it looked like?"

"It was an automatic pistol of some kind. I only know that because I saw the bullets . . . I mean the shell casings, I saw the shell casings fly through the air when he fired his pistol in Mrs. Waring's direction. When all of this was happening, I was so scared of what might happen next that I have no idea why I saw them, but I know I did." Carrie Carnrick paused to wipe away her tears before continuing with her description of what she had seen transpire earlier. "My dad and my boyfriend both like to shoot, and sometimes I go to the range with them. That's how I know the difference between an automatic and a revolver." Carrie proudly offered as she again wiped her runny nose with a now damp tissue.

Then Carrie told the detectives interviewing her two last pieces of information she recalled about the person who had confronted her. It was the last bit of information she offered which caused Wilson to become excited.

"When he first pointed his pistol at me, he tried handing me the pillowcase with his left hand, but I was so scared I didn't take it from him. For a brief moment or two, he just let it dangle in the air in front of me before tossing it at me. When he was holding it up in the air, that's when I noticed he didn't have a thumb on his left hand. For a moment, I thought it was maybe hidden behind part of the pillowcase, but then I saw an ugly scar where his thumb was supposed to be."

Quiet until now, Wilson could not stay that way after hearing what he had just heard. "Miss, if someone like me was to ask you how sure you are about what you saw, about this guy missing his thumb, what would your answer be?"

"I'd tell them I was one hundred percent sure. I may not be as sure about a few other things that happened, but I know what I saw, or maybe what I didn't see is a better way of describing it. But I know for sure he didn't have a thumb on his left hand." The young teller confidently replied.

"Thanks, Miss. I'm going to step outside. I'll leave you with these two detectives for now." Ever the smart-ass, Wilson turned to face Bears and his partner before sarcastically speaking to them. "Keep up the good work, fellas. Report to me when you're done and I'll give you your next assignment."

As he turned to leave, the young teller called to Wilson. "Sir, I overheard you tell the chief before about Donna being a relative of yours. Don't you . . ."

"I'm sorry, Carrie, that was just me being a jerk before," Wilson told her, interrupting the young teller before she could finish with what she had to say. "I'm not really related to her, I just said that so I could hear what you had to say."

Despite hearing what Wilson had said to her, Carrie spoke up before he could get much further away. "Oh, so I guess I should tell these two detectives the part about Paul then? You know, Donna's husband, he's a cop like the three of you are."

Wilson's ears had already started to tune Carrie out, but then perked up at the mention of his friend's name. "What about Paul?"

"Well, this guy . . . the robber guy, he told Donna, I guess he actually threatened her, but he told her he'd come back and hurt her if she tried anything. Said there was nothing either Paul or the good Lord could do to protect her." Then pointing up at the ceiling, Carrie added, "If you look at our surveillance tapes I'm sure you'll see and hear everything that took place this morning. I know how to use the equipment if you want to see what I'm talking about."

Looking at Bears for a brief moment as he stood next to him, Wilson took the young teller up on her offer. "Yeah, I'll take a look-see. This guy wants a look also."

In minutes, Wilson and Bears were both quiet as they watched on a small monitor as Donna's attacker entered the bank. As they did, Wilson took note of the maroon windbreaker her attacker was wearing.

"Son of a bitch, this has to be the same asshole who shot the priest yesterday," Wilson thought to himself as he watched what the cameras had captured. "He's wearing the same freaking type of windbreaker. It has to be him. He's roughly the same size and build as we've been told about." At Wilson's request, the tape was stopped twice. This was done to give both cops the opportunity of seeing Carrie's description of the bank robber had been correct. "This guy is really missing his left thumb!" Wilson quietly mumbled after watching what had transpired earlier.

Finished viewing the tape, Wilson, without giving Bears time to speak, asked the young teller to burn him two copies of what they had watched. After waiting several minutes for this to be done, Wilson, looking at Bears as he did, took possession of the original and one of the two CDs Carnrick had made. "I'm taking the original with me, as well as one copy. You can have the other. The way I look at it, murder beats a bank robbery any day of the week. If you've got a problem with that, have your boss call Pascento." That said, Wilson nodded to the young teller before walking outside to call Bobby Ray and Stine with the news he had learned.

Pulling out his phone to call Bobby Ray, Wilson's eyes caught Pamela Snow and her young son, Billy, walking slowly towards him. Unknown to him, they had witnessed Donna being struck by the Tahoe before it abruptly fled the scene.

"Sir, excuse me," Pamela Snow said quietly, narrowing the distance between her and Wilson as she spoke. As she did, her eight-year-old son held onto his mother's hand. "Are you one of the detectives investigating this terrible incident?"

"Yes, ma'am, I am." Wilson replied as he let his phone slip back into the left front pocket of his pants. "Can I help you with something?"

After explaining how she had come to witness Donna being struck, and that her instincts as both a mother and as a registered nurse had caused her to rush to help tend to Donna's injuries, Snow told Wilson she had stepped back to allow the EMTs to take over when they arrived.

"Thanks for what you did, Mrs. Snow. Donna . . . the lady who was hurt, well, she and her husband are good friends of mine. I'm grateful for the help you offered. I'll make sure they know what you did to help her." Wilson said, smiling politely as he shook hands with Snow.

"Oh, that's not necessary," Snow replied, rubbing her son's hair as she spoke. "I just did what anybody should do when someone gets hurt. She was already unconscious by the time I got to her. I just tried keeping her stabilized until the paramedics arrived."

"No matter what you did or didn't do, Mrs. Snow, you ran to her side to comfort her. That's the important part." Wilson's thoughts now turned back to the investigation at hand, realizing Snow's observations and actions needed capturing in a written statement. "Mrs. Snow, what you've told me, has anyone here taken a statement from you as yet? You know, about what you saw, and how you tried to help Donna. Has that been done yet?"

"No, that's why I came over to see you. I want to tell . . ." Snow was interrupted by Wilson before she could finish telling him what he needed to hear.

"OK, Mrs. Snow. Give me a minute and I'll get someone over here to speak with you."

"But what about my son?" Snow asked, her comment catching Wilson off guard. "He's got something to tell you as well."

Snow's comment froze Wilson in his tracks. Turning around, he walked the few steps back to where Snow and her son were standing on the sidewalk. "Your son?" Wilson asked as he stared down at the young boy.

"I know my son is younger than most of your witnesses, but he has something important to tell you about the license plate we saw on the back of the car, the one that struck the lady from the bank. It was hanging upside down. I'm afraid if he doesn't tell someone about it soon he's going to forget what he saw. No matter how good his memory is."

Curious over what Snow's son wanted to tell him, Wilson knelt down in front of the young boy so he could talk to him at the same eye level. "Billy, your mom says you need to tell me something. I'm guessing that it's maybe something important, perhaps something you saw?" Wilson asked as he shook hands with the young boy. As expected, Billy stood silent for several moments as he stared at the badge and gun strapped to Wilson's belt.

"It was upside down like my mom said, but I saw the letters . . . IBW, and one number. It was a 7." Billy proudly offered, unintimidated by either Wilson's presence or his accoutrements.

Wilson blinked at what he heard, unsure at first of what his young witness was telling him, but then it clicked. "Billy, are you talking about the letters on the license plate?"

"Yes, sir, Mr. Policeman. But it wasn't a car, it was an SUV. It was a Chevy Tahoe, an old one."

Wilson smiled at Billy's politeness as he looked up at the boy's mother, and then back at the boy himself. "Billy, you're pretty good with cars it sounds. Are you sure it was a Chevy Tahoe, or are you just guessing?" Wilson asked, trying to confirm the make and model of the vehicle that had struck Donna.

"It's a Chevy Tahoe for sure. I know what kind of vehicle it was because the old man who lives across the street from our house had one when I was smaller than I am now."

"You convinced me, Billy. Thanks for your help," Wilson said, pulling one of his business cards from a holder in his shirt pocket. Handing it to his young witness, he tried showing him his appreciation. "You call me someday and I'll take you for a ride in a police car. We'll even turn the lights and siren on." Then joking with him as he shot the boy's mother a quick wink, Wilson added, "Who knows, but maybe if your mom behaves herself we'll even let her tag along with us." Standing up, for no particular reason he asked his young witness one last question. "Billy, the man who lives across the street from you, how old do you think he is?"

Billy thought for a moment before answering Wilson's question. "I'm not sure, pretty old, I guess. Maybe thirty-five or forty, not as old as you are though."

"Billy!" Snow's mother yelled loudly, embarrassed over the unintended slight her son had directed at the thirty-eight-year-old cop in front of him. It was one Wilson quickly dismissed with a loud chuckle as he rubbed his chin with his left hand.

"Detective, I know my son is rather young, and while he may not be too good at guessing peoples' ages, I hope you aren't doubting what he told you about the license plate he saw. Billy has a unique talent for numbers and letters for someone his age; it's one even his teachers and guidance counselor can't explain. He's just a young boy who's been blessed with an exceptional talent for remembering certain details he sees, no matter how he sees them. I can't explain it, but if he says the letters on the license plate were IBW, then the letters were IBW. I hope this helps you somehow."

After thanking Billy and his mom for their help, and after making arrangements for a statement to be taken from Mrs. Snow, Wilson walked back to his car to call Bobby Ray.

"Boss, I've got some good news. I just spoke with a young boy and his mom; they saw Donna get struck by our bank robber's vehicle. I'm being told it was an older model Chevy Tahoe. By the sounds of it, I'm pretty sure Donna was intentionally struck. Based on a statement this prick made inside the bank, it looks to me like he was trying to send her a message, a rather deliberate one at that."

After answering a few of Bobby Ray's questions concerning what else all of the witnesses had seen and heard, Wilson told him about the unique descriptor the bank teller had given him. "This shithead is missing his left thumb. The teller told us about it first, but when I viewed the video of this guy shooting the place up I could tell she was right. Just like she told us, the prick is actually missing his thumb." Then Wilson gave Bobby Ray the best piece of information he had. "The first four-digits on our guy's plate are IBW 7. We just need to find out what the last two digits are, shouldn't be too hard to do that. The other thing about the plate is that it was hung upside down. He probably did that to make it look like a plate was there, but he hung it like he did to make it difficult for someone to read. If our young witness is correct about what he saw, we should be able to convince DMV to help us sort this out, even if they have to hand-search through some of their records."

Pleased by what Wilson had just told him, Bobby Ray gave the veteran investigator his next set of marching orders. "I'll make a call to a contact I have at DMV regarding this partial listing you have. I'll also tell them it was seen on a Chevy Tahoe, hopefully that will help them narrow down their search. When you're done at the bank, I want you to hook up with Stine and Wagner. You guys put your heads together when they're done with Betty and the sketch artist." From where he stood outside the hospital, Bobby Ray paused to look at a patient being wheeled into the ER. Doing so allowed Wilson to have time to tell his boss the last piece of good news he had for him.

"OK, consider that done, but hang on a minute. There's more good news you need to hear." Wilson then filled Bobby Ray in on what he had seen on the footage shot by the bank's video cameras.

"You think it's the same guy?" Bobby Ray cautiously asked when Wilson finished. "If it is, then he not only shot our priest, but he likely killed Holland as well. It could very well be that Platek was also killed by this same guy. Certainly seems likely, at least to me it does."

"Has to be him, boss. I mean how many assholes are out there wearing maroon windbreakers when they're shooting priests and robbing banks?"

"Good point, Einstein," Bobby Ray said, offering up a weak and sarcastic acknowledgement to the valid point Wilson had raised. "You call Stine or Wagner about this yet? They're the ones who've watched the video from the church. They'll be able to tell you if it's the same jerk or not."

"Called you first, thought you should know what I just told you before they did. I'll call Blake as soon as we hang up."

"Better get a copy of what you saw after Blake takes a look at it. We're going to need to show Pascento that in the near future.

Renda will probably want a look as well, especially if Blake can confirm for us that it's the same guy who shot Father Guyette. We'll want Lt. Ryan and his PIO staff to see that also. I'll call him later and tell him we want our bank robber's ugly face splashed across the evening news tonight."

"Already done," Wilson proudly responded. "Got the original and one copy in my grubby hands as we speak."

Then Bobby Ray added one last comment. "I'm thinking that maybe the easiest way for us to ID our guy is to conduct a stakeout at the diner for a few mornings. I'd like to get started on it tomorrow morning, so put your head together with Blake and Wags and then call me with a game plan. I want to hear your thoughts on doing that."

14

Later that evening, after a long day of worrying and fear, one he had never personally experienced the likes of before, Paul collapsed into a leather recliner next to Donna's bed. Realizing he was going to be spending many long days by his wife's side, the ICU nurses had arranged for the recliner to be moved into her room. Spending the last several hours dealing with doctors and nurses, and with a handful of hospital administrators who had thrust a variety of troublesome insurance and other forms in front of him to sign, he had just finished speaking with his two sons for the third time before resting his head against the back of the recliner.

With Donna resting next to him as well as could be expected, Paul went over the travel plans his sons had made so they could come see their mother. As he finished doing so, he closed his eyes for his first few moments of rest in hours. Resting comfortably, his grumbling stomach soon reminded him it had been hours since he had last eaten. Having only had several weak cups of coffee and three Coca-Colas since breakfast, he had made it through the strenuous day on strictly adrenaline and caffeine.

"I'll eat something later," Paul thought as he glanced at his watch, a gift from his wife on his last birthday. Seeing what time it was made him realize he would have to wait a few hours longer before eating again. "It's almost ten, too late to eat now." In moments, he was fast asleep. In a deep sleep for only fifteen minutes, Paul was roused by the sound of a voice whispering from the doorway of his wife's room.

Not wanting to bother his wife, despite the fact that she was still in a medically induced coma and still receiving oxygen therapy, but not wanting to ignore his close friend standing in the doorway, Paul motioned for Bobby Ray to enter.

"How's she doing, partner?" Bobby Ray asked as he reached down to touch Donna's hand, one heavily bandaged due to the IV lines that were present.

"Holding her own." Paul softly mumbled as he motioned for Bobby Ray to step out into the hallway with him.

Steering Paul down the hallway to the small visitors' room not far from the entrance to the ICU ward, and speaking softly so he did not disturb any of the other patients, Bobby Ray surprised his friend with a bit of good news. Pointing to the doorway of the small room, he said, "She wouldn't let me come up here without bringing her."

Poking his head inside the room, one filled to near capacity with a couch, two small end tables and several chairs, Paul could not help but smile when he saw the familiar face smiling up at him. Almost as if on cue, he and Betty broke out in tears as they hugged each other.

"How's Miss Donna doing, Paul?" Betty asked in her rich Southern accent, clearly concerned about Donna's welfare. "She gonna be OK, I hope?"

Smiling as he exchanged looks with Betty, and then with Bobby Ray, Paul answered his friend's concerns. As he did, he leaned towards the optimistic point of view. "She's going to be fine, especially when she finds out that you and Bobby Ray were so kind to visit her this late at night." Stopping to compose himself, Paul added, "It also means a great deal to me that you both came up here to see her. You didn't have to do that, but I appreciate it."

Reaching down to pick up a brown paper bag on the table next to where she had been sitting, Betty handed it to Paul. "I wasn't sure if you've had time to think about yourself today so I fixed you a fresh turkey sandwich. There's a bag of chips in there as well. It's not much, but it'll hold you over till breakfast."

Beyond hungry after not having much to eat all day, Paul smiled at his friend's thoughtfulness. "Thanks, Betty. I can sure use this. I'm starving."

For the next twenty minutes as he ate his sandwich, Paul's friends listened as he updated them on Donna's status.

* * * * * *

As Bobby Ray and Betty listened to what Paul had to say, fourteen miles away in Murrells Inlet, the carpenter who showed up late to work that morning began to count the money he had stolen. He did so after dumping the contents of the pillowcase out onto his small kitchen table. On the table next to where he was seated was an opened bottle of Corona and a half-eaten Subway sandwich. Strangely, both sat next to two road flares that had recently been taped together.

Ignoring his sandwich, but soon finishing his beer, Pratt silently completed his task of counting the stolen money. For all of his hard work, he had scored a whopping one thousand and forty dollars. It was an amount that was far less than he had hoped for. Staring at the empty beer bottle, he reminded himself of one important point. The robbery had not been his sole reason for visiting the bank that morning.

Soon finished hiding the money, Pratt knelt down on a small piece of carpet in his messy living room and began praying. Like several other items inside the small trailer he shared with his uncle, he had taken the piece of tan carpeting from a dumpster at the site where he was working. As he knelt, he slowly began reciting the words he had learned from the Koran. But unlike other followers of the sect he had recently joined, he had little understanding of the words he recited. Nor was he even remotely close to pointing in the right direction as he prayed to Mecca.

Like so many other wasted opportunities he had failed at in life, Pratt's latest attempt, at converting to the Muslim faith, would soon prove to be part of his downfall. While he had made serious contact with a handful of true extremists intent on doing America harm, sending them both money and support, like everything else he tried in life, he was already questioning whether he had the degree of fanaticism to follow his plans through to completion. The fire he felt, just like the fires he would set, would only burn bright for a short period of time.

It would last long enough to cost others a considerable degree of pain.

15

The noise of a dog barking a short distance away, as well as a car being driven slowly out on the street, caused Sonny Pratt to drop low along a row of waist-high azalea bushes. Focused entirely on not being seen or caught, or even bitten by someone's dog who felt it was his or her responsibility to defend the neighborhood against an outside invader, Pratt paid little attention to the bright red and pink colors of the flowering bushes. Despite the wee hour of the still dark morning, the bright colors were easily visible, made so by two opposing outdoor flood lights from nearby homes who shared a large common backyard.

Waiting until the dog's curiosity faded and the neighborhood was again quiet, Pratt stared at the wooden shed for several seconds before cautiously making his way towards it. It now sat less than thirty feet away from him.

Living less than a mile from the neighborhood whose backyards he now crept through, he had seen the shed doors open on several occasions when its owners were tending to their lawn. Equating lawn mowers and leaf blowers to gas cans, which Pratt owned none of, he had chosen the shed as the perfect place to boost the small amount of gasoline he needed. With his own small lawn occasionally being taken care of by his uncle's landlord, and not wanting to be captured by any security cameras as he purchased gas at an all-night gas station, the shed was the ideal spot to find what he needed.

Quickly placing the small crowbar he had brought with him through the loop of the shed's flimsy lock, Pratt broke the lock making little, if any, noise. Using a small BIC lighter to help him locate the gas can he was looking for, he quickly realized his choice of a light source had not been well-thought-out.

"Asshole!" Pratt softly whispered to himself after realizing even the smallest of lighters like the one he was using could prove to be an exceptional source of energy when mixed with even the faintest wisp of combustible fumes. "Just what I need, this place going up like a rocket because I used a damn lighter and not a flashlight while I'm trying to steal some freakin' gasoline. Freakin' moron, that's me alright."

Locating a small red plastic container that he quickly confirmed to be containing gasoline, he slowly backed out of the shed. Glancing in several directions to make sure he had not been seen, Pratt quietly closed the shed doors. Pleased over not being seen, and even more pleased the dog he had heard earlier had not elected to warn the neighborhood of his intrusion, he slowly retraced his steps back towards his vehicle.

Unimpeded by the light amount of traffic that was present, or by the handful of traffic lights he encountered, the drive to his next target took less than four minutes. Checking his watch after parking his Tahoe in the large parking lot in Murrells Inlet, he saw the time read 4:27 a.m.. Normally reserved for fishermen and boaters to park their trucks and trailers in while using the public boat launch next to Belin Methodist Church, the parking area at this time of day was nearly deserted. Two pick-up trucks, with their requisite boat trailers attached to the back of them, sat parked on the far side of the lot away from where Pratt parked. Seeing the windows of the other vehicles coated with the early morning's dew told him they had been parked there for some time.

Sitting inside his vehicle for several minutes, both to gather his courage and to allow himself time to calm down, he took his first hit of the still cold beer he had brought with him. As he did, and despite his best efforts to do so, he was far too wired and far too upset to calm down.

"Disrespect me, will ya! Fire me, will ya!" Pratt's angry voice yelled loudly from within the confines of his vehicle. *"I'll teach your sorry mick ass to let me go!"*

After draining the last couple ounces of beer into his still parched mouth, he tossed the crumpled up can into the back seat. Reaching down, he grabbed the plastic container of gas sitting on the passenger's floor. Then pausing just outside his vehicle to make sure he was alone, he reached under the driver's seat, grabbing the two road flares he had placed there earlier.

After cutting through the side yards of two nearby homes, he quickly walked across Murrells Inlet Road. Deserted and quiet, with only the sound of an occasional vehicle passing by off in the distance on Highway 17, it was as if he was in the middle of an abandoned neighborhood.

Cautiously moving towards one particular driveway, Pratt saw his target parked there. Under the moon's bright light, O'Keefe's white Dodge Ram pick-up sparkled in the darkness of the early morning hours. Quickly dousing the truck with the stolen gasoline, he made it a point to pour the last full splash over a few tools left in the truck's bed. Then reaching into one of the pockets of the black cargo style pants he was wearing, he pulled out a Ziploc bag. Hoping to help accelerate the fire he was about to start, he tossed four large handfuls of black gunpowder across the already wet surfaces of O'Keefe's truck. Finished, he placed the empty plastic gas container on the truck's roof, hoping the soon-to-be melted plastic would add additional insult to the injury he was about to inflict.

Ducking low behind a large oak tree off to the right of O'Keefe's driveway, Pratt hid there for several moments to avoid being seen by the driver of a vehicle delivering newspapers in the area. Waiting patiently until the vehicle's taillights could no longer be seen, Pratt peeled off the protective plastic caps of the two road flares he had taped together. Running one end against the coarse surface of the driveway, he ignited the flare on his first attempt. After staring at the brightly lit flare for a brief moment, he tossed it into the bed of O'Keefe's truck and then turned and walked away. In moments, the flares' hot red sparks ignited the gasoline splashed inside it. Soon the flames, burning hot due to the mixture of gasoline and gunpowder, began climbing up the back window of the Dodge onto the roof where the plastic gas container had been left. In moments, the melting plastic began spreading across the burning roof.

"That'll teach you, you piece of shit! Screw with me and I'll screw back even harder!" Pratt mumbled out loud as he adjusted the kufi cap he was wearing. Pausing behind a telephone pole on the other side of the street to watch the fire slowly spread across the truck's surface, Pratt was pleased by what he had done. "Go ahead! Get a new truck, you SOB! I'll come back and burn that one as well!"

Hustling back to his vehicle, Pratt soon drove away, driving off in the opposite direction of the burning truck. As he did, with his windows down and his radio turned up, he allowed himself a hearty laugh.

"I can't wait to see what he buys next. Because like Arnold said, *'I'll be back!'*"

Excited by what he accomplished, and feeling like he had not eaten in days, Pratt stopped at a nearby Kangaroo gas station to nuke a hamburger and to pick up a Coke. As he turned to walk outside after paying for his food, he saw the morning papers stacked neatly across the front of the store. Like two nearby racks full of tabloid magazines, the newspapers sat there waiting to be purchased. The headline he saw on the front page of *The Sun News* read *'Cop's wife survives deadly attack'.*

Walking outside, he took one bite of his burger before tossing it away. Suddenly he was no longer hungry.

16

Over the course of the next three days, Bobby Ray's team of detectives, with help from several uniformed deputies, cops from Myrtle Beach, and from state troopers working the counties around Georgetown, began distributing flyers the GCSD COPS program had made up. While still not aware of their suspect's name, the flyers showed the likeness of the person the cops had come to call 'One Thumb Tom'. It was a likeness Betty and one of her co-workers had given their immediate approval to after seeing the finished sketch.

In addition to the distribution of the flyers taking place locally, Bobby Ray met with several area national television affiliates as another means of getting 'One Thumb Tom's' likeness flashed on the thousands of television screens across the Grand Strand. Similar news stories run by a host of print media outlets, including those in Horry, Georgetown, Charleston, Berkley, and Williamsburg counties, also ran their suspect's likeness.

As all of this was being done, despite a significant loss of staffing due to an early retirement buyout, the South Carolina DMV had already begun the labor intensive process of hand-searching their records for the partial license plate Billy Snow had seen on the back of a Chevy Tahoe.

During their interview with Betty, Stine and Wagner learned their suspect had no real pattern of when he did and did not frequent the diner. The one important detail they learned was that Pratt had never visited the diner after 1pm. Based on what little information they had to go on, Stine reaffirmed to Bobby Ray that a covert surveillance was indeed the best course of action for them to take until someone called in with information on their suspect's identity after seeing one of the posters or news broadcasts.

Soon working out the details of the surveillance with Wagner and Wilson, the surveillance was put into operation. Agreeing it should be put into place for at least ten days, and after deciding the surveillance hours should focus on only the early morning hours as Betty had not told them of their suspect ever visiting the diner after lunchtime, plans were made to staff the surveillance between six to noon each morning.

For the first two days, with Wagner parked near the diner's side entrance so he could see who came and went from that direction, Stine kept close tabs on the diner's front door and the driveway's main entrance. From their respective surveillance locations, both had a clear view of those customers who parked their vehicles in the adjacent gravel parking lot. Patiently they both waited to see if their suspect would visit the small restaurant.

The following day, after finishing his second boring shift of surveillance work, Stine stopped at MBPD to complete some overdue paperwork on an unrelated kidnapping case he was handling. While he was there, he also made plans to pick up his most recent paycheck.

Soon finished writing his supplemental report on a kidnapping which had occurred within a small community inside the Carolina Forest section of Myrtle Beach, Stine dropped it in a wire basket sitting on a supervisor's desk within the department's detective division. Always curious to know about the other cases his fellow detectives were working on, and also wanting to see if any of them had any similar MOs to the case he was currently working on with Bobby Ray, the veteran detective scanned a recent printout listing the newest and more serious cases that had been initiated over the past several days. Three of them immediately attracted his attention.

Reviewing the three case files, as well as one of the computers within the DD, Stine quickly determined two of the recently initiated investigations involved acts of significant vandalism being done to two nearby schools. From his review of the reports, he soon learned that both investigations had already been closed with the arrests of those found responsible for the damage that had occurred. In each of those cases, he also learned, as a result of running a quick check on a nearby Automated Fingerprint Identification System computer - an AFIS machine in cops' lingo, that none of the suspects had been found to be missing their left thumbs. In his quick review of the reports that had been submitted for each case, he also realized no mention of any type of use or display of a Confederate flag had been reported. Satisfied these two cases had no connection to the one he was working, Stine quickly dismissed them.

Stine's review of the third investigation immediately garnered his attention. While nothing had been mentioned within any of the case reports that had been submitted of any connection to a Confederate flag being displayed, or of the victim being connected in any way to any group sympathetic to the late rebellion of the South, such as the Sons of Confederate Veterans or the United Daughters of the Confederacy, another point referenced in one of the reports piqued his curiosity.

After reviewing the case file, one which contained little more than the most basic of information which two busy MBPD street cops had included in the written documentation of what they found at the scene and what they had done to investigate this crime, Stine called the two cops to get a sense of what they had observed at the scene of the truck fire. Satisfied their investigation had determined the arson was not the result of an insurance scam, he then called the victim to set up an interview. Less than an hour later, Stine arrived at the construction project underway within The Market Common community. As was his reputation, the veteran detective was now digging for even the smallest of clues.

******

"Thanks for making the time to meet with me, Mr. O'Keefe. I appreciate it," Stine said as the two men shook hands with each other. While he knew O'Keefe had been the victim of foul play; and not the instigator of it, Stine's training and experience still caused him to evaluate the person he was speaking with. Unlike others he had recently been dealing with, Stine's initial opinion of his witness was a very favorable one.

"Yeah, no problem, detective. Kind of surprised to hear from you though, those first two cops I spoke with didn't seem too interested about my truck having been set on fire. Guess they had more important things to be working on."

Remembering what it was like to be a street cop on days when the radio always seemed to be calling your number to respond to another call, Stine did his best at explaining why the cops who had first responded to the arson of O'Keefe's truck had handled it like they had. His explanation, some of it fact and some of it bullshit, quickly satisfied O'Keefe, who was more than pleased by the follow-up being given to his problem.

"I've read the reports those guys submitted, and while I admit what they wrote was pretty brief, they did cover the basic facts," Stine offered as he stared at several trusses being delivered to a nearby home site. Next to where the trusses were being off-loaded, it was easy to tell the home's concrete slab had just recently been poured.

"At least they agreed it was an arson and not something I was a part of," O'Keefe replied, pleased by the news Stine had told him. "Met with my insurance agent this morning as a matter-of-fact; says she'll have a check to me next week to cover the loss of my truck and the tools that were in it. Driving that for now." O'Keefe pointed across the street at a black Ford pick-up his insurance company had rented for him.

As O'Keefe had pointed, Stine could not help noticing a large colorful tattoo on the construction foreman's upper right arm. "Pretty fancy tattoo you've got there. What are those flags I'm seeing? They look like the Confederate and Irish flags?"

"Yeah, sure are," O'Keefe answered, proudly rolling up his sleeve to fully expose the tattoo for Stine to see. "I was born in Ireland, lived there until I was twenty-four. Had two great-grandfathers, along with three of their brothers, fight in the war after coming to the United States from Ireland in the mid-1850s. Both of my great-grandfathers fought alongside Stonewall Jackson before he was accidently shot at Chancellorsville. Their brothers also fought in Bobby Lee's Army of Northern Virginia. Years ago I was pleased to learn that not only did they all survive the war, they all lived to be old men. I'm proud of both of my homes, that's the meaning behind this tattoo."

"That a fact," Stine replied, more interested in the possible connection of O'Keefe's tattoo to what had happened to his truck and to the other victims than to the history lesson he was receiving. "Think your tattoo had anything to do with your truck being turned into a roaring candle recently?"

It took O'Keefe a moment to figure out what Stine's comment meant, but when he did it caused him a good laugh. "No, not really. Most people don't even know I have it."

"OK, sounds good. I was just asking, that's all. What about any trouble in your life? Having any these days with family or friends? Maybe with a co-worker or two?" Stine asked, well aware that like many homicides, a good number of arsons were often committed by people their victims knew. He did so as another means of trying to find a connection between the tattoo on O'Keefe's arm to his recent truck fire. Then, without using any tact at all, the veteran detective asked, "Anyone at work being a dickhead these days?"

"Family and friends are all good," O'Keefe said as he thought back on whom he might have been having any problems with. "The only problem I've had at work recently was with one of my so-called carpenters showing up to work on time. Had to fire him recently over it, but I'm not sure if he's capable of doing something like that to me. He's never impressed me as being the sharpest tool in the tool shed, if you know what I mean. But I have to admit, I don't know him all that well."

"Doesn't take much to light a match or, for that matter, even a set of road flares, does it?" Stine asked, referring to the burnt stubs of two road flares that had been found in the bed of O'Keefe's truck. "Sounds like whoever torched your truck used the flares to ignite the gasoline that had been poured all over it."

"Suppose not." O'Keefe admitted, toying with a wooden toothpick in his mouth. Having survived a scare with throat cancer several years earlier, the former heavy smoker now chewed on toothpicks to help keep his mind off the nicotine he occasionally still craved.

"Tell me about this guy you fired. Was he harassing you or some of the other employees who work for you? Did you catch him stealing from the job site? Anything else besides his tardiness that caused you to terminate him?" In his day book, Stine began to take notes of what O'Keefe was telling him. Detail-orientated in his approach to his job, Stine even made a written note of O'Keefe's Irish accent.

"Nope, none of that. I simply fired his sorry ass because he couldn't show up to work on time. I had already given the guy several warnings about being late, but despite his bullshit promises that it wouldn't happen again, it did. I've got project deadlines to meet. I can't meet them if my guys decide to show up late to work every day. That's why I fired the prick."

As he continued to take notes of what was being discussed, Stine asked his next question. As he did, a large crane arrived to hoist another series of engineered trusses into place on top of two of O'Keefe's newly framed homes. "Do you remember when you gave this guy his last warning before you terminated him? And, I assume this guy does have a name, correct?"

Distracted by the crane being slowly placed into position in what soon would be someone's front yard, O'Keefe took a moment before answering Stine's question. "Yeah . . . it was . . . it was the same day that bank got robbed in Garden City. I can't recall the date off the top of my head, but it was that same day because the prick was late to work for like the tenth time in less than two months or so. He showed up here at least forty-five minutes late. That's when I told him he was living on borrowed time if he kept showing up late."

"How'd he respond to that?" Stine asked, already believing he knew the answer to his own question.

O'Keefe laughed for a moment as he recalled what occurred that morning. Then, pointing to his tattoo, he said, "The dumbshit basically made a smart-ass comment about my tat more than anything else. He offered up one of his false promises, but that's about it. Later that same day, I chewed him a new ass for goofing off when he should have been working on some trim work that I needed to have done."

Pausing from taking notes of what was being discussed, Stine, in order to keep O'Keefe talking, agreed with his assessment of his former employee. "Sounds like a real pain in the ass. Glad you had to deal with him and not me."

"Yeah, thanks," O'Keefe said sarcastically as he nodded his head at Stine.

Opening his day book back up, Stine asked, "OK, what's this guy's name, and where do I find him?"

"Jerk's name is Carter M. Pratt. Most folks call him Sonny. He's a white guy who's probably around thirty-five years old. He's maybe six feet tall, and fairly skinny. I'll have to get his address from our main office for you as I don't keep those kind of records at the job site. But whatever it is, I doubt it would do you any good. He seems to move quite frequently. Not sure why he does that, unless he's got money problems or he's trying to make it hard for cops like you to find him. Last I heard, I think the prick was living in a beat-up tin can, a doublewide, down in Murrells Inlet. Not sure if he's working another job yet or not, really don't care to know though." As O'Keefe finished speaking, Stine could tell from the construction foreman's body language that he was starting to lose interest in the conversation.

"You said this guy's middle initial is M. Have any idea what that stands for?"

O'Keefe smiled before answering the question. "Yeah, I think it stands for moron."

Stine laughed at O'Keefe's answer, judging it to be a fairly accurate response based on what he had been told about Pratt already. "Anything unusual about this guy? Scars, tattoos, anything like that?"

"No, not really. He's missing his left thumb, but that's about it. I think I was told he lost it in either a hunting or boating accident several years back." Unsure if this was important or not, O'Keefe tossed one more point in Stine's direction. "This guy I fired, it's probably been two weeks now, maybe three, but I remember him showing up to work with a black eye and a few bumps and bruises several days before I canned him. It looked like he took a serious beating from someone."

While intrigued over hearing about the injuries Pratt had sustained, what Stine heard O'Keefe say about his former carpenter's thumb being missing quickly caused him to concentrate even more than he had been. "You sure it's the left one that's missing?"

"Sure as I'm standing here wasting my time talking about this prick. Are we about done?" O'Keefe asked anxiously as he stared at the nearby crane being setup slower than he expected it to be. "I'm not trying to be rude, but that big piece of expensive equipment over there is costing us a ton of money being here this morning. I need to make sure it's out of here ASAP." Growing more and more irritated by the lack of progress being made at the site of one of his new homes, O'Keefe continued to stare at the crane that had yet to lift one truss in place.

"Almost." Stine said, clearly energized by the news he had learned from O'Keefe. "What about Pratt's vehicle? What's he drive? It wouldn't be a Chevy Tahoe, would it?"

Surprised by what Stine had asked him, O'Keefe refocused his attention on the cop standing in front of him. As he did, he flicked the toothpick he had been chewing on several feet away. "How'd you know that?"

"A wild guess," Stine said as he closed his day book for the final time. "You mentioned before that your truck was still parked in your driveway. Would you mind if I stopped by to take a look at the damage the fire did?"

"Nope, not at all. Not sure why you'd want to, but have at it." O'Keefe said, shaking his head to show he had no problem with his truck being looked at.

******

After viewing the damage done to O'Keefe's truck, Stine stood in the driveway making a few notes of the observations he had made. Soon finished, and somewhat frustrated over his efforts not proving to be more fruitful than they were, he was about to walk back to his vehicle when his eyes saw the small black stain on the driveway next to O'Keefe's now flat right rear tire.

Kneeling down next to the stain, a burn mark that he now realized had been caused by something burning extremely hot at the time of the arson; Stine stared at it for a few moments as he reached for his pocketknife. Leaning close enough to the black stain to see if his nose detected any lingering odors, he quickly realized what had caused the burn mark. First taking three photos of the stain with his Smartphone, he then used his small knife to scrape several black flakes onto his white handkerchief. Carefully folding the flakes inside it as he stood up, he then painstakingly inspected the damaged truck a second time, looking for more of what he now suspected had caused the burn mark to appear on the driveway.

"So that's how this truck sustained so much damage that night," Stine thought as he finished his inspection, noting that while the fire had been hot, it had not been hot enough or burned long enough to cause the truck's gas tank to explode.

Placing his handkerchief carefully inside his glove compartment for safekeeping, he knew he would later have to enter this exhibit of burnt black flakes into evidence before turning them over to Vane so they could be sent to the lab for processing.

* * * * * *

The information and evidence Stine found that afternoon, along with what Wilson had learned, would soon begin to help them build their case against a sick and demented individual. One who now thought of himself as both an anarchist and a homegrown Muslim terrorist.

17

As Stine was conducting his interview with O'Keefe, Paul finally managed to doze off in the recliner next to Donna's bed after a restless night of worrying about his wife. Dozing off and on for close to an hour, with his wife resting comfortably next to him, his thoughts briefly turned to the investigation he was helping Bobby Ray with.

Soon woken from his brief power nap by the sounds of a squeaky laundry cart being pushed down the hallway outside of Donna's room, Paul splashed water on his face after checking on his wife. After drying his face with a clean white towel he found in the small private bathroom not far from the end of his wife's bed, he decided to make his way down to the cafeteria for a fresh cup of coffee. Pausing at the foot of the bed, he first made sure the instruments monitoring his wife's pulse and respirations were working to his satisfaction.

Walking outside to a small courtyard adjacent to the hospital's cafeteria after getting his coffee, Paul called Bobby Ray from where he sat enjoying the sun's warmth and his hot drink. Around him, several other patients and staff members were enjoying their early afternoon caffeine fix as well.

"What's up, Yankee Boy?" Bobby Ray asked, answering his phone with a touch of humor in his voice. Then realizing something might be wrong, he anxiously asked, "Everything OK with Miss Donna?"

"Yeah, she's fine. Her doctor looked in on her last night. He's also coming by this afternoon with another surgeon as they've scheduled another CT scan for her sometime later today. They want to see if the swelling in her brain has been reduced at all." Paul said between sips of his still too hot coffee.

Relieved to hear Donna was doing OK, Bobby Ray smiled over what he had been told. "I'll be sure to keep a positive thought out for her today."

"Thanks, Bobby Ray. Listen, I called you about these investigations we're working. You still don't know who our murderer is, do you?"

Unaware of the interview Stine had just finished conducting, Bobby Ray replied in the negative. "Nope, not yet. The boys are working hard on it though."

"OK, then maybe I have an idea which will solve that problem for you. From what you've told me, our first two victims, especially Mr. Holland, they were guys who lived a fairly clean life. By that I mean they hadn't been arrested for anything significant, such as committing a murder or a kidnapping, stuff like that, right?"

"That's correct."

Pleased by Bobby Ray's response, Paul continued with his idea on how to identify their suspect. "If our two guys are that clean, then no one should have had any reason to run their license plates or, for that matter, even their operators' licenses through any DMV computer, should they?"

Not sure where this was going, Bobby Ray partially agreed with Paul's logic. "No, I guess not, but how do we know someone has."

"Simple, you ask. Listen, if someone has run their plates, NCIC would have a record of where the query came from ... their records should be able to tell you what computer terminal ran the query. As you know, it won't matter if the listing was run at a DMV office, at SLED, at one of the highway patrol's field troops, or at any other computer terminal in any police department. Each terminal has an identifier, like SP02 or SP03, or MBPD6, or DMV102, get it?" Paul asked, hoping his friend was catching on to what he was telling him.

"Yeah, you're right. So what you're thinking is once we ID the terminal that was used, that's if our victims' information has been run, then we can also ID who made the query. You're hoping the person who requested the listings is also going to turn out to be the same person who queried the information. Is that where you're going with all of this?"

"You're a genius, Bobby Ray!" Paul said, pleased his friend had caught on with his line of thinking.

"So if we find that our victims' information has been run, we've either found our killer or an accomplice."

Taking another sip of his coffee, one which tasted far better than the last couple of cups he had purchased from the cafeteria, Paul instinctively shook his head in agreement with Bobby Ray's last statement. "My friend, I guess I should hang up now. Looks like you've got some work to get busy with."

******

By day's end, Bobby Ray and Paul, with Stine and Wilson's assistance, would finally start to learn some good news.

18

Two hours after Paul and Bobby Ray had first talked on the phone, the Major Case commander stopped at the hospital to follow up on his friend's earlier idea on how to identify their suspect. During that time, Stine had investigated the two addresses listed on Pratt's DMV op license and registration.

Hot and thirsty from a busy afternoon, Stine stopped at the Markette gas station at the corner of Highway 17 and Wachesaw Road to quench his thirst, and to pick up a box of Garcia y Vega English Corona cigars he always seem to have one of in his mouth. Sitting out of the hot sun in a shady back corner of the parking lot, he used his cell phone to call Bobby Ray. As he waited for the call to be answered, he took his first sip of the cold drink he had purchased.

"What's up, Blake? You have anything special to tell me this afternoon?"

"Yeah, sure do," Stine said, before sucking on the thin plastic straw stuck inside his thick frosty drink. Cheap and flimsy, the straw was already giving him fits. "Where you at? I'd rather tell you what I've found out in person."

"Stopped at the hospital to see Paul for a few minutes, right now we're having coffee in the cafeteria." Bobby Ray announced loud enough for Paul to hear. "I just took a call from Kent. He's meeting us here in about ten, claims he's got some good news to tell us also. Care to join us?"

"Be there in fifteen, don't start the party without me." Frustrated with a straw which did not want to work, Stine tossed it, along with the cup's lid, into a nearly full garbage can on his way out of the parking lot. Anxious to tell the others the good news he had learned, he punched the accelerator hard as he headed north on Highway 17.

******

After exchanging a friendly greeting with the others seated around two rectangular tables that had been pushed together in the cafeteria, Stine, like the others, listened as Wilson began explaining what he had learned earlier. As he did, he advised the others of some frustration he had encountered.

"After being tired of waiting to hear some results on our license plate request, I drove over to the DMV office in Myrtle Beach. At first I thought they were trying to be helpful, but . . . you know, some of those people working there seriously pissed me off today. And they're the ones you told me to go see, Bobby Ray. Freaking bureaucratic assholes, the whole lot of them! That's what they are. Freaking jerks! I'm trying to solve a couple of murders and they're more interested in making sure they get their fifteen-minute breaks than they are in helping me. No wonder state employees always seem to get an unfair rap, it's because of those DMV bastards."

Seeing Paul and Stine smirk as Wilson continued on his tirade against the DMV employees and their lack of cooperation, Bobby Ray added more fuel to the fire by saying, "Kent, don't hold back. Tell us how you really feel."

"Freaking morons. I should . . . no, I am going to write a letter complaining about the lack of help they gave me today." Wilson added before calming down and continuing with what he had to say.

"After I realized these DMV jerks really weren't too keen on helping me, I just went and sat down at one of their computers and started pounding out combinations of license plates, hoping the last two digits I was missing would come back to a Chevy Tahoe." Pausing from the investigative side of his story for a moment, Wilson resumed his tirade against the DMV staff. "Can you imagine that, they let me have access to one of their computers and half of those jerks didn't even know who I was. Hell, I could have been some asshole terrorist or something. If I was there for some nefarious reason, I could have easily placed a virus into every one of their computers."

"I'd have to say they were probably not thinking along the terrorist line, but maybe they were giving some consideration to the other part," Stine joked as he glanced at the others seated around him.

"What part is that?" Wilson asked before realizing what Stine had meant. Quickly he flipped his friend the middle finger salute.

"Go on, let's hear what else you found out today," Bobby Ray said, slipping two sticks of Juicy Fruit gum in his mouth. Like the others, he was enjoying a good laugh over Stine's friendly jab at Wilson.

"When I started entering combinations into their NCIC terminal to go with the letters and number I already had, I was worried that maybe the letters and number on the plate our young witness saw were wrong. I was also concerned that the plate could have been one our shithead bank robber friend might have stolen or had in his possession for some other reason. Luckily for us that didn't turn out to be the case. But for no other reason than just pure luck, I entered the right two numbers we were missing after running about sixty other combinations first. I have to tell you guys, I was quite surprised to find a Chevy Tahoe listed to a guy in Murrells Inlet with the letters the kid gave me earlier. It's listed . . . "

" . . . to a guy by the name of Sonny Pratt." Stine offered rather nonchalantly, trying hard not to smile as he leaned back in his chair before adding one more useful bit of information. "Legally his name is Carter Pratt, but most folks call him by his nickname." From the stunned looks he saw on the faces around him, Stine knew he had just told them all something they had not expected to hear.

Caught totally off guard by what Stine had said, Paul and Bobby Ray stared quietly at him for several moments. Equally surprised by what he had heard, Wilson also stared at his friend for a brief moment before speaking.

"What the . . . how'd you know that?"

"Good police work, I guess." Stine could not help smiling at the bewildered looks he saw on his friends' faces.

"You're telling me I broke my ass this morning sitting at a friggin' terminal punching in numbers and letters and you already knew this prick's name? How'd you learn his name?" Wilson demanded to know as Paul and Bobby Ray waited to hear more about their suspect.

Stine then told the others about how he had come to interview O'Keefe, what he learned from speaking with Pratt's former boss, and about the discovery he made in O'Keefe's driveway. As he finished speaking, he carefully unfolded his handkerchief after taking it out of the clear plastic evidence bag he had placed it in. As he did, he showed the others the black flakes he had scraped off the driveway. Then he showed them the photos he had taken with his Smartphone.

"What do you think it is, Blake?" Bobby Ray asked as he continued to stare at the handful of black flakes.

"Gunpowder, black powder of some kind, that's my guess," Paul interjected, not giving Stine time to answer the question that had been posed to him.

Despite everything that was going on in Paul's life regarding his wife, Stine was not surprised to hear his friend correctly identify what the substance was. "Yep, that's what I'm thinking it is. Probably thrown on the truck when it was burning, maybe before, but done to help the fire burn hot. I'll give this to Doug or Don later when I see them, but I think we need to do something more than just sending these flakes up to the lab to be tested."

Before Bobby Ray could ask his next question, Paul tossed one at Stine. "I assume you gave it a whiff?"

"Correct again, boss," Stine answered, utilizing a term cops often used when addressing not only those in authority, but those they also respected. "Despite the number of days since the arson, the spot I worked on still had the slightest odor of burnt gunpowder present. If I could smell it, there's no doubt one of our canines that's been trained to detect accelerants could do the same thing. We might want to give some consideration to doing that just so we can say we've covered all of the bases."

"Probably was used to accelerate the fire. Mixing gasoline and gunpowder creates an intense fire," Paul offered. As he spoke, he briefly reflected back on one particularly gruesome arson case he had worked back in Connecticut. "What you found on the ground was likely spilled there or unintentionally thrown there in a heavier amount than it was in other locations by whoever started the fire. Possibly by this Pratt guy, I suppose. Whatever was piled up on the ground probably caught fire when a spark ignited it or when some gas dripped on it. Kind of surprised the cops who were first on the scene didn't notice it." Then Paul nodded his head in Stine's direction. "Not surprised you found it though. Good cops like you pick up on small things they find at scenes. Nice job, buddy!"

Paul's comment caused Stine to return the compliment with a brief nod of his head before he continued with what he had to say.

"One more thing about this suspect of ours, his boss also told me he showed up to work several days ago after apparently getting his ass kicked pretty good in a fight. The date of this beating seems to coincide with the date of our first victim being killed. I heard the crime scene boys found two different types of human blood in the vic's driveway. I'm guessing it would be a good idea to check Pratt's blood type against the two that were found at the scene. A simple DNA test will tell us if Pratt was there or not."

Dialing up Detective Davis on his cell phone, Bobby Ray instructed him to start hunting for a DNA sample of Pratt's blood. "Check the hospitals, check the local clinics, check wherever you want to – just find us a DNA sample. When you do, let me know. Then I'll talk to Pascento about getting a search warrant for Pratt's medical records."

As Bobby Ray hung up from talking to Davis, Stine offered up another option for finding a sample of Pratt's blood type. "I'll call O'Keefe when we get done here. Maybe Pratt had to submit to a physical or had to pee in a bottle for a drug test prior to being hired. That might give us what we need. The other option is to have Scozz call his contact with the U.S. Army and see what they can tell us."

Nodding at Stine's suggestions, Bobby Ray then asked him what his other suggestion was. "What's that thing you think we should be doing? Getting a search warrant to process the truck that got torched?"

"Yes, sir. Just so there's no bullshit thrown at us later by any defense attorney. I think we need to send your Major Case van back to O'Keefe's house with Dougie or Don so they can process the truck the right way. It would be too easy for someone to say that I've compromised the evidence I found there today. There's still plenty of it left there, so let's get a search warrant, take some photos and all of that, and seize the evidence the right way. It's your call, but I think that's what we need to do."

"OK, I agree," Bobby Ray said without any hesitation. "Will get on that as soon as we're done here. I'll also make arrangements to have one of our arson dogs take a shot at doing what they do best. We'll run the dog through the scene before we start processing the truck. For now, just so we're all straight on this, we finally have a suspect to start working. This Pratt guy is possibly the same prick who hurt Donna, who set the truck on fire, and, let's hope so for our sake, the same prick who's committed our two murders and the shooting of Father Guyette. Anyone have any other thoughts on this?" Bobby Ray's brief summation was one the others sitting around the table all agreed with.

"Anything else you two want to tell us?" Bobby Ray said, looking at Wilson and Stine.

"Yeah, three things, boss." Stine said, moving his chair closer to the table in front of him. After telling the others more about what O'Keefe had told him regarding Pratt's missing left thumb, a point Wilson quickly corroborated by reaffirming what he had been previously told by the bank teller, Stine spoke about two other important points. "Neither address listed for our guy on both his registration and his operator's license are any good. I've already checked them out. One's a false address and the other's a vacant used car lot just off of Highway 17 in Surfside Beach. Pratt's former boss told me the last he knew our guy was living in a mobile home in Murrells Inlet, but he's not sure where. We'll have to do some serious checking in order to find him. We'll get him, but it may take a few days."

"We've got more work to do based on what Blake and I have found out today, but it's still more than what we knew this morning," Wilson offered, trying to remain positive about the direction the investigation was now heading in. "The first thing we need to do is to run Pratt through NCIC so we can learn if he's ever been arrested. Doing so will tell us if he's ever been violent in the past."

While not completely ignoring Wilson's comments, Paul chose to direct his next question towards Stine. "What's the other thing you have to tell us, Blake?"

Feeling almost guilty about having to answer Paul's question, Stine looked down at the table for several moments before speaking. What he had to tell the others was likely a critical piece of information, but it scared him to have to tell the others the news he had.

"Come on, Blake. Tell us." Bobby Ray said as he watched the color drain from Stine's face. "What can be that bad?"

Looking at Bobby Ray, then at Wilson, and finally at Paul, Stine's next bit of news was something none of the others saw coming. "O'Keefe told me . . . he told me our guy is . . ."

"Is what?" Bobby Ray asked. "What is he?"

"He's a Muslim."

Stine's description of their suspect's religious affiliation quickly flooded through each of the others seated around the table. Even though they each realized that most Muslims were not violent radicalized extremists, the thought of Pratt possibly being one concerned them. The ramifications of Pratt's religious affiliation, as well as the violence he had recently exhibited, caused a host of potential problems to now pass through each of their minds. They were problems that scared the hell out of them.

After several minutes of quiet concern between them, Paul got them back on track.

"OK, let's not speculate on what's going to happen because of this guy's alleged religious affiliation; let's just deal with what we know." Looking at Bobby Ray, he asked, "That sound OK to you?"

"Yeah, as much as this guy Pratt smells bad to me, we have to stick to what we know, just like we always do. Sounds like you have an idea. What is it?"

"First things first," Paul answered calmly. "Like you said a few minutes ago, we already have two dead guys, a priest who's been shot, and my wife who was nearly killed by this Pratt guy. At least we think it was Pratt who ran her over. But for now let's forget about Father Guyette and Donna. If you were going after our first two victims, wouldn't you want to know as much about them as possible? You might already know where they lived just by following them home or by seeing them flying a Confederate flag in their yard, that's if the flag was the reason they were killed, but wouldn't you want to know even more about them before killing them?"

"Like what, Paul?" Wilson asked.

"Like how old they were, like what their exact address was, like what kind of vehicles they owned, and if they owned any weapons. Anyone with access to an NCIC terminal could tell you the answers to all of those questions."

"Good thought, Paul," Stine said, agreeing with the logic that had been put out on the table for them to consider. "Maybe we should have DMV run an audit on our first two victims' op licenses and reg plates. If those vics were fairly clean as we're being told, you'd have to think there wouldn't have been any reason for their personal info to have been queried by anyone recently. An audit would certainly tell us if that had happened or not. If someone did, I think we'd have to have a 'Come to Jesus' meeting with that person. Is that what you're thinking?"

"Exactly. Bobby Ray and I were already discussing the need to contact DMV so they could run an audit for us before you and Kent got here. Seems like an even better idea after hearing about what the both of you found out today."

While farmers and government officials sometimes complain about having to deal with too much water in the wake of a major storm, cops seldom complain about receiving too much information. They never complain when that information relates to the types of murder investigations underway in Murrells Inlet and in other parts of the Grand Strand.

As he sat talking with the others in the now nearly deserted hospital cafeteria, Bobby Ray's cell announced an incoming call from Wagner.

"Doing anything to help the cause today, Wags?" Bobby Ray asked, skipping his normal professional manner of answering his phone.

Intrigued by what he had just learned, Wagner ignored the sarcasm directed his way. "I was down at the office earlier and I saw we had three messages on our Tip Line. I took a moment to play them and I think I've found something substantial for us to run with. You have a moment?"

"Yeah, sure do. Listen, I'm at the hospital with Paul. Blake and Kent are here with us. I'm going to put my phone on speaker so they can all hear what you've got to say. Got that?"

For the next few minutes, Wagner advised the others that one of the calls he had listened to, while anonymous like the other two that had been left, contained an unusual tip that he had just followed up on. A tip involving a call girl and a guy by the name of Sonny Pratt.

After listening to Wagner briefly describe what the anonymous caller had left on the Tip Line, Bobby Ray then told him about what Stine and Wilson had also learned regarding their suspect. "OK, so now you know what we know. Tell us more about this call you followed up on."

"Well, just so you know," Wagner said, still excited over what he had learned, "everyone else was tied up doing something so I grabbed Darren and took him with me as I normally don't like interviewing high-priced call girls by myself. I'm sure you can understand why." Like the others with him, Bobby Ray understood the point being made. A smart experienced cop like Wagner knew it was prudent to have someone with him in order to be able to refute any future allegations of improper conduct when dealing with someone selling her body for a living.

As Stine and the others with him each started laughing over who Wagner had gone to interview, Bobby Ray, despite the cackling going on in the background, spoke to his detective.

"I'm surprised she agreed to talk with you. How'd you manage that?" As Bobby Ray had asked his question, the others around the table with him grew quiet, anxious to hear Wagner's response.

"I used one of our most important tools of the trade; in fact, it's one you taught me."

"Yeah, what's that?" Bobby Ray asked, already convinced the response he was about to hear was not going to be anything but sarcastic in nature.

"I bullshitted her. I had her phone number from the message that was left by our anonymous female caller. She's probably someone who's in the same profession as our girl, and probably someone who's tired of competing against her. So I called this dame just like any of her Johns would and told her I was interested in taking her up on her offer. An offer this anonymous caller said our girl has printed on her business cards. After we spoke for a few minutes on the phone, we agreed to meet at the Hampton Inn on Celebrity Circle, the one behind Broadway at the Beach. When we got there, and based on whom we were going to meet, I had Darren stay in the car so he could take a few shots of her as she arrived. We just happened to park in the right spot as he was also able to grab the plate on her car. I thought it was best to grab it just in the event we needed to contact her again."

"Nice move on both your parts," Bobby Ray said, nodding his head approvingly as he looked across the table at Paul. "So what's this offer this gal's got printed on her cards, and how is she tied into Pratt?"

"As I've told you, I told her someone had given me one of her cards and that I was interested in an afternoon quickie. That's what's supposedly printed on her cards – *Need a quickie? Call Niki!*"

Despite the seriousness of the moment, hearing what Wagner had said caused Bobby Ray and the others to burst out laughing. It was laughter that lasted close to a minute.

"So when I called her, she was the one who suggested the Hampton Inn. Darren and I got there about five minutes before she did. When she walked up to me in the lobby, the first thing she asked me was if I was a cop. That's when I used the other tool of the trade you taught me, I lied. Told her I was just looking for someone to spend part of a nice afternoon with. After she told me she was going to be my girlfriend for the next two hours, and after telling me what I was going to get in return for my three hundred dollars, I showed her my badge and the wire I was wearing. Then I walked her outside to where Darren was waiting for us. Can you imagine that? Three hundred for a quickie from someone who supposedly has a husband and a couple of kids," Wagner said, still somewhat surprised by the cost of an afternoon quickie. "Granted she's a pretty girl with a great figure, but I wonder what it costs to spend a full night with her?"

"That's if she's a girl." Stine wisely offered from his years of having to deal with hookers, pimps and transvestites.

"She talk to you about Pratt?" Paul asked loudly from across the table, making sure Wagner could hear what he said.

"Yeah, but not at first. After I told her we were going to give her a free ride on the prostitution charge in exchange for what we wanted, then she opened up. Besides telling us about having Pratt as a paying customer on at least three occasions . . . twice for sex and once just to talk after he had trouble performing the dirty deed, she described him pretty much as I've already told you. She also told us he's missing one of his thumbs, but she couldn't remember which one it was. When I asked her about it, she took a guess and said it was the left one, but it's just that, a guess. The last thing she told us was that she won't meet with him again, claims he scares her. She thinks he's full of hate. She's afraid he could easily snap and kill her for no reason."

Finished listening to what Wagner had to tell them, Bobby Ray offered up his assessment from the wealth of information that now pointed to Pratt as being their killer. "Well, I guess that about locks Pratt up as being our guy. We still have a bunch of work to do to prove he's our guy, but for now he's our main suspect."

Picking up his phone, Bobby Ray called a friend of his, a deputy commissioner with the South Carolina DMV. As they talked about the audit and why it was needed, Paul got his friend's attention.

"Better order a couple of Blow Backs of our vics, including Father Guyette, and one or two of Pratt as well. I think we're going to be needing them." In cop lingo, Paul had referred to the electronic photos stored by DMV of everyone possessing a South Carolina operator's license.

As this was happening, Wilson, who had been taking in all that was being discussed, brought up two important points. "I understand the logic of having the audit done, but we all know running a query on someone's name to see if they own a weapon is only going to tell you if they've legally registered a weapon as required. We all know there are thousands of unregistered weapons out there, so I'm not too sure that's why someone might be running the names of our victims. My other point is about O'Keefe. We've heard about this guy's tattoo, but he also told Blake he's never flown a Confederate flag at his home. To me, O'Keefe, if it's Pratt we really like for all of this, he's more important than the first two victims are as not too many people likely knew about his Confederate tattoo like Pratt did. I know they had a falling out at work, and while I realize the truck being set on fire could be an act of revenge on Pratt's part for being fired, I can't help wondering if O'Keefe's truck would've been set on fire if he didn't have that tattoo."

"I agree with what you're saying, Kent," Stine offered. "I think O'Keefe's tattoo carries a lot of weight in this whole mess."

＊＊＊＊＊＊

Unlike the first person he had contacted for a favor, less than fifty minutes after first making contact with him, Bobby Ray received a phone call back from his contact at DMV regarding the results of the audit that had been run on all three of their victims.

"Good call on your part, Paul," Bobby Ray said after finishing his call. "My guy at DMV says the registration info for the license plates assigned to both of our first two victims have recently been queried. However, there's no record of any of Father Guyette's information being queried recently, at least not on the one computer they focused on there wasn't. Could be whoever killed them, likely our guy Pratt, may have driven by their homes on a day he saw the flags flying and decided to take them out. Perhaps he's a guy who watches cop shows on television and, like you've said, wanted to know what he was going to be facing in the event his targets confronted him. Unless our killer works at a DMV office, I'm thinking he reached out to someone who has access to a terminal to get the info he needed. This could all be conjecture on our part, but we need to check it out."

"Your guy obviously told you where the plates were run, right?" It was the next logical question to be thrown at Bobby Ray.

"Yeah, sure did. Fortunately for us the queries weren't run by a cop or a dispatcher as that would have been embarrassing for any of our departments to have to explain in front of a bunch of reporters. The good news, if that's what you call it, is they were all run from a terminal at the Myrtle Beach DMV office on 21st Avenue. The best news is that the terminal DMV identified as being the one the queries were run from is assigned to the deputy branch manager. It has a password on it that only he knows, so in all likelihood that means he's the guy responsible for running the registration queries. From what I was just told, he's supposed to use the terminal mainly for running his own audits on the clerks who work for him. As you all know from your own NCIC training, personal queries are clearly prohibited by both federal and state laws. So the question is, if neither of our victims' op licenses or registrations were about to expire, or be suspended, why was their information queried? My guess is that it wasn't for anything good."

Looking at his watch, Wilson asked, "This guy have a name?"

"Yep, already have it. I was told on the phone that he's working there right now," Bobby Ray offered as a smile crossed his face. Looking at Paul, he added, "The Blow Backs have been ordered for us as well. The branch manager has already been told we're coming to see him very soon, he'll hand us the photos when we get there."

"So let's get our butts in gear!" Stine said, standing up from where he had been seated, eager to find out more on Pratt and his associate.

"You're not going with us, Blake. I've got something else I want you to do." Not allowing Stine time to protest his decision, Bobby Ray then told Wilson to contact Scozzafava and Griffin so they could meet them at the DMV office. "Tell them we'll be there in fifteen. I want them to wait for us in the parking lot." Turning back to Stine, Bobby Ray issued him his next set of marching orders. "Blake, I need you to take care of a couple of other needs because Paul's staying here with Donna. First, I want you to get in touch with Dougie and Don. Tell them what you've found, and then tell them you and Edwards are going to contact Pascento for a search warrant on O'Keefe's truck so they can process it for any traces of gunpowder. Darren's just got back from his vacation late this morning. I'll call him to give him an update and then tell him to hook up with you so you guys can prepare the warrant. After you get that all worked out with him, call Davis and tell him I want him to find out everything he can about Pratt at the state and local levels. Also tell him that I'll have Scozz check Pratt out at the federal level due to his contacts and security clearance. I want to know as much about that prick's pedigree as soon as possible."

******

Like any labor intensive murder investigation, bits of credible information often flowed slowly to the detectives working the case. But unlike most days, the hard work of Bobby Ray's detectives had uncovered a wealth of positive information; most notably, information on who their suspect was.

What they now knew, would soon be trumped by information they sweated out of their suspect's accomplice.

19

After greeting Bobby Ray and the others with him as they walked inside the Myrtle Beach DMV office close to closing time, Casey Brown, the branch manager, escorted them to a small conference room across the hall from his office.

A black male in his early fifties, Jones had been assigned to the branch for the past four years. Rising through the ranks, he had held a handful of other management positions with the DMV since first being promoted eleven years earlier. Professional in both his actions and in his appearance, he had already been updated on the situation confronting him by his supervisor, and briefly on the phone by Bobby Ray during his ride over. Feeling betrayed by someone he felt was trustworthy; Jones already had his deputy waiting in the conference room.

"Hey, what the hell's going on?" Ziggy Bagrov loudly asked as he watched four obvious looking cops and his boss enter the room where he had been waiting for Jones to return. With the rest of his employees already gone for the day, and with the building's other doors secured, Jones did not bother closing the conference room door. For now, Bagrov's privacy was no longer a concern.

"Ziggy, these men are police officers. I suggest you listen carefully to what they have to say. Your future with us depends on how you answer their questions. And, if I might add, your future, no matter how you answer their questions, may still be tenuous at best. That said, Captain Jenkins, this is Mr. Zigor Bagrov, or as he's more commonly known to us by, this is Ziggy," Jones said forcefully, realizing his employee's illegal actions had not only compromised his standing with the DMV, but had exposed him to the possibility of being arrested. As he spoke, Jones had stared hard at Bagrov, a third-generation Russian-American whose family still had strong ties to their former homeland. Unlike his parents, Ziggy, a University of Georgia graduate, spoke perfect English. After finishing with his introductions, Jones moved off to a chair located several feet away. It was one which allowed him a full view of the proceedings against his employee.

Deciding he would leave Ziggy's interview up to the two veteran cops present with him, Bobby Ray simply nodded at Wilson and Griffin after Jones had finished speaking. Like others they had learned from, both cops had proven track records in obtaining sensitive information from people who, in most cases, often did not want to give up what they knew about a particular person or event.

Already aware they were going to be conducting the interview, Sgt. Kent Wilson and Detective Frank Griffin elected to come out swinging from the very beginning. With Bobby Ray and Scozzafava intentionally seated behind them and slightly off to one side so they could observe Ziggy's body language and facial expressions, the two cops started by vaguely advising Ziggy as to why they were there. Already aware of the importance of this interview, and the influence it would have over other parts of the investigation, Wilson took care of some administrative needs before formally starting the process of speaking with their suspect.

Reaching into a slightly worn black nylon briefcase that he always had handy, Wilson withdrew a thick generic pre-printed pad that all South Carolina cops used when conducting interviews with suspects and witnesses. Placing the Notice of Rights pad down on the table next to him, he then withdrew a yellow legal pad and an Olympus digital recorder.

Concerned by what he was seeing, Ziggy's eyes focused on the recorder as it was placed down on the table, continuing to stare at it as Wilson populated the Notice of Rights form with Ziggy's name and address, the investigative case numbers assigned to the Platek and Holland murders, as well as the day's date and current time. Finished, he carefully read his suspect his Miranda warnings, a requirement most cops despised having to do.

"OK, Ziggy, do you understand your rights as I've read them to you?" Wilson asked, handing the completed form to Ziggy to sign.

Nervous already, Ziggy was now confused as to why he had been read his rights. Too nervous to speak, he simply nodded his head to indicate he understood what had been read to him.

"Ziggy, I need a verbal reply to my question. I need that just so we know you understood what I've read to you. What I just read to you is what's printed on the form in front of you. Do you understand your rights?" Wilson asked, carefully watching as their suspect anxiously glanced at the forms he held.

"Yes." Was Ziggy's soft response as he nervously signed the form now sitting in his lap.

Picking up his digital recorder, Wilson showed it to Ziggy before turning it on. "Like the form you just signed, this is here to protect both of us. I'm going to turn it on, and then I'm going to make a brief introduction that will include the date and time, where we are, who is present, and then we'll start talking. OK?"

As part of his introduction, Wilson covered a couple of brief additional points before starting the actual interview. His purpose of doing so was to be able to refute any future bullshit allegations that might arise from any of Ziggy's attorneys concerning their client having not been made aware of his rights or being told the interview was being recorded.

"Ziggy, just for the record, you have been advised of your Miranda warnings, and you have been given a copy of that document you signed, correct?"

"Yes."

"And, again just for the record, you have agreed to voluntarily talk to us today, and you have been advised that you can terminate this interview at any point, correct?" Wilson politely asked, then adding one last point before giving his suspect time to respond. "And, you have also been advised as to who each of the five people are in this room with you, and what their ranks and titles are, correct?"

"Yes."

"Ziggy, I'd like you to tell us your date of birth. I need to hear the month, the day you were born, and then the year. When you're done, I'd like you to slide your driver's license across the table to me so I can verify what you've told us."

After taking his license out of his wallet, Ziggy spoke to Wilson as he pushed it towards him. "If you have to look at my license, I guess you don't trust what I'm telling you to be the truth, that about right?"

"That's pretty much it," Wilson admitted as he looked up from looking at Ziggy's photo and DOB printed on his South Carolina issued license. Returning Ziggy's license to him, he added, "Let's see if we can't get started on building that trust between us."

Moments later, after admitting to several perfunctory duties he performed at work each day, Ziggy acknowledged he had been assigned to the Myrtle Beach DMV office for the past several years as the deputy branch manager. Among the facts he admitted to was that he was assigned his own office, which he routinely locked when he was out of the building for lunch and at the end of each working day, and that he, and only he, had access to a NCIC terminal and one other computer in his office. When asked by Wilson, Ziggy also acknowledged that his computers were password protected.

With those issues addressed, Wilson and Griffin went to work on their suspect. Making his first subtle move, one their suspect did not even realize was being done, Wilson asked Ziggy to move this chair to the end of the table so it faced him. After Ziggy had done so, Wilson then moved his directly in front of his suspect's chair. By removing Ziggy out from behind the table, and by placing his chair close to his suspect's, Wilson had intentionally invaded Ziggy's comfort zone, leaving him without a physical barrier to hide behind for the rest of the interview. A court-accepted expert in interview and interrogation techniques, Wilson had set the perfect stage as by now Ziggy's heart rate had climbed even higher than it had been. To add to their suspect's discomfort, Griffin, a large and imposing cop with an athletic build, sat motionless to Wilson's left as he stared at Ziggy.

Wilson's next two questions would prove to be the easiest for their suspect to answer.

"Ziggy, you read the newspaper at all? You know, *The Sun News*, I mean?"

"Sometimes, but not too often. Maybe if I see one lying around the building I will, but I can't say I read it every day."

"How about the news? You watch the local news on television at all?"

"Nope, never. I watch ESPN, some old black and white movies on AMC and TBS once in a while, but not the news, it depresses me. I'm a book reader mostly, I like using my imagination, television doesn't afford me such opportunities."

Nodding his head in response to their suspect's answers, Wilson then went to work. "Ziggy, do you know a white guy by the name of Roger Platek?"

Ziggy's eyes bounced back and forth between the two cops directly in front of him before answering Wilson's questions. For a brief moment, a sense of hope invaded him as he wondered if this had all been a misunderstanding. "No, I don't. Should I?"

"How about a Kevin Holland? He's a white guy also, lives in Murrells Inlet. Know him at all?"

"Can't say I do." Ziggy's eyes continued to fill with hope as he answered the question, buoyed by the thought that he was being asked questions someone else should be answering and not him. Sitting in his chair, he tried figuring out why he was being asked to answer questions about people whose names meant nothing to him.

"How about a priest by the name of Father Jonathan Guyette? Ever hear of him?" Wilson asked, his eyes focused directly on their suspect, hoping to notice even the slightest nervous facial tic Ziggy displayed.

A brief smile broke out over Ziggy's face as he was relieved to have an affirmative answer to a question posed to him. "Yes. I don't know him, but I know the name. Two of the women who work here attend the church the priest is assigned to. They've both told me about him being shot, pretty badly, if I remember correctly."

"So you've heard the priest's name mentioned, but you're telling us you don't know him," Wilson asked as he made it appear as if he was taking notes of Ziggy's responses. His next question was asked to also make it appear that he needed a clarification on his suspect's response, but it was really asked for another reason. "Is that your answer?"

"Yes."

"Don't be upset by this, but did you have anything to do with Father Guyette being shot? Indirectly or . . ."

Upset at being accused of something he had nothing to do with, Ziggy angrily interrupted Wilson before he could finish his question. "No! Why would I shoot someone I don't even know? The man's a priest! You don't shoot priests. People who shoot priests go to hell, I don't care to experience that place! I plan on going to the other place, heaven. You're crazy if you think I had anything to do with him being shot."

" . . . directly." Wilson showed no emotion as he finished asking his question after being interrupted by their suspect's brief but intense outburst.

"No, no, no!"

"What about the other two men I asked you about? Did you have anything to do with them being murdered?"

As five faces stared at him waiting to hear his response, Ziggy slumped back in his chair as an expression of bewilderment crossed his flushed face. "No, of course not! Why are you asking me these questions? What is it that you think I've done?"

Ignoring their suspect's questions, Wilson reached for a file folder sitting on the table next to him. Opening it, he held up the DMV Blow Backs that Brown had handed him when he and the others arrived several minutes earlier. Pulling out two of the photos, he held them up for Ziggy to look at.

"Meet Mr. Platek and Mr. Holland. By the way, they're both dead. I know I've already told you they've been murdered, but I just wanted to make sure you know they're no longer with us," Wilson said, intentionally turning up the pressure Ziggy was already feeling.

As he stared at the photos for a few more moments, Ziggy spoke to Wilson without taking his eyes off of them. "Sorry to hear that about them, but what's that got to do with me? I didn't kill them."

"That's just what you did, asshole!" Griffin said loudly, breaking the calm which had existed in the room up to now. While his thunderous roar had been directed at their suspect, Griffin's loud voice even caught Ziggy's boss by surprise. Playing the role of the bad cop, Griffin waved his thick right index finger in Ziggy's direction before adding, "You may not have killed them per se, but you killed them. You and your asshole friend, Sonny Pratt, killed them!"

Hearing Pratt's name mentioned caused Ziggy to collapse backwards in his chair. With his body temperature quickly spiking

176 | PETER F. WARREN

higher and higher, a sudden cold sweat immediately caused beads of water to form above his brow. Under his dress shirt, sweat began to form under his arms as he finally realized why the cops had come to talk to him. Adjusting himself in his chair, the deputy branch manager quickly tried to disassociate himself from Pratt, and from the violence that had occurred.

"I . . . barely know Pratt. I don't hang around with him, never have. I only know him because I dated his sister for a very brief spell. I swear to God, when I found out that she was as nuts as he was, I dumped her."

Like the others, Bobby Ray and Scozzafava watched as Ziggy used a red handkerchief he had pulled from his pants pocket to wipe away some of the sweat that was now prevalent on his face.

"You know him well enough to run a few license plates for him on your NCIC terminal, don't you? What'd he do, threaten you or something like that if you didn't do what he asked? Is that it, you're scared of him?" Griffin again angrily asked, scaring Ziggy even more this time than he had before.

"I . . . I never ran any plates for him or for anyone. I could get fired for doing something like that," Ziggy responded, trying to distance himself even more from the growing problem he saw piling up in front of him. Finished speaking, he stared at Brown for a sign of confirmation that he had been right in what he said regarding the DMV policy prohibiting employees from using computer information for personal needs or profit. His stare was greeted by the blank expression he saw on Brown's face.

"Sure you did, you liar!" Wilson emphatically replied, playing his trump card by placing several pages from the DMV audit of their suspect's NCIC terminal down on the table in front of him. As he showed Ziggy the pages, Wilson pointed to several specific areas. "See here, this shows the ID number of the terminal that requested the information on our two victim's license plates. I even took a moment to use a highlighter to circle the terminal number on each page, which, by the way, is the one assigned to your office. It's the same one you've already admitted to being the only person who uses it. I've also circled the names and license plates you ran at the request of your accomplice, Sonny Pratt. So tell me we're wrong, but the way we're looking at it it's either you, or maybe it was Sonny Pratt, or maybe it's both of you who are responsible for murdering our two victims. If that's the case, and we suspect one of those possibilities is the right one, then either or both of you are also responsible for shooting the good Father while he was hearing confessions." Pausing a couple of moments to allow his comments to have time to sink in, Wilson then gave Ziggy the opportunity to put some separation between himself and the violence that had occurred.

After a few moments of silence on Ziggy's part, Wilson came back hard at the DMV employee. It was time for him to get what they had come there for. It was also time for Ziggy to implicate himself, and time for him to confirm what Wilson and Griffin already knew.

"You've already admitted no one else uses your computer, and that no one else knows your password, so unless you've got an explanation for how this audit has mistakenly tied our victims' info to your computer, I'm thinking it's time for you to start talking. We're only giving you one opportunity to catch the life ring that's being thrown to you. Take it now or face the consequences that come with being arrested and from being fired by your employer. If we walk out that door over there and you haven't told us what we want to hear, we'll solve these murders on our own, but one thing for sure is going to happen. One or two of us will be back here in a day or two with an arrest warrant and we'll look forward to marching your ass out of this building in handcuffs. Who knows, maybe we'll plan on doing that right in front of your fellow employees, or maybe will invite a couple of news crews to bring their cameras over here when we walk your ass out of here. They'd probably jump at the chance of being able to flash your mug across the evening news that night. Juicy murder stories, especially ones involving a state employee as one of the alleged masterminds, that's the kind of news stories those vultures live for. If there's one thing my partner and I are good at, it's organizing perp walks. No one does it better than us. Right, Griff?"

"No one." Griffin said, sitting with his arms folded across his chest as he stared at their favorite DMV employee.

Ziggy sat quiet for close to a minute, his body trembling as he stared blankly at the photos he now held in his hands. Without looking up, and with tears beginning to stream down his face, he soon began to admit his involvement.

"OK, OK. I admit I ran the plates that Sonny asked me to run for him, but, I swear to you this is the truth; I didn't know he was going to hurt them. He . . . he gave me a couple of bullshit reasons why he needed their info, and I ran the plates because he gave me fifty dollars each time I got him the info he was looking for." Pausing, Ziggy leaned back in his chair to catch his breath. Shaking his head in disgust at the position he had put himself in, his eyes stared angrily at the white ceiling tiles above him as he tried making sense of what he had done. Then, looking at his boss, he directed his next comment to him.

"Casey, please believe me, I'm truly sorry. I've never done anything like this before, but the new house I'm having built has left me with some serious cash problems. I did what I did simply for the money, not to see anyone get hurt. Listen to me, please, I like working for you, but I needed the cash. I'll . . . I'll do anything to keep my job."

Coldly and unapologetically, Brown addressed his employee. "Sorry, Ziggy, but I'm afraid the decision about you keeping your job is out of my hands. That's a decision the executive director and the courts will have to decide now. Guess you should have thought about how much you needed your job before you did what you did."

"What about Father Guyette?" Wilson asked as he pointed to the photo of Guyette that he was now holding up in his left hand for Ziggy to see. "Did Sonny ever ask you to run his license, his registration plates, or obtain his op license info for him?"

"No, no, sir. I just ran the info on those other two guys, I swear. Look . . . look at the audit you've run on my terminal, you'll see I never did that."

"Ziggy, think hard before you answer my next question," Wilson strongly suggested. "I want you to know that we're going to have one of our forensic examiners take a thorough look at this audit that's been done on your computer. I just want you to know that before you respond to what I'm about to ask you." Pausing a brief moment to allow his words to have time to sink in, Wilson then asked, "What about any another terminals? You ever run the priest's name and DOB through any other computer or any other terminals here in the building?"

"No, sir. I swear."

Wilson and Griffin exchanged looks with each other, and then with Bobby Ray before continuing.

"OK, Ziggy, we're almost done here. You just told Mr. Brown that you're interested in keeping your job. While none of us can promise you that's even a remote possibility based on what you've done, a step of good faith towards possibly keeping your job would be to give us a detailed written statement regarding how you have illegally accessed DMV and NCIC computer files for personal gain. Before you tell us if you're willing to do that, you need to know this statement must include the details of how and why you passed on the information you obtained for Pratt. It's what's known as an inculpatory statement, meaning it incriminates you, but it's also your only real hope of showing the court and your employer the remorse you're now telling us you have. Are you willing to give us such a statement?"

"Yes, absolutely," Ziggy replied, answering without a moment of hesitation.

"Even if your statement implicates you in wrongdoing, you're willing to give us a written statement?" Wilson asked, speaking clearly so his digital recorder captured the interaction between Ziggy and himself. "Remember, your statement, if you have any possible hope of keeping your job, and, again, I'm not saying whether you are or are not going to keep it, it has to include the fact that you knowingly knew the money Pratt was offering you was a voluntary act on your part, one which violated both state statutes and DMV policy. You can say whatever else you want to say about Pratt in your statement, but you have to admit your responsibility if you have any chance of us, or even Mr. Brown, remotely speaking on your behalf to the prosecutor after we close our investigation. You still willing to do that?"

Taking an awkward deep breath, Ziggy coughed twice, clearing the nervousness from his dry mouth before speaking. "If I want any chance of keeping my job, as well as showing anyone who reads my statement that I'm sincere about my remorse, I guess I have to give you what you want. It's my only choice."

Smartly, Wilson offered up his next comment. "Ziggy, we're more than agreeable to affording you a reasonable amount of time so you can contact an attorney for some advice before you give us your voluntary statement. Would you like to do that?"

"Nope. Don't have the money for an attorney, and don't trust most of them anyhow. I've made my own bed; I'll take whatever medicine comes my way. I trust you guys to treat me fairly."

"You sure?" Wilson asked.

"Yes, sir. Let's just get this painful part of my life over with." Then looking at Brown, Ziggy spoke to his boss as contritely as anyone who has been caught with their hand in the cookie jar could. "I'm sorry, Casey. Besides myself, I know I've let you down as well. I apologize for doing that."

Still upset by the actions of his employee, Brown chose to remain silent after hearing Ziggy's apology.

After hearing Ziggy's consent to giving them a written statement, Wilson pushed on as he tried wrapping things up. "OK, good. We'll get to that in a couple of minutes. We just have a couple of more questions about Pratt. That OK?"

"Yeah, sure, whatever," Ziggy replied, weighed down by the problems he was now facing. "I really don't think I'm in the position to say no."

Nodding his head, Wilson flashed a brief smile at the beaten man in front of him, realizing it was now time to take his foot off his suspect's throat. Desperate to save his job, he knew Ziggy would give them whatever information they needed.

"Ziggy, do you know where Pratt lives now or where he hangs out?" Wilson asked in a much friendlier tone than he had been using.

"All I know is the guy moves around a lot. He doesn't have much money, least he claims he never does. The reason the asshole doesn't have any money is because he's got a problem keeping jobs. He lives where he lives until the rent becomes past due and then he finds a new place to stay. Honestly, I've lost count of how many times he's been tossed out of the places where he's been staying. He's a deadbeat, that's for sure. Like I already told you, I'm really not sure where he's living these days because I'm not that close to him. I know he was living in a trailer some place in MI, but I have no idea where it is."

"By MI, you're referring to Murrells Inlet, correct?" Griffin asked, seeking clarification on Ziggy's last statement.

"Yeah, sorry. Murrells Inlet."

"What about a phone number? Do you know Pratt's cell number?" Griffin asked before Wilson could ask his next question.

"No, sir. I used to have his number, but that was nearly a year ago. He told me a while back that he changed phones, his number also, because he felt the government was tapping his phone for some reason. I know he's gotten a new phone, but I don't have his new number. He calls me, I don't call him." Then pointing to where his own cell phone rested on the table, Ziggy added, "There's my phone, check it out. Take it with you if you want. You'll see I'm telling you the truth."

"What about when he calls you? Doesn't his number come up on your phone?"

"No, it doesn't. It seems that whenever he calls me the screen on my phone always reads restricted instead by displaying the number that's calling me. He must have a way of blocking his number so people can't read it. Believe me; I'm glad I don't know it. One thing's for sure, I'm never answering a call from that bastard again."

"Where's he hang out? Is he a boozer, a crackhead, a sex fiend . . . any of that?" Wilson asked, trying to get some kind of an idea on Pratt's lifestyle so he and the others could try and figure out where their principal suspect either hung out or lived.

"Depends on which way the wind is blowing, that's what's strange about the dude. I mean, one month the guy's a lush, the next month when he can afford it he's snorting coke like it's going out of style, and the month after that he's into something else. The last I heard, and this was about six or seven weeks ago, he's into religion now. One more thing, the guy is definitely not a sex fiend or a pervert, nor is he gay, but he's not a guy who enjoys chasing skirts for some reason. I know the guy still pines for some gal who killed herself when they were in the army together. I think she overdosed or something like that. From what little I know about her, I think her dying really effed him up in the head. Maybe she's the reason why he doesn't chase women like most guys do, but I'm not really sure on that. He's a smart guy, no dummy by any means, but he's totally a weird dude, that's why I've never been too close to him."

"What about . . . ?"

Excitedly, Ziggy interrupted Wilson before the veteran cop could finish asking his next question.

"Want to know this fool's newest interest?" Ziggy asked without waiting for a response. "Last time I saw him he told me he was converting. Claims he's going to become a Muslim, wants to be radicalized and all of that crap. Claims he's doing it because of what happened to those folks down at that church in Charleston . . . told me he wants to be known as a mujahid, that's a person striving to wage jihad against the United States. He says he's being forced to act because of our nation's immoral sins and because of the political oppression the government forces people like him to live under. Told me he got that from reading the Quran or whatever it is they call their bible. Sonny also told me that he believes the people who still support the Confederacy were behind the shooting in Charleston, and that those same folks are planning to rise up again against the North. Last time I saw him, when he told me all of this nonsense, he claimed that he believes anyone who still supports the Confederacy, even someone who still shows any support for their family's Southern heritage, was evil and it was his job to put an end to it. I'm not really sure what he meant by all of this stuff he was saying, but I . . . I . . . I honestly didn't know he was actually going to start killing and shooting people."

Taking in all that Ziggy had said, Scozzafava now took a run at him. "What about becoming a Muslim? Does Pratt attend a mosque or go to any prayer meetings?"

Scozzafava's questions, while logical ones for the FBI agent to ask, drew a brief laugh from Ziggy. "Are you kidding me? Sonny go to church or a mosque. No way he's doing that, at least the Sonny I once knew never would. Sonny's simply a screwed up guy who goes through so many different phases in life that I've lost count of how many there's been. Sonny talks a good game, but unless he's hiding it real good he's about as much of a Muslim as you and I are. He may be reading the Koran or Quran or whatever it's called, but I seriously doubt he'd make it as a terrorist. If you ask me, I think the guy's a nut job more than anything. Maybe an intelligent nut job at that, but he's still a nut job." Ziggy paused to laugh at a mental picture that had formed in his head. "My man, Sonny, covering his head with a scarf and dressing up like some camel jockey? No friggin' way, man, never gonna happen!" Despite the many problems facing him, Ziggy laughed again at the idea of Pratt becoming a Muslim.

While they were somewhat relieved by Ziggy's statement about their prime suspect not being a Muslim extremist, Bobby Ray and the others also knew anything was still possible due to the lack of contact between Pratt and his DMV contact over the past several weeks. Each of them knew they would have to perform their own due diligence to rule Pratt out as an actual member of any terrorist group.

Like the others, Scozzafava was relieved by what Ziggy had told them, but he still sought to learn more about Pratt. "What about guns? Your buddy own any weapons that we should know about?"

"Probably, maybe, but I'm not sure. I saw him with some kind of rifle once, and I know he used them in the army, but I'm not really sure what he does or doesn't own."

"What kind of work did Pratt do in the army, any idea?" Scozzafava asked, following up on Ziggy's statement about his friend.

"I'm not sure if I ever believed this because I remember thinking at the time that he was just bullshitting me, but he told me he taught other soldiers, new recruits I think he meant, to learn how to shoot. He also told me he never went overseas, claimed he was assigned to some base here on the east coast. He might have told me Fort Bragg, but I really don't remember. The only other thing

I know about his being in the army or about his interest in guns is that I know he used to get a kick out of firing black powder guns, you know, the kind they used to use in the Civil War and before that. He used to make his own bullets or whatever they were called, but I'm not sure if he's still into that or not. Reloading, that's a term I know he used to toss around quite a bit, but what little I know about that stuff that's more for modern weapons than it is for those black powder rifles he liked to fire, isn't it?"

Thinking about what Ziggy had told them about Pratt's career in the army, and his interest in black powder guns, caused everyone to let their suspect's last question go unanswered.

After giving Bobby Ray and the others a quick look to see if they were done asking questions, Wilson closed the notebook he had been writing in. "OK, Ziggy, I believe we are done." Then catching one more thought, Wilson asked his last question before shutting off his digital recorder. "We know that Pratt's worked recently as a carpenter. To the best of your knowledge, is he still in that line of work?"

"Yeah, I mean I guess so. That's the only kind of work I've ever really known him to do. He had his own plumbing business a few years back, if that's what you want to call it. Excuse me for saying it this way, but that went down the drain like so many of his other harebrained schemes."

"Remember the name of his business?" Griffin asked with little more than a passing interest.

"Sure don't, detective. It was several years back."

After finishing up with Ziggy, Bobby Ray directed Wilson to contact the Garden City Police Department detectives working the robbery at Donna's bank.

"Now that we've got our focus on Pratt, they need to know that. Do what needs to be done, but make sure they know we like him as our suspect, and make sure they get a copy of his pedigree. You also need to give them at least one copy of Pratt's DMV Blow Back. They'll likely want to show it to Donna's co-workers for ID purposes. I'm going to be calling Davis in a couple of minutes to have him get with our folks so they can put Pratt's picture on some new Wanted Posters. If they want to keep the sketch on the posters, that's fine with me, but I want Pratt's mug on it for the world to see."

* * * * * *

Having listened carefully to what Ziggy had told them, each of the four cops who walked out of the DMV office now realized even more the importance of what Stine had found near the burnt shell of O'Keefe's truck. After they finished talking a few minutes later, they stood near their vehicles in the parking lot as Bobby Ray handed out his next set of orders.

"We need to find our boy, Sonny Pratt, like now. This just became a full-out RTC effort. I'm going to put everyone, and I mean everyone, including Davis and our newest detective, Jim Dzamko, on this right now. Everything else that Bruce and the others have been working on besides this case gets put on hold for now. If anything, this investigation will give Dzamko some much needed experience. I'm also going to have Edwards and Wagner team up." Looking at Wilson and Griffin, Bobby Ray then added, "You guys have already put in a full couple of days. Go grab some chow and a few hours of sleep. I'm going to need you both when we find Pratt." Turning to Scozzafava, Bobby Ray gave him his marching orders. "Scozz, I need you to access whatever federal databases you can. Find out if our boy ever served in the army like this guy Ziggy said he did. If he did, I want you to identify every Podunk place where this no-good son of a bitch served. Even if he was stationed in some far out place that didn't have a coffee shop or a freaking traffic light, I want to know about it. While you're doing that, find out what, if any, expertise or special training he received, and then look for whatever other bullshit you can find on him." As his language reflected, Bobby Ray was beyond fed up with Pratt's actions and by the carnage he had strewn across Murrells Inlet.

As he started walking to his vehicle, Bobby Ray's cell announced an incoming call. Hearing his phone ring caused the others to hold their positions as they waited to see what kind of news the call brought. After speaking to the voice on the other end of the call for several minutes, Bobby Ray slid his phone back into his pants pocket. Turning to look at the others, he said, "Father Guyette's dead. Died an hour ago of complications from pneumonia. Guess we all know what brought that on, don't we? Poor guy died a terrible death after serving others for so many years."

"Guess we have three murder victims now, don't we?" Griffin asked, already knowing the answer to his question.

"Guess we do, Griff. Guess so." Bobby Ray said rather sadly as he opened his car door. "I'll call the others about this so they know what's happened. If you guys don't hear from me before then, meet me at the Murrells Inlet sub-station tomorrow morning at six. We need to get a surveillance going on our guy as soon as possible, but we have to find the prick first. That's the first thing on our list of things to get done." Pausing a brief moment, Bobby Ray then added, "For the sake of everyone else still flying the Confederate flag these days, let's hope we find our guy soon."

20

As his brother cops worked feverishly throughout the rest of the afternoon and into the evening hours to locate Sonny Pratt, Paul spent his time at the hospital watching over Donna. At roughly the same time his friends were interviewing Ziggy, Dr. Ellis, along with Dr. Randolph Tillengast, the neurosurgeon who had operated on Donna's head injury, met with Paul in their patient's room. Also present was Donna's personal physician, Dr. Catherine Engle, an exceptionally warm and caring practitioner who had made it a point during her rounds each day to stop and visit her seriously injured patient. On her own, she had also made it a point to contact Ellis several times for professional updates on her patient.

"The swelling in your wife's brain has subsided quite nicely, Paul," Dr. Tillengast said, pleased by the progress his patient was making. "I'm going to order another CT scan just to play it safe, but, just as my colleagues here are, I'm encouraged by what I'm seeing. I don't want to give you any false hope because we're certainly not out of the woods as yet, but I'm pleased by her progress. We'll see what the new scan shows us and then we'll make a decision about whether or not to continue with the medication she's under. For now, we all agree that keeping her sedated is the best course of action for keeping the swelling down inside her brain. I'm also quite pleased by her overall appearance as it appears the

PEG tube we inserted into her gastrointestinal tract is delivering a sufficient amount of nutrition to her. Earlier I checked the area around her stomach where we inserted the tube. I did not see anything amiss. By that I simply mean I did not see any signs of leaks or infections."

"Well, that certainly sounds like good news, but obviously I'm . . . we're all still concerned about her brain injury and what affect it will have on her ability to walk or talk or on her ability to function on her own," Paul said as he gave a look at each of the three doctors standing around his wife's bed. "Any of you care to tell me what to expect? I mean, you must have some kind of an educated guess based on the number of patients you all have treated with injuries similar to hers. I'd just like to know if you believe she's going to be facing any limitations in the years to come."

As Ellis and Engle exchanged looks with each other, Tillengast ignored them, choosing to tell Paul some of what he wanted to know. "None of us, as much as we would like, can tell you what to expect. Each head injury, just like each patient, is different in so many ways. Each patient who sustains a traumatic brain injury responds differently in the end. It all depends on the degree of the blunt trauma, what the angle of the force was upon impact, how far the patient might have fallen, what the patient's health was at the time of the injury, and so on. For now," Tillengast added, looking straight at a husband who was genuinely worried about his wife's welfare more than anything else in his life, "how about we deal with those issues, like her motor skills, when we know what we're facing. Personally, I don't like speculating on what the future is going to bring for one of my patients, at least not until I've had the chance to give them a thorough examination. In your wife's case, I haven't had the opportunity to do that yet."

Pausing for a moment, Tillengast then added, "Over the years I've learned that hypothetical promises aren't fair for anyone as they sometimes lead to disappointment and false hope. I don't subscribe to that practice. Fair enough?"

"Fair enough, doc." Paul said in response to what he had been told. As he did, he glanced down at the various IV lines, at Donna's feeding tube, and at the tracheal tube that were all helping to keep his wife alive. Turning to look back at the others at the foot of her bed, he added, "I hope this isn't too much to hope for, but I just want her back like she was. She was perfect that way."

With his boys back home, Paul had been left to deal with his wife's medical problems, his own needs, and, when time allowed, with the murders that had occurred in Murrells Inlet. With all of those issues taking up most of his time, the sleep he had gotten over the past many days had been little. It had come from bits of time he stole while keeping close watch over his wife. Mentally and physically fatigued, he fell into a deep sleep in the recliner in Donna's room less than fifteen minutes after being briefed by his wife's doctors on her condition.

* * * * * *

Sleeping in his recliner, Paul's restful sleep was first disturbed by the sound of an ICU crash cart being slowly wheeled down the hallway outside of Donna's room, its squeaky wheels growing more and more annoying as it grew closer to where he rested. Moments later, a soft polite knock on Donna's door forced Paul to open his eyes partway.

"Mr. Waring?" The elderly female volunteer's voice quietly asked from where she stood in the doorway, respecting the privacy of the person she saw lying in the bed next to where Paul sat.

"Yes, ma'am. Can I help you?" Paul sleepily asked, slightly irritated over his nap being disturbed. Slipping his sneakers back on, he slowly sat up in his chair.

"My name is Paula, I'm a volunteer here." Pointing to her cart, she added, "I have some flowers for your wife, they were just brought here a few minutes ago. I have to tell you what a lovely arrangement this is. The colors are beautiful."

Looking around his wife's already crowded room as he was handed the floral arrangement, Paul sought to find space among the many other arrangements that had been delivered over the past several days. Moving a large vase of red and yellow roses off to one side, Paul set the newest arrangement down next to a growing pile of unopened get-well cards. Piled on a window shelf close to his wife's bed, he was saving the cards for Donna to hopefully open someday soon.

Speaking meekly from where she remained just outside of Donna's room, Paula got Paul's attention by asking, "Mr. Waring, can I tell you something? Perhaps out here in the hallway, I don't want to disturb your wife."

After thanking her for delivering the flowers, Paul listened to the elderly woman's complaint.

"That man who brought those flowers to us, well, I know he's a friend of yours, but, well to tell you the truth, he was downright rude . . . demanding as well!"

While he was not sure of whom Paula was referring to, Paul still sought to apologize for what had occurred. "Miss Paula, I'm not sure which of our friends you might be referring to, but I apologize if one of them acted inappropriately towards you or any of your fellow volunteers. Do you remember his name? The only reason I'm asking is because I'd like to have a talk with him about how he treated you."

Despite Paul's apology, the elderly volunteer continued to describe what had occurred just outside the small office she and her fellow volunteers worked out of. "He was very rude to Helen; I saw and heard the whole thing. He talked rudely to her when she told him the ICU ward was off-limits to most people, except, of course, for immediate family and special guests. Despite that, and despite him telling her several times that he knew your wife was brought here after she had been injured, he kept demanding to know your wife's room number, but Helen held her ground," Paula said, laughing briefly as she recalled the unpleasant exchange she had witnessed. "She told him to go home and learn some manners before he ever came back here again. Then she told him she was calling Security. He didn't much care for that, so he just stuck one of his business cards inside the flower arrangement before leaving in a huff. Old Helen," Paula added as she softly laughed again, "she's almost ninety-two, but she's a tough old buzzard. She never takes much guff from anyone, especially when they have bad manners."

"Miss Paula, this friend of ours, did he say how he knew my wife was at this hospital?"

Nodding her head, the elderly volunteer replied by saying, "Said he read about her being here in the papers."

Looking back at the arrangement he had just set on the shelf, Paul stared at it for a few moments before apologizing to Paula again as she began to slowly make her way back to the hospital lobby. After watching her make her way through the ICU's double set of automatic doors, he walked back inside his wife's room. Curious to find out which of their friends had been so rude, Paul fished through the arrangement looking for the business card Paula had told him was placed there.

Soon finding it, he drew a blank on who had brought the flowers for Donna as the name printed on the card meant nothing to him. For several moments he tried jogging his memory, but the name he continued to stare at on the card made no sense. "*Palmetto Boys Plumbing?* Who the hell are they? I've never even heard of them." Looking at the logo on the card, as well as the Pawleys Island business address that was listed, did little to help figure out who the rude visitor in the lobby had been. "Maybe Donna hired this company to fix something when I was out of town traveling or something, but I can't ever recall using them. I certainly don't know anyone who works there."

Trying to recall Paula's words as he went to sit down, Paul's law enforcement instincts suddenly kicked in. Staring out into the hallway, he struggled to recall the exact words the elderly volunteer had used.

"That's it! That has to be it!" Paul thought as he finished putting the pieces of his conversation with Paula together.

Excited by what he now judged to be something of a significant concern, and too awake to be able to fall back asleep, Paul made his way down to the cafeteria for something light to eat and drink. Waiting for an elevator outside the ICU ward, he continued to focus on the details of his newest problem. As he did, two elderly women, both at the hospital to visit a mutual friend, walked up and continued on with their chatter as they waited for the elevator less than three feet away from where Paul stood. What they soon said to each other, like the heavy amount of make-up and perfume one of the women was wearing, quickly got Paul's attention.

"Eloise, this is just horrible." Eloise's friend, Kathleen Bannon said, waving her hands in disgust as she spoke. As she did, her gestures exposed Paul to another unwanted strong whiff of the excessive amount of Eternity perfume she had earlier put on. "I don't know what the world is coming to, but just before I left to come over here to meet you I heard on the television the priest in Pawleys Island, the one who was shot by some maniac, that he died. It's just terrible! Imagine shooting a priest like that when he was just serving the church by hearing confessions."

Like Paul, Eloise had not heard of Guyette's death. "Oh, how sad! My goodness, you're right, what is this crazy world coming to?"

As the two women walked inside the elevator, followed closely by Paul and two others, Kathleen added to the conversation they were having. "It was bad enough to read about the poor Father being shot, but then I was forced to read that horrible story about the poor woman who was run over in the parking lot of her bank. My goodness, what kind of a man would do something like that to a defenseless woman."

"I agree," Eloise added, "it's terrible. There was another story in the paper about her today. From what I read, it sounds like she's being treated right here for her injuries. Let's hope she makes it." Then, as the elevator doors opened to let her and her friend off at their floor, Eloise, totally out of character, added one last comment concerning Donna's attacker. "I hope they catch the bastard and fry his ass!"

As Paul took note of the conversation he had just overheard, he realized it was likely connected to the flowers that had been delivered to Donna's room minutes earlier. Like the past several days, he had been far too busy, and far too tired, to find time to read the morning newspaper. "I need to read that article in the paper those ladies were referring to," he thought as the elevator made its next stop.

"Afternoon, Mr. Waring!" Ray Smith said cheerfully as he stepped inside the elevator, extending his hand at the same time to shake hands with someone he had recently met. Lost in thought, Smith's friendly greeting caught Paul by surprise.

Snapped out of his thoughts, Paul returned the friendly greeting with one of his own as he shook Smith's hand. "Ray, good afternoon. I'm sorry, I was kind of lost in space there for a moment. How's the day going? And, by the way, it's Paul. Mr. Waring was my father."

Smith chuckled at Paul's comment. "OK, it's Paul. Sir, ma'am, Mr. and Mrs., those are just habits I can't break from my days in the service. I'll work on calling you by your first name though."

"Sounds good," Paul responded, punching the button for the elevator doors to close so it would take them to the floor he had already selected. "I'm heading to your world famous cafeteria for a snack and a cup of coffee. Can I buy you one?"

After a few brief friendly exchanges as they exited the elevator, Smith answered Paul's previous question. "You know, despite this one problem I have to address in about thirty minutes, today has been a pretty good day. How's it going for you?"

"Not bad. My wife's doing as well as we can expect for someone in her condition. Her doctors actually think she's improving a little. I'm grateful for that, of course." Then Paul asked Smith, the hospital's director of security, about his problem.

For the past fourteen years, Ray Smith, a tall and well-built former Marine who had just celebrated his sixty-ninth birthday, had been employed at the hospital. Hired as the hospital's first black security guard, the former lance corporal, who had lost part of his left leg in August 1968 after being blown up while walking point on a patrol in Vietnam's Quang Tri Province near Da Nang, quickly proved to be one of the best employees the hospital ever had. Outgoing, friendly, and ambitious in life, Smith, despite the loss of his leg, had been determined to succeed in life. While he had first been promoted to a supervisor's position four years after being hired, and then to his current position five years later, one of Smith's proudest achievements had been the college degree he obtained after going back to school on a part-time basis for six years. That degree, along with his work ethic, had earned him his current position.

"It's not that big a deal," Smith replied in response to Paul's question about the issue confronting him later that afternoon. "I just have to deal with one of the idiots who works for me. Guess that comes with the territory, doesn't it? From our talk the other day, you know all about that, right?"

"Sure do. I've certainly had my share of employee-related problems to deal with as well. No one really thinks about it, but I guess it's part of the gig when you sign on to take the big bucks." For a brief few moments, Paul reflected back on a couple of employee-related issues he had been forced to deal with in Connecticut. Like others he worked with, unless laws had been broken or people's rights violated, he had never relished having to dole out discipline.

Smith laughed at Paul's response as they carried their coffees to a small round laminated table near one of the cafeteria windows. As they sat down, Smith spoke to Paul about the family ties his own family had in Connecticut. "Hey, I'm not sure I told you this the other day, but I've got folks back in Farmington. You never arrested any of them when you were a state cop, did you?"

"Yeah, I did, Ray," Paul said with a laugh of his own as he finished taking his first sip of coffee. "And they deserved it too! Even mentioned your name, but that just got them in deeper trouble with me."

After several more moments of pleasantries and laughs, Paul spoke to Smith about the murder investigations he had been helping Bobby Ray with. As he did, he also told Smith about the flowers that were delivered to Donna's room earlier. As he sat there discussing this with Smith, someone he felt comfortable talking with from the moment they had met, Paul realized his new friend's background in the security field, plus the three years he had spent as an MP, made him the perfect person to be bouncing his thoughts off of. As Paul had hoped for, the more Smith listened to the details of what had transpired, the more indignant he became.

"That's terrible, Paul. Now I'm upset by what you've told me," Smith said as he leaned forward in his chair. "I know I shouldn't be saying this because I hardly know you, but I'm starting to take this personal, and I think you know why. Yeah, I'll be glad to help . . . 24/7 . . . whatever and whenever." Finished speaking, Smith slid one of his business cards across the table. "My cell number is on the back. Call me anytime, and I mean anytime! I live right down the street practically, at the Dunes Club. Even if it's in the middle of the night, I'm no more than four minutes away."

Pocketing the business card after giving it the once-over, Paul nodded at Smith's offer. "Thanks, Ray. Your offer is much appreciated." As he finished speaking, he saw a smile break out on the security director's face.

"Hey, wait a minute!" Smith said, looking at Paul as he pushed his empty coffee cup off to the side. "Now I've got it. I knew I had heard your name before, but I couldn't place it until now. You . . . you were the guy some friends of mine told me about. In fact, they've told me they've played some golf with you. You were the one who found the lost Confederate treasury a few years back. Yeah, that was you, wasn't it? Man, I followed that story in the papers every time they ran something. I loved that story!"

A small smile now creased Paul's face as he listened to Smith describe an event that had taken place five years earlier. While still pleased by what he and his friends had found during that remarkable discovery, Paul, like he had done on many previous occasions whenever the subject had been brought up, did his best at distancing himself from unwanted attention. With other more important things on his mind right now, he tried deflecting some of the credit for the discovery towards others. "Yep, that was me, but I was part of a team that found it. Despite what you've read, it wasn't just me. Other people, my wife included, deserved a bunch of the credit for finding that with me. Unfortunately my wife is lying in your ICU ward right now, but you already know that, don't you?"

"Yeah, sure do, Paul. Not to minimize what we've already talked about concerning her status here, but that was a wild find you made, finding all of that money and all. Wild! I know my buddies were real excited to hear you talk about it a couple of times."

With too much already happening in his life, including the events of the afternoon, Paul paid little attention when Smith made mention of his golfing buddies. Until his wife's prognosis was known, thoughts of golf, and even of his pontoon boat, had been pushed to the far recesses of his mind. But for some reason that was important to him, Smith let Paul know who he was referring to.

"You know these guys I'm talking about, right? Taylor, Bob and Ed; they're my neighbors. They've told me you've played a couple of rounds of golf with them over the past year or two. Is that true, or have they been bullshitting me again?" As he waited for Paul's response, a wide grin stretched across Smith's face. He was pleased to be sitting with someone whose adventures he had closely followed in the papers.

Leaning back in his chair as he stretched his arms out wide to either side of him, Paul let out a tired yawn, one caused by too many days of far too little sleep. "Oh, yeah, I know those guys," Paul said after polishing off what little coffee remained in his Styrofoam cup. "They're friends of yours, huh? I would have thought you were someone who kept better company than those guys."

Laughing at Paul's good-natured comment, Smith's toothy smile and body language gave his new friend the first impression of how he felt about his occasional golfing partners and full-time neighbors. With his palms wide open and his arms raised up high above him as if he was praying, Smith said, "Neighbors are like your relatives, most times you don't have a say in who they're going to be. At least in my case, I love my family!" Smith's humorous comment caused both men to enjoy a good laugh together.

"While I have played a few rounds with them, and don't get me wrong on this," Paul said, "they're all great guys, but they're all far too competitive, too intense, for me. I know you've probably seen this happen a dozen or more times if you've played golf with them as much as you say you have, but why are Taylor and Ed always arguing about who's the better left-handed golfer between them. Who cares? All three of them keep me amused, if that's the right way to describe it, with their cursing and club throwing and other antics, but that's not me. I'm a rather low-key kind of guy when I play. If I hit a good shot, I hit a good shot. If I don't, I don't worry about it. Even if I'm totally stinking the place up, I don't let it bother me. My friend, Bobby Ray, he's like me. We go out to relax, to enjoy some fresh air, and to have a few Jack and Cokes over lunch. Don't get me wrong, he and I try our best, but at the end of the day we really don't care what our scores turn out to be. I'll admit that I'm as competitive as the next guy when it comes to trying to find a Confederate treasure, or when I'm trying to catch a killer, but not so much when I'm playing golf. When I play, I look at it as a day to just chill."

"I hear what you're saying, those boys are intense when it comes to golf, that's for sure," Smith said, agreeing with Paul's description of their mutual friends. "Believe it or not, another one of my neighbors is even more intense than those three guys are. Doesn't really matter though, I still enjoy their company. However, I'm more like you it sounds when it comes to playing golf, Paul. I just enjoy being out there whacking that little white ball around. The game is frustrating at times, but it lets me get rid of some of my frustrations while I'm collecting my side bets from my playing partners. I just love taking their money." For the next few minutes, Smith described a betting game that he and his neighbors played during their weekly golf game. As he did, Paul barely paid attention. Worried about his wife's safety, his thoughts were now once again focused on the flowers which had been delivered earlier that afternoon. Flowers that had come from someone he did not know.

Wanting to get back to his wife, Paul stood up to throw his empty cup in the garbage, but then decided to keep it. "Tell you what, Ray. After Donna gets back on her feet, how about you and I ask Taylor, or Mister Head Starter as he likes to be called, to hook us up with a round at Caledonia? We'll get him and Bob to round out our foursome." Then shooting Smith a wink, Paul added, "Or maybe we'll just have Taylor make all of the arrangements for us and then we'll leave him home so the other two guys can play with us. That work for you?"

"Sounds good, I like the way you think," Smith said, glancing at his watch. "I've got that meeting in two minutes, so I've got to run. You have my number, call me for golf, but definitely call me for the other thing we talked about whenever you need me." As the former Marine turned to leave, he looked back over his shoulder at Paul. "Oorah, brother! Bring it on! Oorah!"

Refilling his coffee cup before heading back to Donna's room, Paul was pleased by how comfortable he now felt about letting Smith know of his latest concern.

* * * * * *

The one aspect Paul was unsure of was how and where he and the others would soon confront Sonny Pratt. Whether their killer was a schizophrenic, a psychopath or even a sociopath with a limited conscience did not matter. What mattered was stopping him before he could claim another victim, and another victory against what he had once believed in.

Stopping in the doorway of Donna's room, Paul stared at the various floral arrangements sent to his wife by their family, friends, and several of her co-workers. All had come from people he was familiar with; all, that is, except one. Focusing his attention on the arrangement which had come earlier that afternoon caused Paul's concern to now intensify.

Turning to look at his wife resting comfortably in her bed, Paul softly whispered a prayer out loud. "Lord, I hope I'm wrong about this. Please, I beg you, please let me be wrong this time."

21

The following morning, Paul tried reaching out to Bobby Ray before his friend's day jumped into high gear. Advised about this the previous evening, he knew Bobby Ray was planning on meeting early with Stine, Wilson, and with the other detectives assigned to the growing investigation. What had started out as four separate investigations had now become one large massive and complex investigation.

"Jenkins here, but you knew that already, didn't you, Yankee Boy!" Pleased by some earlier good news he had received that morning, Bobby Ray was in a pleasant mood as he pulled into the parking lot of the GCSD's Murrells Inlet sub-station. "What's up, my man? Donna doing OK?"

"Yep, she's fine. I've gotten some good news from her doctors over the past twenty-four hours so I'm trying my best to stay optimistic after hearing all of that news. I'll tell you more when I see you, but that's not why I'm calling. Got a minute?"

"Sure do. Just got to the sub-station. What's up?" Bobby Ray asked again. Waiting for his friend's response, he placed his sunglasses down on the passenger's seat next to him.

"I've given some thought to what Blake found in the driveway where the truck was set on fire. I'm thinking the truck should have been seized as evidence far earlier than it hopefully has been. If it hasn't, and I know it's been sitting outside in the elements since the fire, I still think you need to seize it. Maybe tarp it first so nothing blows off of it, and then have it towed back to your garage. It probably would be a good idea to have Dougie or Don go over it with a fine-tooth comb. I know we've talked about this already, but it has to be seized."

Bobby Ray lingered outside his vehicle as he listened to Paul finish his thoughts. When he was finished, the Major Case commander told him what had already been done. "Paul, I'm glad you think this way, but we had all of that taken care of last night. I had Doug and Don process the truck first, and then they took care of doing the same with the scene. Oh, yeah, one more thing. Just as we expected, one of our arson dogs hit on the spot where Blake took his scrapings from. The dog's handler also showed the guys several other spots his dog hit on. Small samples they took at the scene all tested positive for the presence of nitrates found in gunpowder. Blake's already confirmed this with the truck's owner, but there's no doubt someone else carried that stuff to the scene as our victim claims he's never transported any gunpowder in his truck, nor has he used any kind of blasting equipment at work. Wags took care of following the flatbed back to the garage. Once they got there, he made sure what's left of O'Keefe's truck was secured inside. I believe the guys are going to give the truck another once over later today. The good news is they found enough of a sample on the driveway to send it up to SLED's lab for identification and comparison needs. While they were there, they also took scrapings off the truck's surface in three other locations for comparison needs. We should know those results fairly soon as I've asked SLED to put our evidence on the fast track."

"OK, good. I wasn't doubting you," Paul said as he listened to what Bobby Ray told him about having the truck seized as evidence. "I just wanted to make sure you were following up on our discussion from yesterday."

* * * * * *

"OK, let's get this meeting of you alleged detectives started so you can get back to work! We have a lot to get done today." Bobby Ray hollered loudly as he walked inside the sub-station, trying as he did to quell the morning chatter taking place among his staff as they sat waiting for him.

Over the next fifteen minutes, Bobby Ray updated the others on everything that had happened since yesterday afternoon. Included within his update was news of Sonny Pratt's vehicle finally being located.

"Davis, along with his newest protégé, Jimmy D, found it early this morning. They're still sitting on it as we speak." Turning to look at Wilson and Griffin, sitting next to each other in the second row of a group of hastily arranged chairs, Bobby Ray issued his first order of the day. As he did, he advised everyone present of the exact location of the surveillance, and of the fact that he had already taken care of notifying the Horry County Police Department, the Horry County Sheriff's Department, and the highway patrol of what was occurring at the location Davis and his partner currently had under surveillance. He had done so in an attempt to avoid the location from being accidentally compromised by a patrol car innocently passing through the area or by a deputy challenging any of Bobby Ray's cops as they sat in their vehicles staking out Pratt's vehicle.

"Griff, you and Kent are next up on surveillance. When we're done here, you guys go relieve the D & D boys so they can go home and get some rest. When you see them, tell them I want them back to work by 1700 hours at the latest. Have them call my cell when they sign on."

Just as Bobby Ray was about to have each of his detectives give a brief update on the part of the investigation they had been working on, Sheriff Renda, in full view of everyone, entered the large meeting room. His unexpected presence immediately caused the room to briefly go quiet.

Nodding to the others present, Renda, who Bobby Ray had given a partial update to earlier on the status of the investigation, took a seat next to Griffin. After giving Griffin a friendly pat on his left knee, Renda, realizing his presence had unintentionally interrupted the flow of information taking place, said in his somewhat gruff way, "Carry on, fellas, I'm not here to be more of an interruption than it appears I've already been. For what it's worth, I didn't mean for that to happen. I'm just here to sit and listen to what you folks are working on. I'm gonna let my ears do all the work this morning, so you boys carry on with what y'all have been discussing about this here case of ours."

After listening to the brief updates the others gave, Bobby Ray handed out several other assignments related to the surveillance of Pratt's vehicle. Then, after assigning two teams of two detectives each to visit the Myrtle Beach area mosques in an attempt to determine if their suspect was or was not affiliated with either of them, Bobby Ray handed out one last assignment after confirming an important point with Stine. As he did, he made sure Renda heard the compliment he directed towards the Myrtle Beach detective.

"Just so you hear this publicly from me, Blake, that was a great job you did yesterday. Making that extra effort to go visit O'Keefe, and then to go inspect his damaged truck, that was huge for us. Great job!"

As expected from within this mostly tight group of veteran detectives, Bobby Ray's praise immediately drew a friendly round of sarcastic barbs and catcalls from the others seated around Stine. Hearing what was being said made Renda laugh. It also caused Stine to direct a few good-natured insults back at those around him.

After receiving the clarification he was seeking from Stine, Bobby Ray took a long hit on the Dunkin' Donuts coffee sitting next to him. Having sat ignored for close to ten minutes, the once hot beverage was now lukewarm at best. Soon dismissing the others so they could get to work on what needed to be done, Bobby Ray directed his next comment at Renda.

"Sheriff, Tommy Scozz and I have a few things we think you ought to know."

As the others filed out of the building, Bobby Ray had Scozzafava update Renda on what he had found out concerning Pratt's military career. While most of it was fairly routine information, the FBI agent's briefing included two important points.

"The army's personnel officer I spoke to at the National Personnel Records Center in St. Louis advised me of two concerns. While neither is all that important on their own, when coupled together with what we're facing with these murders that's when they become troubling. First thing I learned was that Pratt, by all accounts, was a decent soldier during his initial three-year enlistment period. But then, during the first six months of his re-enlistment, he started having serious performance problems, especially when dealing with his superiors. His temper, which had begun to surface during his initial stint, resulted in him serving two stints in the brig at Fort Bragg before he was drummed out. The officer I spoke with, when I told him we were looking at Pratt for a couple of murders, told me our guy even spent some time at WRAMC when he first starting having problems." Seeing the confused look on Renda's face caused Scozzafava to realize he had used an acronym the sheriff was not familiar with. "Sorry, sir, Walter Reed Army Medical Center is what it's more commonly referred to as."

After answering several questions the sheriff had, Scozzafava continued with what he learned regarding Pratt's background.

"The next point I learned is perhaps the most disturbing point, especially if you think of it in relation to what Blake found yesterday. Apparently our friend at DMV was correct when he told us Pratt had been responsible for training other soldiers on how to shoot during basic training. I was told the army spent a whole lot of time and money training our guy to be a firearms instructor after identifying some basic skills Pratt was very proficient at. As the army had hoped would happen, this training made him a valuable soldier to try and retain after his initial enlistment period was up. However, I found this quite strange as the early aptitude tests the army gave him had determined he was likely not going to be anything special as a soldier. It was because of his increasingly poor attitude, as well as the decline in his performance, they went through the expense of sending him to Walter Reed. As you probably realize, they were trying to save someone who had acquired a bunch of useful skills. Apparently at one time they thought pretty highly of him."

"So what's the other bad news?" Bobby Ray asked.

"The other bad news is that near the end of Pratt's time working at the range, Fort Bragg experienced two significant thefts. The likes of, I was told, they had never experienced before. Apparently one weekend when Pratt was somewhat in charge of three weapons vaults where a variety of small arms were stored, several of those weapons went missing. I was told the army did their usual thorough investigation, even spent time trying to determine if our guy was fencing the weapons for cash or drugs, but they could never develop enough PC to put the theft on him. The officer who told me all of this said the army eventually needed to have their pound of flesh over this theft so they ended up demoting two of Pratt's superiors who were officially in charge of the vaults and range that day. Even though they apparently still believed our guy was responsible to some degree for what had happened, they never demoted or punished him at all. Another strange thing as well, apparently these stolen firearms have never turned up. Not on any NCIC hits, not in any police departments, not in any pawn shops, and not in any other place either. Weird, huh?"

"Very." Bobby Ray acknowledged before listening to the rest of what Scozzafava had to tell him.

But before allowing Scozzafava time to continue, Renda asked a logical question. "What's the possibility of this Pratt fellow shipping these weapons overseas or selling them someplace else, like to some unscrupulous gun dealer right here in the U S of A?"

"Either possibility is likely a pretty darn good one, sheriff," the FBI agent readily admitted. "Because of the time that's passed since the theft, I know I wouldn't be surprised if someone told me one or two of them were found in Mexico or Pakistan or Iraq or in some other shithole like those places."

"What else do you have for us, Scozz?" Bobby Ray asked, steering the conversation back to the investigation they were currently working on.

"The other bad news is that near the end of Pratt's tenure at the range, Fort Bragg experienced one other significant theft. For us, that theft is the worst of the two, especially when you consider what happened to O'Keefe's truck."

It took a moment, but Bobby Ray quickly caught on to what Scozzafava was alluding to. "They lost gunpowder?"

"Yes, sir, and quite a bit of it, actual black powder to be precise, one hundred and seventy-five pounds of it. The stolen powder actually did not belong to the army per se, but was owned by an army sponsored shooting club whose members were all retired military. The army lets this club, they still do in fact, store their rifles, assorted small arms such as revolvers and pistols, gunpowder, and other supplies in a weapons vault that is no longer being used as part of any formal training. The facilities are all owned by the army, but the equipment, including the powder, was and is privately owned."

Thinking back to the first issue Scozzafava had told them about, Renda asked the FBI agent one question. "You sure they never found out who stole those weapons?"

"Yes, sir, like I said before, the army believed Pratt was involved to some extent, but they could never prove it. I was told they looked long and hard at him for both incidents, but could never make anything stick. They even executed a couple of search warrants at an apartment house he sometimes stayed at, and later did the same for one of his trucks, but they never found anything to implicate him as being involved in any manner."

"Great," Bobby Ray sighed, "not only do we have a first-class nut job as our only suspect, but he's someone who likes to play with guns and kill people. That's when he's not stealing from the army and shooting priests of course. What more could we ask for?"

"You forgot to factor into the equation that he's a Muslim," Scozzafava said, chuckling as he added to Bobby Ray's woes.

Responding to the FBI agent's unpleasant comment, Bobby Ray slowly shook his head. He was already expecting more of the worst from their suspect. "Yeah, you're right. How could I have forgotten that wonderful tidbit of happiness?"

Then Renda caught his Major Case commander and Scozzafava completely by surprise. What he said was something they never expected to hear him say.

"I know we know who this jerk is, and while we still haven't arrested him, I know we're going to. But what about the FBI? Do we need their help with all of this?"

Renda's off the cuff comment caught Bobby Ray totally unprepared to answer what had been directed primarily at him. Then, sensing his degree of frustration rising, he did his best at answering Renda's questions with a simple, but snide remark. He did so rather incredulously.

"The FBI? The same FBI you've hated for years? Why bring them in now?" Finished, the Major Case commander turned and looked at Scozzafava. Like Bobby Ray, the FBI agent was not sure what direction Renda's questions were heading in.

"What about their Behavioral Analysis Unit at Quantico? Don't they have analysts or profilers there to assist departments like ours with violent crimes? I mean, we've got a guy who likes to murder people, don't we? He's got to be a whacko as he's already shot a priest. And correct me if I'm wrong, but this same guy, if I heard you right a few minutes ago, he's someone who's probably intending to murder a few more folks with some pipe bombs he's likely constructing right this very minute. Why in the hell are we not involving them?" Stressed from receiving far too many phone calls about the actions of their killer, Renda no longer cared about how he felt regarding the Federal Bureau of Investigation. For now, he simply wanted results, positive ones.

"It's not that I don't want their assistance, sheriff," Bobby Ray replied, "it's just that we don't need the help of their BAU personnel right now. We've identified our suspect, and we've finally put him under surveillance, so all is good. For right now, we're just giving him enough rope to hang himself. Besides, Scozz and I have already discussed this between ourselves. We both agree we don't need their help, or the help of their ViCAP Unit, at this time as they're not going to be able to tell us anything we don't already know. For what it's worth, and I say this because I know how much you value his opinion on matters like this, Paul agrees with us."

Rocking back and forth on his heels, Renda stood quietly for several seconds, taking in what Bobby Ray had told him. Unable to remain quiet for long, he asked, "You both sure on this? Because if you aren't, I'm gonna be pissed off like I've never been before."

"Yeah, we're sure," Bobby Ray replied, dismissing Renda's idle threat as he had done countless times before. "Maybe after we arrest our guy I'll have Scozz contact them so they can have some background on Pratt, but for now, we're good. We just need him to make a move so we can pop him."

For the next several minutes, Bobby Ray, with Scozzafava's help, spoke with Renda regarding the sheriff's concerns. After filling him in with a few other details, Renda concurred with Bobby Ray's plan on how they planned to arrest Pratt.

* * * * * *

What Bobby Ray and the others had learned about their suspect over the past two days, while far more than what they had known before that, was still not everything they needed to know about Pratt.

He would soon surprise them once again.

22

After making a quick stop at a local Kangaroo Express to grab four coffees, Griffin and Wilson drove the short distance to where Davis and Dzamko had been keeping an eye on their suspect's vehicle.

"Morning, ladies! Say hello to the 'A' Team," Wilson joked as he and his partner both slid into the back seat of Dzamko's unmarked Ford Taurus. As they did, two hot cups of coffee were passed forward to the tired occupants sitting there. Taking a moment to settle in, Wilson and Griffin soon put eyes on Pratt's Tahoe. Parked between two doublewide mobile homes just off of Deltron Drive, a narrow but paved road inside the Waterford Mobile Home Park, the vehicle looked nearly as bad as a few of the surrounding mobile homes did. Like several others in the small mobile home park, neither of the two homes Pratt's vehicle sat between had either been mobile or cared for in years. The same was true for the mobile home Pratt's uncle had rented for the past seven years. It was, by far, the most run-down of all the homes in the small mobile home park.

"Great job finding asshole's car, guys," Griffin said, offering a well-deserved compliment to Davis and Dzamko between sips of his coffee. "How'd you find it? Shit luck or good police work," the veteran cop asked before adding, "I'm betting on shit luck."

"Shit luck," Davis admitted, looking over his left shoulder at his two friends in the back seat. "We were just riding through the neighborhood after being told he might be staying in a tin can down in this neck of the woods. That's when Jimbo here saw the Tahoe. Hasn't moved since we first saw it and neither has our guy. At least, not to our knowledge he hasn't."

Pointing to the right of the Tahoe, to a mobile home whose once dark brown exterior had now faded to a light tan color due to years of neglect, as well as from too much exposure to both the sun and salt air, Dzamko told Wilson and Griffin another piece of information. "When we first setup shop here the trailer had two lights on inside it, but they went out around three this morning. Like Bruce said, we believe our boy is still inside it, but, to be totally honest with you, we don't know if he is or isn't. After searching so hard to find that piece of shit he's driving, we didn't want to chance being seen too close to it as we weren't sure if our guy has friends living nearby or not."

"I went up the street around four to stretch my legs and to eyeball the place a little closer," Davis offered as he again stared down the street at where Pratt's vehicle was parked. "I didn't see anyone moving around inside when I walked by the dump he's staying in, but I did hear a radio or something like that playing. The radio or whatever it was had been turned off when I walked back that way about an hour later. It's been quiet there ever since."

After exchanging a few other pieces of information, along with a couple of crude jokes that Griffin had recently heard, Davis and his partner left to get some much-needed sleep. As they did, Griffin took a position near the intersection of Charlotte Drive and Atlantic Avenue, while Wilson moved his vehicle into a driveway of a mobile home that was advertised as being for sale.

Doing so allowed the two of them to keep tabs on all four sides of the dilapidated trailer their suspect was holed up in.

At just after ten that morning, Griffin saw the first sign of movement inside the small trailer when a curtain facing his position was pushed open ever so slightly. Using his encrypted portable radio, he advised Wilson of what he had just seen.

Then, at exactly 1030 hours, Griffin radioed Wilson again, making sure his partner was watching Pratt as he exited the trailer. As their suspect stood next to his vehicle, Griffin, wanting to confirm it was actually Pratt they were watching, used a set of binoculars to confirm the facial features on Pratt's DMV Blow Back matched those of the person he was watching. He soon confirmed they did. "That's our boy for sure," Griffin said over the radio to his partner as they watched their suspect start up his Tahoe and then slowly back it off the section of lawn he had parked it on.

Watching Pratt as he drove west on Atlantic Avenue, Griffin allowed a pick-up truck and a FedEx van to move in directly behind Pratt's Tahoe so his vehicle was not constantly being viewed in their suspect's rear view mirror. Following close behind his partner, Wilson soon elected to cut down Charlotte Drive to Treasure Avenue before entering Highway 17. Like Griffin, Wilson did so to avoid having his vehicle constantly being seen by Pratt.

For the next hour, the two detectives followed Pratt as he stopped to buy gas and a cold drink at a gas station in Surfside Beach, before later following him up to where he had last worked in The Market Common. There they watched from a short distance away as their suspect picked up his last paycheck. As they watched him, they saw Pratt become involved in a brief shouting match with an unknown white male, an incident which soon escalated into an even briefer pushing and shoving match. Moments later, as their suspect drove away from the scene, with Griffin following not far behind him, Wilson stayed behind to determine what had occurred between Pratt and one of his former co-workers. As both cops had correctly surmised, Wilson soon learned it was O'Keefe who had been arguing with his former employee.

Then, to the surprise of both detectives, Pratt drove to Pawleys Island, parking his vehicle in the parking lot of an ACE Hardware store on Highway 17 before going inside. As they watched him walk inside, Wilson called Bobby Ray with an update.

"I'm going to jump in with Stine," Bobby Ray said in response to the news Wilson was telling him, "we're just leaving the sub-station, so stay with our guy. We'll be there in five. I'm also sending McKinney and Odom your way. When Pratt leaves the hardware store let them pick him up and then you and Griff can sit back a distance in the event he makes them."

A fourteen-year veteran of the Horry County Police Department, Detective Roy McKinney had just joined the investigation a day earlier. Like the others already working the investigation, he had been assigned to the expanding investigation at Bobby Ray's request. Realizing the rest of his detectives were already spread too thin due to the surveillance that was now taking place, the Major Case commander had contacted Renda for additional assistance. Like his partner, Trooper Edward Odom, a twenty-eight year veteran of the South Carolina Highway Patrol who had worked two similar cases with Bobby Ray's crew in the recent past due to his knowledge of the area and of the people living there, McKinney had worked with most of the others during the Melkin investigation two years earlier. Bored from having spent the better part of the past two weeks with several other cops and forensic experts testifying in an unrelated murder trial being held in Conway, McKinney was ready to get back to work. The same was true for Odom, who, despite his numerous protests, as well as the light duty assignment he was finishing up, had been holding down the fort in Georgetown while the others were hard at work pounding the pavement regarding the three murders that had already occurred.

Arriving only moments before Pratt walked out of the hardware store, Bobby Ray watched as their suspect placed his purchase in the backseat of his Tahoe before driving away. From where they were parked, McKinney and Odom had done the same. As he watched their suspect drive north on Highway 17 back towards Murrells Inlet, Bobby Ray made sure McKinney and his partner were in position to follow him.

"Yeah, we've got him," McKinney said over the secure radio channel. "We'll stay with him for a few miles and then we'll drop back so Kent and Griff can take the lead again. Not to worry, we'll coordinate this between ourselves."

Curious as to why their suspect had driven all the way to Pawleys Island to visit a hardware store, Bobby Ray radioed the others to advise them that he and Stine would be inside the store for several minutes.

Walking inside, Bobby Ray was surprised to see Henry Holmes, an off-duty GCSD deputy standing near the register. A fairly new member of the department, Holmes had just recently completed his field training program after graduating from the South Carolina Criminal Justice Academy. Because of his new job, one with a steady paycheck and a somewhat stable future to it, and with help from his parents, Holmes had just purchased a small home in Georgetown County.

"Thanks, Carl. I appreciate you mixing this paint for me this morning," Holmes said as he put his debit card back in his wallet. "I needed one more gallon to finish off the two bedrooms I'm painting." Carl Adkins, the owner of the hardware store nodded at what one of his newest customers was telling him as he placed a wooden paint stirrer on the can of paint. As Holmes picked the can up off the counter, he saw Bobby Ray walking towards him. Flustered by the Major Case commander's unexpected presence, he nervously fumbled for the right words to greet him with. Seeing the young deputy's nervousness caused Stine a fair degree of amusement.

"Morning, Captain Jenkins, sir." Holmes uttered too fast and too loud as he panicked, wondering if he should salute one of the senior members of his department or not.

"Morning, Deputy Holmes!" Bobby Ray said in a friendly tone, sensing the young deputy's nervousness as he glanced down at the can of paint Holmes was holding in his left hand. "Looks like you have a project going in that new house of yours. I heard you recently purchased a fixer-upper. Good luck with all of that." Not waiting for a response, Bobby Ray reached over the counter and shook hands with the store's owner.

"Morning, KD, how's the world treating you this fine morning?"

"Not bad, Bobby Ray, just helping one of your newest deputies with some paint he needed. Kind of quiet otherwise." Like Stine, Adkins was equally amused by the nervousness he saw Holmes exhibiting.

For the next several minutes, Bobby Ray and Carl Adkins, better known as KD to a small circle of friends, joked and caught up with each other. Friends since their days at Georgetown High

School, the two had not seen each other for the past several months. Soon finished with their trip down memory lane, and with Stine and Holmes still standing within hearing distance, Bobby Ray told his longtime friend why he was there.

"KD, I need to talk to you about that last customer of yours who just left here. Please forgive me for having to say this, but I have to be careful with what I can and can't tell you about him. Let's just leave it for now that he's a pretty bad dude. He's a guy we're interested in for something, something obviously pretty bad. Know what I mean?"

"Yep, sure do. I'm guessing you want me to tell you what I know about him and how I know him. You probably also want to know what he just purchased, don't you?" Adkins said as he replaced a thin elastic band at the end of his long ponytail with a thicker one.

"You're a smart man, KD," Bobby Ray replied, glancing briefly at Stine and Holmes with a slight smile on his face.

"Well, to start with, I've got a bad case of CRS disease at times when it comes to remembering names of fellas I haven't seen for some time." As he spoke, Adkins painfully shifted his weight from his left foot to his right due to a badly sprained ankle he had sustained the night before while playing basketball at the YMCA. As he did so, he looked at the young deputy on the other side of the counter, asking him if he knew what CRS disease was.

"No, sir, I sure don't. I hope it isn't serious though." Holmes' reply drew a round of loud laughs from the others standing around him.

"*Can't remember shit*, kid. That's what CRS stands for." Grinning widely after explaining what his acronym meant, Adkins watched with the others as Holmes' embarrassed face turned a bright red.

Pointing to the far end of his long front counter, one filled with a variety of products for impulse buyers to purchase as they stood in line waiting to pay for what they had originally come in to his store to purchase, Adkins pointed to a variety of different business cards displayed there. "I can't remember that fella's name, but I do remember him leaving a handful of his cards there maybe a year or so ago. He had a small plumbing business for a few years, that's what you'll see on the card under all of that dust down there. Didn't think he was still doing that kind of work though as I haven't seen him in months. Maybe the bastard's been buying what he needs at Home Depot or at one of them other no-good box stores. Those big national chain stores are ruining my business; same is true for plenty of other small folks around here like me," Adkins lamented, frustrated by how business had dropped off in his small hardware store over the past few months.

As Stine went to look for the business card Adkins had referred to, Bobby Ray asked his next question. "What he buy, KD?"

Without hesitation, and without having to check his cash register receipts, Adkins told his friend what Pratt had purchased. "He picked up four three-quarter by twelve inch pieces of threaded steel pipe and eight threaded steel caps. Said he needed two of them for a repair job he was working on in Murrells Inlet. Kind of funny about that, isn't it?"

"You mean him driving all the way down here for that little amount of pipe when he could have gotten it cheaper up in the inlet at Home Depot?" Realizing what he had just said, Bobby Ray kicked himself after making the reference to the cheaper prices the big box store offered. "Sorry about describing it that way, KD. No offense meant."

"None taken, partner. What you said is true. It's sad, but it's true."

"That may not be the reason why he drove all the way down here," Stine said, jumping into the conversation as he eyed the hardware store's walls and ceilings. "Seeing what I'm not seeing?" His comment caused a moment of confusion for Bobby Ray and Adkins, but then the Major Case commander caught on.

"No cameras. I see the two that are mounted over the front and rear doors, but there aren't the excessive number that all of those box stores have mounted on their ceilings. I certainly understand why they have so many of them watching you as they do, but they seem to follow you everywhere you go." Paying particular attention to the area above the cash register and front counter, Bobby Ray asked, "KD, any others we're not seeing or are those the only two cameras you have?"

"Just those two. The back one is frozen in position, barely records anything these days. It just captures the back left corner where the paint is. Like everything else these days, it costs too much to have the unit fixed or replaced. I'll probably end up regretting not having it looked at, but I just can't afford to put any money into repairs right now."

After spending a few moments sympathizing with Adkins on how the high cost of living continued to hurt the average businessman and home owner, Bobby Ray looked at Stine. "You might be right on that summation of yours, Blake." Nodding his head as he continued to stare at the camera mounted over the front door, Bobby Ray looked back at his friend. "KD, we already know what our guy purchased here, you told us that. But I'm going to send a couple of my guys here later to have a look at what your camera caught. They'll want to make a copy of it so we can put our guy in your store. You good with that?"

"Yep."

"I'd appreciate you also burning a copy of your cash register receipt for my guys when they come in. I wouldn't be asking you for all of this if this wasn't something serious we're looking at with this guy."

"No problem, Bobby Ray. If it's that important I'm glad to help."

"KD, that brings up another question. It's one I probably already know the answer to, but let me ask it anyway. Yesterday's paper ran a sketch of our guy, and I know the local television stations also began running the same sketch on their evening news. I didn't get a chance to see the news last night, so they may have even started running his photo as well. Any chance you saw either one of those?"

Adjusting his ponytail, KD told Bobby Ray the answer he expected to hear. "I'm a positive person in life, so I don't tend to read much of the negative and biased news the newspapers like to stuff inside their papers. I guess you now know the answer to the first part of your question, don't you? From knowing me as well as you do, I believe you know I haven't owned a television since the last black and white one I had. Sitcoms, reality television, news controlled by the politically driven media . . . especially the damn liberals who are so far left of norm that no one, me included, gives a hoot about the daily rhetoric they spew at us. That also goes for those Viagra commercials and all of that other bullshit that's being peddled on television; none of that crap excites or interests me. I spend most of my nights playing my guitar . . . sometimes my wife joins in with me or some nights a couple of friends will stop in and join us, but I seldom even see a television. Maybe when I go to a bar for a couple of beers, but even then I don't pay them much attention. Music is my entertainment."

Growing nostalgic for a couple of moments, Bobby Ray's high school friend added, "I remember when you use to play a pretty mean guitar back in the day. You should come over some night so we could play together. It doesn't have to be anything fancy, just for some laughs and fun and a couple of beers."

"I just might do that, brother. I just might. Sounds like a plan." Not having touched his guitar in months, it took Bobby Ray a few moments to remember where he had stored it inside his home after last playing it.

The description of what their suspect had purchased at the hardware store finally caused Bobby Ray and Stine to exchange concerned looks with each other. They were looks Adkins immediately took notice of.

"Bobby Ray, don't tell me that SOB is using them . . ." Realizing what the small pieces of steel pipe were going to be used for caused Adkins to loudly utter a brief but strong disapproval. "*Shit!* I should have seen that coming."

Shaking hands with his friend, Bobby Ray thanked him for his help. "KD, as always, it's been a pleasure. Thanks for the help this morning. I promise, we'll get together with our guitars real soon." As he turned to follow Stine outside, Bobby Ray asked Adkins one last question. "Cash, correct?"

"Yeah, he paid cash." Adkins replied, now even more upset over what his earlier customer had planned to use his purchase for.

Standing in the parking lot with Stine, and far too busy processing what Adkins had just told them, Bobby Ray paid little attention to the young deputy standing nearby. Despite him doing so, Holmes soon worked up the courage to ask the first of his two questions.

"Captain, it's not really any of my business, but I'm guessing the news Carl told you about that customer of his, that's likely connected to those murders you're working on, isn't it?"

"That a guess on your part, deputy, or do you know something we don't know?" Stine asked, slightly pissed off not only by Holmes' continued presence, but by the question he had also asked.

"Neither." Holmes answered, aware of his intrusion being unexpected and slightly unappreciated. "I'm just hoping to become a detective someday, that's all." Despite his question going unanswered, Holmes summoned the courage to ask his next one.

"Captain, the old man who owns the hardware store, his name is Carl, but you kept calling him KD. Why's that?" Holmes asked, ignoring the intense stare from Stine.

"You calling me old, kid?" Bobby Ray asked with a slight laugh as he answered the question Holmes had posed. "That old man is the same age as I am, so you'd better be careful about calling him old again, you hear?"

Embarrassed for the second time, Holmes tried apologizing, but his attempt was waved off.

"No worries, Holmes, but KD and I did go to high school together a few years back. KD is Carl's nickname; he's had it since our first year at Georgetown High. In fact, a couple of our friends and I coined that name for him. KD has led an interesting life since our school days, maybe even more so back then. We started calling him Doobie at first because he smoked and sold a ton of weed during those four years at our beloved alma mater. Believe me when I tell you that because it was probably pretty darn close to being a ton of weed that went through his hands. That boy just loved to smoke and sell weed for some reason. Well, one thing led to another and Doobie became King Doobie and then, in an effort to try and hide his nickname from the teachers and a few others, it simply became KD."

As the Major Case commander finished with his explanation, and unsure if he was being screwed with or being told the truth, Holmes excused himself, politely telling Bobby Ray and Stine that he had to get back to his painting. As they briefly watched him drive off, Stine shook his head as he looked at his friend.

"You are so full of shit! You had that kid believing every word you told him."

Climbing into Stine's car, Bobby Ray could not help feigning disappointment over Stine's description of him. "Me? Full of shit? Why would you say that?" Bobby Ray's comment was quickly followed by one of his deep-chested laughs.

Barely noticing the smirk that Stine gave him, Bobby Ray's attention was now focused on the business card he had been handed. Of all the cards that had been stacked at the end of the counter in Adkins' store, the card Bobby Ray now held was the only one which had advertised a variety of plumbing services. All of the others had advertised a wide range of electrical, roofing, and lawn services from a variety of small local businesses. Now the Major Case commander looked closely at the name printed on the card he was holding.

"*Palmetto Boys Plumbing*? Who the hell are they?" Bobby Ray mumbled softly to himself, unable to ever recall seeing any of their vehicles or advertisements in the Georgetown or Pawleys Island area before. As he continued to stare at the unfamiliar name, he made a mental note to have someone follow up on the address and phone number listed on the cheaply produced white-colored business card.

******

As Stine drove his Dodge Durango north on Highway 17 towards Myrtle Beach, where their suspect had momentarily stopped at a Sonic Drive-In, Bobby Ray called Solicitor Pascento with an update on what they had recently learned about Pratt.

"I agree with you, Bobby Ray, you certainly have more than enough PC for a couple of search warrants for both the mobile home he's staying at and for the vehicle he's driving. Tell you what, have someone run the warrant applications up to me this afternoon. I'll find us a sympathetic flag-waving judge to sign them for us."

"OK, Joe, sounds good. I'll have Tommy Scozz and someone else start working on them. They should have them in your hands by late afternoon. I'll have them call you when they start your way. Listen, even after these warrants get issued this investigation is far from being over. There are still a number of issues we need answers to. Because of that, and I'm sure you'll agree with me on this, but I'd like you to ask whatever Judge signs them to order the warrants to be sealed for now, at least until after we get this prick arrested. You good with that?"

"Already planned to do that. That won't be a problem, I'll take care of it," Pascento replied confidently, agreeing with the logic surrounding the sensitivity of the complex investigation. Like his counterpart had, he would also request that the PC listed in each of the warrant applications be kept sealed until after Pratt had been arrested. "But for now, I have a question for you. What about the FBI? You've already been told two things that have caused at least one red flag to be raised, at least in my opinion it has."

"You're referring to the points about Pratt allegedly being a Muslim, and the fact that we've been told he's purchased some steel pipe this morning."

"I am."

"Joe, with all due respect, I'm not calling the feds in on this yet for two reasons. First, I don't think it's risen to that level yet; nor does Scozz, our resident FBI agent. If it does, I'll do that, but first I need some confirmation that Pratt's a terrorist or something else along those lines. He may be a killer, but let's just wait until we know what he's really all about before we call the feds in on this. Besides, I'm not interested in playing Chicken Little at this point, it's too early to do that."

Pascento laughed at Bobby Ray's folk tale reference. "OK, sounds good, but if I see this going in that direction much further then we'll have no choice but to call them in." Like Bobby Ray, the veteran prosecutor knew what the ramifications would be if the media found out Pratt had been labelled a terrorist and neither he or his friend had reached out to the FBI or Homeland Security for assistance. Concerned over a significant event occurring from this point forward, especially one reflecting badly on his office and on Bobby Ray's, Pascento knew the shitstorm would be especially bad if one of Pratt's pipe bombs hurt any innocent civilians.

"OK, understood." Bobby Ray said, dutifully taking note of Pascento's concerns.

"What's the other reason you don't want to call the FBI in now?" Pascento asked, recalling his friend had said he had more than one reason for not doing so.

"Because Renda hates the FBI. He'd kick my ass for days if I was to call them in now." Bobby Ray then told Pascento about the earlier conversation he and Scozzafava had with Sheriff Renda regarding the FBI's Behavioral Analysis Unit.

After listening to what he was being told, Pascento laughed again, well aware of Renda's significant disdain of the FBI. Then the solicitor asked his most important question. "How's Paul's wife doing? I stopped at the hospital the other day, but Paul was busy with her doctors. I didn't want to interrupt them so I just left a card for her with the nurses. I hope she's improving."

"She's holding her own. I understand some of the swelling in her brain has subsided as her doctors had hoped for, but she still has some tough times in front of her."

"I'll say a prayer for her. Please let Paul know I was asking about her. I'll reach out to him in the next day or two."

******

After finishing his call with Pascento, Bobby Ray contacted Scozzafava, advising him to prepare search warrants for Pratt's vehicle and for the mobile home where their suspect was staying. As they spoke, he gave the FBI agent one other task to complete.

"I'm holding onto a business card that I believe our boy left at a hardware store in Pawleys Island. The name on the card reads Palmetto Boys Plumbing. It has a Pawleys Island address listed on it, but when Blake and I drove by the location a few minutes ago it's a vacant storefront. I've lived in this neck of the woods my entire life so I kind of know what's going on, but I can't ever recall a plumbing business being at that address. I'm going to call one of our analysts and have her see what she can find out about this company. Do me a favor, use some of your contacts and do the same thing. Maybe this is nothing, but something stinks about this card."

* * * * * *

While Pascento and Bobby Ray had an interest in securing search warrants that day, observations made by the two surveillance teams of some additional suspicious activity on Pratt's part put the submission of the warrant applications on hold temporarily. Learning of this new activity, Bobby Ray made plans to extend the surveillance of their suspect. For now, the search warrants would have to wait.

But despite those plans, in late afternoon traffic, and despite the best efforts of the surveillance teams, Pratt and his Chevy Tahoe disappeared. Frantically the teams hunted for their suspect. As they did, they were soon assisted by Bobby Ray and Stine.

Even with what they thought they already knew about him, Pratt would soon confound the cops watching him on at least three more occasions.

23

Twelve hours after unfairly being chewed out for their part in losing visual contact with Pratt, Wilson and Griffin struggled to keep their eyes open after working for nearly twenty hours straight. Like the others working this labor intensive investigation with them, they had worked far too many hours over the past three weeks. Sitting down the street from the mobile home they had seen their suspect at the previous morning, Wilson scanned the still dark neighborhood from where he sat slumped behind the steering wheel of his vehicle. Next to him, Griffin dozed on and off as his tired body tried fighting off the fatigue it felt from having recently worked far too many hours.

Like the others responsible, in Bobby Ray's opinion, for blowing the surveillance on Pratt, Wilson and his partner had spent several long and excruciating hours unsuccessfully searching through several neighborhoods, bars, and restaurant parking lots for their suspect. Early on in their search, they had spent a significant amount of time cruising one particularly notorious section of Myrtle Beach. Unlike the other places they checked, this location housed a variety of bars, strip clubs, tattoo parlors, and other forms of adult entertainment. But like the other locations they checked during their fruitless night of searching, they failed to locate Pratt or his vehicle among the neon lights of Seaboard Street.

Now, for the past two hours, as the others continued to scour several depressed neighborhoods along the Grand Strand trying to find their suspect, places where people like Pratt often liked to frequent while trying to hide in plain view of others, Wilson and Griffin gambled on him returning home. Bored and tired of doing what he had been doing for the past several hours, Wilson's eyes became mesmerized as they watched the brake lights of a mini-van as its owner delivered the morning newspaper to several homes in the area. Doing so nearly caused him to miss seeing Pratt's vehicle as it slowly made the turn from Atlantic Avenue onto Deltron Drive. Rousing Griffin from his brief nap, the two cops watched as Pratt walked quickly inside the pitch-black mobile home.

Confident their suspect was as exhausted as they were, Griffin contacted Davis and Dzamko, advising them that Pratt had returned home. For the last hour of their extended shift, the four detectives watched Pratt's vehicle closely, determined not to let it or their suspect escape from their view again.

******

Usually an early riser, Stine decided to sleep in after a late night of trying to help locate their missing suspect. As he enjoyed a rare morning of doing so, the musical ringtone of his cell phone annoyingly announced an incoming call. As he looked at the unfamiliar number displayed on his phone, he also took note of the time.

"Who the hell is bothering me at this time of the morning?" Stine groused as he fumbled to answer his phone. "Yeah, who is this?" Like his partially opened eyes, Stine's raspy voice was still full of sleep.

"Detective Stine? I'm sorry for waking you, but I've got a problem, a huge one at that. I need some help, *please!*" The frantic voice on the other end of the call pleaded.

"Who the heck is this?" Stine's voice demanded to know as he forced his tired body to sit up in bed.

"It's Mickey O'Keefe. I've got some trouble here at the house. I need your help."

In a matter of moments, O'Keefe quickly explained the problem confronting him so early that morning. It was one which quickly garnered Stine's full attention.

"You found what!" Stine said loudly. Jumping out of bed, he searched for clothes to put on. With his phone tucked between his ear and left shoulder as he put on his pants, he continued to listen to what he was being told. Minutes later, after rushing out the door of his condo, he headed for Murrells Inlet.

******

Finding the street outside of O'Keefe's home already cordoned off from the response of several uniformed deputies and two fire trucks, Stine ducked under a single line of yellow crime scene tape ringing O'Keefe's property. Along with three deputies, the ubiquitous yellow tape helped to keep a handful of curious early morning onlookers a safe distance away. As Stine cleared the outer perimeter, further down the street a loud air horn announced the impending arrival of a large specialty vehicle. It was one that had been specially built for the needs of the Horry County Bomb Squad.

Walking to where O'Keefe stood on the far side of his yard, Stine saw the small pipe bomb lying on the ground directly under

O'Keefe's new Ford F-150 pick-up truck. After learning the construction foreman had found the bomb as he walked to his truck earlier that morning, Stine then spoke with Lieutenant Jill Patton, the commander of the Horry County Special Operations Division. A former instructor at the prestigious U.S. Army – FBI Hazardous Devices School, and a graduate of the International IEDD Training School at the Army School of Ammunition, the former army ordnance disposal specialist was now only one of four female commanders across the country currently heading up emergency services units for their respective police departments.

"Guess we got lucky with this one," Patton said several minutes later as she watched Sergeant Charlie Shaw, her most experienced bomb tech, carefully load the now inert pipe bomb into their bomb truck. Like Patton, Shaw had received a wealth of experience from handling a variety of explosive devices since graduating several years earlier from FBI-sponsored courses at the Redstone Arsenal in Huntsville, Alabama. "That thing is small, but it could have easily ripped apart that nice new truck over there, along with its owner, into a whole bunch of pieces if it had been installed correctly. I take it your vic must be having a beef with someone?"

"No chance of it going off now?" Stine warily asked before briefly cluing Patton in with the details surrounding O'Keefe's problem. As they spoke, and unfazed by the task he had just completed, Shaw casually stood next to the large specialty vehicle as he joked with two of his fellow bomb techs. Unlike Stine, the experienced bomb tech gave little thought to what was resting inside the vehicle next to him.

"Nope, not really. I had Sergeant Shaw and his guys x-ray it before we moved it, but we're good now," Patton said, taking note of Stine's reluctance to get too close to her bomb truck. "Besides the usual gunpowder, it looks like it's packed with some ball bearings and nails. What we've got here is a typical homemade pipe bomb that someone made in their basement or garage; we're just lucky whoever taped it to the vehicle's frame did a shitty job doing that. The connection they made between the bomb's fuse wire to the truck's wiring harness was also done pretty poorly. Maybe whoever did it was rushed, or maybe they thought someone saw them, but when the duct tape holding the pipe bomb failed it tore the fuse wire from its intended source of juice. It's a good thing it did. If it hadn't, I guess you'd be talking to the coroner right about now and not with me."

"Damn!" Stine said after listening to Patton explain why the bomb had failed. As he stood there, he realized just how close O'Keefe had come to being Pratt's fourth murder victim.

******

What Stine and the others would soon learn was that O'Keefe was not the last of Pratt's targets. While another person already had been, two others would soon become the focus of a deranged man's rage. For one of them, it would be their second encounter with him.

24

As he closed the dust-covered blinds of the window he had been looking out of, Sonny Pratt stared at the specks of dust lingering in the air. Like the rest of the trailer he was staying in, the blinds had not been cleaned in years. All around him stacks of old newspapers, junk mail, food wrappers, and empty beer cans contributed to the almost hoarder-like mess inside his uncle's mobile home.

Walking down the narrow hallway from the bedroom window he had been watching the cops from, Pratt stopped to open the door of the home's unused second-bedroom. Ignoring the room's foul musty odor, as well as the drawn and cobweb-covered curtains that once had been a light blue in color, he grinned as he moved closer to the old refrigerator he had placed in a corner of the small room three months earlier. As he did, he could barely hear the motor running as it kept its contents cold. Inspecting the several layers of grey duct tape he had previously wrapped around the unit, he was pleased to see the tape still held the refrigerator door securely shut. A quick check of the tape showed no signs of it having been tampered with since his last inspection several days earlier.

"Maybe if you had spent some time cleaning this place up once in a while you wouldn't have found yourself on ice, Uncle Johnny!"

Pratt angrily yelled as he ran his fingers over the outside of the refrigerator. "Guess you should have spent more time doing that instead of being a royal pain-in-my-ass, isn't that right, little man?"

Laughing to himself over how he had hidden his uncle's body in the refrigerator after killing him in a fit of rage eleven days earlier, Pratt paused in the doorway for a brief moment before turning out the room's single overhead light. Looking back at the refrigerator, he loudly whispered, "Have a good day, Johnny! Talk to you later!"

Like the rest of his family and friends back in the hill country of South Carolina, Sonny Pratt had grown up dirt-poor. Raised by two abusive parents, whose principal goals in life were getting their daily buzz on from smoking ditch weed and drinking whatever kind of spirits they could get their hands on, including an occasional bottle or two of NyQuil when nothing else was available, Pratt barely managed to survive. He did so only due to the kindness of a handful of other adults who came and went on a regular basis during the early years of his life.

Despite his poor grades, Pratt, a disinterested student for most of his academic career, had been pushed through high school like several others he knew. While not lacking the common sense gene like other members of his family, he had simply been bored with school. To the dismay of several teachers who had tried working with him, he graduated with a reading level which had not risen past the eighth grade. Partially due to his lack of academic success, he had bounced from menial job to menial job for two years after graduating until he could no longer tolerate the life he was living. At age twenty, after listening to a slick sales pitch made by an army recruiter, he joined the army hoping to tour the country, if not the world.

Even though he had been exposed to a harsh upbringing, Pratt had never been in trouble with the law; nor had he been an abuser of illegal substances. However, that all changed during the first year of his reenlistment. From that point on, a series of arrests and military violations, coupled with a lack of confidence and bouts of depression, caused him to drift through life aimlessly. After being drummed out of the army, life had once again become difficult for Sonny Pratt. Soon a series of jobs that were far too many in their number to remember followed. Strangely, and for reasons he often questioned, after his military career had come to an abrupt ending, Pratt had become a voracious reader.

Early in his military career, the abused son of a father and mother who had also been physically and mentally abused during their childhood, Pratt had finally started to grow as a person. Army life, full of its many wonderful opportunities, and full of people from all walks of life who were just as eager to make new friends as he was, quickly agreed with him. It was also, for the first time in his life, a time when he had enough to eat on a daily basis.

Life in the army had also allowed him to experience what it was like to fall in love. Volunteering to work one night at a family event at Fort Bragg, one he had conveniently failed to mention to any members of his own family, Pratt met Lynn Burke, a fellow soldier.

Hailing from Boone, North Carolina, and raised in a dysfunctional family like her soon-to-be new boyfriend, Burke had been the eighth of nine children. Growing fond of each other during the weeks following their chance encounter, they began spending as much of their off-duty time together as possible. However, Burke soon proved to be everything Pratt was not, including being an abuser of alcohol and Oxycontin; two substances which never mixed well together. Unknown to her new boyfriend, Burke had been extremely promiscuous in high school. Now surrounded by a large number of male soldiers, she continued with her ways; often involving herself with some of her boyfriend's best friends. This was a side of her that Pratt knew nothing about.

Despite the difficulties of sometimes having to put up with Burke's shortcomings, Sonny Pratt enjoyed spending time with his girlfriend. Until that fateful day, Burke had been the love of his life.

Eighteen months after first meeting his girlfriend, Pratt was enjoying breakfast in the mess hall on a rare Sunday off when he was summoned to his company commander's office. Stunned to learn of his girlfriend's death, from a long night of hard drinking and drug use, Pratt's heart was then further ripped out of his chest when he was told all there was to know about her death. Found naked in a hotel bathtub with another soldier, both had died from a heroin overdose.

Already beginning to show signs of being at odds with life in the army before his girlfriend's death, Pratt grew even more angry and confused over the next several weeks after feeling betrayed by someone he loved. As he began to question life in the army more and more, he also began to question his faith in the Catholic Church. Several months later, after being kicked out of the army, Pratt distanced himself even further from the remaining members of his estranged family by moving to Myrtle Beach. It was there, despite his best efforts to stay with the church, often the sole source of comfort during his difficult teenage years at home, he began to distance himself from it and from his acceptance of the American dream. Developing a passion for questioning authority, he soon began to question decisions made by anyone entering his life. It was during this time that he also began his self-proclaimed mission of cleansing his adopted hometown of enemies.

******

Drawing the drapes tight over the kitchen sink after taking one last look at the cops parked down the street, Pratt laughed as he pulled back the small throw rug covering part of the kitchen floor. Kneeling down, he lifted up the small trap door his uncle had built into the floor several years earlier. Reaching into one of the several plastic tubs he had placed under the mobile home weeks earlier, he lifted four smaller sealed containers up onto the kitchen floor.

Sitting at a small kitchen table, Pratt smiled as he momentarily stared up at the kitchen window he had been looking out of minutes earlier. Donning plastic latex gloves, he smirked as he began his work, insulting the cops who sat a few mere yards away from where he was carefully working. "Do you really think keeping me under surveillance is going to stop me from doing what needs to be done?"

Picking up a small length of steel pipe which he had already capped on one end, Pratt carefully placed a handful of small nails and an even larger number of ball bearings inside it. With a piece of duct tape covering the small hole he had previously drilled in the pipe, he filled the remaining voids with gunpowder. Finished, he wiped down the exposed threaded end of the pipe with a damp cloth in an effort to reduce the possibility of friction causing an accidental explosion. From reading articles on how to build effective pipe bombs, Pratt was aware that even the slightest amount of gunpowder settling within the steel threads could cause an explosion to occur when the last cap was screwed in place. Despite knowing he had been careful as he poured the explosive powder into the pipe's interior, Pratt had no interest in losing any of his fingers or either of his hands. Taking his time, he slowly screwed the last cap in place over the still damp threads. Off to his right, a small kitchen timer, two thin short lengths of electrical wire and a 9-volt battery sat waiting to be attached to the small length of pipe. Finished making his first bomb, he soon repeated the process two more times. Pleased by what he put together while sitting at the table, Pratt used his Smartphone to take three pictures of the devices he had carefully constructed.

"You cops just try and stop me from what I'm about to do! Just try!" Pratt hollered as he placed the remaining items back inside the plastic containers before securing them in the plastic tub from where they had come. Reaching into another plastic container, he removed a satellite phone before placing the trap door and throw rug back in their respective places.

Standing up, the self-admitted fan of old black and white movies smiled as he placed the sat phone in one of his pants pockets. Weakly, he tried imitating Edgar G. Robinson, one of his favorite gangsters from a variety of 1950s era movies he often watched. "Just try and stop me, coppers! Just try!"

One hour later, and using the phone he had been supplied with, Pratt followed the instructions he had been given a week earlier and made the first of his two calls. As he would later do during his second call, he advised his overseas contacts that his plans were proceeding as scheduled.

25

Two hours after Pratt was seen arriving back at home, Solicitor Pascento signed search warrant applications for their suspect's Chevy Tahoe and for Uncle Johnny's mobile home. While the language of both warrants was very similar, Wilson and Griffin carefully worded them to demonstrate the degree of probable cause needed for each warrant. They did so by vaguely outlining how and where each of the murders had occurred, the manners and causes of each victim's death, information regarding O'Keefe's truck being set on fire, and some of the observations made by Bobby Ray's detectives during the surveillance of their suspect. Both warrants also included several important details regarding the robbery of Donna's branch office, details on how Donna had been injured, and how those two acts were connected to each other. The application also reflected how Pratt was directly responsible for hurting her. Additionally, the warrants also laid out another critical piece of information in the case against Pratt as they detailed how Ziggy Bagrov had assisted his friend by illegally supplying him with confidential information obtained from DMV computers. As required, the warrants also listed the address of the locations to be searched, and the fact that Pratt was temporarily residing within the mobile home rented by his uncle. At Pascento's insistence, the PC outlined in each of the warrants also included information concerning Pratt's disciplinary records while in the army. Almost as important as the other information it contained, the warrant applications also contained the fact that their suspect's elderly handicapped uncle had not been seen by any of his neighbors for the better part of the past two weeks.

Putting the warrant applications down on his desk after reading them, Judge L. Robert Harding looked over the top of his reading glasses at Pascento, and then at Wilson and Griffin, the warrants' two affiants. A native South Carolinian, Harding's reputation for being pro-law enforcement was well-known across Georgetown and Horry counties. This was especially true when he was dealing with defendants accused of intentionally trying to harm a police officer. He was even harsher when handing down verdicts against gangbangers and other degenerates when they had been caught illegally possessing firearms when robbing small family-run businesses within his jurisdiction. Leaning back in his chair, Harding asked, "You really believe this Pratt fellow is using gunpowder to construct such horrible weapons as you've described? Why would he do such a thing?" Finished asking his questions, Harding withdrew his favorite pen from inside the pocket of his suit coat.

"From what we can tell, Your Honor, our suspect is . . . well, to put it bluntly, and in terms we're all becoming too familiar with these days, for some reason he's decided to start his own holy war right here along the Grand Strand. Someone or something has obviously set him off, and we believe, as we've tried to articulate within the warrants, that he's about to step up his reign of terror even more by using pipe bombs. As the warrants show, we can prove where and when he purchased some of the materials needed to make those bombs," Wilson said, answering the questions Harding had posed.

Sitting behind his desk, Harding closed his eyes momentarily as he contemplated what Wilson had told him. "Hmm, I see. I'm not questioning anything you've written in the applications, sergeant, I'm just horrified to learn what this fellow seems to have planned, that's all. I've never been described as being naïve, at least to my knowledge I haven't, but I'm having trouble grasping the fact that the world's problems have now shown up on the doorstep of the Grand Strand. To me, pipe bombs, murder, and all of that associated violence is not what our community is all about. I had hoped we were above all of that foolishness." Sitting silent for several moments, Harding toyed with his pen as he reflected back on what he had just read.

"Your Honor, obviously we need these warrants so we can search the place where Pratt's staying. Doing so will hopefully help us determine what the actual scope of his plan is. We've asked for the warrant for his vehicle because we saw him use it when he picked up some of his bomb-making supplies at the hardware store. He's also used it to help facilitate some of his other plans, and it's also likely that he's used it to transport other equipment needed to make his bombs," Wilson said, offering up some additional information for Harding to consider. As he did, he took a brief look at Pascento. "It's clearly, at least in my opinion it is, an instrumentality of the crimes he's trying to perpetuate." Finished with what had to be said, Wilson hoped his polite but respectful response had not come across as being delivered too emphatically.

Looking up for a brief moment as he carefully signed and dated the various pages of both warrants to properly reflect he had granted their issuance, Harding again looked over the top of his glasses at Wilson. "Are you an attorney, son?"

"No, sir. Just like my partner here, I'm just your plain old average street cop. We're just trying to get the job done before anyone else gets hurt."

Even though he had never met Wilson before, Harding knew of the veteran cop's reputation as being both an outstanding police officer and a well-respected expert witness. Hearing Wilson's response as he finished approving the warrants caused a smile to crease Harding's face. "You're hardly an average street cop, sergeant. Just like your friend here, it sounds like you're a pretty darn good one. Maybe you should think about a career change as you've just made a good argument for a cause you obviously believe very strongly in. I might add it was well done, very well done, indeed. Come see me if you decide to change careers."

******

The warm sunny afternoon flooded many of the streets in Murrells Inlet with a slow steady flow of traffic. While much of it in several locations was beach traffic, others clogging the streets were simply looking to get an early jump on the start of their weekends. Included in the mix were hundreds of motorcycles whose operators were among the first wave of every imaginable kind of enthusiasts arriving for the start of Bike Week. Like most of the surrounding streets, Atlantic Avenue, one of the main arteries running to and from the beach, was packed with traffic. It was also a street running parallel to the neighborhood where Pratt was living.

The bumper to bumper traffic also caused one other problem to Bobby Ray's plans of executing the two search warrants at their suspect's home. Watching Pratt earlier as he had climbed into his Tahoe, Davis and Dzamko were caught completely off guard when their suspect sped across a neighbor's lawn on the other side of the street from where his uncle's home was located. Driving through a narrow twenty-foot gap separating two other mobile homes from each other, Pratt narrowly missed hitting one of the homeowners as he mowed his front lawn. Driving recklessly after leaving the mobile home park, and despite clipping the front end of a Honda Civic, Pratt managed to somehow make his way out to Highway 17. As he entered the busy roadway, his surveillance teams struggled to follow him. Driving down the grass median just north of where Glenns Bay Road intersects with Highway 17 South, Pratt ran the red light as he turned onto the busy secondary road. For the second time, the surveillance teams no longer had their suspect in sight.

As others continued to hunt for their suspect, Bobby Ray was forced to alter the designated time he had set for executing the two search warrants. He did so out of concern for both the area homeowners and passing traffic. As word quickly got out to all of the cops assigned to executing the warrants, including those assigned to the three search teams, that the time had been adjusted from 3pm to 6pm, Bobby Ray hoped for something else to happen. Quietly he prayed that when the warrants were executed they would catch their normally nocturnal suspect at home grabbing a few late afternoon hours of sleep.

******

At 5:30 pm, with Paul present after being chased out of the hospital earlier by his wife's nurses so he could get some much-needed rest at home, Bobby Ray prepared to search the mobile home their suspect had been staying in. To his and everyone's regret, Pratt had not yet returned home.

With the neighbors on either side of the mobile home already evacuated due to Bobby Ray's concern over their suspect possibly having placed booby traps and motion sensors in and around the perimeter of his uncle's property, the go-ahead was given for the bomb squad's robot to enter the small residence. With one exception, the robot soon began sending back images of each of the rooms inside the residence to Dell computers mounted inside the Major Case Squad's crime scene processing van and to others within the Bomb Squad's command vehicle. A similar live feed was also being broadcast to a laptop computer being monitored by Patton, Shaw, Bobby Ray, and several detectives. After viewing these images with Patton, and after a quick sweep of the interior by Shaw and two other bomb techs, Bobby Ray gave the all clear signal to his detectives.

After allowing Elmendorf, Vane, and two of their evidence techs time to photograph and videotape the interior of the small residence, Bobby Ray's detectives began their search. As they did, Stine was the first to notice the refrigerator that had been placed inside the closed bedroom.

"What the hell is this doing in here and what's with the layers of duct tape wrapped around it?" Stine wondered out loud as he and the others stood looking at the large appliance Pratt had placed there. As they did, Elmendorf opened one of the two windows within the small room in an effort to clear the musty dank smell that was present.

"I'm thinking we may have just found Uncle Johnny," Paul offered as he visually inspected the still plugged in refrigerator. His words immediately received the attention of the others present.

Realizing what was likely inside it, and after Shaw determined it was safe to do so, Bobby Ray made the refrigerator their first priority. Pointing at it, he sarcastically offered up, "OK, Doug, Donnie, have fun! Let's get this sucker open so we can find out if Paul's right."

After carefully cutting the grey duct tape on both sides of the door, doing so to minimize the loss of any fingerprints that may have been left on the tape, Vane slowly opened the refrigerator door. As he did, Uncle Johnny's cold and pale left arm greeted him as it freed itself from within the tight confines of the old Kenmore refrigerator.

Surprised, but not shocked by what they found, Stine, Wilson, and the others soon began their systematic search of the rest of the rooms as Vane and Elmendorf began processing the room where Uncle Johnny's body had been found. As they began their search, they specifically looked for any of the items listed on the two warrants. Among them were gunpowder, small sections of threaded steel pipe, threaded steel caps, blasting caps, duct tape, BBs, ball bearings, nails, road flares, and any souvenirs their suspect might have taken from any of his victims. As their search progressed, Bobby Ray, made aware of Solicitor Pascento and one of his inspectors recently arriving at the scene, went outside and briefed them on what they had just found inside the mobile home. A call to Sheriff Renda soon followed.

After finishing with his updates, Bobby Ray moved further down Uncle Johnny's driveway and closer to the road as he called to McKinney and his partner, Trooper Ed Odom. Three homes further down the narrow road, the two cops stood in a neighbor's driveway putting the finishing touches on their neighborhood canvass. Like McKinney, Odom, a tall and balding law enforcement veteran who had spent most of his career conducting a variety of criminal investigations involving violence, had recently returned to work after being injured in a car accident three months earlier.

"Learn anything important, I hope?" Bobby Ray asked, nearly pleading with the two senior cops to tell him some additional good news as they joined him where he was standing near the edge of the driveway. Less than twenty-five feet away, the search of the mobile home was still taking place.

"Not much. How about you guys? Find anything inside you didn't expect to find?" McKinney asked after taking a long hit on the bottle of Powerade he had been carrying in his back pocket.

"Yeah, kind of," Bobby Ray snorted, trying hard not to find any humor in having found Pratt's uncle packed inside his own refrigerator. "We found the uncle dead in there. Looks like he's been that way for some time. Poor bastard still had his wallet inside one of his pockets. It's him for sure; we made a positive ID from his driver's license."

"Damn!" Odom said as he looked up from the notes he had taken during the canvass. "No pun intended, but that's freaking cold, wasting your own uncle like that."

"Bobby Ray, that couple you saw us talking to, they're both retired cops from Philly. They live in that trailer over there, the one with the yellow flowers in the flower beds," McKinney said, pointing to one of the few well-kept doublewides on the street. In another of the home's small flower beds, three pink plastic flamingos stood motionless as they stared at McKinney. "Both of them told us they haven't seen the uncle for at least the past two weeks or so. They also told us the old man, this Uncle Johnny character of yours, is pretty much a loner, likely due to his poor health. They've also noticed that his car, a red Chevy Impala, is missing. They claim it's been gone for about four or five days now. They both thought that was kind of strange because the old guy barely ever drove it."

"They ever see our guy, Uncle Johnny's nephew, coming or going?" Bobby Ray asked, staring back at the pink flamingos he just now saw standing in the flower bed.

"Yeah, they have," McKinney replied, "and both of them, being ex-cops and all, apparently had him pegged as being bad news since the first day they met him. Especially the ex-female cop, she told us she knew he was a shithead right from the start." Chuckling, McKinney added, "I guess once you're a cop you never lose the instincts the job teaches you about people. In this case, I'd have to say they're correct in their feelings about this guy we're working."

After hearing what else they had learned during their canvass, Bobby Ray instructed McKinney to contact the GCSD Dispatch Center, telling them to issue a BOLO on both their suspect's and his uncle's vehicles, and on Pratt himself. "Make sure whoever enters the info into NCIC, and in the message being sent out via our in-car computers, that Pratt is listed as someone who is to be considered armed and dangerous. Have them copy the NCIC message Special Attention to each of the area departments, including the highway patrol."

Besides a few of Pratt's written rants against recent actions taken by the United States government in the Middle East and in other locations in Europe, as well as a handful of similar rants and drawings against the Catholic Church, Bobby Ray's detectives found several other interesting items of evidence inside the home Pratt had shared with his uncle. Among the incriminating items were two slightly torn and bloodstained Confederate flags. Both had been found hanging inside a small hallway closet. One other item, a new brightly polished nail, was found by Elmendorf on the home's filthy kitchen floor.

Standing in the small kitchen with Bobby Ray and Elmendorf as they discussed the need to have the blood found on the flags typed for DNA needs, Paul was disgusted by the accumulation of dirty dishes, food waste, dirt, and the piles of junk mail and old newspapers. At one end of the kitchen counter a small army of palmetto bugs were hard at work attacking the remnants of an Entenmann's coffee cake. Too focused on what they were doing, they worked undisturbed, ignoring the presence of several large law enforcement officers who occasionally watched them as they crawled in and out of the opened food container.

As he stood there, Paul began to question why a brand new shiny nail had been found on the floor. As he thought more about it, his eyes focused on a small rug covering a section of the linoleum floor adjacent to the stove. More importantly, they focused on how the floor's accumulated dust and dirt seemed as if it had been pushed to each side of the rug in small rows. Carefully walking back and forth over the rug so as not to disturb the debris on either side of it, his feet sensed the floor giving slightly.

Now on the phone with Pascento, who had left the scene several minutes earlier, Bobby Ray was finalizing a few details regarding the issuance of a murder warrant for Pratt for killing his uncle when he noticed what Paul was doing. Curious over what he was seeing, he quickly ended his conversation with Pascento.

"You got something there, Yankee Boy?" Bobby Ray asked, his rich southern drawl revealing itself as it always did when he was excited about something.

Looking at Elmendorf, and then at Scozzafava who had just walked back inside, Paul pointed to the small rug and to the filth around it. "Either of you see anything unusual here?"

Grasping what Paul was referring to, Scozzafava carefully knelt down and lifted the rug up and out of the way. As he did, the others quickly saw the trap door the rug had hidden from view.

Minutes later, Bobby Ray had the bomb squad remove some of the mobile home's exterior skirting so they could access the area underneath the trailer. After carefully inspecting the crawl space, it was soon determined that no explosive devices or trip wires had been set to go off if the trap door had been opened improperly. With that determination made, Vane put his evidence techs to work. Despite being aware that no explosive devices had been found, the techs worked nervously as they lifted six plastic tubs up and onto the kitchen floor from under the home. Unknown to Bobby Ray and his staff, each of the tubs had been placed there weeks earlier.

"Looks like we found what we were looking for," Bobby Ray said as his eyes moved from tub to tub, looking at what was stored inside them. "I'm seeing a whole lot of gunpowder, some blasting caps, electrical wire, some pieces of pipe bomb length steel pipe, some ball bearings and nails, a couple of packs of BBs, some homemade fuses, a few steel caps for the sections of pipe, and a handful of batteries." Being facetious, he added, "This looks like someone was planning on making a few pipe bombs."

"Or already has." Stine said from the kitchen doorway where he stood watching.

"Or already has." Bobby Ray quickly concurred with Stine's assessment, noticing as he did the several sheets of paper Stine was holding onto.

Reaching into one of the tubs, one of the evidence techs soon held up four items of particular interest. The first item, a worn kitchen towel, was not as important as the next three. What was carefully wrapped inside it, a .22 Smith & Wesson pistol, was the first thing that quickly received everyone's attention. Like the pistol, the third item being held up also received a significant amount of their attention. It was a maroon-colored windbreaker. The fourth item was a partially full resealable plastic bag of white cotton.

Putting the papers he had been holding down on a nearby countertop, Stine said, "Well, lookie at what we just found, boys!" As he held up the windbreaker in front of him, he examined the pockets for anything left inside them. "I'll bet this is the jacket your girl down at the diner told you about. The same one ol' Mr. Pratt's been wearing when he's out murdering folks." Not finding anything inside the pockets, Stine then checked the jacket for any names or identifying marks. "Hey, anyone know who Dennis is? Anyone care to guess if that's someone's first or last name?"

After briefly examining the windbreaker, being cautious as he did not to mar any fingerprints or to lose any hair follicles that might still be present, Stine directed his next thought to no one in particular. He did so as he stared at the pistol Pratt had hidden inside one of the plastic tubs.

"If this is the gun we think it is, then why has our guy left it here for us to find? Even a shithead like Pratt has to be smart enough to realize that once we identified him we'd be getting a warrant to search his home."

"Maybe he only carries it when he's out taking care of business," Paul offered, closely inspecting the weapon without touching it. "Could be he knows we're after him and he didn't want to take a chance of us finding it on him when we caught him. Besides, hiding it under your mobile home in a plastic bin is a pretty safe place to hide it. We found it purely by accident, but I doubt many other cops would have looked as hard for it as we did."

Remembering what Stine had been holding a few minutes earlier caused Bobby Ray to ask, "Those papers I saw you put on the counter before, they anything important?"

"No, not really," Stine replied as a slight smile crept across his face. Picking the papers up to take another brief look at them before telling the others what they were about, he then added, "They're just papers our boy apparently downloaded off some computer someplace, maybe at a library or a friend's house."

"Nothing important about them?" Bobby Ray asked.

"No, not really. They're just your basic instructions on how to construct pipe bombs and other anti-personnel devices. You know, the stuff most people have lying around their homes. Probably just some light reading for him to enjoy while he was sitting on the throne."

Grabbing the papers out of Stine's hands as the others around them laughed over the mental picture of Pratt sitting on the toilet reading instructions on how to build pipe bombs, Bobby Ray immediately knew the importance of what Stine had found. Handing the papers to Vane so they could be included with the other evidence being seized, the Major Case commander said, "This is just another nail in our boy's coffin. Maybe anarchists might do this, but most normal people don't have shit like this lying around their homes. Based on what we already knew about what he had purchased at the hardware store, and everything else we found before Blake found these papers, I have to say I like our guy even more than I already did. Without a doubt, he's the person responsible for all of these murders."

As they gave Uncle Johnny's home a final walk-through to make sure they had not missed anything, Elmendorf and Vane concentrated on the small kitchen as Stine, Scozzafava, and the others focused on the bedrooms, the living room, and the home's one bathroom. Going over the kitchen for a second time, Vane found hidden from view in a large ceramic bowl on top of one of the cabinets four exterior colored photographs of the Myrtle Beach Convention Center and a rough drawing of the facility's loading dock area. The unfinished drawing, done in pencil on a small sheet of white paper, had what appeared to be several reference points and measurements marked on it. After showing what he found to Elmendorf, Vane hollered down the small hallway for Bobby Ray to come see what they had found.

"What the hell's this all about?" Bobby Ray asked as his eyes scanned what Vane had laid out on a section of the kitchen table. "This son of a gun planning something or what?"

Like Stine, Paul focused more on the drawing than he did on the photos. What he saw immediately concerned him. Realizing the importance of what they were looking at, Paul gave Bobby Ray his strongest recommendation possible. It was one Stine and Scozzafava quickly concurred with.

"Bobby Ray, you not only need to get a couple of your folks up there to do some interviews and to flash our sketch of Pratt around with the folks working at the convention center, but you need to contact MBPD ASAP on this so they can start protecting this facility. While you and your folks are out hunting Pratt, MBPD needs to start putting a plan together to protect the convention center and everyone who's using it."

Nodding his head, but saying nothing in response to Paul's suggestion, Bobby Ray walked outside to start advising Renda,

Pascento, and MBPD of what they had just found inside Uncle Johnny's home. After doing so, he contacted Detective Darren Edwards on his cell phone. With three others, Edwards had spent most of the day in Myrtle Beach running down leads concerning Pratt's possible connection with any of the area mosques.

With eleven years of total service with the Georgetown County Sheriff's Department, Edwards had spent the last two years working for Bobby Ray. Large in stature and with a personality nearly as big, the young detective had been a welcome addition to the Major Case Squad. Like most of the others working this investigation, he had also worked the North Litchfield murders several months earlier.

"Darren, you still have Wagner, Nanfito, and Lancelot with you?" Bobby Ray asked after making contact with Edwards.

"Yes, sir. Wags is with me and the other two guys are right down the street finishing up an interview. Need something?"

After advising Edwards of the photos and the drawing of the convention center they had found during the search of Uncle Johnny's home, Bobby Ray directed him and the others to start interviewing the employees working there to determine if they had ever seen Pratt hanging around the facility.

"Listen, I've just contacted the chief's office at MBPD so they know all about this," Bobby Ray advised Edwards. "They're taking this as serious as you and I would so expect to see some of their folks showing up there real soon. It's their show, but work with them. Keep using our sketch, but I'd rather you ask MBPD to print a few copies of Pratt's DMV Blow Back for you guys to use. Flash them both to as many of the convention center employees as possible to see if they've ever seen Pratt there. If they have, get as many details about their encounter with him as possible. I've got my hands full down here, but let me know what you find out."

Soon finished, Bobby Ray moved back inside where the others stood waiting for him. As he did, he saw Vane and Elmendorf had already completed packaging up what they had found within the ceramic bowl.

Realizing the importance of all of the items they had found, especially the windbreaker and the pistol, but also realizing the importance of any DNA evidence that might still be on them, Bobby Ray watched as Vane and Elmendorf carefully packaged the evidence in plastic evidence bags. Slow and meticulous in the approach to what they were doing, they were cautious to protect any transfer or DNA evidence still present. As Bobby Ray expected from two of his most trusted cops, both of whom having more time processing crime scenes than most cops on the job ever would, they had already swabbed the windbreaker's sleeves and chest area for GSR purposes. Both areas had field-tested positive for the presence of nitrates and other chemicals commonly found in gunpowder. When they were finished, Bobby Ray gave his next order to Stine and Scozzafava.

"After these guys get this windbreaker packaged up, tomorrow morning I want you to show it to Betty. Don't unwrap it or anything like that, but let her take a look at it so she can tell you if it's the jacket she told us about. When you do, ask her if she knows who this Dennis guy is."

As he continued to think about what had just been found in Uncle Johnny's kitchen, Paul gave Bobby Ray a couple of suggestions to pass on to MBPD.

"We pretty much know that Pratt is responsible for murdering two men in Murrells Inlet. We also are pretty certain he's responsible for shooting Father Guyette down in Pawleys Island, and we're also pretty sure he's the guy we like for robbing Donna's bank in Garden City, and for hurting her. Now we've just learned that he may have plans to do something else in Myrtle Beach. If we have it figured out correctly, what he's planning to do may be something even more horrific than what he's already done. It's your call, but maybe you need to suggest to MBPD that they should consider programing their surveillance cameras with Pratt's information. They already have a bunch of these cameras mounted at the various intersections in and around the area of the convention center. They use them for other events like Bike Week, so why not use them to our advantage with this mess we're facing. Doing so would obviously give them a heads-up if something happens, especially if Pratt tries returning to the area to do any more surveillance work or, God forbid, something worse. Come to think of it, it also wouldn't be a bad idea if they posted a few of their patrol cars that are equipped with license plate readers in the area. The electronic readers would tell them if Pratt's vehicle is seen approaching the convention center or any other nearby location. The readers will be an even bigger help in the event he tries to do something stupid like mounting his plate on another vehicle. You might want to suggest to them that they should also consider programing their readers with the information that's related to Pratt's vehicle and his uncle's. Not knowing which vehicle he's driving at any given time, I guess it's better for us to be safe than sorry."

Slightly miffed at himself for not coming up with these same ideas, Bobby Ray was still pleased his friend had. "OK, partner, I'll do that. If they haven't already thought of doing this on their own, I'm sure they'll take these suggestions of yours and run with them. I'll give MBPD a call in just a couple of minutes."

* * * * * *

Finished processing Uncle Johnny's mobile home for evidence, and having already made arrangements to have two uniformed deputies posted on the property until further notice, Bobby Ray assigned Griffin and Wilson the responsibility of preparing the arrest warrant application charging Sonny Pratt with the murder of his uncle. Then, with Vane and Elmendorf headed back to the office to process and label the evidence they had seized, including the refrigerator which had held Uncle Johnny's body, Bobby Ray sent the rest of his detectives out to find their suspect.

"He's a sick son of a bitch, a sick and demented cocky son of a bitch who probably thinks he's smarter than we are. That's why I think we're still going to find him in the area, and not in Arkansas or some other godforsaken place. Let's go, I want this prick found tonight!"

As Bobby Ray challenged his detectives to find Pratt, Paul stood off to the side reflecting on the crimes their suspect had recently committed. As he did, his earlier concern flashed through his mind. Suddenly it caused him to break out in a cold sweat. Concerned about his wife, he loudly mumbled, "Oh my God!" Then he ran to his truck.

* * * * * *

Paul's concern over what could happen was a real and viable one, it was also one which now concerned him even more than it had earlier that afternoon. For now, unlike earlier in the day, Pratt's movements were no longer being watched by members of the Georgetown County Sheriff's Department.

26

After the search of Uncle Johnny's mobile home had been completed, Bobby Ray worked like everyone else until nearly four in the morning. As a result, he had only managed to grab a mere three hours of sleep before meeting Paul for breakfast at the Waccamaw Diner. Like the lack of sleep his tired body had been receiving lately, he had eaten little the day before. A lousy tasting chicken sandwich from a fast food restaurant and two Cokes just before the execution of the search warrant, followed by a mild case of indigestion and a handful of Tums, had been the extent of his caloric intake before falling asleep at home very early that morning.

Like his friend, Paul had also experienced a late night at the hospital before falling asleep in the recliner in Donna's room. Concerned about his wife's safety, he had fallen asleep only after placing one of the chairs in his wife's room near her partially closed door. Worried over not hearing someone enter, he had done so hoping the noise of the door striking the chair's metal frame as it was being pushed open would warn him of anyone entering during the night. Despite his own fatigue, and his own failure to eat a proper meal the day before, he was in far better condition than his friend was as they arrived for breakfast. Even without much sleep, after shaving and showering, and after putting on a clean shirt and a pair of pants that he had only worn once since they were last washed, Paul arrived at the diner fresh and happy. For unlike Bobby Ray, Paul knew this particular Saturday was going to be a good day for him and Donna.

After updating Betty on Donna's condition, Paul and Bobby Ray enjoyed the day's first cup of coffee as they waited for their morning meal to arrive. As they did, Bobby Ray told his friend about the lack of success his detectives had experienced during the night concerning their hunt for Pratt.

"We've got BOLOs out on Pratt, on his and his uncle's vehicles, but despite that, and despite the boys humping their asses trying to find this prick, we ended up with squat. I stayed out with them for a good part of the night, but we never even had one lousy sighting of the bastard. MBPD hasn't seen hide nor hair of him either. I mean, you would think we would have found one of the cars parked some place, wouldn't you? The asshole can't be driving both of them at the same time, right?"

His mouth full of warm blueberry pancakes, Paul, at first, only managed to nod his head at Bobby Ray's metaphorical question before washing them down with some coffee so he could speak. After two healthy swigs, he finally managed to say, "You'll find him or the vehicles somehow, Bobby Ray. I'm sure of that. For obvious reasons, you'd rather it was the Tahoe you found first and not the uncle's Impala."

After finishing their first good meal in three days, the two friends sat talking about the investigation before Bobby Ray moved their conversation in another direction. "Hey, let's talk about something else besides this nonsense. Today's the big day, right?" Despite his fatigue, Bobby Ray allowed a wide smile to cross his face.

"Yeah, sure is," Paul said, checking his watch to see where he stood timewise. "I'm meeting with Donna's doctors in just about an hour. So far, they're all pleased by the results from her latest round of tests. So unless there are any last minute changes in her condition that I'm not aware of, the plan is to bring her out of her medically induced coma this afternoon. They've been keeping her sedated with propofol, but, the good Lord willing; she'll be done with that after today."

"Good news, brother, great news actually." Bobby Ray said as he waved for Betty to bring their check over. "Keep me posted when you know more."

"Will do, but I'm not expecting any miracles today. I'm just going to be pleased when she wakes up. To be honest, I'm kind of anxious to see how long it's going to take her to regain consciousness," Paul freely admitted. "Once that happens, the doctors will have a better understanding of any speech problems she may be experiencing or what the degree of loss is with any of her other cognitive skills. Whatever happens is fine. I just want her back with me. I have to be honest with you; I've missed the small things in life ever since she was hurt, like just being able to talk with her." Paul's eyes teared up momentarily as he finished speaking, but it mattered little to him if Bobby Ray or others saw him crying. His wife's condition, good or bad, was all that concerned him now. As he composed himself, Betty returned to their booth to begin clearing away their dishes.

"Seeing what time one of your buddies was here this morning, you boys are kind of getting a late jump on the day, aren't you?" Betty said, setting the breakfast bill down on the booth's table directly in front of Bobby Ray. "He was already here when I pulled into the parking lot at five-fifteen. I don't mind telling you that he scared the bejesus out of me when I saw him standing in the dark by his car. Figured it was somebody up to no-good at first."

While Paul was at a loss over who she was referring to as he had not been told of Stine and Scozzafava's assignment, Bobby Ray knew who it was that Betty was talking about. Despite that, he was puzzled over something he had heard.

"One of our buddies? There should have been two of them who came to see you."

"Nope, just one, the cute one. Blake's his first name. While we were talking earlier, I found out he's single," Betty said with a devious smile on her face.

"What about the windbreaker he showed you, was that the same one you told us about? Was it the one you had seen hanging on the coat rack?" As was to be expected, Bobby Ray was far more interested in hearing about the windbreaker than in Betty's hope of having Stine ask her out.

"I told him it definitely looked like the one I had told y'all about. When we were talking about it, he told me about finding the name inside the windbreaker."

"And?" Bobby Ray asked after a prolonged silence. As he waited impatiently to hear Betty's answer, with his palms up he extended his hands and arms slightly out in front of him. It was another way of asking '*did you recognize the name he gave you?*'

"Well, I told him I don't know any of my customers who use Dennis as their first name. Least, not with me they don't. The only person I know with the last name of Dennis is an old black guy who comes here once in a great while. I barely know him as he's rather quiet, doesn't say much when he's in here, I just call him Peacock like everyone else does. As I understand it, Peacock's a nickname; it's not his given name."

"Thank goodness for that." Paul chuckled.

"The way I understand it, folks started calling him Peacock because he used to raise peacocks for quite a spell, had over two hundred of them at one time out on his property on Sandy Island. I don't think he has many left now. He's kind of getting up there in years."

"Where'd your future husband go after he left from here? Sandy Island, I hope." Bobby Ray asked, teasing Betty at the same time about her interest in Stine.

"Not sure about that, may have, I guess. After what he had for breakfast, I figured he may have gone home and gone back to sleep. I mean, who eats what he ate for breakfast so early in the morning? He must have a cast-iron stomach or something."

Paul laughed at Betty's description of Stine's odd but notable eating habits. Out of curiosity, he asked, "What'd he have for breakfast?"

"Before six this morning, your buddy ate a loaded bacon double-cheeseburger with three pieces of Swiss cheese, a large order of fries, a side order of slaw, and then he washed it all down with a chocolate shake. I'd be sucking on Tums all day if I ate what he ate for breakfast."

Less than five minutes later, as Paul and Bobby Ray finished drinking their coffee, Stine joined them in the booth after speaking with the Dennis family.

Knowing Stine had been out on his own this morning, but also knowing he had assigned Scozzafava to assist him, Bobby Ray asked about the whereabouts of their missing FBI agent. "Where's Tommy Scozz? I told him to help you with what you were doing this morning."

Munching on a small pack of cheese crackers he had opened, Stine explained Scozzafava's absence. "He called me early this morning, around two I think it was. Said the hot water heater in his condo was leaking water all over the place and that he wouldn't be able to make it this morning. Said he had to wait for a plumber friend of his to show up, he's going to meet me later." Still chewing what was left of the crackers in his mouth, Stine added, "Shit like that happens. I didn't want to bother anyone else so early, so I just took care of business on my own. No big deal, I managed to get the info we needed."

"So I guess you had a nice boat ride out to Sandy Island this morning by yourself, didn't you?" Bobby Ray asked, well aware the unincorporated community, one still populated by descendants of former slaves, was only accessible by boat. A newly purchased, but gently used pontoon boat ferried the island's residents and guests, including schoolchildren, to and from the mainland several times a day.

"Sure didn't," Stine answered, nodding his head at Betty who had just set a coffee down in front of him. "Me and boats don't go together. People who ride in boats sometimes drown, and some of them even get bitten by the gators living out there. The real unlucky ones get eaten and that's not going to happen to me."

Trying hard not to laugh over Stine's apparent phobia, one he had not known of before now, Paul asked how he had spoken to Dennis.

"Initially I spoke with his wife on the phone, but then I told her I needed to speak with her at the boat landing, told her it was important." Stine said after picking up his cup to take another sip of the still hot coffee.

"OK, but why her and why not this Peacock fella Betty told us about?"

Stine's face quickly displayed a slight smirk. "Because dead men can't speak, at least the ones I've been around can't."

"Peacock's dead?" Bobby Ray asked without a hint of any emotion. "What the wife have to tell you then?"

"She told me her husband, this Mr. Peacock fellow, died about two weeks ago. Died in his sleep apparently. The old man was ninety-two, spent most of his life working a small farm out on the island and raising peacocks like Betty's told you. Raised other animals as well from what his wife told me, but peacocks and pheasants mostly. When I was finally able to get her to stop talking about their farm animals, I showed her the windbreaker. As soon as she saw it, she positively identified it as being Jerome's, that's Mr. Peacock's given name. She'd like it back when we're done with it, but I told her that may not be for some time. I also asked her about her husband visiting the diner where the coat was stolen from. She claims he went there maybe once or twice a month for a grilled cheese sandwich and a root beer. Sounded like that was a big treat for him. She described the late Mr. Peacock as being a real quiet kind of a guy, never spoke much to strangers so that's why Betty probably didn't know him too well."

"Well, it certainly sounds like ol' Peacock certainly wasn't part of any dastardly plan that our guy is involved in," Paul wisely surmised. "The ol' guy must have simply forgotten his jacket one day when he was here. Guess that gave Pratt the opportunity to steal it."

Several minutes later, as the three of them walked out the front of the diner, Bobby Ray's cell loudly announced an incoming call from Detective Davis.

"Morning, Bruce. You and Jimmy D . . ."

Anxious to give his boss the morning's good news, Davis reluctantly interrupted Bobby Ray's greeting. "Boss . . . we found Pratt! We've got eyes on him now. He's up in the inlet . . . right now he's driving the red Impala, the uncle's car."

Elated by the good news, Bobby Ray quickly excused himself from Paul, wishing his friend good luck for what was going to happen later at the hospital. As the two friends turned to leave in different directions, Bobby Ray hollered a brief vote of confidence to Paul. While what he hollered had something to do with Donna's condition, it mostly had everything to do with his friend's safety. "It's all going to work out like we talked about, but you be careful, hear!"

Pointing his finger at Bobby Ray to acknowledge he had heard his friend's warning, Paul responded by saying, "Yep, I got it. Thanks!"

"And give your pretty wife a kiss for me!"

Finished saying what had to be said as he opened his car door, Bobby Ray was quickly back on the phone with Davis.

"Bruce, you guys stay with him for now. I'm going to get Griff and Wilson, and maybe a couple of the others headed your way. Keep me posted with any changes. I'm coming your way with Blake as soon as I'm done on the phone. I just need to give Pascento and Sheriff Renda a quick update."

* * * * * *

Wanting to let Paul's hunch play out, Bobby Ray made a gutsy call. Instead of having Pratt arrested, something that would have pleased Sheriff Renda greatly, he chose to have the surveillance teams stay on the red Impala for the balance of the day. As they did, the two teams switched vehicles several times in an effort to keep their suspect off guard.

As they continued to follow, both teams took notice as their suspect slowly drove the Impala through one particular neighborhood on four separate occasions. Despite the Chevy's heavily tinted windows, it was Wilson and Griffin who first picked up on one important observation; quickly they advised Bobby Ray of what they and the others had observed.

At 2 pm, both teams watched their suspect park the vehicle he was driving in a Walmart parking lot just off the Garden City Connector. Moments later, the teams watched as Pratt, dressed in an orange-colored sweatshirt, brown cargo pants, and wearing a Red Sox hat, walked inside the large box store through an entrance located next to the garden center.

Parking their vehicles in different sections of the large parking lot so they could keep the store's entrances and exits under constant surveillance, while at the same time maintaining a close watch on the vehicle Pratt had been driving, Wilson and Griffin waited for their suspect to emerge from the store. As they did, Bobby Ray slipped into the backseat of Wilson's Ford Taurus. Nearby in another section of the large parking lot, Davis and Dzamko also waited anxiously for the rest of the afternoon to play out.

"I don't know about you guys, but I'm feeling a whole lot better this afternoon since Bruce called me with the news that he and Jimmy D had found our guy," Bobby Ray said as his eyes scanned the large parking lot around him. As he did, the veteran cop made sure there were no counter-surveillance operations setup watching them as they targeted their suspect.

"Yeah, boss, we know how you feel," Wilson replied, his eyes never moving off the store's exit he was watching. "Let's just hope we don't lose this stupid prick again."

"If we do, I guess you'll both be working for someone else pretty soon." Bobby Ray replied, chuckling lightly over the situation now confronting him.

"Sounds like Renda is not too pleased by the call you've made, that about right?" Griffin asked.

"That's the polite way of putting it, Griff. He calmed down a bit after I told him why I wanted to follow Pratt a bit longer, but it's safe to say if this thing blows up in my face I won't be on the sheriff's Christmas card list any longer."

"Screw him! He needs to grow a pair. That's why we all like working for you, boss. You aren't afraid to take chances when the situation warrants," Wilson said, offering up an honest opinion of how he and the others thought about their current boss. "Most people in your position would have gone for the kill, the easy way to end this mess we're all so tired of working. But you haven't done that. Personally, I'm not sure why you didn't, but I'm confident you'll tell us why when you're ready. Besides, I hear Renda's Christmas cards aren't that special anyhow. You won't miss getting one."

Like Griffin, Bobby Ray laughed at Wilson's subtle comment about Renda canning him if things went wrong with the day's surveillance of their suspect.

"I received some other good news this morning after I called you guys," Bobby Ray offered up as he watched Griffin turn around to look at him from where he sat in the passenger's seat. "One of the forensic scientists I know up at SLED called me with the results of the tests they ran on the residue Stine found in O'Keefe's driveway. Looks like he and Paul were right, turned out the residue tested positive for nitrates found in gunpowder."

"How'd they determine that?" Griffin asked.

"Pretty sophisticated testing, that's how. Those guys at the lab are pretty slick, a heck of a lot smarter than the three of us. I was told they dissolved the samples Donnie and Doug found in the driveway in a solution called diphenylamine and then the solution was examined under a Scanning Electron Microscope . . . it's commonly referred to as a SEM E-Dex microscope . . ."

"A what?" Griffin asked as he stared incredulously at Bobby Ray.

"A Scanning Electron Microscope, one with a Dispersive Reaction Analyzer which has the capability of detecting elements like sulphur, potassium, and combined potassium, that's a combination of both nitrates and sulphur. Then once those particles were found, and obviously in our sample they were, SLED conducted a micro-chemical test by applying a nitron chemical reagent to the solution being tested on a slide under the microscope. It was on that particular slide they found the presence of what they have referred to as spikes, something always present in nitrates found in gunpowder."

"You're shitting me, right?" Like his partner, Griffin sat open-mouthed as he stared back at their boss. "All I wanted to hear was that they had found the shit we wanted them to find after looking at it under one of their fancy freaking microscopes. I wasn't looking for a lecture on the chemical components of gunpowder, nor did I have to hear about whatever kind of microscope it was they had used." Griffin burst out laughing as he looked at his partner and then back at Bobby Ray. "How the frig did you remember all of that bullshit anyhow?"

"Impressive, aren't I? Sometimes I even impress myself. If you'd like me to, I can amaze you even more by reciting the tabular arrangement of the periodic table." Bobby Ray said jokingly before joining the others in a quick laugh. Then he added, "At least we know what our arsonist mixed with the gasoline when he set O'Keefe's truck on fire."

Then Bobby Ray told them the other good news he had learned. "When I was riding up here, I was also told by one of SLED's firearms examiners the S&W .22 we found was the same weapon that fired the shell casings and slugs we've found. The markings on the shell casings and the bullets have all been positively matched to this pistol. After test-firing the pistol they were able to positively match the markings on the test casings to the marking on the ones the guys found at the church. But that's not even the best news I have for you. The best news is they found Pratt's prints on the gun barrel, and a partial print of his on the trigger guard. You know what that means, right?"

"Yeah, sure do." Griffin answered as he opened the window next to him to let in some fresh air. "It means the pistol and the bullets were both at the church when our priest got whacked. More importantly, it means Pratt was inside the church as well."

"Correctamundo!" Bobby Ray said smiling. "The cotton is a different story for now as they can't say definitively yet that the cotton we found at the church matches the stuff we found at Pratt's home. They're still giving it a go, but they aren't confident they'll be able to say with any certainty it's an exact match. That's OK, we've got the other good stuff all sealed up just like we wanted."

Concerned their suspect had now been out of sight for nearly fifteen minutes, Bobby Ray radioed the third surveillance team with instructions on what he wanted done. Unlike the other two teams, Detectives Ron Nanfito and Doug Lancelot were parked around the corner in a Walgreens parking lot. Working together off and on throughout their careers, the two detectives had been friends since joining the GCSD seventeen years earlier. Like his friend, Nanfito was normally assigned to other duties within the department, serving as one of two detectives in the department's Juvenile Division. Now, due to manpower needs, he and Lancelot, the head of the department's K9 Unit, were temporarily assigned to the investigation for the remainder of it.

"Ron, you copy?" Bobby Ray asked Nanfito over the encrypted radio channel.

"Yes, sir, loud and clear," Nanfito answered enthusiastically, clearly excited over working a surveillance of this magnitude for the first time in quite a while. Unlike most of his fellow detectives, Nanfito was a fairly impressionable cop who was still full of piss and vinegar. Like he was on most days, the former navy petty officer was eager to get to work.

"I want you two guys to change your position." Bobby Ray said before pausing to survey the parking lot he was sitting in for a good place to situate the third surveillance team. "Park off to the far left of the store's main entrance, and then I want just you to walk inside and find our guy. He's been out of view for far too long now. Go find him and then call me on my cell, but don't let this prick know you're watching him."

"Roger that. Stand by."

Within minutes, Nanfito was inside the large retail store trying to find Pratt. Growing concerned several minutes later after unsuccessfully sweeping the store twice, Nanfito was about to call Bobby Ray with the disturbing news when he caught sight of a male walking away from one of the check-out lines. Seeing the orange sweatshirt as it moved towards the exit, he called Bobby Ray with an update. As he did, Wilson and Griffin listened to what one of the investigation's newest detectives was telling their boss.

"Boss, our guy is walking outside right now. I saw him as he was leaving, but I didn't have a chance to get a good look at his face due to where I was when I saw him. It has to be him though; he's wearing the orange sweatshirt the guys saw him wearing before. He's also wearing a pair of tan cargo pants and a shitty-looking Red Sox hat. Unless you tell me otherwise, I'll hang back in the store for a couple of moments so our guy doesn't see me eyeballing him."

With his ears already perked up over Nanfito's description of the male walking out of the store, Bobby Ray issued his next set of instructions over his portable radio. As he did, Wilson and Griffin watched as the male in the orange sweatshirt weaved his way through several rows of parked cars.

"Bruce, you and Jimmy D see our guy yet?" Bobby Ray asked anxiously.

"Our view of him isn't the greatest, but we've got him. He just threw on a pair of tinted sunglasses," Davis replied from where he sat two rows away from the red Impala Pratt had been driving. "He's less than twenty feet from his car and headed straight for it."

Pleased to again have their suspect in sight, Bobby Ray barked his next set of instructions to the surveillance teams. "Bruce, you two guys pick him up as he leaves. I'll have Nanfito and Lancelot follow you guys, but they're going to hang back until you tell them to take the lead. Griff and Wilson will be tagging along a mile or so behind you guys, so use them when you need them. Keep me posted on my cell of any problems. I've got a couple of things that need taking care of."

"OK, sounds good. We're making a left out of the parking lot as we speak and headed west on the connector towards the by-pass," Davis replied before making sure the back-up teams heard what he had just said.

* * * * * *

As the others headed off to follow their suspect, Bobby Ray soon left to make plans so he was ready to prevent Pratt's next attack from occurring. But before he did, unlike the others who had been with him in the parking lot, he radioed Stine a set of instructions. He did so as he had picked up on something Nanfito had said when their suspect walked out of Walmart. Smiling to himself as he patiently waited for the right moment, he thought, "Looks like Paul got it right again."

Inside the large box store, someone else grinned as he watched the caravan of vehicles exiting the parking lot. They had reacted just as he expected they would. All that is, except for one of them.

27

Less than an hour after leaving the Walmart parking lot, Bobby Ray was contacted by Detective Edwards regarding the interviews he and the others had conducted at the Myrtle Beach Convention Center.

"Boss, it's like I told you yesterday after we got done speaking with the staff members who were there, outside of confirming that the drawing you guys found was actually one of the loading dock area, we didn't learn much more today. That's until we spoke with a guy by the name of Sal Abbott, then our luck changed."

"Praise the Lord!" Bobby Ray joked, thankful for finally hearing some good news for a change.

"Just like we had done when we spoke with several of Sal's fellow employees, we showed him both the sketch and Pratt's photo when we started talking with him about an hour ago. To say that opened the floodgates would be an understatement as this Sal fellow told us that not only did he recognize Pratt, but he also told us he threw him off the property four days ago after seeing him acting funny near the loading dock area. Sal here claims to have seen Pratt jotting down some notes on a piece of paper after he watched him pace off a few measurements by the loading dock area. I'm guessing that's probably the same piece of paper Vane found. Anyhow, when Sal challenged him on what he was doing, Pratt tried telling him he was there working on an estimate to power wash the rear of the convention center where all the delivery trucks drop off their loads. Right away Sal said he knew Pratt was lying to him because he knows the convention center's maintenance staff does all of that kind of work themselves, they never hire any sub-contractors to do work like that."

"This Sal guy ever tell anyone about seeing Pratt acting suspiciously?" Bobby Ray asked.

"No, he didn't. He realizes now he should have done just that, but at the time he was satisfied when he saw Pratt leave."

"Is he sure the person he looked at in the sketch is the same guy he gave the boot to that day?" Bobby Ray asked, assuming it was the sketch, and not Pratt's photo, that Edwards' newest witness had made the positive ID from.

"Yep, one hundred percent. Even told us when he watched Pratt leave, he saw him driving away in a Chevy Tahoe. The good thing is he mentioned the make and model of Pratt's vehicle before we could even bring it up. Pretty hard to believe it wasn't Pratt he saw."

"Guess you're right about that, Darren. He tell you anything else that's helpful?"

"No, sir. He did give us a pretty good description of Pratt though; it's one that matches the description of our guy pretty damn close."

"OK, that's fine. MBPD on top of all of this, I hope?"

"Like stink on you know what," Edwards replied, doing so more politely than a few of Bobby Ray's other cops would have done.

"They're taking this real serious, just as we had hoped they would. I was just told a few minutes ago they're planning on posting two cops per shift here until Pratt is found. They've also taken our sketch, as well as Pratt's DMV photo, and printed a mess of them for their folks to take out on patrol. The plan is for their street cops to show them to as many people as possible. Likewise, I also believe they've sent copies of both to every in-car computer they have, and they've posted other copies in each of their various commands. Just before I called you, I updated Deputy Chief Carney and one of MBPD's PIO staff members on what we've recently learned from our witness. Carney is on his way right now to meet with his boss and Mayor Polk about what I've told him. I don't know about you, but I'm not sure we could them ask to be doing anything more than what they're already doing. They want Pratt as bad as we do."

"Guess not," Bobby Ray admitted. "OK, you guys keep working that angle up there. Give MBPD any help they need. Call me if anything pops."

******

As Edwards and Bobby Ray spoke, less than two miles from the convention center, Sonny Pratt was cruising the area around the eastern end of Highway 501. As he did, he finally located the run-down three-bay garage he had been told about. Parking his vehicle in the parking lot of a strip club the courts had recently ordered closed due to its presence being considered a blight on the neighborhood, Pratt took notice of his surroundings. Dotted with a variety of adult bookstores, as well as with a handful of bars which only hookers and other low-lifes frequented, as well as a few ethnic restaurants, the neighborhood was one that tourists paid little attention to. Like nearby Seaboard Street, 3rd Avenue

South, a busy two-lane street running from Highway 501 to Highway 17 on its eastern end, was the home of several small ethnic and minority-owned businesses. On a daily basis, in one of the most depressed neighborhoods in Myrtle Beach, they each struggled hard to stay open. Up and down the street, a variety of older homes, many unkempt in their appearances, also lined the busy thoroughfare.

Eating a pre-packaged breakfast pastry he had purchased earlier from a nearby mini-mart, Pratt watched as several customers came and went from the garage that two local mechanics rented space at. As he expected from a run-down location crammed with a variety of vehicles which had all seen better days, those he saw working there or bringing their vehicles in for repairs were not well off. Having worked and lived with the same kind of people he now saw coming and going from the garage, it was easy for him to tell the customers he was watching were not the kind who would call the cops, AAA, or anyone else if the repairs to their vehicles had not been done to their satisfaction. Doing so, in a neighborhood full of illegal immigrants, would only cause unwanted attention being directed at them, their families, and at others living nearby.

More interested in those who came to the garage for other reasons, Pratt sat amused as several males and two females came and went after briefly interacting with a surprisingly tall and well-built Mexican male. In the not too far distant past, Sonny Pratt had lived the lifestyle he was now watching. As such, he knew the purpose of each brief handshake that now took place across the street. Unlike the mechanics he saw working there, the Mexican's clothes, despite being ridiculously colorful, were clean, pressed and very neat in their appearance. While the mechanics did most of their work inside the building, Pratt quickly determined the male he was watching did not. Like several other vehicles parked there, the Mexican's office was an older model Ford Explorer whose right front tire was missing. In its place, a large cinder block kept the vehicle propped up.

Waiting for the right moment, Pratt soon walked across the street. As he did, his eyes stayed focused on his target.

"Yo, you Taco?" Pratt asked the Mexican he had been watching. As he did, his eyes scanned the area around the poor excuse of a repair facility. Like everyone else who was there, Pratt had little interest in being confronted by any undercover cops.

"Who wants to know?" Rueben Hernandez, an illegal from Rio Rico, Mexico, asked in broken English. Better known to his family and street friends as Taco, the twenty-nine-year-old's nickname had been placed on him years earlier due to his fondness for eating large quantities of the Mexican delicacy bearing the same name. From his size, it was easy to tell Taco's fondness for the folded corn tortillas had not diminished.

"Doesn't really matter, does it?" Pratt asked, his eyes still scanning the high-crime neighborhood for cops and unseen trouble. "All that matters is this." Held in place by two rubber bands, Pratt held up a fairly thick green roll of twenties and fifties he had pulled out of one of his pants pockets. The roll of cash equaled nine hundred dollars.

"Looking for love?" Taco asked, barely paying any attention to the money the white boy in front of him was holding up.

"Something like that, bro, but not the shit you're selling out of that ride of yours," Pratt said, referring to the small bags of cocaine and crack Taco was dealing. Nodding at the Explorer, he added, "Those days are over for me. I'm looking for something else, and I want you to get it for me."

Still not sure of whom he was dealing with, Taco remained quiet, leaving the stranger in front of him to do most of the talking.

"I was told you can get things for people, things like that," Pratt said, pointing at a rusty old Toyota pick-up truck parked on the edge of the garage's property.

"Why you interested in a piece of junk like that?" Taco asked, his strong accent still present despite years of living north of the border. Leaning against the Explorer as he gave the stranger in front of him the once-over for a second time, his eyes glanced twice at the roll of bills being casually tossed in the air. Almost immediately, the streetwise entrepreneur recognized the opportunity now confronting him. Quickly his opinion of the rusty old pick-up changed dramatically. "It may not look like much, but that's a fine ride, amigo. Things like that cost money, so does my time. My interest in helping you get what you want, that's if I have any, that costs even more. Comprende, my friend?"

"Comprende, bro. That's what this is for." Pratt said, casually tossing the rolled up bills in the air as if he was playing catch with a ball.

Sensing an opportunity to make a fast buck off someone who vaguely looked familiar to him for some reason, Taco took a gamble on the situation confronting him.

"You got a name for me, Holmes?" Taco asked, still somewhat suspicious of why Pratt had come to see him. "And one more thing, before you tell me something that's pure bullshit about why you need a ride like that, you best not be a cop." Nodding in the direction of where his own lookout stood watching over him, Taco warned Pratt about messing with him. "Because if you are, badge or no badge, payback is going to be a bitch. Hear me?"

Pratt smiled for a moment after hearing the threat that had been directed at him. "No worries here, my man. I've got my own problems; I'm not about bringing any down on you. This is strictly a business deal to benefit both of us, but just one thing, amigo," Pratt said as he took a step closer to the Mexican standing in front of him, "don't screw with me either, Taco. You don't know shit about me, but trust me when I tell you this. Mamacita isn't going to be too happy with you if you can't keep delivering the mail to her. Comprende?"

As Pratt had, Taco smiled at Pratt's threat of harming a part of his anatomy if he screwed with him. The other thing it told him was that the white boy was not a cop.

"OK, Holmes," Taco said, trying to talk more like a gangster than he actually was. "How much you got for that truck you want? And, when you need it by?"

Tossing the rolled up bills to Taco, Pratt told him what he was looking for. "I don't need anything fancy. Just make sure it has a plate on it and that it runs." Then pointing across the street at a pick-up that had just pulled into the parking lot of a small bodega whose window signs advertised a variety of Mexican, Guatemalan and Hispanic food items on sale, Pratt made two more requests concerning his needs.

"See that large plastic container sitting in the bed of that truck? That's used for water and other shit by losers who power wash homes for a living."

Smirking at Pratt's description of what the plastic container was used for as he counted the bills that had been rolled up, Taco quickly snapped at Pratt as he slid the money into one of his pockets. "You think I don't know what that thing is used for, white boy? You think I'm stupid because I'm a Mexican, is that it? Besides, my cousin, he power washes lots of things, homes and boats mostly. Are you also saying he's a loser like them other people?"

"He is what he is, bro," Pratt said, refusing to be intimidated by Taco. "Listen, when you deliver my truck, I'll expect to find one of those containers in the bed. I don't care if it's dented or anything like that, just as long as it doesn't leak."

Laughing over the additional demands being placed on him, Taco shook his head as he pulled Pratt's money back out of his pocket. "Nine hundred for a truck, that's something I can do, my man. But I ain't in the FedEx or pressure washing business. Those are extras, bro, expensive extras."

"This cover your time and one of those containers?" Pratt asked, unfolding a sheet of white paper before handing it to Taco. On the paper was a photocopy of a .357 Colt Python.

Eyeing the photo, and then Pratt, Taco asked, "This hot?"

"Very. That matter?" Like others like it, the Colt had been missing from Fort Bragg for several years.

Realizing the position of power he had over Pratt in negotiating a deal for the truck, Taco countered with an offer of his own. "If this is hot, then I'll need two of them to make it all happen like you want. The way I'm looking at it, I'm the one taking all the risks."

"Nine hundred, the Colt, and a S&W .357 that's in mint condition. That's my offer, take it or leave it." Pratt growled, growing tired of haggling with someone he had little respect for.

"Where's it going and how am I getting the balance of what you owe me?"

Handing Taco a slip of paper with an address and a unit number written on it, Pratt explained how he wanted the deal to play out. "That's the number of a storage unit I just rented in Murrells Inlet. When I stop by there later today, I'll expect to find everything I want inside it. There's a lock on it already." Reaching into one of his pockets, Pratt handed Taco a key. "Inside the unit you'll find your two presents inside a plastic box, it'll be the only thing that's there. When you're done doing what you have to do, leave the key for the lock on the truck's front seat. Put the lock back in place just like you found it. That work?"

"Works fine. It'll all be there by six this evening."

Not bothering to shake hands with his new business partner, Pratt smiled, nodded at Taco's other partner, and then walked back across the street to where he had parked his Tahoe. Pleased by the deal he had worked out; Pratt was out of the run-down neighborhood in less than three minutes.

******

After watching Pratt drive away, Taco gave his lookout friend several instructions. With his friend soon on his way to find a truck to steal, Taco walked the short distance to the small neighborhood restaurant he often ate his lunch at. Walking inside Fajitas y Albondigas Mexican Restaurant, a small family-run business whose customer base was mostly a mix of Mexicans, Latinos and Guatemalans living and working in the area, Taco ordered a cold cerveza after placing his order to go.

As he enjoyed his beer, Taco's attention was drawn to a poster mounted on one of the walls just inside the restaurant's front door. While the large *Reward for Information* wording at the top of the poster was what initially attracted his attention, the artist's sketch of a white male the police were looking for caused him to inspect the wanted poster up close.

"I knew I had seen your ugly face some place, amigo," Taco thought to himself as he read the rest of the wording on the poster hanging in front of him. "Perhaps you are a bad hombre like you said you were."

Smiling as he pulled his cell phone out of one of his back pockets, Taco's eyes continued to study the sketch mounted in the middle of the poster as he waited for his call to be answered.

"Talk to me, Taco. You have something good for me?" The male voice on the other end of the call asked.

"Yeah, something *very* good for both of us. Maybe the best thing ever. But not on the phone, you know where I'll be. Remember . . . I like Benjamins the best, new ones especially."

* * * * * *

Rueben 'Taco' Hernandez was fussy about many things in life. The one thing he was not fussy about was who lined his pockets with pictures of dead presidents. Like many others, he had a special fondness for crispy new Benjamins, even those he collected from the cops.

<u>28</u>

Paged by one of the ICU nurses after she had seen the first real sign of Donna regaining consciousness, Donna's doctors stood quietly with Paul as he gently spoke to his wife, trying to coax her out of her extended rest.

"Paul . . . Paul," Donna softly uttered, momentarily gasping for breath after being temporarily taken off oxygen for the first time in weeks. With her throat dry and irritated, Donna's raspy sounding voice scared Paul at first. Sounding as if she had a bad sore throat, the irritation in her throat had first been caused by the presence of an early feeding tube, and then by the prolonged presence of a tracheal tube that had helped to maintain the proper exchange of oxygen and carbon dioxide during her induced coma. Confused and disorientated, and still far too groggy despite being weaned off the narcotic which had helped to keep her brain activity reduced from what it normally was, Donna tried speaking one more time. "Paul, what's . . . what's happened to me? Where . . . where am I?"

Holding his wife's hand, Paul gently kissed Donna's forehead before speaking. "Honey, you're in the hospital. You've have had a bad accident, but you're fine now. I'll tell you everything you want to know later on, but for now I'm going to let Dr. Ellis and Dr. Tillengast speak with you. Dr. Engle is here also, she's been watching out for you just as these two fine gentlemen have been doing." Pausing to nod at the others gathered around her bed, Paul finished by saying, "Don't worry, I'll be right here just like I have been."

Aware their patient would likely only be awake for a short period of time, and far too fatigued to comprehend much of anything they told her, Donna's small team of doctors did little more than reassure their patient that she was doing well. Moments later, as Donna drifted back to sleep, her doctors spoke with Paul in the hallway outside her room.

"Paul, not to understate the obvious, but the good news is Donna has woken up. As you saw, she's still beat-up and exhausted from what her body has been put through, but I'm optimistic from what little I've seen so far." Ellis said as he looked back into the room where Donna was already fast asleep.

As was his nature, Dr. Tillengast spoke slightly more cautiously, not wanting to give Paul a false sense that his wife was totally out of the woods from her serious and still lingering medical problems. "Paul, let's just leave it that I'm pleased by what little I heard your wife say a few moments ago. I'm actually more pleased by how easily she said what she did than what it was she said. I hope that makes sense to you. Her first few words were clear and easy to understand, that's a positive start. When she gains a little more strength, maybe by late Monday afternoon, we'll run her through a couple of easy mental tasks so we can monitor her brain activity. Doing so will help us determine what, if any, impact her injury has had on her cognitive skills. Unless I hear of a problem she's experiencing over the weekend, I'll be back to see her with Dr. Ellis around two or so on Monday afternoon. We'll know more then for sure." Tillengast had barely finished speaking when Ellis, a bit of a techie, opened up the scheduling icon on his iPhone 6 and began populating his calendar with the date and time he and his colleague planned on seeing their patient next.

After stressing to Paul the importance of not taxing his wife's physical and mental endurance over the next several days, the three doctors left to attend to their other patients.

Ten minutes later, as Paul stood at the foot of his wife's bed watching her sleep, Donna woke for a brief few minutes. Quietly, in a room that had been left somewhat dark to lessen the impact on her eyes, Donna stared at Paul's face. In the darkness of her room, and still somewhat woozy from her meds, it took her a few moments to recognize her husband.

"Paul, . . . is that you?" Donna asked softly, barely getting the words through her dry and parched lips as she awkwardly tried pushing the oxygen mask off her mouth.

Moving to the left side of his wife's bed, Paul placed a cold damp washcloth against his wife's lips, allowing her to gently suck some of the water out of it. "Welcome back, honey, I've missed you. You had me scared there for a while." Like he had done several minutes earlier, he again bent down and kissed Donna's forehead. Stroking her cheek with his right hand, he talked to her about the many floral arrangements and get well cards their family and friends had sent her.

"Paul, I can feel the casts on my arm and leg, and I know my head is wrapped in some kind of bandages, but am I . . ." Tears filled Donna's eyes as she tried finishing a question she was afraid to ask.

"You're going to be just fine," Paul said, trying to reassure his wife that all was well. "A couple of weeks of some good rest, followed by a couple or three weeks of occupational therapy and who knows what else, and you'll be doing cartwheels again."

Smiling for the first time in weeks, Donna gently chided her husband for fibbing to her. "I . . . I could never do cartwheels before, so what makes you think I'll be able to do them now?"

Chatting for a few more brief moments, Donna asked her husband the question any mother would ask after not seeing or talking to her children for an extended period of time. "The boys . . . are they OK? Do they know what's happened to me?" As she finished speaking, Donna coughed twice due to the dryness still in her throat.

Reassuring his wife their sons were doing well, and that they would both be down to see her by the end of the week, Paul wisely suggested she needed to rest. "I'll be right here when you wake up, but for now you need to sleep."

As Donna drifted off to sleep, Paul sat down in the recliner next to her bed. After finished texting his sons with the day's good news about their mother, he put his head back to allow his tired mind to have time to rest. He had barely closed his eyes when a gentle knock on the door aroused him from his brief rest. Opening his eyes, he saw Ray Smith standing just inside Donna's room.

"You ready to do this, Paul?" Smith whispered, asking his question with a big smile on his face.

Careful not to disturb his sleeping wife as he rose from his chair, Paul walked to where Smith stood. 'Been waiting on you, my friend. You take care of everything?"

Walking back out into the hallway, Smith pointed at a room diagonally across the hall from Donna's. Doing so partially answered his new friend's question. "That's going to be her new home for the next week or so. I've got everything else we need setup in the room to the right of hers. Before we get started, I want to show you something. Follow me."

Walking into the room adjacent to where his wife was going to be moved to, Paul saw Smith had set it up perfectly. Three closed circuit television monitors were already up and running; their split screens capturing the live feed sent to them from ten CCTV cameras situated in different locations across the hospital's property. Next to them a digital recorder was already at work making a permanent record of what the monitors were displaying. A remote sitting next to one of the monitors allowed Smith to turn on or off any number of the hospital's other cameras that were ready to feed the monitors with a live view from any other location than the ones currently being displayed. It would also allow him to disable or isolate any camera he chose to. On a small table setup in the room, Smith pointed to another monitor. "Take a look at this."

For the next few minutes, Paul stared at the monitor as Smith played video footage of an incident he had not yet seen until now. It was footage of what had caused he and Smith to now be standing where they were, and to be doing what they were about to do. "Thought you'd like to see that before the party starts," Smith said as the previously recorded footage of Pratt arguing with the hospital volunteers came to an end.

"Yeah, I did. I appreciate that. If your intention for showing me that was to motivate me even more than I already am, it worked. Thanks."

A gentle rap on the door caused both men to look in the direction of where two male nurses now stood. Between them, the ICU's head nurse stood with her hands on her hips as she peered over the top of her glasses looking at Paul and Smith. Dressed in her white uniform, an outfit most nurses no longer wore, Nurse Mary Sullivan's red eyeglass frames sat perched on the end of her nose as she briefly stared at the equipment that had been setup in a room normally occupied by one of her patients. A nurse for over twenty years, Sullivan had already been briefed on what was about to unfold within her unit. Then, just moments before the chaos was about to begin, she confidently spoke to the two cops standing a few feet away. "The cavalry just arrived. You ready for our help?"

Twenty minutes later, with two machines still monitoring her vital signs and with a stainless steel stand holding two plastic IV bags which were still delivering pain medication to his wife, Donna's bed was carefully rolled across the hallway to her new room. As it was, Paul wheeled the stand carrying the medication Donna still needed for pain and to help her sleep. After pushing her bed in place, the three nurses made sure the monitors and IV lines were operating properly. As they did, Paul and Smith wheeled an empty bed into Donna's former room.

"What time you think this is going to happen?" Smith asked, glancing at his watch after making sure everything was ready.

"Not sure, but I'm guessing sometime after seven tonight, not much after that I wouldn't think." As he spoke, Paul looked to see if either Stine or Scozzafava had texted him to let him know when to expect them. As he did, and almost as if on cue, both cops came walking through the ward's double set of automatic doors.

Closing the door to Donna's former room so they did not disturb the operations of the ICU ward any more than they already had, and to give them the privacy they needed, Paul finalized the night's plan with his three friends. Looking at the hospital's director of security as he finished going over the plan, Paul asked, "Got it with you, Ray?"

* * * * * *

Several miles away, Bobby Ray's detectives watched from a distance as the suspect they had been following sat parked in a restaurant parking lot across from the MarshWalk in Murrells Inlet.

"What's this asshole doing?" Dzamko asked his partner, frustrated by their suspect's recent lack of movement and by the Impala's deeply tinted windows. The deep tint rendered useless the binoculars the young detective was trying to use. "He's been sitting there for at least an hour, maybe longer. Think he's waiting for someone?"

Davis sat quiet for another moment before answering. Like his partner, he had also been wondering similar thoughts. "Not sure what he's doing, maybe just killing time, who knows. Guess we'll find out soon enough, won't we?"

Less than five minutes later the driver's door window of the car they were watching was partially lowered to allow a cigarette butt to be flicked outside. As this happened, the two cops, along with their back-up team, managed to catch a brief glimpse of the driver's head as he answered a call on his cell. Two minutes later, with the cell call terminated the red Impala was on the move.

"Team two to teams one and three, we're mobile." Davis said over the secure radio channel. "He's headed south down Business 17. Stand by for further updates."

* * * * * *

With their suspect again in motion, Bobby Ray began putting his plan in gear. As he did, he let Paul know what was happening.

29

Earlier that afternoon, Bobby Ray had spent time listening to what his surveillance teams were telling him regarding their suspect's movements. As he did, he had paid close attention when they referenced the point about having seen their suspect's vehicle pause each time he drove by one particular residence on Planters Trace Loop in Murrells Inlet. Doing so not only convinced him their suspect had selected this particular home to be his next target, but also convinced him their suspect's next attack was likely only hours away.

Calling ahead to make sure the owners were home, Bobby Ray had Griffin and Wilson meet him at the small home owned by Jim and Gail Barone. The neat but simple home, located at 186 Planters Trace Loop, was situated just off of Wachesaw Road and just east of a recent roundabout the county had built at a nearby busy intersection. Highway 17, the main traffic artery running north to south through the Grand Strand, sat slightly more than a stone's throw away from the Barone residence.

As the three cops exited their vehicles, Bobby Ray easily saw what had attracted the attention of both their suspect and the surveillance team members earlier that afternoon. Approaching the pick-up truck owned by Jim Barone, Bobby Ray paused to view the bumper stickers displayed on the left side of the truck's rear bumper. The colorful stickers, mostly done in red and white, reflected their owner's support of two organizations who quite often did not receive the same type of support from others. As he stared at the two stickers, one supporting the right to fly the Confederate flag and the other extremely pro-NRA in its wording, Bobby Ray nodded his head as he spoke to the two detectives standing by his side. "I've got to give it to this guy for standing up for what he believes in. These bumper stickers, as well as that Confederate flag I see mounted by his front door, are not the most popular symbols to be supporting these days." As he spoke, a bright red and white nylon version of the Stars and Bars flapped gently in the wind from where it was mounted against the light brown-colored vinyl siding of the Barone residence.

Meeting with the Barones, a childless couple in their late forties, Bobby Ray explained why he and the others had come to see them. As he did, he tactfully outlined, in some detail but not fully, three of the four recent murders that had occurred. For now, because of a couple of reasons he felt reluctant to publicly talk about, he chose not to tell them about the murder of Father Guyette. What he soon explained to the couple frightened Gail, but only served to incense her husband, an individual extremely proud of his family's Southern heritage. Like most men, he was someone who was equally as proud of his ability to defend his home.

Despite his desire to stand his ground, Jim Barone, who was coughing and sneezing badly from the annual influx of pine pollen which had just begun to invade the area, agreed to cooperate with Bobby Ray's request for him and his wife to leave their home for the next two days. In doing so, he gave Bobby Ray permission to use their home to whatever degree was needed so he could put an end to the recent violence occurring in the area.

"I recall reading about that lady who was run over in the bank parking lot recently," Gail Barone volunteered as she and her husband spoke with Bobby Ray near the Confederate flag displayed in the front of their home. Off to the side, Wilson and Griffin listened intently to what was being said. "Do you folks really believe this crazy nut did that to her intentionally?"

"Yes, we do." Wilson confidently replied. "In fact, we're sure of it."

"Then shoot the son of a bitch right here on my front lawn and let's put an end to this asshole's life!" Jim Barone's loud voice offered after again wiping his nose from sneezing due to the pollen problem.

* * * * * *

With the Barones safely tucked away at a relative's home in the Carolina Forest section of Myrtle Beach, and with the neighbors on either side of their residence advised of what might happen later that evening, Bobby Ray began putting his personnel in place. Knowing their first victim had been murdered shortly after sunset, and wanting his detectives manning their posts prior to that time period, six detectives on foot, supported by four others on roving patrol, soon took their assigned positions. Doing so while it was still light out allowed each of them time to acclimate themselves with their immediate surroundings. This was especially critical for those assigned to a specific post in either the Barone's yard or in one of their neighbors' yards.

As twilight soon turned to dusk, Bobby Ray waited, albeit impatiently, in the darkness alongside the Barone's garage for the expected to happen. As the others with him adhered to his order of maintaining radio silence, the minutes slowly passed. As they did, barely any activity stirred out on the narrow road less than sixty feet away from where he stood.

Then, nearly an hour later than when the first murder had occurred, a loud scream from the front yard of a nearby home pierced the night's stillness. Immediately it changed the focus of the cops guarding the Barone residence.

30

Sitting in his living room reading after working a day of overtime at the local golf course he worked at, Joseph Horn was happy just to be relaxing at home for the evening. With his wife, Maria, a nurse at Waccamaw Hospital, at work, and his daughter, Jenna, a nineteen-year-old sophomore at Coastal Carolina University, sitting on the other side of the living room texting her friends, Horn buried himself in a biography of Franklin Delano Roosevelt. An amateur historian, he especially loved reading anything he could find on Roosevelt, Thomas Jefferson, George Washington, and Abraham Lincoln.

Horn had been reading for roughly thirty minutes when he first noticed the shadow slowly creep across his living room carpet. Behind him and slightly off to either side of where he sat reading in his favorite chair were two windows. Both faced the road outside his home. Immediately outside, his covered front porch was lit by three recessed lights. Noticing the dark shadow once, then once again, and then once more, he watched each time as the shadow, unimpaired by the sheer white curtains his wife had hung in each of the windows, slowly moved back and forth across his carpet.

Walking to his front door with the thought that one of Jenna's testosterone-driven boyfriends had come calling unannounced,

Horn slowly opened it without making any noise. Stepping outside, he surprised both himself and the intruder who had just finished removing a wooden flagstaff from its metal mounting bracket. On the flagstaff was a Confederate flag the Horn's had recently started displaying. Like another one displaying another similar sized flag, both brackets had been mounted on two of the three vinyl-covered posts holding up the porch's roof. Slow to react at first, Horn soon followed the intruder off the porch as the uninvited visitor attempted to get away by vaulting over the waist-high wooden railing. Landing awkwardly, the intruder, dressed in black clothing, fell to one knee. Doing so gave Horn time to chase him down.

A football player during his college days, Horn, who had played sparingly in two semi-pro leagues after finishing school, tackled the male figure as he tried rising to his feet. For the next several minutes, on a dark front lawn lit only by what little light the porch lights cast out, the two men exchanged a series of powerful blows and kicks between them.

As her father had been, Jenna had also been slow to react to her father's calls for help. Now walking out onto the porch, she saw her father stagger backwards after being struck twice by two powerful blows to the right side of his face. As he struggled to defend himself, Horn heard his daughter scream loudly as she started to move towards him.

"Jenna, no! Go back. Lock the doors and call 911," Horn yelled as he fell to the ground punching and kicking the person who was now intent on trying to kill him.

Stunned by what she was seeing, Jenna hesitated for a brief moment before running inside to call the police. But then, as she neared her phone, she changed her mind. Sprinting to her bedroom, she was soon back out the front door. Coming to a stop less than fifteen feet from where her father now stood, she watched for a brief moment as her father's attacker held him firmly in a chokehold, trying desperately to choke the last few remaining ounces of strength from him.

"Daddy! Daddy!" Jenna yelled as loudly as she could. *"Thunder, daddy! Thunder!"*

Despite the extreme fatigue he was feeling, and with blood running down the side of his face from a deep laceration next to left eye, Horn immediately recognized the word his daughter had used. Quickly, he allowed his body to go limp. His attacker, now too exhausted himself to hold Horn's weight up, pushed him to the ground.

As her father's body hit the ground, Jenna Horn fired a quick and deadly three-shot burst from her Beretta 92FS 9mm pistol. Her first shot quickly tore off the thumb of the attacker's right hand as he raised it in a foolish and desperate last-ditch attempt to defend himself from what he saw coming. After quickly dispatching the attacker's thumb, Jenna's first shot continued on, ripping through the exposed right side of the stranger's chest. It was an area no longer being protected by the now ripped side panel of the Point Blank body armor he had been wearing. Fired less than a hundredth of a second after the first one, Jenna's second shot slammed into the attacker's throat, quickly severing his spinal cord before exiting out the back of his neck. Lifeless, but still momentarily upright, Jenna's third shot blew the back of the attacker's head off as his body convulsed in mid-air before crashing to the ground.

✶✶✶✶✶

Hearing Jenna's screams and then the three loud explosions that followed, Bobby Ray immediately barked orders to the six detectives stationed around the Barone residence.

"Hold your positions! Stay put! Until we know if those screams were real or not, I want you staying right where you are. I'll get back to you ASAP!"

Running down the road in the direction of where the screams and gunshots had come from, Bobby Ray was quickly passed by Wilson and Griffin. From where they had been parked in Griffin's vehicle, they also heard the loud female voice as it screamed for help. Now as they passed him, they heard the same voice scream loudly again.

"Daddy! Daddy! Help! Help us! We need help here!"

Exiting their vehicle as the one Davis and Dzamko were riding in skidded to a stop in front of 168 Planters Trace Loop, Wilson, his weapon drawn and aimed at the body he saw lying on the front lawn, scanned the immediate area around him for any additional trouble. As he did, Griffin, off to the right of his partner, cautiously moved across the lawn to where Jenna stood, her weapon still clutched in her hand as it hung next to her right leg. As they did this, despite bleeding badly, Joseph Horn struggled to his knees as he fought hard to catch his breath.

"My daughter . . . that's my daughter!" Horn said, fighting through his injuries to protect his daughter. *"Don't hurt her, she . . . she saved my life!"*

Quickly realizing most of what had happened, Bobby Ray radioed for an ambulance as the others diffused what remained of the brief, but intense situation. After making sure the scene was stable, he used his cell phone to contact the GCSD's Dispatch Center, making arrangements for a coroner to come to the scene and for uniformed deputies to establish a secure perimeter around the once quiet neighborhood. Then he used his radio to contact McKinney and Odom.

"Tell the others I want them to remain at their posts for now until we get this mess sorted out down here, but I need you two guys down here pronto!" Bobby Ray had just finished on the radio when Wilson's voice boomed a loud and frightening warning.

"Bomb! Bomb!" Wilson yelled as he scrambled to put distance between himself and the dead intruder's body. *"This guy's got two pipe bombs wired to his chest! Move!"*

✶✶✶✶✶✶

Taught years earlier by others on how to draft a functional and thorough Op Plan for events requiring a fair amount of planning and coordination, it was Paul who had taught his friend to plan for contingencies.

Earlier that afternoon, and still using a copy of an Op Plan that Paul had crafted years earlier to help quell a prison riot in Somers, Connecticut, Bobby Ray made three smart inclusions in his own plan for the evening when he put it together. Anticipating problems to arise if their suspect decided to fight it out instead of fleeing or being captured, Bobby Ray's plan had included staging an ambulance, the Horry County Bomb Squad, and a dozen uniformed deputies and state troopers at a seldom used strip mall less than a mile from the scene. Doing so now allowed him to put them to work immediately without having to wait for them to be called out.

With EMS personnel already tending to the Horns a safe distance away from their front lawn, and with the bomb squad working to neutralize the pipe bombs, Bobby Ray put his deputies and the troopers to work. Out of concern for the safety of others, he did so by having them evacuate the homes within a six hundred yard radius around the Horn residence, doing so due to the potential, and yet unknown, destructive powers of the pipe bombs.

As all of this was being done, and after contacting both Renda and Pascento with news of what had happened, Bobby Ray called for Griffin, Wilson, Davis, and the others to meet with him a safe distance away from where their suspect lie dead.

As he walked to where the others were waiting for him in the middle of the road, Bobby Ray heard the conversation taking place over the confusion of the two street numbers assigned to the Barone and Horn residences.

"We clearly were at the right house when all of this shit happened," Wilson said, still confused over what had occurred at the Horn residence. As he spoke, he carefully referred to the notes he had made earlier in his pad. "Look, when we were following this guy earlier I had written down the house number for the Barone residence as being 186. That's the house the prick stopped in front of each time he drove down the street earlier today. He never even paused in front of this one. So if that's the case, then why is he attacking the guy who lives at 168? What's this prick, dyslexic or something?"

"Maybe just freakin' stupid." Griffin added as he visually measured the short distance separating the Barone and Horn residences.

Having been busy with a host of details since responding to Jenna Horn's cries for help, Bobby Ray had not yet had time to view the dead suspect lying nearby. His response to what Wilson was about to tell them was one that startled his detectives.

"Bobby Ray, that jihadist son of a bitch lying dead over there," Wilson said as he pointed to the body lying in Joseph Horn's front yard, "whoever the hell he is, he's not Pratt." Stunned by what they had heard, Wilson's words caused everyone around him to quietly stare at him in disbelief for a couple of moments. The only exception was Bobby Ray.

Even though he had yet to view the body up close, Griffin was still surprised by what his partner had just said. "What the hell are you talking about, Kent?" Griffin asked as he wiped sweat from the evening's excitement off of his forehead. "It has to be our guy; he's the only one we've all been working."

Like Griffin, Davis and Dzamko were also quick to dismiss Wilson's comment.

"Of course, it's Pratt," Dzamko offered, still shaking his head over what he had heard. "Maybe it just looked like someone else due to the lack of light when you first took a look at him or maybe it's because you were distracted when you saw the bombs wired to his chest. But like Griff just said, it has to be Pratt."

Adamantly, Wilson again told the others what he had seen. "That dead guy over there is not our guy. Even with the back of his freaking head blown off I can tell it's not him. Pratt doesn't even look remotely close to what this prick looks like. That guy dead over there is a real life camel jockey, you know . . . a Muslim-looking guy. Go see for yourselves if you don't believe me. Have at it!"

"He's right," Bobby Ray suddenly interjected into the conversation. "That's not Pratt lying over there, it's someone else. Maybe the guy's an accomplice of his, maybe he's another son of a bitch fanatic like Pratt, who knows, but it's definitely not Pratt." Then he surprised the others by adding, "Paul figured this out about six or seven days ago. We just didn't know when or how our friend over there was going to act until this morning." Pausing a moment, Bobby Ray answered a question posed to him by a state trooper regarding the outer perimeter being established around the neighborhood. "This morning, that's when all of you should have picked up on the fact that it wasn't Pratt who walked out of Walmart in the orange-colored sweatshirt."

Puzzled by what he and the others were hearing, Griffin sought a clarification on how they should have known it was not Pratt they had been following.

"You guys were following him, that's until he walked inside the store. That's when the bad guys made their switch. You were all so focused on picking Pratt up again when he came outside that you didn't listen close enough to what Nanfito said when he briefly described the clothing he saw the guy wearing," Bobby Ray said as he pointed towards the Horn's front lawn. "He's the same guy who is lying dead over there. What you all failed to pick up on was the difference in the color of the pants Pratt and this guy were wearing. I'll grant that it's a subtle difference, but Nanfito clearly described the difference. It wasn't Ronnie's fault that he didn't pick up on the difference as he never had a chance to see what Pratt was wearing when our guy walked inside the store. I hate to say this, but Pratt got one over on you guys. Maybe you will and maybe you won't, but you have to admit that was a pretty slick move on his part. Maybe this guy's smarter than we've been giving him credit for."

As they slowly digested what Bobby Ray had told them, Wilson spoke up, irritated over being kept in the dark until now. "Then why the hell didn't you say something if you knew this was happening?"

"Because at that time I really hadn't completely bought into Paul's theory. That's why I stayed behind when y'all left to follow our friend over there. Paul's theory was that something strange was going to happen, something like a wrinkle being thrown into the surveillance so we'd get thrown off Pratt's trail. I stayed behind after I heard the different colored pants being described as I figured Pratt had either changed pants or one of his co-conspirators had come outside to drive off in the vehicle you had seen Pratt park in the parking lot. Less than ten minutes after y'all left to follow this dead guy, Pratt walked out of the store. I followed him to where he had stashed his Tahoe, but then Blake and I lost him because I was on foot. He was out of sight by the time Blake managed to pick me up."

Despite understanding what they were being told, looks of confusion were still exchanged amongst Bobby Ray's detectives for several more moments. As they were, Davis spoke up. Like Wilson, he was less than pleased about being kept in the dark until now.

"So where's Pratt now? And, for that matter, where's Stine and Tommy Scozz? Are they bird-dogging Pratt while we're all standing around here with our thumbs up our asses?" These were questions all of the others had started to ask themselves as well.

Bobby Ray smiled at his curious and slightly pissed-off group of detectives. Not completely sure of where their principal suspect was at this exact moment, he toyed over what he should tell them before answering Davis' questions.

"Where's Pratt? That I'm not totally sure of at this exact moment, but I believe he's going to be attending a party Paul's hosting later this evening. Maybe a couple of you should follow me over there later as we're all invited to it."

Already confused by the switch that had occurred, and by not having a clue as to who was lying dead not far from where they stood, Bobby Ray's reference regarding a party Paul was hosting later that evening thoroughly confused those standing around their boss.

* * * * * *

Once given the all clear signal by Patton and her bomb techs, Bobby Ray's detectives went to work processing the scene outside the Horn residence. As they did, Bobby Ray listened in on the interview Wilson and Griffin were conducting with Joseph Horn on his front lawn.

As he spoke, among the points Horn raised was the fact that he and his daughter were avid target shooters. Describing his family as survivalists, he further explained how they had rehearsed certain drills in the event of a home invasion or similar social disturbance taking place like the one which had just occurred on their front lawn.

"One of code words is thunder," Horn explained as he sat on the ground being treated for his injuries by two EMTs. "Thunder means if one of us is in a jam, like the one I was in tonight, then we're to immediately drop to the ground as whoever's called that word out is ready to terminate the threat the other one of us is facing. As we all now know, my daughter had the tactical advantage at that moment and she used her advantage to terminate the threat I was facing." Pausing a moment, Horn pushed the hand away of one of the EMTs tending to his head injury so he could glance over at his daughter sitting on the front steps of their porch. As she sat there, McKinney and Odom stood by as a female EMT made sure she had not been hurt. "Probably pretty much of an understatement at this point," Horn said smiling, "but that little girl can flat out shoot. Shoots almost as good as I can. At least that's what I keep telling her, but that's just me joking with her. She's a far better shot than I am, and I've got no problem telling anyone that." Again, Horn paused from speaking to allow one of the EMTs to place a bandage on his bloody face. Then continuing with what he had to say, he added, "You folks may not agree with me on this, but I'm glad she took that asshole out. Simply put, that bastard got what he deserved. Nothing more, nothing less. If you boys would let me, I'd walk over there right now and piss on his face for making my little girl do what she had to do."

Nodding his head in agreement to what Horn had said, Bobby Ray offered up his own opinion. "You don't hear me or my guys disagreeing with you, do you?"

"No, I don't. I appreciate that." Bobby Ray's response pleased Horn greatly.

Despite hearing what Bobby Ray said, Horn, still fearful over his daughter's safety, asked the veteran investigator his next question. "You fellas going to arrest my daughter for shooting that son of a bitch?"

"Not likely," Bobby Ray replied without a moment of hesitation. "The way I'm looking at it, South Carolina's Stand Your Ground law was put to proper use by your girl tonight. The law clearly says we all have a right to defend our home, and that's what she did. Using your own words, Joe, she defended her home and her father from an uninvited invader, nothing more and nothing less. I'll explain all of this to the solicitor when I talk with him later, but I'm quite confident he'll see our side of it. But if he doesn't, which I don't see happening, then he can come down here and arrest her himself because none of us are going to do that. Talk's cheap, but don't worry, she'll be fine."

Both exhausted and upset from what he had been through, Horn's eyes now stared at his Confederate flag lying on the ground close to where he and the intruder had done battle. At first, as he continued to stare at the flag, he simply nodded in response to what Bobby Ray had just said. Growing more concerned over what had happened, Horn pointed at the controversial symbol of the Confederacy. Like it had been on two other recent occasions, it was again the apparent cause of the evening's trouble. "Maybe I should think about taking down my flag. It's not something I want to do, but I don't care to put my family through something like this again."

"Then don't," Bobby Ray suggested. "We all know what happened in Charleston, and we all know that some folks don't like that flag you and others fly, but others do. For what it's worth, I'm one of those people who likes seeing that flag flying. That flag, just like the gun that was used that night in Charleston, didn't kill those innocent people, a sick mentally unstable person did. Like many others, I agree that the state of South Carolina shouldn't be flying the Stars and Bars over the statehouse as it sends the wrong message, but there's no reason folks like you shouldn't keep flying it if you want. It's part of our heritage . . . . part of our nation's history, so keep flying it. If you and others are flying it as a racist symbol, then that's wrong, but if you're flying it for the reasons I just mentioned, then I hope you'll keep flying it." Understanding he had been caught up in the moment, Bobby Ray smiled as he looked at Horn before finishing his thoughts. "Excuse me for preaching, but as far as I'm concerned this country has become too politically correct. If you and others stop flying that flag, then we let the other side win. I'm not a racist, nor am I remotely close to being someone who is because I hate those kinds of people. I'm just someone who believes we should be able to fly the Stars and Bars in our own front yards if we want to and that we shouldn't have to justify why we do. The history of the South is just that, it's our history. Whether you're *fer or again it* as some of our old-timers like to say, it's still our history and the flag is indeed a controversial part of that history."

Bobby Ray's comments, like they had moments earlier, pleased Horn greatly. After glancing at his daughter, Horn offered a weak smile in Bobby Ray's direction. As he did, he gave the Major Case commander a thumbs up. "I appreciate hearing your thoughts. Like you, I'm not a racist either, nor is anyone in my family. I'm a history buff who just has an appreciation for the South's fight for independence, that's why I fly my flag. I'm hardly trying to offend anyone by doing so. I'll talk this over with my family, but after listening to what you said I think we'll keep flying our flag."

******

Finished with what he had to do at the scene, and with a veteran group of cops taking care of all that needed to be done, Bobby Ray walked to his vehicle. Moments later, he drove away. Like Pratt, he had a party to get to.

31

By the time he finally neared the hospital, Sonny Pratt was so pissed off that he could barely think straight. "That no-good freakin' Mexican bastard!" Pratt angrily yelled inside the confines of his Tahoe. "I'm going to kill that asshole next, and then I'll take care of his son of a bitch lookout. If I can make it happen, neither one of them will live to see the sun set tomorrow night. Freakin' illegal bastards, freakin' thieves, that's just what those two are!"

Less than an hour earlier, Pratt had gone to inspect his storage unit, expecting to find both the truck and the large plastic container he had paid for inside it. Instead, he found the unit empty. To make matters worse, missing from it were the two handguns he placed there earlier, handguns he had agreed to compensate Taco with. With no truck and no large container left in its bed for him to use later that evening, Pratt's plans for the rest of the day had now been altered considerably.

"Freakin' greaseball son of a bitch! First he steals my money, and now he steals my guns!" Pratt mumbled loudly as he tried composing himself. "Soon that rat bastard is going to die a miserable death. So is his faggot asshole lookout!"

Realizing the task at hand now needed to be the sole focus of his attention; Pratt forced himself to take a few deep breaths in order to momentarily forget all that had gone wrong. "I'll deal with that other shit later," he thought, finally starting to calm down from the screwing he received earlier.

Parking in a spot close to where the construction project was taking place, one not far from the hospital's ER entrance, Pratt scanned the area around him before exiting his vehicle. As he did, he caught himself staring in his rearview mirror.

"Not bad, not a bad job at all," he said, smiling at his full head of bleached-blond hair. Earlier, in effort to look more like the person he was representing himself to be, Pratt had bleached both his hair and his eyebrows, turning them blonde from their natural dark color.

Smoking a cheap cigar he had just purchased at a nearby mini-mart, he puffed hard on it as he slipped on a white knee-length lab coat. Like the blue surgical uniform he was wearing, he had purchased the coat at a local uniform supply store in Myrtle Beach three days earlier, using some of the money he had stolen from the bank the day Donna had been injured. As he made his way across the nearly deserted parking lot, he casually slung a blue canvass backpack over his left shoulder.

A large dumpster, one used by the various sub-contractors working on a section of the hospital's new wing, sat less than one hundred feet from where Pratt had parked. Now working his cigar even harder as he made his way across the dimly lit section of the parking lot, he walked directly towards the metal dumpster sitting there.

Hours earlier, dressed as one of the many workers working on the new wing, Pratt had strategically dumped four commercial size paint cans inside one corner of the dumpster. Each can, no longer filled with paint but now with gasoline, had been sealed with lids that had been intentionally perforated with a series of small holes. They were holes designed to allow the combustible fuel inside of them to slowly seep out. Along with them, he tossed in four uncapped road flares and three used canning jars he had packed tightly with gunpowder. Unlike the paint cans, the lids to the jars had intentionally been left off of them.

Pausing in the dumpster's shadow, one created from the light emitted by a nearby High Pressure Sodium light mounted high above him in the parking lot, Pratt casually peered around the corner he was standing near to see if he was being watched. Soon satisfied he was not, he took one last hard draw on his cigar before tossing it inside the dumpster. Almost immediately, the cigar's hot embers caused a collection of gasoline-soaked wood scraps, papers, rags, and bits of carpeting to catch on fire. Quickly spreading to several other items in the nearly full dumpster, the intensely hot fire soon heated the fumes escaping from the cans Pratt had thrown inside earlier.

Making his rounds as he passed through the still uncompleted ground floor of the new wing, Security Officer Tyrone Jackson, a newly hired member of the hospital's security force, felt the concussion caused by the explosion of the remaining gasoline inside three of the paint cans Pratt had thrown in the dumpster earlier. Heated to the proper flash point, and fueled by both the gunpowder and the intense heat emitted by the road flares, as well as other partially full cans of flammable solvents and lubricants that had been improperly discarded by workers working on the new wing, the explosion blew the dumpster's large heavy door off its hinges. Almost immediately, the metal door crushed the right side of a nearby Chevy Camaro before coming to rest against a backhoe that had been left in the lot overnight. Frightened and inexperienced, Jackson reacted even better than Pratt had hoped for. Using his portable radio, he contacted the switchboard operator, ordering her to activate the hospital's seldom-used emergency plan.

Walking inside by way of the ER entrance, Pratt confidently made his way further inside the confines of the hospital by way of a connecting hallway. At the far end of the hallway sat a bank of elevators. As he made his way towards them, the switchboard operator calmly announced over the intercom system a warning to her fellow co-workers. Repeating the emergency plan's discreet code name three times - *'Dr. Black - Please dial 00, stat. Dr. Black - Please dial 00, stat. Dr. Black - Please dial 00, stat'* - the switchboard operator alerted her fellow co-workers to the hospital's emergency plan being activated. Less than a minute later, she began repeating the same warning. As this was being repeated over the intercom system, fire doors in each of the hallways began to close automatically. As they did, several unobtrusive flashing white lights strategically placed throughout each of the hallways simultaneously activated, further warning staff members of an existing crisis. Despite working as they had been designed, each of the emergency signals, like the repeated page for Dr. Black, now added to the confusion the explosion had already caused.

Approaching a security officer stationed close to the main bank of elevators, Pratt casually flashed the stolen hospital ID card he had pilfered days earlier. Wanting to make it seem as if he belonged in the hospital when he was ready to activate his plan, Pratt had made it a point to conduct a reconnaissance mission so he could calmly make his way around the many connecting hallways after his plan had been put into action. After purchasing two magazines at the hospital's gift shop and then using them to bluff his way inside that day as he posed as a visitor visiting a sick relative, he had stolen an official hospital photo ID card after seeing it clipped to a lab coat inside a small empty office. Once back home, he had carefully sliced open the laminated card and replaced the photo of a blond-haired Doctor Zealor with one of his own after dying his hair in an attempt to match Zealor's. Unlike the other plastic bins Bobby Ray and his detectives had found, one other small bin had not been found during the search of the mobile home as it had been cleverly hidden inside a false ceiling in one of the bedrooms. Stored inside it was a laminating machine, several laminating pouches, a handful of colored headshots of Pratt wearing different shirts and disguises, several nearly perfect computer-generated Social Security cards, and one small box of South Carolina DMV blanks. Like the DMV information he had been illegally given, Pratt had received the DMV blanks from the same source.

As he waited for one of the elevators to arrive, Pratt looked back with contempt at the security guard dealing with the chaos existing in the hallway. As he did, he watched as the guard patiently answered questions from nervous staff members and patients. Continuing to watch with disdain as the guard performed his duties, Pratt mumbled a comment that only he could hear. "If you're going to be a security officer, then do your job better than you're currently doing it, you freakin' jerk!"

Moments later, after Pratt walked inside one of the elevators to take it up to the next floor, Detective Doug Lancelot, posing as a member of the hospital's security force, and the same guard Pratt had flashed his fake ID card to, placed a call on his cell phone. Quickly it was answered.

"He's in the building," Lancelot calmly announced. "He's headed your way on elevator two."

"Got it. I saw him walk in," the voice on the other end of the call replied. "Hold your position for five minutes. Then I want you to go find our suspect's vehicle. When you locate it, call the number I gave you earlier, its Jill Patton's. Tell her where Pratt's vehicle is located and she'll be up to help you as soon as she can. Remain with the vehicle until help arrives, but be careful, we don't know if he's placed any booby traps inside it. Wait for the bomb techs to take a look at it before you go and touch it. When you can, grab a couple of security guards and start sealing off the parking lot so no one gets hurt."

Watching Pratt on the CCTV monitors the hospital's IT department had setup in the room next to Donna's, Paul, along with Ray Smith and Tommy Scozz, now watched as their suspect held open the elevator door with his foot. Staring at one of the monitors, they saw Pratt reach inside his backpack. Moments later they watched as Pratt tossed two smoke grenades, one inside the elevator and one down an adjoining hallway. Almost immediately, orange smoke filled the screens of two of the monitors being viewed.

"Those will add to the confusion we're already seeing," Scozzafava said calmly, realizing Pratt had come to the hospital better prepared than they had expected. Even more than they already had, Paul and the others with him now anticipated Pratt's arrival inside the ICU ward. As they did, Smith turned off the camera feeds which were no longer needed, keeping activated only the four directly in Pratt's path.

Two minutes after being notified of Pratt's presence inside the hospital, Smith phoned the ICU nurses' station from where he stood behind a door that had been purposely left ajar. "He's here. Tell your staff to stay away from this end of the hallway until I give you the all clear. If you see any orange smoke, don't panic, it's only smoke from a smoke grenade. It won't hurt you." As Smith did this, Paul sent a similar warning to Stine by way of a text message.

As Smith finished his call, Paul watched Pratt on one of the monitors as their suspect cautiously entered the quiet and nearly deserted ICU ward. Hours earlier, six of the eight ICU patients had been temporarily moved to two other floors. Only Donna and one other patient, an elderly comatose male who was too ill to be moved, now occupied the ward. Then, as their suspect slowly started down the hallway, Paul spoke softly to the hospital's security director.

"I've got to give it to this asshole, Ray. He's obviously gone to great lengths to pull this off. He's created two really effective diversions, one that was even good enough to cause your staff to put the hospital's emergency plan in motion. He's also wearing the right clothes to make it look like he belongs here. I wonder where he stole that official-looking photo ID I see him wearing."

"Hear that?" Smith said as he briefly turned to look at Paul. "That hissing sound is diversion number three. He just tossed another smoke grenade down the hallway towards the nurses' station." Looking at the monitor capturing what was occurring just outside the room they were in, both men could easily see orange smoke rapidly filling the hallway. In moments, Smith uttered the words Paul had waited to hear. "His hands are on the door."

Watching Pratt as he slowly pushed open the door to Donna's former room, Smith waited patiently as their suspect scanned the hallway, then the room itself, for any unwanted visitors before disappearing from view. Once inside the partially dark room, Pratt cautiously pushed the door partway closed. Quickly scanning the room again, he saw the many floral arrangements displayed around the room, smirking as he located the one he had dropped off a few days earlier. Focusing on the figure lying in bed, Pratt's attention was momentarily distracted by the red digital lights of the heart monitor as it closely monitored the vital signs of the patient it was hooked to. As he stared at the lights displaying the patient's heart and pulse rates, as well as the current blood pressure reading, he heard the soft rhythmic breaths being taken by his target.

Reaching into his backpack, Pratt removed a large serrated survival knife he had been issued in the army years earlier. Placing his backpack on the recliner, he unsheathed the knife as he took two steps closer towards the bed. Raising it in his right hand, Pratt was suddenly aware of the door behind him being violently pushed open. Quickly the once dark room was bathed in bright white as three sets of fluorescent lights came to life, the sudden brightness causing Pratt to blink rapidly several times as his eyes strained to adjust to the change in lighting. As they did, a small amount of orange smoke began filling the room.

"Drop it, Pratt! Drop it now!" Smith's loud voice commanded.

With his eyes quickly recovering from the change in lighting, Pratt turned to face the voice which had startled him. As he did, Stine, acting as a decoy in the room's bed, threw back the sheets he had been hidden under. Momentarily sitting upright in bed, his head still wrapped in white bandages to mimic the injury Donna had sustained, Stine aimed his Glock .40 caliber pistol at the back of Pratt's head as he began to stand up.

As he glanced back at Stine, Pratt realized his options were limited. Hoping to make his escape from the now crowded room, he charged at the large black male blocking his escape. As he did, Smith, in full combat position, fired once.

Responding immediately to the command given them, Smith's Taser fired two dart-like electrodes at the charging target. Fired less than ten feet away, the barbed electrodes quickly implanted themselves in Pratt's skin after easily passing through the disguise he was wearing. Immediately the electrodes delivered a massive dose of electrical current, the intense shock causing Pratt to immediately drop to the floor near the foot of the bed Stine had been hiding in. As he did, the serrated survival knife released from his grip. Twice it harmlessly bounced on the floor before coming to rest close to where Smith stood. Screaming in agony as his body experienced neuromuscular incapacitation, a complete and total loss of its voluntary muscle control, Pratt's body convulsed out of control for several moments.

Careful to avoid making contact with Pratt while he was still connected to the heart monitor, Stine laughed as he noticed the spike in his heart rate, a spike caused by a few intense moments of action. Like Stine and his bandaged head, the heart monitor and the movement of Donna from one room to another had all been parts of the orchestrated ruse Paul had thought up.

Brushing by Smith as the security director withdrew the two electrodes from Pratt's chest, Paul stood over their suspect for a brief few moments as Pratt slowly began to recover from the debilitating shock his body had experienced. After determining it was safe to do so, Paul reached down and grabbed Pratt by the shirt, lifting his head several inches off the tiled floor.

Emotionally upset, Paul's face was flushed with anger as he stared down at the person who had tried to kill his wife. Filled with a kind of rage that he had never experienced the likes of before, his words were angrily and loudly delivered. "That was my wife you ran over with your car a few weeks ago. This . . . this is the very room where our sons and I thought we might lose her."

Doing something he had never done before in his thirty-plus years in law enforcement, Paul reached back and delivered a crunching blow to Pratt's face. Satisfied by what he had done, he released his grip, allowing Pratt's limp body to fall back on the floor. Then looking down at the crumpled mess at his feet, he spoke one last time to the person he hated the most in life. "That's from my wife, asshole! She wanted me to tell you she said hello."

******

As Stine and Scozzafava handcuffed their prisoner, Paul thanked Smith for his assistance before walking across the smoke-filled hallway to his wife's room.

After leaning down to kiss Donna's forehead, Paul knelt down next to her as she slept, unaware of all the excitement that had transpired just across the hall. In a hushed tone, he thanked the good Lord for saving his wife's life. As he continued to pray, Bobby Ray stood watching from the doorway. Along with Davis and Dzamko, he had arrived in time to see their dazed and handcuffed suspect marched outside the ICU ward.

Touched by the scene in front of him, Bobby Ray slowly moved back out into the hallway, unwilling to disturb the moment he knew Paul and Donna deserved to spend alone.

32

Twenty minutes after Pratt had been packaged up in the back of Stine's vehicle for the ride back to Georgetown, Bobby Ray steered his own vehicle out of the ER parking lot. While it would soon prove to be an even longer night than even he had expected it to be, it would soon prove to be an even longer night for Pratt.

Notified of what had happened at the hospital, Wilson and Griffin waited in Georgetown for the real party to start. As they waited, they were told they would be joined in a few hours by a team of domestic terrorism experts from the FBI's field office in Charleston, and then by others from the Department of Homeland Security.

While the original plan was for Pratt to be interviewed with at least one representative present from both the FBI and Homeland Security, Bobby Ray soon instructed Wilson and Griffin to conduct a preliminary interview with their suspect shortly after his arrival in Georgetown.

Looking across the narrow table that separated he and his partner from the person who had committed so much violence over the past several weeks, Wilson realized the physical description O'Keefe had provided Stine with had been fairly accurate. Appearing to be slightly over six feet in height, Pratt's rawboned physique was hardly a remarkable one. As he thought about this, Wilson also realized their suspect's physicality belied the degree of hatred Pratt had recently exhibited.

While their suspect's face showed the stubble of not shaving for the past few days, it was also clear to the two cops who were about to interview him that areas along his jawline had been badly pockmarked. Like his partner, Wilson attributed these rough-looking facial features to be the result of acne scarring during Pratt's teenage years or from a childhood infection that had been caused by chicken pox. Besides one other feature they noticed, a thin prickly-looking moustache below their suspect's thin narrow nose, they also saw the feature that a young bank teller had first told Wilson about. It was the ugly scar where Pratt's left thumb had once been.

Setting up the interview like he had done with their suspect's DMV accomplice, Wilson started the interview by reading Pratt his Miranda warnings. Despite his efforts to have him do so, Pratt refused to sign the warning form. Moments later, Wilson showed Pratt the same digital recorder he had used during the interview with Ziggy Bagrov. Like the camera mounted on the wall directly above Wilson's chair, one focused directly on their suspect, it quickly started to record everything inside the small interview room.

Then, despite their best efforts of trying to interview Pratt on several points, their suspect refused to cooperate. Still smarting from being punched in the face by Paul, Pratt rubbed the side of his jaw several times; ignoring the questions he was being asked.

Realizing the obstinate and defiant position Pratt was taking, Wilson knew he had to stick to the game plan he had formulated. That included letting their suspect they know they already knew about every little detail he had carefully planned to accomplish that evening.

"Heard from your buddy lately?" Wilson asked as he placed two photographs upside down on the table in front of their shackled prisoner. He did so as a means of trying to annoy Pratt even more than their presence was already doing.

"Just out of curiosity, what buddy is that?" Pratt asked, quickly bored by the efforts of the two cops who were trying to squeeze him for as much information as possible.

"Nice try, asshole!" Griffin's loud voice startled Pratt for a brief moment. Not the least bit pleased by their suspect's arrogant facial expressions, or by the slouched way he sat facing them, Griffin kicked one of the legs of the table just hard enough to make Pratt's head fall out of the hand that was propping it up.

"Unfortunately for your buddy, you're doing a whole lot better than he is right about now. You know the one I'm talking about, right? Your shit-for-brains jihadist pipe bomb wearing asshole friend, that's who I'm talking about." Like he always had, Griffin was again playing the role of a bad cop to near perfection.

Like the others watching the interview take place from behind a one-way mirror mounted in the room, Wilson laughed at his partner's description of Pratt's friend. He did so contemptuously, intentionally trying to show Pratt the disdain he and his fellow cops had for people like him.

Angry at being talked to as he was, Pratt angrily lashed out at the cops across the table from him. "Maybe you've caught him, or maybe you haven't, but I'm sure Kaliq has fulfilled his mission for Allah."

"What's your definition of the words caught and fulfilled?" Griffin smugly asked. As he did, Wilson turned over the photos he had placed in front of Pratt a few moments earlier.

"Yeah, we caught Kaliq. Too bad for him we did. I guess you can kind of tell two things about him from those photos your eyeballs are staring at," Wilson said as soon as he saw the upset look on Pratt's face beginning to grow even more intense than it had been. "In case you haven't figured it out yet, Mr. Kaliq, well . . . he's dead. Too bad about that, I'm sure he's going to be missed." Wilson's sarcasm was obvious to everyone listening to what he was saying. Then pointing to one of the photos, Wilson added, "The other thing that's obvious in this photo you're looking at is the pipe bombs your buddy was wearing are still strapped to his chest. Guess you've figured out your dead friend wasn't able to fulfill his promise to Allah, or to anyone else. He didn't kill anyone because after his dumb ass went to the wrong house, he was shot and killed by a young girl. Come to think of it, knowing how much some of your dickhead Middle Eastern friends like to disrespect women so much, your buddy must be really pissed off right about now by how he died."

Seeing some of the fire leave Pratt's eyes as he continued to sit staring in disbelief at the photos in front of him, Griffin sought to irritate Pratt one more time in an attempt to get their suspect to start talking.

"You just told us your towel-head wearing friend's first name was Kaliq. Which, by the way, was more than what we already knew about him. So what's your buddy's surname? Smith, Jones, White . . . something like that?"

"Screw you!" Pratt softly responded, his eyes still staring at the photo of his dead terrorist friend.

"OK, enough about Kaliq for now." Wilson said, trying to restore some semblance of order in the room. "Let's talk about the Myrtle Beach Convention Center, shall we? What were you planning on doing there? Despite what you told one of the people who works there, we all know you weren't there to write up an estimate for power washing the loading dock. What were you really doing there? Were you planning on blowing up the building or something like that?"

Wilson's comments caught Pratt totally unprepared. "What?"

Continuing with his line of questioning, Wilson peppered Pratt with several questions and statements, all designed to make their suspect feel the pressure that was being applied to him. "Obviously you have to know we've searched the mobile home your Uncle Johnny rented. The same one we found his body stuffed inside a refrigerator in. While we were there we also found your drawing of the loading dock area at the Myrtle Beach Convention Center. You know . . . the one with measurements written all over it. It's the same one you tried hiding by placing it on top of one of your kitchen cabinets. What were you going to do, maybe copy what Timothy McVeigh did to the Alfred P. Murrah Building in Oklahoma City? Was that what you were going to use the truck for?"

"What truck?" Pratt weakly asked, trying to engage Wilson in a conversation so he could learn what the cops did and did not know about him.

But Wilson, far too experienced and far too street savvy, refused to bite. Now he went at Pratt, hammering him with details of his life, details that he hoped would make their accused suspect crumble. If anything would, Wilson knew the very last comment he was about to toss in Pratt's face would likely decide the outcome of the interview.

"Do you want me to spell it all out for you, Sonny? I mean, we can sit here and talk for hours if you want. We'll talk about the truck, the large plastic container you were interested in buying, and everything else that you and Taco talked about. We can even talk about how much money you paid him . . . it was nine hundred dollars, right? And, we can even talk about the two stolen guns you left for him in your storage unit. By the way, those are guns that are now in our possession. If you don't believe me, we can show them to you. They're right down the hallway in our Evidence Room; it won't take but a minute to fetch them so you can see them one last time. If we start running out of things to talk about, we'll talk about the pipe bombs we know you've been making. Hell, we can talk about anything you want. We're in no hurry; we're just trying to get to the bottom of this entire mess that you've created. Just one thing, though. Don't freaking lie to us, OK? Because we know everything there is to know about you. We even know about Lynn Burke and her drug habit. You remember her, don't you?"

Pratt continued to sit motionless in his chair for several moments. As he did, he chose to remain quiet, his eyes staring hard at Wilson.

"In case you don't remember her, she's the girl you once loved; the one you thought you were having a monogamous relationship with. I guess she thought otherwise as we were told she was involved in at least two other relationships. One was with illegal drugs, and the other, probably the more painful one for you, was with a host of other soldiers she was screwing behind your back. That must have been painful to learn about. Right, Sonny?"

As he continued to stare at Wilson in silence, almost glaring at the cop on the other side of the desk, Pratt, at first, remained motionless. Beaten down by the events of the evening, and also frustrated from listening to Wilson grate on him, Pratt then leaned forward in his chair. Like the desk in front of him, the chair had also been bolted to the floor. Sitting there, his head drooped as he stared at the scuffed concrete floor. Almost immediately several thoughts flooded through his tired head.

"If only I had shot the bitch at the bank and not tried running her over. I should have also made sure the freakin' priest was dead, and should have taken care of that asshole O'Keefe and not his truck. If I hadn't been so stupid the cops would have had three less people to talk to. If only . . ."

"We could also talk about this."

Wilson's words caused Pratt to look up. Quickly his eyes took notice of the red label that had been affixed to the outside of a small clear plastic bag, one that Wilson was holding in his right hand. The large black letters of the word EVIDENCE told him what the bag contained. On the table to Pratt's right sat a slightly larger plastic bag that had a similar label attached to it. Inside the larger of the two bags, Pratt saw the rolled up wad of bills he had paid Taco with hours earlier.

"Shit!" Pratt softly muttered. It was a response Wilson took note of, but one he elected not to comment on directly.

"Just in case you don't recognize what's inside this bag," Wilson said, turning it around so Pratt could see what was inside it, "it's the key to your storage locker. It's the same key you gave to Taco so he could park the truck you wanted him to steal inside it. Too bad you didn't know that he likes to play both sides of the street on occasion . . . the good side *and* the bad side. He's developed a fondness for Benjamins, and, most times, he doesn't care where they come from."

As Wilson spoke, his eyes directed Pratt's stare towards the bag containing the rolled up wad of cash. Like his previous comments, the two evidence bags and what they each contained told their suspect they knew everything about him.

Feeling fairly good over what they had confronted Pratt with, Wilson and Griffin, like the others listening in on the interview, were suddenly stunned by what their suspect said next. What he told them was both unexpected and unsolicited. It was even better than the confession Wilson had hoped to get.

"Can anybody here offer me any guarantees?" Pratt asked as he glanced at the one-way mirror mounted on the wall off to his left.

Realizing Pratt was likely testing the waters regarding something significant he had to say, Wilson quickly surmised their suspect was looking for the best deal possible. Looking at the photos of the two guns he had earlier tried engaging their suspect in conversation about, Wilson took a gamble. Holding up one of the photos, he asked, "We talking about the rest of these?"

Stoically, Pratt looked at the cops sitting across from him. As he did, he did his best at playing stupid. "I'm not sure I know what you're talking about. Maybe if you tell me there's a deal on the table, and maybe if you explain what that deal encompasses, then maybe my memory might improve. Until that happens, I really have no idea what you're referring to."

"We can't go to bat for you, Sonny, if you don't tell us what you have to offer." Tactfully, Wilson then added, "Give us something to talk to the bosses about. Just enough to show them you have something we're interested in."

Nodding his head to show he understood the point Wilson was making, Pratt sat quiet for a few moments as several sets of eyes stared at him. "Let's just say you might have been fairly warm with that lucky guess of yours a few moments ago. We'll leave it at that. For now, that's all I have to say, detective, the ball is in your court."

Ignoring the demotion Pratt had given him, Wilson and his partner excused themselves from the Interview Room. Meeting down the hallway with Sheriff Renda and Bobby Ray, as well as with Ralph Harrison, the Special Agent in Charge of the FBI's Charleston Field Office, they spoke briefly regarding what Pratt had put on the table. After doing so, the others kept Wilson and Griffin waiting for nearly thirty-five minutes as the three of them burned the phone lines, making a series of calls to Pascento, to Harrison's boss, to two federal prosecutors assigned to the Department of Justice, and to the Army Criminal Investigation Command at Fort Bragg. They did so to give Pratt's interviewers the information they needed to hammer out a deal with him.

Fifteen minutes after the flurry of phone calls had come to an end, and after a brief meeting between all of them, Wilson and Griffin reentered the room where Pratt had been kept waiting. On the table next to their prisoner sat two empty Coke cans. Both had been drained by Pratt during his brief wait. As he had earlier, Wilson again took the lead with their suspect.

"Sonny, the deal on the table is this. In exchange for you turning over the rest of the weapons we all know you stole from Fort Bragg, as well as you turning over the balance of the stolen gunpowder, we can assure you that you will not be prosecuted for the thefts that occurred. That's a take it or leave it deal. If you refuse to take it, and we later find the stolen weapons on our own, then you'll likely be charged with stealing them. It's this simple; if you take the deal you won't be prosecuted." Finished speaking, Wilson picked his chair up and moved it closer to where Pratt was seated. Looking at the person he was committed to getting some answers from, he calmly spoke again. "Sonny, not only have you embarrassed yourself by all that you've done, but you've embarrassed the shit out of the army's criminal investigators long enough. They don't like the fact that they haven't been able to find the weapons we all know you stole. They also don't like the fact that they haven't been able to get enough dirt on you to prosecute you for stealing what you did. If I were you, I'd take the deal. It at least shows some good intention on your part to cooperate with us."

Cautiously, Pratt eyed Wilson, still leery of trusting someone he had an immense dislike for. As he did, he gave thought to what he had just been told. "I assume someone's going to put what you've said in writing. Am I correct in making that assumption?"

"You have my word that is going to happen. I was told this promise will be reduced to writing by some assistant federal prosecutor who's assigned to the DOJ. If you want to think about this for a few minutes, or if you want to contact an attorney, my partner and I are good with that." Then Wilson added one last important part of the deal. "Sonny, the only stipulation that comes with this deal, and this is strictly coming from the folks at Fort Bragg, is that you have to admit in writing that it was you who stole the weapons and the gunpowder from the base. This is just so the army's investigators can close out their investigation. I assure you there are no tricks being played as this is too important for all of us."

Twenty minutes later, after repeatedly assuring Pratt that all was on the level, the prime suspect in the theft of fifteen handguns and one hundred and seventy-five pounds of gunpowder admitted it was he who was responsible for stealing the items from Fort Bragg.

Early the next afternoon, in front of DOJ officials, army personnel from Fort Bragg, FBI Agent Thomas Scozzafava, and Captain Bobby Ray Jenkins, Pratt formally admitted his guilt in writing. It was a deal totally removed from each of the four murders he had committed, as well as the assault on Horn, and his other related crimes.

Two days later, with help from the FBI, US Army investigators, and the Spartanburg County Sheriff's Office, Wilson and Griffin used a pick and shovel to dig behind a weathered tombstone in a small neglected cemetery in rural Spartanburg County, South Carolina. Less than fifteen minutes after they started, a large plastic container holding a slightly smaller version of the same style container was gently lifted out of the ground. Years earlier, the smaller of the two containers had been carefully wrapped in plastic and layers of duct tape to protect the valuable contents stored inside it. Inside the container, one remarkably free of dust and moisture, the rest of the stolen handguns sat wrapped in three separate plastic bags.

Even though it was difficult to read after years of being exposed to the sun and all types of weather, the name on the tombstone read Jeremiah Carter Pratt. Dying two years prior to the birth of his great-grandson, Sonny Pratt's great-grandfather never had the chance of meeting him.

* * * * *

Later that week, as Pratt continued to cooperate with Wilson and Griffin, and then with a team of federal investigators, his legal team pressed on with their efforts to halt his degree of cooperation. Concerned over the possibility of the original DOJ agreement being withdrawn, and despite several verbal assurances their client would not be facing the death penalty, Pratt's attorney's feared the favorable agreement would not be recognized by the courts in the future. Because of that concern, they continued to argue with him regarding the position he had taken. The position his attorneys' now took changed dramatically three days after the handguns had been unearthed in South Carolina.

While the final forensic lab report had yet to be written, SLED, in conjunction with Solicitor Pascento's office, announced the findings on the testing of Pratt's blood. The strongly-worded announcement included the fact that the testing had positively found traces of Pratt's DNA on Platek's driveway and on the two bloodstained Confederate flags found during the search of Uncle Johnny's mobile home. Additionally, SLED also announced that DNA evidence belonging to Platek and Holland had been found on the flags taken from their homes. Coupled with the recent written statements taken from O'Keefe and Taco Hernandez, as well as the mountain of other evidence that was now stacked up against their client, Pratt's legal team finally elected to allow their client to continue cooperating with the authorities. By now, even they realized their client had been the evil menace who had terrorized the Grand Strand for several weeks.

The day after the DNA findings had been announced, the once wannabe terrorist revealed to Wilson and Griffin, as he later did to others, a handful of secrets he and several other low-level jihadists had planned for a few locations along the Grand Strand. Among them were plans to blow up the Myrtle Beach Convention Center, along with several other buildings and restaurants at Broadway at the Beach, one of the main tourist destinations in Myrtle Beach. They were plans which none of the so-called domestic terrorism experts at the FBI or Homeland Security knew anything about.

In the final negotiated agreement that was soon hammered out between Pratt's court-appointed attorneys, the United States Department of Justice, and Solicitor Pascento's office, in exchange for pleading guilty to all of the charges facing him in South Carolina, Pratt agreed to continue telling state and federal authorities interviewing him as much as he knew about what his fellow jihadists had planned. It was an agreement which assured Pratt that neither the state of South Carolina nor the federal government would seek the death penalty for the four murders he committed. It was an agreement that also assured him he would serve the rest of his life in a federal prison after being convicted of the charges against him. Additionally, in return for having the death penalty being taken off the table, Pratt also agreed to identify who his regional and foreign contacts were, and where their funding came from in the United States.

Pratt's follow-up interviews would span four intense days, first in Georgetown and then in Washington. Within days, the information Pratt's interviewers learned during that period would soon send tremors through the nation's intelligence community. Quickly it proved to many that neither the FBI nor Homeland Security were capable of properly vetting most of the immigrants seeking asylum in the United States. To those law enforcement agencies and others who already knew this, it further proved that neither agency had the ability to properly identify sleeper cells already imbedded within so many of our nation's communities.

Despite that concern, in the last year of his administration, just as he had done during his previous seven years in office, the president again chose to ignore the valuable intelligence that had been generated from the exhaustive interviews conducted with Pratt. As he had in the past, the president continued with his biased policy of not listening to the recommendations of his senior military and criminal justice advisors. Instead, he chose to open even wider the doors of our great country to those intent on harming our freedoms.

The president's troubled policy, one which continued to foster a less than ideal approach of being able to stem the flow of Islamic radicals into the country, would continue to create a variety of challenges for Paul, Bobby Ray, and the rest of America's law enforcement agencies for years to come.

33

Thirty-three days after being transferred from the hospital to the Murrells Inlet Health Care Center so she could receive close to a month of intense occupational therapy, Donna was finally cleared to go home by her doctors. Despite her time at the rehab center being an extremely positive experience while her injuries continued to heal, Donna was anxious to return home.

Her recovery from her traumatic brain injury, by far the most serious of all of her injuries, had gone very well. Even Dr. Tillengast, normally reserved in the evaluation of his patients' recovery times, had been impressed by the remarkable recovery Donna was making. At the time of her release from the hospital, the impact of her brain injury on her speech and thought processes had been deemed negligible. However, her balance, as well as the use of her left hand, had not been as fast to return to what they had been prior to her injury.

Now after a month of hard work, Donna's balance had nearly returned to what it had been, and the use of her left arm had improved remarkably since being released from the hospital. As she prepared to return home that morning, her physical therapist assured her she would soon regain full use of her arm.

"Donna, it's been a pleasure working with a patient so dedicated and hard-working as you have been with your therapy. I hate to say this because I know how anxious you are to go home, but I'm already looking forward to seeing you next week for your first outpatient session," Marla Wilkins, Donna's physical therapist said as she leaned down to hug the patient she had grown fond of.

Minutes later, despite his wife's protest that she could manage on her own, Paul pushed her wheelchair out the front doors of the rehab center to the private ambulance he had hired to bring her home. Soon loaded aboard the ambulance while still in her wheelchair, Donna waved to the nurses and aides who had come outside to see her off.

Less than twenty minutes later, with Paul riding in the back of the ambulance with her, Donna was finally back home. After her wheelchair was lowered onto the driveway, she saw for the first time the colorful streamers, signs and balloons that her family, neighbors and co-workers had adorned her front porch with. As Paul wheeled her closer to the crowd standing and cheering as they welcomed her back home, she finally saw her sons and daughters-in-law waving to her. Almost in tears from the reception she was being given, Donna laughed when Lauren, her pregnant daughter-in-law, held up a homemade sign as she pointed to her large pronounced belly. While the simple sign made her cry even harder than she already was, it also reinforced to her that she was finally home. It was also a sign referring to something positive that was soon going to happen in her life.

The wording on the simple homemade sign read '*WELCOME HOME, GRANDMA!*'

* * * * * *

Two days after Donna arrived back home, Paul and Bobby Ray, along with Stine and Wilson, met with Solicitor Pascento and members of his staff at the courthouse in Conway regarding some of the evidence seized during the Pratt investigation. This was done to clarify a few points that had been raised during Pratt's interview. It was also being done so Pascento's assistants could draft a response for the solicitor to sign, a response refuting several baseless allegations Pratt's legal team had raised during their efforts to get their client the best deal possible. After finishing up, and wanting to stretch his legs before his next appointment began, Pascento walked outside with Paul and Bobby Ray to enjoy a few minutes of fresh air.

While enjoying the morning sunshine and a brief few laughs with Bobby Ray and Paul, Pascento soon shook hands with both of them. As he did, he smiled at Bobby Ray before speaking to him.

"I didn't want to say anything in front of Blake or Kent, Bobby Ray, but from what I was told earlier this morning I guess any thoughts you've recently been giving towards retiring have been postponed. I suppose a different kind of congratulations are now in order, aren't they?" Smiling over the news he had been told earlier, Pascento added, "It's well-deserved, I'm happy for you. I was pleased to hear you'll be staying with us."

Somewhat surprised by what Pascento already knew, Bobby Ray managed a polite but somewhat embarrassed response. "Thanks, Joe. I appreciate that. I hope it's the right move, but I guess time will tell, won't it?" Ignoring the confused look on Paul's face, Bobby Ray asked Pascento a simple question to satisfy his own curiosity. "How'd you hear about this?"

"Your boss called me this morning on something totally unrelated to why we were meeting here this morning. He just brought it up in conversation." Seeing the confused look still displayed on

Paul's face, Pascento added, "I hope I haven't said anything I shouldn't have. I wouldn't want to ruin any surprises for you."

"No, not at all," Bobby Ray answered. As he did, he shot an awkward glance in Paul's direction.

"You two guys mind telling me what it is you're talking about?" Paul asked, realizing something significant had happened. "I'm standing here in the bright sunshine but I kind of feel like I'm standing in the dark. What gives?"

Slightly embarrassed about not yet telling his friend the good news, Bobby Ray, at first, stammered slightly as he told Paul what had happened. "Renda's asked me to become his undersheriff, he's promoting me to be his second-in-command. I . . . I was going to tell you, but I haven't had time this morning."

Despite wanting to give his friend a friendly but sarcastic reply over how he had been kept in the dark regarding the good news, Paul held off on doing so. Instead, he smiled at his friend as he patted him on the back. "Great news, Bobby Ray, I'm happy for you!" Then, in true Paul fashion, he asked, "Your boss couldn't find anyone else more qualified than you?"

After leaving Pascento laughing on the front steps of the courthouse, Paul and Bobby Ray began the drive back to Murrells Inlet to meet the others for a hastily arranged lunch at the Waccamaw Diner.

Forty minutes later, as they walked to where Stine, Wilson, Griffin, and several others, including Davis and Vane, were sitting, both of them noticed Sheriff Renda had taken them up on their offer of having lunch with them. Having another appointment in less than thirty-minutes, Renda was already halfway through a bowl of Hoppin' John, one of his favorite afternoon meals. As he sat eating, a white linen napkin tucked behind his tie protected the front of his clean dress shirt from being stained.

"How'd the meeting go?" Renda asked, looking up from his bowl of black-eyed peas, rice, onions, and bacon. "Joe raise any concerns?"

"Went fine, no problems at all. Hope we didn't hold you up too much," Bobby Ray joked as Renda got back to business with his bowl of Hoppin' John.

"Nope, not at all." Renda said between bites. "I told the boys here that I have to get going in a few minutes, that's why I ordered before y'all got here."

As Betty handed the others their menus and took their drink orders, Renda, finished with his lunch, wiped his mouth with his napkin before speaking.

"These boys know the good news yet, Bobby Ray?"

"Paul does. I was going to tell the others over lunch, that's unless you want to do the honors."

Never one to pass up an opportunity for being the center of attention, Renda jumped at Bobby Ray's offer. Trying to be humorous as he spoke to everyone seated around the large table that had been setup for them to have lunch at, the sheriff soon gave everyone the news regarding their boss being promoted. Along with their handshakes and hearty congratulations, everyone joined Paul by raising their glasses of either sweet tea or soft drinks in an impromptu salute to someone they all genuinely liked and respected.

Anticipating the obvious question concerning who was going to fill the commander's position within the Major Case Squad, a vacancy obviously created by Bobby Ray's promotion, Renda winked at Bobby Ray before addressing his next comment across the table to Paul.

"Paul, I've already spoken with Bobby Ray about this, and just so you know, he's on board with me about this. If it helps any, so is Joe Pascento. I told him about this when we spoke earlier this morning on other matters. So, without beating around the bush any longer, I'd like you to be the new commander of the Major Case Squad. Besides the great job you've done for us since the Melkin investigation, you've got the background and experience this position requires. More importantly, everyone seated at this table likes and respects you, even Bobby Ray," Renda joked as he finished speaking. As he did, the others around him warmly seconded Renda's request. Moments later, as they continued to echo their support, everyone around the table quietly started chanting, "Take it, take it!"

"Talk about being caught off guard," Paul said smiling. Then his thoughts turned back to Donna and to her recovery. "I'm honored by the offer, but I'm not sure I can accept it. I'd have to speak with my wife first and I'm . . ."

Then, to add to his friend's growing list of surprises for the day, Bobby Ray told Paul what he had learned. "First of all, you're taking the job. Whether you want to or not, you're taking it. I guess there are two things I didn't tell you today. The first you already know about. The second is that after the sheriff and I spoke about you taking over my job, I stopped to see Donna yesterday when you were out and told her what was going to be offered to you today. She understands how much you mean to us and how good you are at your job. She's going to tell you this when you get home, but she's given her full blessing to this offer we're making you."

Not giving Paul time to speak, Renda told him of his other plans. Before he did, he paid everyone seated around the table a compliment. "I doubt that many departments here in South Carolina have faced what we've had to face over the past two years since the time of the Melkin murders. Each of you folks, starting with that lengthy investigation and then continuing with the terrible tragedy that happened to those young men in North Litchfield last year, and now with this mess that's recently been cleaned up, well, y'all have done a fabulous job solving each of these very complex cases. Thinking back on all that has happened has caused me to realize what a wonderfully talented group of folks y'all are. The people of Georgetown County should be proud of the nice group of folks who are seated right here at this table with me. That's why I want to keep y'all together for as long as I can. With Bobby Ray's help, I'm going to make that happen. Over the next few weeks, I'm planning on reorganizing the structure of my department for a couple of reasons. I want each of you to help us complete that task, and to show you how much this means to me, I'm giving Paul the choice of picking the person he wants to fill the vacancy that's existed since the time of Audrey Small's death. It's high time we filled that spot." Then Renda qualified his offer, pointing at Stine, Wilson, and Griffin as he did. "Paul, you pick whoever you want . . . as long as it's one of these three fellas."

"But they don't work for you, sheriff; they each work for different departments than yours." Paul said as he looked at each of the faces now staring at him. Like he was a few moments earlier, they were now stunned by what they were each hearing.

"For now they do, but not for long. You pick who you want to be your XO and then I'll make an offer to the other two, one that will benefit each of them in the long run. Whoever you don't pick," Renda said as he again glanced at Stine, Wilson, and Griffin, "I'll make them an offer to come and be an important part of my reorganization. I'm going to need a new narcotics commander and I'm going to need a commander for the bomb squad we're going to be adding to our Emergency Services Unit. But it all starts with you. I want you to be a part of what I'm planning." Then grinning at Bobby Ray, Renda added, "Unlike in the recent past, I need to know my Major Case commander knows what he's doing when shit hits the fan."

As Renda expected, his comments drew a brief, but appropriate round of comments directed at Bobby Ray. Like he always did, the target of those friendly comments and insults took them very well.

"Wow! You've given me a lot more to digest than just the lunch I thought I was coming here to enjoy." Paul said, smiling at Betty who had come to take their lunch orders.

After everyone had placed their orders, Paul responded to Renda's offer. As he did, he stared at Stine for a brief moment before looking at Renda. "OK, sheriff, if Bobby Ray's not lying to me like he generally does, and as long as my wife gives her blessing to this offer of yours, I'll take the job as long as you assure me of a few things. First, you'll need to compensate me properly for my experience and skills; second, you'll have to assure me that you're not going to be looking over my back second-guessing every decision I make; and third, I'll take this job for a minimum of two years, maybe three or four tops, as long as you make one promise to me in front of everyone seated here."

Not exactly sure what Paul had up his sleeve, Renda decided to test the waters before totally committing himself to any arrangement. "I normally don't sign blank checks, Paul, so why don't you enlighten me a little bit on what you're referring to."

"Fair enough, sheriff," Paul said, shooting a smirk at Bobby Ray as he did. "Besides the investigative side of this new job you're offering me, I'm going to be spending a great deal of my time teaching my new XO how to manage the operation for times when I'm not around. I don't want that time to be wasted, so I'd like you to promise me one thing. That whoever I pick to be my XO, that person becomes your next Major Case commander when I decide to leave."

While not a person who liked having demands placed upon him, Renda quickly agreed to Paul's requests, promising him and everyone else at the table that he would promote, in the absence of any disciplinary problems, Paul's pick to be his next Major Case commander. "OK, OK, I agree," the sheriff said as he stood up to put his coat back on. "But this is my department and I have to answer to the people who live here. I'll always be looking over your shoulder because that's what's expected of me. The only thing I'll promise you in that regard is that I'll try not to be too much of a pain in the ass to you on those occasions when I am looking over your shoulder."

Satisfied with what he heard Renda say, Paul stood up from where he had been seated. Shaking hands with the sheriff, he said, "In that case, I guess you've found your guy. Thanks, sheriff, I appreciate the offer." Then looking at Wilson and Griffin, Paul added, "I think I have a couple of recommendations for you for those two other positions you want to fill." Glancing at Elmendorf and Vane, the new Major Case commander spoke one last time. "I also have a few ideas on how we can better use Don and Doug's combined talents."

"That's fine, Paul, I'll be looking forward to hearing your thoughts on who should be selected. As for your thoughts on those other two fellas, I'm all ears. They both deserve whatever it is that we can do for them." As Renda finished speaking, he waved for Betty to come over to where he was standing.

"Yes sir, sheriff, what can I do for y'all?" Betty asked. Like a couple of others, she was amused over how Renda had managed to find a way to stain a small section of his shirt with his lunch.

"Well, to start with young lady, I want to express my thanks for the huge help you gave us during this recent string of murders we've been working on. Some of these folks sitting here have told me how helpful your tip was regarding a windbreaker that you knew had been stolen from here. Thanks so much for all of your help."

"I'm glad you arrested that creep, sheriff. I hope the bastard gets what he deserves for doing what he did to all of them nice people."

Then Renda surprised everyone seated around the table for a second time that day by taking his American Express card out from his wallet. Well-known as both a publicity hound and as a cheapskate, Renda handed the card to Betty. "Buy these boys lunch on me. They've earned that and a lot more for what they've just done for the folks living around here. When you put the bill together, throw a nice tip on there for yourself. Bobby Ray likes spending my money; he'll sign the bill when it's ready."

As the sheriff walked away, those who knew him the best, including Bobby Ray and Vane, feigned heart attacks over the unusual generosity Renda had directed towards them.

For the first time in six weeks, it was the first good laugh they all shared together.

34

The first three months of Paul's new job proved to be unremarkable, allowing him time to become familiar with the policies and procedures of his new department, and to get settled in his office. During that time, Donna had continued to progress well with both her physical therapy and from her injuries. Like most women, she was now at the point where she spent more time worrying about her hair growing back than she did about her ongoing therapy sessions.

Due to the generosity of her bank, as well as help from the South Carolina Victim Assistance Program and her insurance company, Donna's medical expenses had all been satisfied without any financial obligations being incurred by her or Paul.

Because of her steady recovery, Donna had also recently started discussions with her boss regarding her interest in returning to work on a part-time basis. Telling her it was just as important for her to heal mentally as it was for her physical injuries to heal, Donna finally convinced her boss to allow her to come back to work for three days a week for the first month. Between them, they agreed on a return date of October 1st.

* * * * * *

After returning to his office from a late lunch with Detectives Nanfito and Lancelot, Paul's quiet day was suddenly turned upside down by two successive phone calls. The first, the more important of the two, came from further down the hallway from Bobby Ray.

"Yankee Boy, you sitting down?" Bobby Ray asked from where he sat in his own office.

"Should I be?"

"I'll let you decide that after you hear what I just learned from a friend of mine who works in D.C. for the U.S. Marshal's Service. Depending on how you look at what I'm about to tell you, I guess it could be considered either good or bad news."

"OK, I'm sitting down now, Bobby Ray. Fire away," Paul said as he leaned back in his chair inside his office. Like the rest of the meager furnishings present, the black faux leather chair he sat in had seen better days.

"Our boy, Pratt, is dead. The marshal's office and a couple of D.C. cops were transporting him back to prison from a court appearance he had in federal court earlier today when the vehicle he was riding in took a direct hit from a shoulder-fired RPG. I was told Pratt and the two uniformed cops in the vehicle with him were killed instantly. One of the other vehicles sustained some damage from being hit by shrapnel from the vehicle Pratt was in, but no one else was injured too seriously. They shut down a seven-block section of the city as soon as it happened. They've found parts of the discarded launcher, and from what I'm being told they believe they've got two suspects holed up in an abandoned apartment building. My buddy said he'd call me back with an update as soon as he hears more. Pretty wild, huh?"

"Holy smokes, I'll say." Paul yelled out as he sat upright in his chair, his excited voice easily being heard across the large bullpen outside his office where several of his detectives were working on a variety of case reports. In moments, Nanfito, Lancelot, Wilson, Vane, and two others filled the doorway of Paul's office, aware that something out of the ordinary had happened.

Holding one hand over the phone as Bobby Ray continued to talk, Paul told the others the bare essentials of what he had just learned. As he finished clueing them in, Nanfito and Vane exchanged high fives with each other. As they did, Wilson started singing the words to Queen's popular song '*Another One Bites the Dust*'.

"*Another one bites the dust, another one bites the dust,*" Wilson cheerfully sang off-key, happy someone who had caused so much misery in the lives of several others was now dead. As he finished, Nanfito and Lancelot repeated the song's lyrics two more times.

Over the phone, Bobby Ray asked, "You know what this means, Paul, don't you?"

"Yeah, I do. Besides nothing positive, it means this was a message Pratt's former comrades sent him, and to America. It's a message that not only says to Pratt and to other jihadists like him that if you betray us we'll come and get you, but it's one that also says to everyone across the country that these ISIS bastards are already here. They're daring us to come find them before they wreak more havoc on us."

Slamming his hand down on his desk, Bobby Ray angrily responded to Paul's comment. "And our wonderful president won't do squat about it. He'll continue to tie the hands of law enforcement while at the same time leaving our borders wide open for these terrorist pricks to march in whenever and wherever they want. I can't wait for January to happen. That shithead can't get out of the White

House fast enough for me." Calming down a few moments later, and with more than just a little hint of concern still left in his voice, Bobby Ray asked, "Do you really think it was some of those ISIS assholes who killed Pratt?"

"Either them or their jihadist sympathizers," Paul answered. "I can't imagine who else would have done this. All the publicity Pratt's arrest has received is likely well known by everyone in ISIS now. I'd have to guess they either told someone here to shut his mouth for them or they sent someone here to do it. Whoever they had do it, they did it violently, even more so than the Mafia would have done."

"I'll bet the powers to be in the FBI, Homeland Security, and in the U.S. Marshal's Service are walking around with their butts in a knot over this. I have to imagine the pucker factor in D.C. is pretty damn high right about now." Bobby Ray offered, summarizing the news he had learned as only he could. As he did, he tried finding on his office television any updates that CNN or FOX were broadcasting about the breaking news story.

As Bobby Ray did so, Paul's cell phone announced an incoming call from Detective Davis. Hanging up on Bobby Ray, Paul answered his second call of the afternoon. Like the first one, it did not bring good news.

"Paul, one of my snitches, Sandy McDavid, the gal who's helped us a few times; she just called me with some disturbing news. Seems she and her husband are out on the Waccamaw River on their boat just east of the Sampit River Bridge. They've found two bodies, one male and one female, floating belly down in the river. She told me they didn't get too close, but got close enough to see the victims' hands are handcuffed behind them. I've asked her to wait there until we can get some folks on the scene."

"OK, that's more *great news* I've been told this afternoon, Bruce," Paul said sarcastically as he realized he was now facing his first homicide investigation as the department's new Major Case commander. "I'll get everyone headed that way. I'll meet you there as soon as I can."

✳✳✳✳✳✳

As he walked to his car, Paul could not help thinking of the news Bobby Ray had told him regarding Pratt's death. As he continued to think about it, he wondered how he would break the news to his wife, also wondering if she would react to the news of his death as Wilson had.

Closing his car door, Paul realized life as a cop, no matter where you worked, had now changed for the worse. Cell phone cameras, the growing lack of disrespect for law enforcement, liberal politicians, and the biased media had now changed how so many honest cops did their jobs.

Even worse, however, was his feeling that cops in New York, California, Colorado, Connecticut, and so many other places across America, including Georgetown County, South Carolina, now had more to worry about than just speeding tickets and investigating traffic accidents. Now they also had to worry about terrorists and sleeper cells harming the age-old principles so many of us still cherish so dearly.

Starting his car, Paul headed towards the Sampit River Bridge to meet with Davis and the others. As he did, he hoped the murder investigation they were about to commence would be a boring and mundane one. For now, just like those working for him, he had experienced enough with terrorists like Sonny Pratt.

While Paul's wish for a routine murder investigation would play out like he had hoped, another horrific event would soon confront him. The person responsible for this new tragedy would make Sonny Pratt look like an altar boy.

CPSIA information can be obtained
at www.ICGtesting.com
Printed in the USA
JSHW061356210822
29486JS00001B/4

9 781478 779117